Praise for the Dresden Files

Changes

"Fast-paced and compelling. . . . Butcher throws one high-stakes curveball after another at his hero. . . . Butcher is deft at relieving some of the tension and grimness with bursts of gallows humor that keep readers coming back for more." —*Publishers Weekly*

"The taut and sometimes twisty plot is full of surprises and changes for Harry and his friends and family. *Changes* is a compelling installment in what continues to be an outstanding series. . . . After the cliff-hanger ending, readers will be clamoring for the next book. A can't-miss entry in one of the best urban fantasy series currently being published." —*Booklist*

"An action-packed adventure full of desperation, leavened with a few sharp bits of humor, and some tantalizing new developments." —*Locus*

"Butcher never fails to present a dark, dramatic, and suspenseful experience. . . . With fast-paced thrills, magic, and mayhem, this series is easily one of the best in urban fantasy." —*SciFiChick.com*

"There's plenty to like in this most recent volume in the Dresden Files. Harry continues to be a complex character who marches to his own drummer."

—*Romantic Times*

continued . . .

"Wow. Just wow. . . . *Changes* is a defining novel for the Dresden Files and contains some of Butcher's finest writing for the series . . . a fantastic novel that guarantees Dresden Files fans begging for more." —LoveVampires

Turn Coat

"Butcher . . . spins an excellent noirish detective yarn in a well-crafted, supernaturally charged setting. The supporting cast is again fantastic, and Harry's wit continues to fly in the face of a peril-fraught plot." —*Booklist*

"Both fans and newcomers will get into the fast-paced action." —*Publishers Weekly*

Praise for the Other Novels of the Dresden Files

"Think *Buffy the Vampire Slayer* starring Philip Marlowe . . . a fast and furious adventure with winking nods to Bugs Bunny and John Carpenter."
—*Entertainment Weekly*

"Fans of Laurell K. Hamilton and Tanya Huff will love this series." —*Midwest Book Review*

ALSO BY JIM BUTCHER

THE DRESDEN FILES

Storm Front
Fool Moon
Grave Peril
Summer Knight
Death Masks
Blood Rites
Dead Beat
Proven Guilty
White Night
Small Favor
Turn Coat
Side Jobs

THE CODEX ALERA

Furies of Calderon
Academ's Fury
Cursor's Fury
Captain's Fury
Princeps' Fury
First Lord's Fury

JIM
BUTCHER

CHANGES

A NOVEL OF THE DRESDEN FILES

A ROC BOOK

ROC
Published by New American Library, a division of
Penguin Group (USA) Inc., 375 Hudson Street,
New York, New York 10014, USA
Penguin Group (Canada), 90 Eglinton Avenue East, Suite 700, Toronto,
Ontario M4P 2Y3, Canada (a division of Pearson Penguin Canada Inc.)
Penguin Books Ltd., 80 Strand, London WC2R 0RL, England
Penguin Ireland, 25 St. Stephen's Green, Dublin 2,
Ireland (a division of Penguin Books Ltd.)
Penguin Group (Australia), 250 Camberwell Road, Camberwell, Victoria 3124,
Australia (a division of Pearson Australia Group Pty. Ltd.)
Penguin Books India Pvt. Ltd., 11 Community Centre, Panchsheel Park,
New Delhi - 110 017, India
Penguin Group (NZ), 67 Apollo Drive, Rosedale, North Shore 0632,
New Zealand (a division of Pearson New Zealand Ltd.)
Penguin Books (South Africa) (Pty.) Ltd., 24 Sturdee Avenue,
Rosebank, Johannesburg 2196, South Africa

Penguin Books Ltd., Registered Offices:
80 Strand, London WC2R 0RL, England

Published by Roc, an imprint of New American Library, a division of Penguin
Group (USA) Inc. Previously published in a Roc hardcover edition.

First Roc Mass Market Printing, March 2011
10 9 8 7 6 5 4 3 2 1

Copyright © Jim Butcher, 2010
All rights reserved

 REGISTERED TRADEMARK—MARCA REGISTRADA

Printed in the United States of America

Chapter

One

I answered the phone, and Susan Rodriguez said, "They've taken our daughter."

I sat there for a long five count, swallowed, and said, "Um. What?"

"You heard me, Harry," Susan said gently.

"Oh," I said. "Um."

"The line isn't secure," she said. "I'll be in town tonight. We can talk then."

"Yeah," I said. "Okay."

"Harry . . ." she said. "I'm not . . . I never wanted to—" She cut the words off with an impatient sigh. I heard a voice over the loudspeaker in the background, saying something in Spanish. "We'll have time for that later. The plane is boarding. I've got to go. About twelve hours."

"Okay," I said. "I'll . . . I'll be here."

She hesitated, as if about to say something else, but then she hung up.

I sat there with the phone against my ear. After a while, it started making that double-speed busy-signal noise.

Our daughter.

She said *our daughter*.

I hung the phone up. Or tried. I missed the base. The receiver clattered to the floor.

Mouse, my big, shaggy grey dog, rose up from his usual napping spot in the tiny kitchenette my basement apartment boasted, and came trotting over to sit down at my feet, staring up at me with dark, worried doggy eyes. After a moment, he made a little huffing sound, then carefully picked the receiver up in his jaws and settled it onto the base. Then he went back to staring worriedly at me.

"I . . ." I paused, trying to get my head around the concept. "I . . . I might have a child."

Mouse made an uncertain, high-pitched noise.

"Yeah. How do you think I feel?" I stared at the far wall. Then I stood up and reached for my coat. "I . . . think I need a drink," I said. I nodded, focusing on nothing. "Yeah. Something like this . . . yeah."

Mouse made a distressed noise and rose.

"Sure," I told him. "You can come. Hell, maybe you can drive me home or something."

I got honked at a lot on the way to McAnally's. I didn't care. I made it without crashing into anyone. That's the important thing, right? I pulled my battered, trusty old Volkswagen Bug over into the little parking lot next to Mac's place. I started inside.

Mouse made a whuffing sound.

I looked over my shoulder. I'd left the car door open. The big dog nosed it closed.

"Thanks," I said.

We went into the pub.

Mac's place looks like Cheers after a mild apocalypse. There are thirteen wooden pillars irregularly spaced around the room, holding up the roof. They're all carved with scenes of Old World fairy tales, some of them amusing, more of them sinister. There are thirteen ceiling fans spinning lazily throughout the place, and the irregularly shaped, polished wooden bar has thirteen stools. There are thirteen tables in the room, placed in no specific pattern.

"There're a lot of thirteens in here," I said to myself.

It was about two thirty in the afternoon. No one was in the pub except for me and the dog—oh, and Mac. Mac is a man of medium height and medium build, with thick, bony wrists and a shining smooth pate that never shows signs of growing in. He could be anywhere between thirty and fifty and, as always, he was wearing a spotless white apron.

Mouse stared intently at Mac for a moment. Then he abruptly sat down in the entryway at the top of the little stairs, turned around once, and settled down by the door, his chin on his paws.

Mac glanced toward us. "Harry."

I shambled over to the bar.

Mac produced a bottle of one of his microbrews, but I shook my head. "Um. I'd say, 'Whiskey, Mac,' but I don't know if you have any whiskey. I need something strong, I think."

Mac raised his eyebrows and blinked at me.

You've got to know the guy. He was practically screaming.

But he poured me a drink of something light gold in a little glass, and I drank it. It burned. I wheezed a little, and then tapped a finger next to the glass.

Mac refilled it, frowning at me.

I drank the second glass more slowly. It still hurt

going down. The pain gave me something to focus on. Thoughts started to coagulate around it, and then to crystallize into definite shape.

Susan had called me. She was on the way.

And we had a child.

And she had never told me.

Susan had been a reporter for a yellow rag that covered supernatural news. Most of the people who worked there thought they were publishing fiction, but Susan had clued in to the supernatural world on her own, and we'd crossed trails and verbal swords several times before we'd gotten together. We hadn't been together a terribly long time—a little less than two years. We were both young and we made each other happy.

Maybe I should have known better. If you don't stand on the sidelines and ignore the world around you, sooner or later you make enemies. One of mine, a vampire named Bianca, had abducted Susan and infected her with the blood thirst of the Red Court. Susan hadn't gone all the way over—but if she ever lost control of herself, ever took another's lifeblood, she would.

She left me, afraid that if she didn't, I'd be the kill that turned her into a monster, and set out into the world to find some way to cope.

I told myself that she had good reason to do so, but reason and heartbreak don't speak the same language. I'd never really forgiven myself for what had happened to her. I guess reason and guilt don't speak the same language, either.

It was probably a damned good thing I had gone into shock, because I could feel emotions that were stirring somewhere deep inside me, gathering power like a storm far out to sea. I couldn't see them. I could only feel their effects, but it was enough to know that whatever was rising inside me was potent. Violent. Dangerous. Mindless rage got people killed every day. But for me, it might be worse.

I'm a professional wizard.

I can make a lot more things happen than most people.

Magic and emotions are tied up inextricably. I've been in battle before, and felt the terror and rage of that kind of place, where it's a fight just to think clearly through the simplest problems. I'd used my magic in those kinds of volatile circumstances—and a few times, I'd seen it run wild as a result. When most people lose control of their anger, someone gets hurt. Maybe someone even gets killed. When it happens to a wizard, insurance companies go broke and there's reconstruction afterward.

What was stirring in me now made those previous feelings of battle rage seem like anemic kittens.

"I've got to talk to someone," I heard myself say quietly. "Someone with some objectivity, perspective. I've got to get my head straight before things go to hell."

Mac leaned on the bar and looked at me.

I cradled the glass in my hand and said quietly, "You remember Susan Rodriguez?"

He nodded.

"She says that someone took our daughter. She says she'll be here late tonight."

Mac inhaled and exhaled slowly. Then he picked up the bottle and poured himself a shot. He sipped at it.

"I loved her," I said. "Maybe love her still. And she didn't tell me."

He nodded.

"She could be lying."

He grunted.

"I've been used before. And I'm a sucker for a girl."

"Yes," he said.

I gave him an even look. He smiled slightly.

"She'd be . . . six? Seven?" I shook my head. "I can't even do the math right now."

Mac pursed his lips. "Hard thing."

I finished the second glass. Some of the sharper edges had gotten softer. Mac touched a finger to the bottle, watching me. I shook my head.

"She could be lying to me," I said quietly. "If she's not . . . then . . ."

Mac closed his eyes briefly and nodded.

"Then there's this little girl in trouble," I said. I felt my jaw clench, and the storm inside me threatened to come boiling up. I pushed it down. "My little girl."

He nodded again.

"Don't know if I ever told you," I said. "I was an orphan."

Mac watched me silently.

"There were times when . . . when it was bad. When I wanted someone to come save me. I wished for it so hard. Dreaming of . . . of not being alone. And when someone finally did come, he turned out to be the biggest monster of all." I shook my head. "I won't let that happen to my child."

Mac folded his arms on the bar and looked at me intently and said, in a resonant baritone, "You've got to be very careful, Harry."

I looked at him, shocked. He'd . . . used grammar.

"Something like this will test you like nothing else," Mac said. "You're going to find out who you are, Harry. You're going to find out which principles you'll stand by to your death—and which lines you'll cross." He took my empty glass away and said, "You're heading into the badlands. It'll be easy to get lost."

I watched him in stunned silence as he finished his drink. He grimaced, as though it hurt his throat on the way down. Maybe he'd strained his voice, using it so much.

I stared down at my hands for a moment. Then I said, "Steak sandwich. And something for the pooch."

He grunted in the affirmative and started cooking. He took his time about it, divining my intentions with a bartender's instincts. I didn't feel like eating, but I had a little time to kill while the buzz faded.

He put my sandwich down in front of me. Then he took a bowl with some bones and some meat out to Mouse, along with a bowl of water. I ate my sandwich and idly noted that Mac never carried food out to anyone. Guess he was a dog person.

I ate my sandwich slowly and paid Mac.

"Thanks," I said.

He nodded. "Luck."

I got up and headed back for the car. Mouse followed beside me, his eyes lifted, watching me to see what I would do.

I marshaled my thoughts. I had to be careful. I had to be wary. I had to keep my eyes open. I had to keep the storm inside me from exploding, because the only thing I knew for certain was that someone—maybe Susan, maybe my enemies—was trying to manipulate me.

Either way, Mac was right.

I was heading into the badlands.

Chapter

Two

Susan arrived at around one in the morning.

I had gone back home from the pub and straight to my lab in the subbasement, and made with the wizardry, which demanded an intense focus on my tasks. Over the next several hours, I prepared a couple of things that might come in handy in the immediate future. Then I went back up the stepladder to my apartment and put on my force rings. Each of them is a braid of three individual rings, and I had enchanted them to store up a little kinetic energy every time I moved my arm. They were pretty efficient, but it wouldn't hurt to top them off, so I spent half an hour beating the tar out of the heavy bag hanging in one corner of my apartment's living area.

I showered, cleaned up, made some dinner, and generally never stopped moving. If I did that, thoughts might start to creep in, and I wasn't sure how I would deal with them.

I didn't even consider trying to sleep. It just wasn't going to happen.

So I stayed in motion. I cleaned the kitchen. I bathed Mouse and brushed out his coat. I picked up my living room, my room, my bathroom. I changed out my cat

Mister's litter box. I tidied up the fireplace, and set out fresh candles to illuminate the room.

It took me a couple of hours of that to realize that I was trying to make my apartment look nice because Susan was coming over. Old habits die hard, I suppose.

I was debating with myself whether or not I might need to clean Mister up (and having a narrow-eyed glare bestowed upon me from his perch atop my highest bookshelf) when there was a polite knock at the door.

My heart started being faster.

I opened the door and found Susan facing me.

She was a woman of medium height, which meant she was about a foot shorter than me. Her features were leanly angular, except for her mouth. She had dark, straight hair and even darker eyes, and her skin had a sun-bronzed tone to it far deeper than I had ever seen on her before. She looked thinner. I could see the tendons and muscles beneath the skin of her neck, and her cheekbones seemed starker than they had before. She wore black leather pants, a black T-shirt, and a leather jacket to complement the pants.

And she had not aged a day.

It had been most of a decade since I had beheld her. In that time, you expect people's appearances to change a little. Oh, nothing major. A few more pounds, maybe, a few more lines, a few silver hairs. People change. But Susan hadn't changed. At all.

I guess that's a nifty perk of being a half-turned vampire of the Red Court.

"Hi," she said quietly.

"Hi," I said back. I could meet her eyes without worrying about triggering a soulgaze. She and I had looked upon each other already.

She lowered her eyes and slipped her hands into her jacket pockets. "Harry . . . can I come in?"

I took half a step back. "I dunno. *Can* you come in?"

Her eyes flickered with a spark of anger. "You think I crossed over?"

"I think that taking unnecessary chances has lost its appeal to me," I said.

She pressed her lips together, but then nodded in acquiescence and stepped over the threshold of my apartment, the barrier of magical energy that surrounds any home—an action that simply would not have been possible for a vampire without first receiving my permission.

"Okay," I said, backing up to let her enter before I shut the door again. As I did, I saw a sandy-haired, plain-looking man seated casually on the top step of the concrete stairwell that led down to my apartment. He wore khakis, a blue denim jacket, and was reclining just enough to display the lines of a shoulder holster beneath the jacket. He was Susan's ally and his name was Martin. "You," I said. "Joy."

Martin's lips twitched into the faint and distant echo of a smile. "Likewise."

I shut the door on him and, just to be obnoxious, clacked the dead bolt closed as loudly as I could.

Susan smiled a little and shook her head. She looked around the apartment for a moment—and then suddenly froze as a growl came rumbling from the darkened alcove of the minikitchen. Mouse didn't rise, and his growl was not the savage thing I had heard once or twice before—but it was definitely a sound of polite warning.

Susan froze in place, staring at the kitchen for a moment. Then she said, "You got a dog."

"He kind of got me," I replied.

Susan nodded and swept her eyes around the little apartment. "You redecorated a little."

"Zombies," I said. "And werewolves. Place has been trashed a few times."

"I never understood why you didn't move out of this musty little hole."

"Musty? Little? My home this is," I said. "Get you something? Coke, beer?"

"Water?"

"Sure. Have a seat."

Susan moved silently over to one of the easy chairs framing the fireplace and settled down on its edge, her back straight. I got her some ice water, fetched myself a Coke, and brought the drinks over to her. I settled down in the other chair, so that we partly faced each other, and popped the tab on my drink.

"You're really going to leave Martin sitting outside?" she asked, amusement in her voice.

"I most certainly am," I said calmly, and took a sip of my drink.

She nodded and touched her glass to her lips. Maybe she sipped a little water.

I waited as long as I could stand it, maybe two or three whole seconds, before I broke the heavy silence. "So," I asked casually, "what's new?"

Her dark eyes regarded me obliquely for a moment before her lips thinned slightly. "This is going to be painful for both of us. Let's just have it done. We don't have time to dance around it."

"Okay. Our child?" I asked. "Yours and mine?"

"Yes."

"How do you know?"

She smoothed her face into a nonexpression. "There hasn't been anyone else, Harry. Not since that night with you. Not for more than two years before that."

If she was lying, it didn't show. I took that in for a moment and sipped some Coke. "It seems like something you should have told me."

I said it in a voice far calmer than I would have thought possible. I don't know what my face looked like when I said it. But Susan's darkly tanned skin became several shades lighter. "Harry," she said quietly, "I know you must be angry."

"I burn things to ash and smash holes in buildings when I'm angry," I said. "I'm a couple of steps past that point right now."

"You have every right to be," she said. "But I did what I thought was best for her. And for you."

The storm surged higher into my chest. But I made myself sit there without moving, breathing slowly and steadily. "I'm listening."

She nodded and took a moment to gather her thoughts. Then she said, "You don't know what it's like down there. Central America, all the way down to Brazil. There's a reason so many of those nations limp along in a state of near-anarchy."

"The Red Court," I said. "I know."

"You know in the abstract. But no one in the White Council has spent time there. Lived there. Seen what happens to the people the Reds rule." She shivered and folded her arms over her stomach. "It's a nightmare. And there's no one but the Fellowship and a few underfunded operatives of the Church to stand up to them."

The Fellowship of St. Giles was a collection of the supernatural world's outcasts and strays, many of them half vampires like Susan. They hated the Red Court with a holy passion, and did everything in their power to confound the vampires at every opportunity. They operated in cells, choosing targets, training recruits, planting bombs, and funding their operations through a hundred shady business activities. Terrorists, basically—smart, quick, and tough because they had to be.

"It hasn't been Disneyland in the rest of the world, either," I said quietly. "I saw my fair share of nightmares during the war. And then some."

"I'm not trying to belittle anything that the Council has done," she said. "I'm just trying to explain to you what I was facing at the time. Teams from the Fellowship rarely sleep in the same bed twice. We're always on the move. Always planning something or running from something. There's no place for a child in that."

"If only there had been someone with his own home and a regular income where she could have stayed," I said.

Susan's eyes hardened. "How many people have gotten killed around you, Harry? How many hurt?" She raked her fingers through her hair. "For God's sake. You said yourself that your apartment has been under attack. Would that have gone any better if you'd had a toddler to watch over?"

"Guess we'll never know," I said.

"I know," she said, her voice suddenly seething with intensity. "God, do you think I didn't want to be a part of her life? I cry myself to sleep at night—when I can sleep. But in the end, I couldn't offer her anything but a life on the run. And you couldn't offer her anything but a life under siege."

I stared at her.

But I didn't say anything.

"So I did the only thing I *could* do," she said. "I

found a place for her. Far away from the fighting. Where she could have a stable life. A loving home."

"And never told me," I said.

"If the Red Court had ever learned about my child, they *would* have used her against me. Period. As a means of leverage, or simple revenge. The fewer people who knew about her, the safer she was going to be. I didn't tell you, even though I knew it was wrong. Even though I knew that it would make you furious because of your own childhood." She leaned forward, her eyes almost feverish from the heat in her words. "And I would do a thousand times worse than that, if it meant that she'd be better protected."

I sipped some more Coke. "So," I said. "You kept her from me so that she would be safer. And you sent her away to be raised by strangers so that she would be safer." The storm in me pushed up higher, tingeing my voice with the echo of its furious howl. "How's that working out?"

Susan's eyes blazed. Red, swirling tribal marks began to appear on her skin, like tattoos done in disappearing ink, only backward—the Fellowship's version of a mood ring. They covered the side of her face, and her throat.

"The Fellowship has been compromised," she said, her words crisp. "Duchess Arianna of the Red Court found out about her, somehow, and had her taken. Do you know who she is?"

"Yeah," I said. I tried to ignore the way my blood had run cold at the mention of the name. "Duke Ortega's widow. She's sworn revenge upon me—and she once tried to buy me on eBay."

Susan blinked. "How did . . . No, never mind. Our sources in the Red Court say that she's planning something special for Maggie. We have to get her back."

I took another slow breath and closed my eyes for a moment.

"Maggie, huh?"

"For your mother," Susan whispered. "Margaret Angelica." I heard her fumble at her pockets. Then she said, "Here."

I opened my eyes and looked at a little wallet-sized portrait of a dark-eyed child, maybe five years old. She wore a pink dress and had purple ribbons in her dark hair, and she was smiling a wide and infectious smile. Some calm, detached part of me filed the face away, in case I needed to recognize her later. The rest of me cringed away from looking any closer, from thinking about the image as anything but a bit of paper and ink.

"It's from a couple of years ago," Susan said quietly. "But it's my most recent picture." She bit her lip and offered it to me.

"Keep it," I told her quietly. She put it away. The red marks were fading from her skin, gone the way they had come. I rubbed at my eyes. "For now," I said slowly, "we're going to forget about your decision to edit me out of her life. Because chewing over it won't help her right now, and because her best chance is for us to work together. Agreed?"

Susan nodded.

I spoke the next words through my teeth. "But I haven't forgotten. Will never forget it. There *will* be a reckoning on that account later. Do you understand?"

"Yes," she whispered. She looked up at me with large, shining dark eyes. "I never wanted to hurt you. Or her. I was just . . ."

"No," I said. "Too late for that now. It's just wasting time we can't afford to lose."

Susan turned her face sharply away from me, to the

fire, and closed her eyes. When she opened them again, her expression was under control. "All right," she said. "For our next step, we've got some options."

"Like?"

"Diplomacy," she said. "I hear stories about you. Half of them probably aren't true, but I know you've got some markers you could call in. If enough of the Accord members raise a voice, we might get her back without incident."

I snorted. "Or?"

"Offer reparations to the Red King in exchange for the child's life. He doesn't have a personal interest in this matter, and he outranks Arianna. Give him a bribe big enough and she'll have to let Maggie go."

"Right off the top of a building, probably," I growled.

Susan watched me steadily. "What do you think we should do?"

I felt my lips do something that probably didn't look like a smile. The storm had settled somewhere around my heart, and heady tendrils of its fury were curling up into my throat. It was a good ten seconds before I could speak, and even then it came out in a snarl.

"Do?" I said. "The Reds stole our little girl. We sure as hell aren't going to pay them for *that*."

A hot and terrible hunger flared up in Susan's eyes in response to my voice.

"We find Maggie," I said. "We take her back. And we kill anyone who gets in the way."

Susan shuddered and her eyes overflowed. She bowed her head and made a small sound. Then she leaned over and gently touched my left hand, the one still covered in slowly fading burn scars. She looked at my hand and winced, beginning to draw away.

I caught her fingers and squeezed hard. She settled

her fingers against mine and did the same. We held hands for a silent moment.

"Thank you," she whispered. Her hand was shaking in mine. "Thank you, Harry."

I nodded. I was going to say something to stiff-arm her and keep the distance, but the warmth of her hand in mine was suddenly something I couldn't ignore. I was furious with Susan, furious with an intensity you can feel only when someone you care deeply about hurts you. But the corollary of that was unavoidable—I still cared, or I wouldn't be angry.

"We'll find her," I said. "And I will do everything in my power to bring her back safe."

Susan looked up at me, tears streaking her face, and nodded. Then she lifted a hand and traced her fingers lightly over the scar on my cheek. It was a newer one, still angry and colorful. I thought it made me look like some old-school German character from Golden Age Hollywood with a dueling scar on his cheek. Her fingertips were gentle and warm.

"I didn't know what I was going to do," she said. "There was no one willing to stand up to them. There was no one."

Our eyes met, and suddenly the old heat was there between us, quivering out from our joined hands, from her fingertips against my face. Her eyes widened a little, and my heart started pounding along rapidly. I was furious with Susan. But apparently my body just read that as "excited" and didn't bother examining the fine print. I met her eyes for a long moment and then said, through a dry throat, "Isn't this how we got into this mess?"

She let out a shaking sound that was meant to be a laugh, but was filled with awareness of the inherent irony, and drew her hands away. "I . . . I'm sorry. I didn't mean to . . ." Her voice turned wry. "It's been a while for me."

I knew what she meant. I took several slow, deep breaths, separating mind from body. Then I said quietly, "Susan, whatever happens from here . . . we're done." I looked up at her. "You know that. You knew it when you chose not to tell me."

She looked brittle. She nodded slowly, as if something might break off if she moved any more quickly than that. She folded her hands in her lap. "I . . . know that. I knew it when I did it."

Silence stretched.

"Right," I said finally. "Now . . ." I took another deep breath, and told myself it would help. "The way I see it, you didn't fly into Chicago just for a chat with me. You wouldn't need Martin for that."

She lifted an eyebrow at me and nodded. "True."

"Then why?"

She seemed to gather herself, her voice more businesslike. "There's a Red outpost here. It's a place to start."

"Okay," I said, rising. "Let's start."

Chapter

Three

"I hope there are no hard feelings," Martin told me as he pulled out of the little gravel lot next to the house I board in.

Susan had yielded the passenger seat of the rental car to me, in deference to my storklike legs. "Hard feelings?" I asked.

"About our first meeting," Martin said. He drove the same way he did everything—blandly. Complete stops. Five miles an hour under the limit. Wherever we were headed, it was going to take forever to get there.

"You mean the way you used me to attempt to assassinate old Ortega?" I asked. "Thereby ensuring that the Code Duello was broken, the duel invalidated, and the vamps' war with the White Council continued?"

Martin glanced at me, and then into the rearview mirror at Susan.

"I told you," she said to Martin. "He's only dense in the short term. He sees everything eventually."

I gave Susan a slight wry tilt of my head in acknowledgment. "Wasn't hard to realize what you were doing in retrospect," I said. "The Red Court's war with the White Council must have been the best thing to happen to the Fellowship in ages."

"I've only been with them for slightly over one hundred years," Martin said. "But it was the best thing to happen in that time, yes. The White Council is one of the only organizations on the planet with the resources to seriously threaten them. And every time the Council won a victory—or even survived what should have been a crushing defeat—it meant that the Red Court was tearing itself to shreds internally. Some of them have had millennia to nurse grudges with rivals. They are appropriately epic in scale."

"Call me wacky," I said, "but I had to watch a few too many children die in that war you helped guarantee. No hard feelings?" I smiled at him—technically. "Marty, believe me when I say that you don't want me to get in touch with my feelings right now."

I felt Martin's eyes shift to me, and a little tension gather in his body. His shoulder twitched. He was thinking about his gun. He was pretty good with firearms. The night of my duel with the Red Court vampire named Ortega, Martin had put a round from one of those enormous sniper rifles into Ortega about half a second before the vampire would otherwise have killed me. It had been a gross violation of the Code Duello, the set of rules for resolving personal conflicts between individuals of the nations who had signed the Unseelie Accords.

The outcome of a clean duel might have put an early end to the war between the Red Court and the White Council of Wizards, and saved a lot of lives. It didn't turn out that way.

"Don't worry, guy," I told him. "Ortega was already in the middle of breaking the Code Duello anyway. It would have fallen out the way it did regardless of what you had done that night. And your being there meant that he ate a bullet at the last second instead of me. You saved my life. I'm cognizant of that."

I kept smiling at him. It didn't feel quite right, so I tried to do it a little harder. "I'm also aware that if you could have gotten what you wanted by putting the bullet in *my* back instead of his chest, you would have done it without blinking. So don't go thinking we're pals."

Martin looked at me and then relaxed. He said, "It's ironic that you, the mustang of the White Council, would immediately cling to its self-righteous position of moral authority."

"Excuse me?" I said quietly.

He spoke dispassionately, but there was a fire somewhere deep down behind the words—the first I'd ever heard in him. "I've seen children die, too, Dresden, slaughtered like animals by a threat no one in the wise and mighty Council seemed to give a good goddamn about—because the victims are poor, and far away, and isn't that a fine reason to let them die. Yes. If putting a bullet in you would have meant that the Council brought its forces to bear against the Red Court, I would have done it twice and paid for the privilege." He paused at a stop sign, gave me a direct look, and said, "It is good that we cleared the air. Is there anything else you want to say?"

I eyed the man and said, "You went blond. It makes you look sort of gay."

Martin shrugged, completely unperturbed. "My last assignment was on a cruise ship catering to that particular lifestyle."

I scowled and glanced at Susan.

She nodded. "It was."

I folded my arms, glowered out at the night, and said, "I have literally killed people I liked better than you, Martin." After another few moments, I asked, "Are we there yet?"

*   *   *

Martin stopped the car in front of a building and said, "It's in here."

I eyed the building. Nothing special, for Chicago. Twelve stories, a little run-down, all rented commercial space. "The Reds can't— Look, it can't be here," I said. "This building is where my office is."

"A known factor, for Red Court business holdings purchased it almost eight years ago," Martin said, putting the car in park and setting the emergency brake. "I should imagine that was when you saw that sudden rise in the rent."

I blinked a couple of times. "I've . . . been paying rent to the Red Court?"

"Increased rent," Martin said, with the faintest emphasis. "Duchess Arianna apparently has an odd sense of humor. If it's any consolation, the people working there have no idea who they're really working for. They think they're a firm that provides secure data backups to a multinational import-export corporation."

"But this is . . . *my building.*" I frowned and shook my head. "And we're going to do what, exactly?"

Martin got out of the car and opened the trunk. Susan joined him. I got out of the car on general principles.

"We," said Martin, definitely not including me, "are going to burgle the office and retrieve files that we hope will contain information that might point the way toward Arianna's locations and intentions. You are going to remain with the car."

"The hell I will," I said.

"Harry," Susan said, her tone brisk and reasonable, "it's computers."

I grunted as if Susan had nudged me with her elbow. Wizards and computers get along about as well as flamethrowers and libraries. All technology tends to behave unreliably in the presence of a mortal wizard, and the newer it is, the wonkier it seems to become. If I went along with them, well . . . you don't take your cat with you when you go bird shopping. Not because the cat isn't polite, but because he's a *cat*. "Oh," I said. "Then . . . I guess I'll stay with the car."

"Even odds we've been spotted or followed," Martin said to Susan. "We had to leave Guatemala in a hurry. It wasn't as smooth an exit as it could have been."

"We didn't have days to spare," Susan said, her voice carrying a tone of wearily familiar annoyance. It was like listening to a husband and wife having an often-repeated quarrel. She opened a case in the trunk and slipped several objects into her pockets. "Allowances have to be made."

Martin watched her for a moment, selected a single tool from the case, and then slid the straps of a backpack with a hard-sided frame over his shoulders. Presumably it had computer things in it. I stayed on the far side of the car from it and tried to think nonhostile thoughts.

"Just watch for trouble, Harry," Susan said. "We'll be back out in twenty minutes or less."

"Or we won't," Martin said. "In which case we'll know our sloppy exit technique caught up to us."

Susan made a quiet, disgusted sound, and the pair of them strode toward the building, got to the locked front doors, paused for maybe three seconds, and then vanished inside.

"And I'm just standing here," I muttered. "Like I'm Clifford the Big Red Dog. Too big and dumb to go inside with Emily Elizabeth. And it's *my building*." I shook my head. "Hell's bells, I am off my game. Or out of my mind. I mean, here I am talking to myself."

I knew why I was talking to myself—if I shut up, I would have nothing to think about but a small person, terrified and alone in a den of monsters. And that would make me think about how I had been shut out of her life. And that would make me think about the beast in my chest that was still clawing to get out.

When the local Red Court badass, the late Bianca, had stolen Susan away and begun her transformation into a full-fledged vampire of the Red Court, it had been the vampire's intention to take my girlfriend away from me. One way or another she had succeeded. Susan as she had been—always joking, always laughing, always touching or kissing or otherwise enjoying life in general and life with me in particular—was gone.

Now she was somewhere between Emma Peel and the She-Hulk. And we had loved each other once. And a child had been born because of it. And Susan had lied to—

Before I could begin circling the block a few more times on *that* vicious cycle, a cold feeling went slithering down my spine.

I didn't even look around. Several years of tense missions with Wardens not old enough to buy their own beer had taught me to trust my instincts when they went insane in a darkened city at two in the morning. Without even thinking about it, I crouched, reached into the air surrounding me, and drew a veil around myself.

Veils are subtle, tricky magic, using one of several basic theories to render objects or people less visible than they would be otherwise. I used to suck so badly at veils that I wouldn't even try them—but I'd had to bone up on them enough to be able to teach my apprentice, Molly Carpenter, how to use them. Molly had a real gift and had learned quickly, but I'd been forcing her to stretch her talents—and it had taken a lot of personal practice time for me to be able to fake it well enough to have credibility in front of the grasshopper.

Long story short—fast, simple veils were no longer beyond my grasp.

The street darkened slightly around me as I borrowed shadow and bent light. Being under a veil always reduced your own ability to see what was happening around you, and was a calculated risk. I figured it was probably worth it. If someone had a gun pointed my way, I had a long damned run before I could get around the corner of a nice thick building. It would be better to be unseen.

I crouched next to the car, not quite invisible but pretty close. The ability to be calm and still was critical to actually using a veil. It is *hard* to do when you think danger is close and someone might be planning to part you from your thoughts in a purely physical fashion. But I arrested the adrenaline surge and regulated my breathing. *Easy does it, Harry.*

So I had a dandy view of half a dozen figures that came darting toward the office building with a hideous, somehow arachnid grace. Two of them were bounding along rooftops, vaguely humanoid forms that moved as smoothly as if they were some kind of hunting cat. Three more were closing on the building from different angles at ground level, gliding from shadow to shadow. I couldn't sense much of them beyond blurs in the air and more shivers along my spine.

The last form was actually scuttling down the *sides* of buildings on the same street, bounding from one to the next, sticking to the walls like an enormous spider and moving with terrible speed.

I never got more of a look than that—flickering shadows moving with sinister purpose. But I knew what I was looking at.

Vampires.

Red Court vampires.

They closed on my office building like sharks on bloody meat.

The tempest in my chest suddenly raged, and as I watched them vanish into the building—*my* fricking building—like cockroaches somehow finding a way to wriggle into places they shouldn't be, the anger rose up from my chest to my eyes, and the reflections of streetlights in the window glass tinted red.

I let the vampires enter the building.

And then I gathered up my fury and pain, honing them like immaterial blades, and went in after them.

Chapter

Four

My blasting rod was hanging from its tie on the inside of my coat, a stick of oak about eighteen inches long and a bit thicker than my thumb. The ridges of the runes and sigils carved into it felt comfortably familiar under the fingers of my right hand as I drew it out.

I went up to the building as silently as I could, let myself in with my key, and dropped the veil only after I was inside. It wasn't going to do anything to hide me from a vampire that got close—they'd be able to smell me and hear my heartbeat anyway. The veil would only hamper my own vision, which was going to be taxed enough.

I didn't take the elevator. It wheezed and rattled and would alert everyone in the building to where I was. I checked the index board in the lobby. Datasafe, Inc., resided on the ninth floor, five stories above my office. That was probably where Martin and Susan were. It would be where the vampires were heading.

I hit the stairs and took a risk. Spells to dull sound and keep conversations private were basic fare for wizards of my abilities, and it wasn't much harder to make sure that sound didn't leave the immediate area around me. Of course, that meant that I was effectively putting myself in a sonic bubble—I wouldn't hear anything coming toward me, either. But for the moment, at least, I knew the vampires were here while they presumably were unaware of me. I wanted to keep it that way.

Besides, in quarters this close, by the time I reacted to a noise from a vampire I hadn't seen, I was as good as dead anyway.

So I murmured the words to a reliable bit of phonoturgy and went up the stairs clad in perfect silence. Which was a good thing. I run on a regular basis, but running down a sidewalk or a sandy beach isn't the same thing as running up stairs. By the time I got to the ninth floor, my legs were burning, I was breathing hard, and my left knee was killing me. What the hell? When had my knees become something I had to worry about?

Cheered by that thought, I paused at the door to the ninth-floor hallway, opened it beneath the protection of my cloak of silence, and then dropped the spell so that I could listen.

. Hissing, gurgling speech in a language I couldn't understand came from the hallway before me, maybe right around the corner I could see ahead. I literally held my breath. Vampires have superhuman senses, but they are as vulnerable to distraction as anyone. If they were talking, they might not hear me, and regular human traffic in this building would probably hide my scent from them.

And why, exactly, a voice somewhere within the storm in my chest whispered, *should I be hiding from these murdering scum in the first place?* Red Court vampires were killers, one and all. A half-turned vampire didn't go all the way over until they'd killed another human being and fed upon their life's blood. Granted, an unwilling soul taken into the Red Court found themselves at the mercy of new and nearly irresistible hungers—but that didn't change the fact that if they were a card-carrying member of the Red Court, they had killed someone to be there.

Monsters. Monsters who dragged people into the darkness and inflicted unspeakable torments upon them for pleasure—and I should know. They'd done it to me once. Monsters whose existence was a plague upon millions.

Monsters who had taken my child.

The man once wrote: *Do not meddle in the affairs of wizards, for they are subtle and quick to anger.* Tolkien had that one mostly right.

I stepped forward, let the door bang closed, and snarled, "Fuck subtle."

The gurgle-hissing from around the corner ahead stopped at a confused intersection of speech that needed no translation: *Huh?*

I lifted the blasting rod, aimed it at the corner ahead of me, and poured my rage, my will, and my power into it as I snarled, *"Fuego!"*

Silver-white fire howled down the hallway and bit into the corner ahead, blowing through it as easily as a bullet through a paper target. I drew the line of fire to my left, and as quickly as that, the fire gouged an opening as big as my fist through several sections of studs and drywall, blasting through to the perpendicular hallway where I'd heard the vampires talking. The din was incredible. Wood tore and exploded. Drywall flew into clouds of dust. Pipes screamed as they were severed as neatly as if I'd used a cutter. Wires erupted into clouds of popping sparks.

And something entirely inhuman let out a piercing shriek of pain, pain driven by unnaturally powerful lungs into a scream that was louder than gunshots.

I screamed in answer, in challenge, in defiance, and

pelted forward. The runes on my blasting rod shone with white-hot fire, throwing brilliant silver-white light out ahead of me into the darkened building as I ran.

As I rounded the corner a shape was already in motion, coming toward me. My shield bracelet was ready. I lifted my left hand, fingers contorted into a gesture that had nothing to do with magic but that was generally considered insulting. My will poured into the charm bracelet hung with multiple tiny shields, and in an instant my power spread from there into a quarter-dome shape of pure, invisible force in front of me. The black shape of the vampire hit the shield, sending up concentric circles of blue light and white sparks, and then rebounded from it.

I dropped the shield almost before he was done rebounding, leveled the blasting rod with a flick of my wrist, and ripped the vampire in half with a word and a beam of silver fire. The pieces flew off in different directions, still kicking and thrashing hideously.

In the middle of the hallway was a second bisected vampire, which I'd apparently hit when firing blindly through the wall. It was also dying messily. Because I've seen too many bad horror movies and know the rules for surviving them, the instant I'd made sure the hallway was empty of more threats, I swung the rod up to point above me.

A vampire clung to the ceiling not twenty feet away. People have this image of vampires as flawless, beautiful gods of dark sex and temptation. And, while the Red Court can create a kind of outer human shell called a flesh mask, and while that mask was generally lovely, there was something very different underneath—a true, hideous, unrepentant monster, like the one looking down at me.

It was maybe six feet tall when standing, though its arms were scrawny and long enough to drag the backs of its claw-tipped hands along the ground. Its skin was rubbery and black, spotted here and there with unhealthy-looking bits of pink, and its belly hung down in flabby grotesquerie. It was bandy-legged and hunchbacked, and its face was somewhere between that of a vampire bat and something from H. R. Giger's hallucinations.

It saw me round the corner, and its goggling black eyes seemed to get even larger. It let out a scream of . . .

Terror.

It screamed in fear.

The vampire flung itself away from me even as I unleashed a third blast, bounding away down the hall, flinging itself from the ceiling to the wall to the floor to the wall and back again, wildly dodging the stream of ruinous energy I sent after it.

"That's right!" I heard myself scream. "You'd better run, pretty boy!" It vanished around the next corner and I shouted in incoherent rage, kicked the still-twitching head of one of the downed vampires with the tip of my steel-toed work boots, and rushed after it in pursuit, cursing up a storm.

The entire business had taken, at most, six or seven seconds.

After that, things got a little complicated.

I'd started half a dozen small fires with the blasts, and before I'd gone another half a dozen steps the fire alarms twittered shrilly. Sprinkler systems went off all around me. And at the same moment, gunfire erupted from somewhere ahead of me. None of that was good.

The alarms meant that the authorities would be on the way—and except for the smartest guys in CPD's Special Investigations, they just weren't ready to deal with a vampire. They'd be little more than victims and potential hostages to the supernatural predators.

The falling water wasn't good, either. Running water grounds magical energies, and while it wouldn't shut me down completely, it would make everything harder to do, like running through soft sand or over wet clay. And the gunshots weren't good because a pair of bullets came through the wall not six feet away, and one of them tugged hard at the hem of my jeans over my left ankle.

"Ack!" I said.

Fearless master of the witty dialogue, that's me.

I twisted my left wrist across the front of my body, brought my shield up again. A couple of bullets that probably wouldn't have hit me anyway popped off of it, concentric circles of flickering blue light spreading from the points of impact. I dashed down the hall and around the corner, the blasting rod in my right hand lifted and ready.

There were two vampires in front of a door to an office. One of them was on the floor, thrashing and hissing in agony, clutching at its flabby belly. It was leaking blood all over the floor. Several dozen bullet holes—exit holes—in the door explained why. The injuries wouldn't kill the vamp, but they were painful and robbed it of the source of its supernatural power—the blood it had devoured. The other was crouched to the side of the doorway, as if debating with itself whether or not it should try to rush the door as its companion apparently had.

My runner went by them, wailing in fear.

I slid to a stop on the rapidly moistening floor, lifted the rod, and cut loose with another blast. It howled down the hallway, and the running vamp seized the wounded one and pulled it up to intercept the shot I'd meant for it. The wounded vamp screamed and absorbed just enough of the energy to let the runner plunge through the drywall at the end of the hall. It vanished from sight, and a second later I heard the sound of glass breaking as it fled the building.

The luckless vampire was dead, or on the final approach to it, since the beam had sliced off almost everything to the left of its spine. The final vampire whirled toward me, hesitating.

It proved fatal. The wall behind it suddenly exploded outward, and Martin, his skin livid with dark tattoos, came crashing through it. He drove the vampire across the hallway and slammed it into the wall. One hand snaked around the surprised vampire's belly, and a knife gleamed. Scarlet gore fountained against the wall, and the vampire collapsed, screaming breathlessly.

Martin leapt clear before the thrashing creature got lucky with one of its claws, snapped his gaze up and down the hallway, saw the hole in the far wall, and said, "Damnation. You let one get away?"

Before I could answer him, Susan appeared, slipping out through the hole in the wall. She had the computer backpack slung over one shoulder and a smoking gun in her hand, a .45 automatic with an extended magazine. She took a look at the vampire on the ground and lifted the gun, her dark eyes hard and cold.

"Wait," I said. "There were six. He's number four."

"There are always six of them," Susan said. "Standard operations team."

She calmly pulled the trigger, letting loose a short, precise burst of automatic fire, and blew the wounded vampire's head into disgusting mulch.

Martin looked at his watch. "We don't have long."

Susan nodded and they both started down the hallway, toward the stairs. "Come on, Harry. We found floor plans. The building's wired."

I blinked and ran after them. "Wired? To what?"

"The explosives are on the fourth floor," Martin said calmly, "placed all around your office."

"Those *jerks*," I said. "They told us they were cleaning out asbestos!"

Susan barked out a short laugh, but Martin frowned her down. "When that runner gets them word about what happened, they'll set them off. I suggest we hurry."

"Holy crap," I breathed.

We sprinted for the stairs. Going down them took a lot less time than going up, but it was harder to control. I stumbled once and Susan caught me by the arm, her fingers like bands of rigid steel. We reached the bottom together.

"Not out the front!" I barked. "Inbound authorities!"

I pounded past them and led them down a short hallway and out a side door, into an alley. Then we sprinted to the back of the building, down another alley, and away.

We had made it to the next block when light flashed and a giant the size of the Sears building hauled off and swatted us all with a pillow from his enormous bed. We were flung from our feet. Susan and Martin landed in a roll, tumbling several times. By contrast, I crashed into a garbage can.

It was, of course, full.

I lay there for a moment, my ears putting out a constant, high-pitched tone. A cloud of dust and particles washed over me, mixing with whatever hideous stew was in the trash can and caking itself to my body.

"I am not playing at the top of my game," I mused aloud. I felt the words buzz in my throat, but I couldn't hear them.

A few seconds later, sounds began to drift back in. Car horns and car alarms were going off everywhere. Storefront security systems were screaming. Sirens—lots and lots of sirens—were closing in.

A hand slipped beneath my arm and someone helped me stand up. Susan. She was lightly coated with dust. It filled the air so thickly that we couldn't see more than ten or twenty feet. I tried to walk and staggered.

Martin got underneath my other arm, and we started shambling away through the dust. After a little while, things stopped spinning so wildly. I realized that Martin and Susan were talking.

"—sure there's not *something* left?" Susan was saying.

"I'll have to examine it sector by sector," Martin said tonelessly. "We might get a few crumbs. What the hell was he thinking, throwing that kind of power around when he *knew* we were after electronic data?"

"He was probably thinking that the information would be useless to the two of us if we were dead," Susan said back, rather pointedly. "They had us. And you know it."

Martin said nothing for a while. Then he said, "That. Or he didn't want us to get the information. He was quite angry."

"He isn't that way," she said. "It isn't him."

"It wasn't him," Martin corrected her. "Are you the same person you were eight years ago?"

She didn't say anything for a while.

I remembered how to walk, and started doing it on my own. I shook my head to clear it a little and looked back over my shoulder.

There were buildings on fire. More and more sirens were on the way. The spot in the skyline where my office building usually sat from this angle was empty except for a spreading cloud of dust. Fires and emergency lights painted the dust orange and red and blue.

My files. My old coffee machine. My spare revolver. My favorite mug. My ratty, comfortable old desk and chair. My frosted-glass window with its painted lettering reading, HARRY DRESDEN, WIZARD.

They were all gone.

"Dammit," I said.

Susan looked up at me. "What was that?"

I answered in a weary mumble. "I mailed in the rent on my office this morning."

Chapter

Five

We got a cab. We got out of the area before the cops had cordoned off a perimeter. It wasn't all that hard. Chicago has a first-rate police department, but nobody can establish that big a cordon around a large area with a lot of people in the dead of night quickly or easily. They'd have to call and get people out of bed and onto the job, and pure confusion would slow everything down.

By morning, I knew, word of the explosion would be all over the news. There would be reporters and theories and eyewitness interviews with people who had sort of heard something happen and seen a cloud of dust. This hadn't been a fire, like we'd seen a few times before. This had been an explosion, a deliberate act of destruction. They would be able to find out that much in the aftermath.

There would be search and rescue on the scene.

I closed my eyes and leaned my head on the window. Odds were good that there was no one else in the building. All the tenants were businesses. None of them was prone to operating late at night. But all of them had keys to get in when they needed to, just like I did. There could have been janitors or maintenance people there—

employees of the Red Court, sure, but they didn't know that. You don't explain to the janitorial staff how your company is a part of a sinister organization with goals of global infiltration and control. You just tell them to clean the floor.

There could very well be dead people in that building who wouldn't have been there except for the fact that my office was on the fourth floor.

Jesus.

I felt Susan's eyes on me. None of us had spoken in front of the cabbie. Nobody spoke now, until Martin said, "Here. Pull over here."

I looked up. The cab was pulling up to a cheap motel.

"We should stay together," Susan said.

"We can go over the disk here," Martin said. "We can't do that at his place. I need your help. He doesn't."

"Go on," I said. "People"—by which I meant the police—"are going to be at my place soon anyway. Easier if they only have one person to talk to."

Susan exhaled firmly through her nose. Then nodded. The two of them got out of the cab. Martin doled out some cash to the driver and gave him my home address.

I rode home in silence. The cabbie was listening to the news on the radio. I was pretty beat, having tossed around a bunch of magic at the building. Magic can be awfully cool, but it's exhausting. What was left buzzing around me wasn't enough to screw up the radio, which was already alive with talk of the explosion. The cabbie, who looked like he was vaguely Middle Eastern in extraction, looked unhappy.

I felt that.

We stopped at my apartment. Martin had already paid him too much for the ride, but I duked him another twenty on top of that and gave him a serious look. "Your name is Ahmahd?"

It was right there on his cabbie license. He nodded hesitantly.

"You have a family, Ahmahd?"

He just stared at me.

I touched my finger to my lips in a hushing gesture. "You never saw me. Okay?"

He grimaced, but dipped his head in a nod.

I got out of the cab, feeling a little sick. I wouldn't hurt the guy's family, but he didn't know that. And even if he did, that and the bribe together wouldn't be enough to keep him from talking to the cops if they came asking—though I suspected it would be enough to keep him from jumping up to volunteer information. Buildings were exploding. Sane people would want to keep their heads down until it was over.

I watched the car drive away, put my hands in my coat pockets, and shuffled wearily home. I'd cut into my physical and psychic resources pretty hard when I'd turned all that energy loose on the vampires, and now I was paying the price. I'd unintentionally poured soulfire into every blast I'd leveled at them—which was why I'd had the nifty silver-white blasts of flame instead of the red-orange of standard-issue fire. I felt like falling into bed, but it wouldn't be the smart move. I debated doing it anyway.

I had time to get a shower, take Mouse out for a much-needed trip outside, put on a pot of coffee, and was just finishing up cleaning the debris and trash from my leather duster with some handy-dandy leather-cleaning wipes Charity Carpenter, Molly's mother, had sent over, when there was a knock at the door.

Mouse lifted his head from where he lay near me, his

brown eyes wary and serious. Then his ears perked up, and his tail began to wag. He got up and took a step toward the door, then looked at me.

"Yeah, yeah," I said. "I'm going."

I got up and opened the door. It stuck halfway. I pulled harder and got it open the rest of the way.

A woman a little more than five feet tall stood at my door, her face weary and completely free of makeup. Her hair was golden blond, but hanging all over her face and badly in need of attention from a brush and maybe a curling iron. Or at least a scrunchie. She was wearing sweatpants and an old and roomy T-shirt, and her shoulders were hunched up in rigid tension.

She stared at me for a moment. Then she closed her eyes and her shoulders relaxed.

"Hiya, Murphy," I said.

"Hey," she said, her voice a little feeble. I enjoyed the moment. I didn't get to see Murphy's soft side often. "Do I smell coffee?"

"Made a fresh pot," I said. "Get you some?"

Murphy let out a groan of something near lust. "Marry me."

"Maybe when you're conscious." I stepped back and let her in. Murph sat down on the couch and Mouse came over to her and laid his head shamelessly on her lap. She yawned and scratched and petted him obligingly, her small, strong hands making his doggy eyes close in bliss.

I passed her a cup of coffee and got one for myself. She took it black with a couple of zero-calorie sweeteners in it. Mine came with cream and lots and lots of sugar. We sipped coffee together, and her eyes became more animate as the caffeine went in. Neither of us spoke, and her gaze eventually roved over my apartment and me. I could hear the wheels spinning in her head.

"You showered less than an hour ago. I can still smell the soap. And you just got done cleaning your coat. At four in the morning."

I sipped coffee and neither confirmed nor denied.

"You were at the building when it blew up," she said.

"Not *at* it," I said. "I'm good, but I don't know about having a building fall on me."

She shook her head. She stared at the remainder of her coffee. "Rawlins called. Told me that your office building had exploded. I thought someone had gotten to you, finally."

"We on the record?" I asked. Murphy was a detective sergeant with Chicago PD's Special Investigations division. It was the dead-end department of CPD and the only one with any clue whatsoever about the supernatural world. Even so, Murphy was a cop to the bone. She could stretch the line when it came to legality, but she had limits. I'd crossed them before.

She shook her head. "No. Not yet."

"Red Court," I said. "They bought the building a few years back. They wired it to blow if they wanted to do it."

Murphy frowned. "Why do it now? Why not blow you up years ago?"

I grunted. "Personal grudge, I guess," I said. "Duchess Arianna is upset about what happened to her husband when he tangled with me. She thinks it's my fault."

"Is it?"

"Pretty much," I said.

She swirled the coffee around the bottom of the cup. "So why not just kill you? Click, boom."

"I don't know," I said. "She figured it wasn't enough, maybe. Click-boom is business. What I have going with her is personal."

My jaws creaked a little as I clenched them.

Murphy's blue eyes missed little. "Personal?" She looked around again. "Your place looks too nice. Who was it?"

"Susan."

Her back straightened a little. It was the only sign of surprise she showed. Murphy knew all about Susan. "You want to talk about it?"

I didn't, but Murphy needed to know. I laid it out for her in sentences of three and four words. By the time I'd finished, she had set her mug on the coffee table and was listening to me intently.

"Jesus and Mary, Mother of God," she breathed. "Harry."

"Yeah."

"That . . . that *bitch*."

I shook my head. "Pointing fingers does nothing for Maggie. We'll do that later."

She grimaced, as if swallowing something bitter. Then she nodded. "You're right."

"Thank you."

"What are you going to do?" she asked.

"Martin and Susan are seeing what they can get off the disk," I said. "They'll contact me as soon as they know something. Meantime, I'll get a couple hours horizontal, then start hitting my contacts. Go to the Council and ask them for help."

"That bunch of heartless, gutless, spineless old pricks," she said.

I found myself smiling, a little, at my coffee.

"Are they going to give it to you?" Murphy asked.

"Maybe. It's complicated," I said. "Are *you* going to get CPD to help me?"

Her eyes darkened. "Maybe. It's complicated."

I spread my hands in a "there you are" gesture, and she nodded. She rose and paced over to the sink to put her cup down. "What can I do to help?"

"Be nice if the police didn't lock me up for a while. They'll realize that the explosives were around my office eventually."

She shook her head. "No promises. I'll do what I can."

"Thank you."

"I want in," she said. "You're both too involved in this. You'll need someone with perspective."

I started to snap back something nasty, but shut my stupid mouth because she was probably right. I put my own coffee cup in the sink to give me an excuse not to talk while I tried to cool down. Then I said, "I would have asked you anyway, Murph. I need a good gun hand."

Tiny Murphy might be, but she'd survived more scrapes with the supernatural than any other vanilla mortal I'd ever met. She'd keep her head in a crisis, even if the crisis included winged demons, howling ghouls, slavering vampires, and human sacrifice. She'd keep anyone—by which I meant Martin—from stabbing me in the back. She'd keep her gun up and firing, too. I'd seen her do it.

"Harry . . ." she began.

I waved a hand. "Won't ask you to break any of Chicago's laws. Or U.S. laws. But I doubt we're going to be in town for this one."

She absorbed that for a moment, folded her arms, and looked at the fire. Mouse watched her silently from where he sat near the couch.

She said, "I'm your friend, Harry."

"Never had a doubt."

"You're going to take Maggie back."

My jaw ached. "Damn right I am."

"Okay," she said. "I'm in."

I bowed my head, my eyes abruptly burning, the emotion clashing with the storm in my belly.

"Th—" I began. My voice broke. I tried again. "Thank you, Karrin."

I felt her hand take mine for a moment, warm and steady.

"We *will* get her back," she said, very quietly. "We *will*, Harry. I'm in."

Chapter
Six

I didn't sleep long, but I did it well. When my old Mickey Mouse windup alarm clock went off at seven, I had to fight my way up from a deep place on the far side of dreamland. I felt like I could use another eighteen or twenty hours.

It was another instance of my emotions getting the better of me. Using soulfire on pure, instinctive reflex was a mistake—potentially a fatal one. The extramortal well of power that soulfire offered was formidable in ways I understood only imperfectly. I don't know if it made my spells any more effective against the Red Court—though I had a hunch that it sure as H-E-double-hockey-sticks did—but I was dead certain that it had drawn upon my own life energy to do it. If I pulled on it too much, well. No more life energy kinda means no more life. And if that energy was indeed the same force that is commonly known as a soul, it might mean oblivion.

Depending on what actually happened when you got to the far side, I guess. I have no idea. And no mortal or immortal creature I had ever met had sounded like he knew for sure, either.

I did know that powerful emotions were an excellent source of additional energy for working magic, sort of a turbocharger. Throw a destructive spell in the grip of a vast fury, and you'd get a lot more bang for your effort than if you did it while relaxed on a practice field. The danger, of course, was that you could never really be sure how much effect such an emotion would have on a spell—which meant that you ran a much higher risk of losing control of the energy. Guys operating on my level can kill others or themselves at the slightest mistake.

Maybe the soulfire came from a similar place as the emotions. Maybe you couldn't have one without at least a little bit of the other. Maybe they were all mixed together, like protein powder and skim milk in a health smoothie.

Didn't matter, really. Less than sixty seconds of action the night before left me exhausted. If I didn't get a handle on the soulfire, I could literally kill myself with it.

"Get it together, Harry," I growled to myself.

I shambled out of bed and out into the living room to find that my apprentice, Molly, had come in while I was sleeping and was profaning breakfast in my tiny kitchen.

She wore a simple outfit—jeans and a black T-shirt that read, in very small white letters, IF YOU CAN READ THIS, YOU'D BETTER HAVE BOUGHT ME DINNER. Her golden hair was longer—she'd been letting it grow—and hung down to her shoulder blades in back. She'd colored it near the tips with green that darkened to blue as it went down.

I'm not sure if Molly was "bangin'," or "slammin'," or "hawt," since the cultural catchphrase cycles every couple of minutes. But if you picked a word meant to be a term of praise and adoration for the beauty of a young woman, it was probably applicable. For me, the effect was somewhat spoiled, because I'd known her since she was a skinny kid somewhere between the ages of training wheels and training bra, but that didn't mean that I didn't have an academic appreciation for her looks. When she paid any attention, men fell all over her.

Mouse sat alertly at her feet. The big dog was very good about not taking food off the table or from the stove or the counter or on top of the refrigerator, but he had drawn a line on the linoleum: If any bits fell to the floor, and he could get to them first, they were his. His brown eyes tracked Molly's hands steadily. From the cheerful wag of his tail, she had probably already dropped things several times. She was a soft touch where the pooch was concerned.

"Morning, boss," she chirped.

I glowered at her, but shambled out to the kitchen. She dumped freshly scrambled eggs onto a plate next to bacon, toast, and some mixed bits of fruit, and pressed a large glass of OJ into my hand.

"Coffee," I said.

"You're quitting this week. Remember? We had a deal: I make breakfast and you quit morning coffee."

I scowled at her through the coffeeless haze. I dimly remembered some such agreement. Molly had grown up being interested in staying healthy, and had gotten more so of late. She was careful about what she ate, and had decided to pass that joy on to me.

"I hate morning people," I said, and grabbed my breakfast. I stalked over to the couch and said, "Don't feed Mouse anything. Not good for him."

Mouse didn't twitch an ear. He just sat there watching Molly and grinning.

I drank orange juice, which I found a completely inadequate beginning to my day. The bacon turned out to be made of turkey, and the edges were burned. I ate it anyway, along with toast that was not quite done enough.

The grasshopper had talents, but cooking was not among them. "Things are up," I said.

She stood at the sink, scrubbing a pan, and looked up at me interestedly. "Oh? What?"

I grunted and thought about the matter carefully for a moment. Molly was not much for combat. It just wasn't her field. The next few days would certainly be hazardous for me, and I could live with that. But if Molly got involved, they might well be murderous.

I'd seen both sides of the "ignorance is safety" line of thinking in action. I'd seen people die who wouldn't have if they hadn't been told about the supernatural and its hazards, and I'd seen them die because they'd been forewarned, and it just wasn't enough to really impress the scale of the threat upon them. There was just no way to know what would happen.

And *because* I had no way to know what would happen, I'd come to the conclusion that, absent factors that might make me believe to the contrary, I just wasn't wise enough to deny them the choice. Molly was a part of my life. This would affect her strongly, in one way or another. The only responsible thing to do was to let her decide for herself how she wanted to live her life. That included endangering it, if that was what she felt was appropriate.

So, much as I had for Murphy, I laid it out for the grasshopper.

By the time I was finished, Molly was kneeling on the floor next to where I sat at the sofa, her blue eyes wide. "Wow, Harry."

"Yeah," I said.

"Wow."

"You said that."

"This changes everything."

I nodded.

"How can I help?"

I hoped that she hadn't just chosen to get herself killed. "You tell me. What's the smart move, padawan?"

She chewed on her lip for a moment and then peered up at me. "We need information. And we need backup. Edinburgh?"

I drank the last swallow of my orange juice, resented its healthiness, and said, "Bingo."

We took the Ways to Edinburgh, taking advantage of the weird geography of the spirit world to cover a lot more physical distance in the material world. Only certain previously explored routes were safe and reliable, and you had to have some serious supernatural juice to open the door, so to speak, between the real world and the Nevernever, but if you could do it, the Ways were darned handy. The Chicago-to-Edinburgh trip took us about half an hour.

The headquarters of the White Council of wizards is a dull, dim, drafty sort of place—not unlike the insides of the heads of a great many people who work there. It's all underground, a network of tunnels, its walls covered in carvings of mystic runes and sigils, of stylized designs and genuinely beautiful artistry. The ceilings are kind of low for me in places. Some of the tunnels are pitch-black, but most of them are bathed in a kind of ambient light without a visible source, which is an awfully odd look— sort of like one of those black lights that makes certain other colors seem to glow.

We passed two security checkpoints and walked for another five minutes before Molly shook her head. "How big is this place?" Her subdued voice echoed down the empty tunnels.

"Big," I said. "Almost as big as the city above, and it has multiple levels. Way more than we actually use."

She trailed her fingers over an elaborate carving in the stone as we passed it, a mural depicting a forest scene, its edges and lines crisp and clean despite the smoke from occasional torches and the passage of centuries. Her fingers left little trails in the light layer of dust coating the wall. "Did the Council carve it out?"

"Nah," I said. "That would have been too much like work. Rumor has it that it used to be the palace of the lord of the Daoine Sidhe. That the original Merlin won it from him in a bet."

"Like, *Merlin* Merlin?" she asked. "Sword in the stone and so on?"

"Same guy," I said. "Doubt he was much like in the movies."

"Wrote the Laws of Magic, founded the White Council, was custodian of one of the Swords and established a stronghold for the Council, too," Molly said. "He must have been something else."

"He must have been a real bastard," I said. "Guys who get their name splashed all over history and folklore don't tend to be Boy Scout troop leaders."

"You're such a cynic," Molly said.

"I think cynics are playful and cute."

There was no traffic at all in the main corridor, which surprised me. I mean, it was never exactly crowded, but you usually bumped into *someone*.

I headed for Warden country. There was a large dormitory set up for the militant branch of the White Council, where I could generally be confident of finding a surly, suspicious face. It was also very possible that Anastasia Luccio, captain of the Wardens, was there. The cafeteria and the administrative offices were nearby, so it was hands down the busiest part of the stronghold.

Warden country and the cafeteria were both empty, though there was a deck of cards spread out on a table in one of the lounges. "Weird," I muttered. "All the checkpoints are business-as-usual or I'd think something was wrong."

Molly frowned. "Maybe someone got into the heads of the sentries."

"Nah. They're jerks, but they're not incompetent jerks. No one around here is going to get away with mental buggery for a while."

"Buggery?" Molly asked.

"Hey, we're in the United Kingdom. When in Rome."

We went across the hall to administration and, finally, found someone: a harried-looking woman who sat at an old switchboard—the kind with about a million holes and plugs that had to be manually inserted and removed to run it. She wore a pair of ancient-looking headphones and spoke into an old radio microphone. "No. No, we have no word at this time. When we learn something, you will be informed." She jerked the wire out, plugged it in under another flashing light, and repeated her spiel. I watched that half a dozen times before I literally waved a hand in front of her face to get her to notice us.

She stopped and blinked up at me. She was a matronly-looking woman, iron grey woven smoothly through her brown hair, which meant that she could be anywhere between forty-five and two hundred years old. Her eyes flicked over me and then Molly, and I saw her body tense. She eased her rolling chair a few inches back from us—like most of the older crew of wizards, she probably regarded me as a sociopath looking for a nice bell tower. The switchboard lights blinked on and off steadily. They were the old kind that made little clicking sounds as they did.

"Ah," she said. "Wizard Dresden. I am quite busy."

"It looks like it," I said. "Wizard MacFee, right? Where is everybody?"

She blinked at me again, as though I had spoken in Ewok. "Why, they're in the Senior Council's residence hall. It was the only place big enough for everyone who wished to witness it."

I nodded pleasantly and tried to remain calm. "Witness what?"

"The ambassador," MacFee said, impatience touching her voice. She gestured at the switchboard. "You haven't heard?"

"Was sort of busy yesterday," I said. "Heard what?"

"Why, the Red Court, of course," she said. "They've sent an ambassador plenipotentiary." She beamed. "They want to change the cease-fire into a genuine peace. They've sent no less than Duchess Arianna Ortega to ask for terms."

Chapter

Seven

I felt my stomach flutter around inside me.

The duchess was playing dirty. As the Red Court envoy, of course she'd have some advance knowledge about her people's intentions. There was no way in hell that this was a coincidence. It was too perfect.

If the Red Court was offering a return to the status quo—and older wizards love status quo, let me tell you—and adding in something to sweeten it to boot . . . the Senior Council would never authorize an action that would jeopardize such a peace. Not for some random little girl—and certainly not for the offspring of the White Council's most famous maybe-psychotic problem child, Harry Dresden, and a half-vampire terrorist.

Plenty of the people on the Council thought I should have been beheaded when I was sixteen. It made the younger wizards think I was cool and dangerous, which probably explained my popularity with them. The older members of the Council, though, held the lion's share of its influence and authority. That set would be happy to take any reasonable excuse to leave me hanging in the wind, and Duchess Arianna clearly planned to give it to them.

She was cutting me off.

It wasn't until then that I noticed that while my brain had been calmly paddling down the stream of logic, the raging cauldron in my belly had overflowed, and I was walking with smooth, swift strides down a hallway, my staff in my left hand, my blasting rod in my right, and the runes and carvings of both were blazing with carmine light.

That was somewhat alarming.

Someone was shaking my arm, and I looked down to see that Molly was hanging on to my left arm with both hands. I was dragging her sneakers forward across the stone floor, though she was clearly trying to stop me.

"Harry!" she said desperately. "Harry! You can't!"

I turned my face away from her and kept walking.

"Harry, please!" she all but screamed. "This won't help Maggie!"

It took me a few seconds to work out how to stop walking. I did it, and took a slow breath.

Molly leaned her forehead against my shoulder, panting, her voice shaking. She still held on tight. "Please. You can't. You can't go in there like this. They'll kill you." I heard her swallow down a mouthful of terror. "If we have to do it this way . . . at least let me veil you."

I closed my eyes and took more deep breaths, concentrating on pushing my anger back down. It felt like swallowing acid. But when I opened my eyes, the runes on the staff and rod were quiescent once more.

I glanced at Molly. She looked up at me, her eyes reddened and afraid.

"I'm okay," I told her.

She bit her lip and nodded. "Okay."

I leaned over and kissed her hair gently. "Thank you, Molly."

She offered me a hesitant smile and nodded again.

I stood there for a moment more before I said, gently, "You can let go of my arm now."

"Oh, right," she said, releasing me. "Sorry."

I stared down the hallway in front of me, trying to order my thoughts. "Okay," I said. "Okay."

"Harry?" Molly asked.

"This isn't the time or the place to fight," I said.

"Um," Molly said. "Yes. I mean, clearly."

"Don't start," I told her. "Okay. So the duchess is here to play games. . . ." I clenched my jaw. "Fine. Game on."

I started forward again with a determined stride, and Molly hurried to keep up.

We proceeded to the White Council's ostentatiatory.

I know. That isn't a word. But it should be. If you'd seen the quarters of the Senior Council, you'd back me up.

I strode down the hall and nodded to the squad of twelve Wardens on guard outside the chambers of the Senior Council. They were all from the younger generation—apparently there were grown-up things happening on the other side of the large double doors, to which the children could contribute nothing but confusion.

For once, the Council's geriatocracy had worked in my favor. If they'd left one of the old guard out here, he would certainly have tried to prevent me from entering on general principles. As it was, several of the doorkeepers nodded to me and murmured quiet greetings as I approached.

I nodded back briskly and never slowed my steps. "No time, guys. I need to get in."

They hurried to open the doors, and I went through them without slowing down and stepped into the chambers of the Senior Council.

I felt impressed upon entering, as I always did. The place was huge. You could fit a Little League baseball field in it and have room left over for a basketball court. A rectangular central hall splayed out in front of me, its floor made of white marble with veins of gold running through it. Marble steps at the far end swept up to a balcony that circled the entire place, which was supported by Corinthian columns of marble that matched the floor. There was a quiet waterfall at the far end of the chamber, running down into a pool, surrounded by a garden of living trees and plants and the chirp of the occasional bird.

A platform stage had been erected in the middle of the room, complete with stagelike lighting from a number of brightly glowing crystals, plus another mounted on a wooden podium that would, I took it, provide amplified sound for anyone speaking near it. The place was packed with wizards standing on the floor in a miniature sea of humanity, with more of them lining the balcony above, filling the place to its capacity.

All in all, the ostentatiatory was so overdone that you couldn't help but be impressed, which was the point, and though my brain knew it was hundreds of feet underground, my eyes insisted that it was lit by natural sunlight.

It wasn't, though: There was a vampire standing on the platform stage, beside the newest member of the Senior Council, Wizard Cristos. He stood at the podium, smiling and addressing the assembly. The rest of the Senior Council, resplendent in their black formal robes and purple stoles, looked on with their hoods raised.

". . . another example of how we must meet the future with our eyes—and minds—open to the possibility of change," Cristos said. He had a great speaking voice, a strong, smooth baritone that rolled effortlessly through the enormous chamber. He spoke in Latin, the official language of the Council—which ought to tell you something about their mind-set. "Humanity is already beginning to move away from the cycle of unthinking violence and war, learning to coexist with its neighbors in peace, working together to find solutions to their mutual problems, rather than allowing them to devolve into bloodshed." He smiled benevolently, a tall, spare man with a mane of flowing gray hair, a dark beard, and piercing dark eyes. He wore his formal robes open, the better to display the designer business suit beneath it.

"It is for this reason that I requested a telephone conference with the Red King," he continued. He used the English word for *telephone*, since there wasn't a proper Latin noun for it. It garnered a reaction from the assembled Council watching the proceedings. Such things were not done. "And after speaking with him for a time, I secured his support for a clearly defined, binding, and mutually acceptable peace. Creating the peace is in everyone's best interests, and it is for this reason that I am pleased to present to you, wizards of the White Council, the Duchess Arianna Ortega of the Red Court."

Several wizards not far from Cristos's position on the stage began clapping enthusiastically, and it spread haltingly throughout the chamber, eventually maturing into polite applause.

Arianna stepped up to the podium, smiling.

She was gorgeous. I don't mean "cutest girl at the club" gorgeous. I mean that she looked like a literal goddess. The details almost didn't matter. Tall. Dark hair. Skin like milk, like polished ivory. Eyes as blue as the twilight sky. She wore a gown of red silk, with a neckline that plunged gorgeously. Jewels touched her throat, her ears. Her hair was piled up on her head, occasional loose ringlets falling out. Hers was a beauty so pure that it was nearly painful to behold—Athena heading out on a Friday night.

It took me a good five or six seconds of staring to realize that there was something beneath that beauty that I did not like at all. Her loveliness itself, I realized, was a weapon—such creatures as she had driven men literally insane with desire and obsession. More to the point, I knew that her beauty was only skin-deep. I knew what lurked beneath.

"Thank you, Wizard Cristos," the duchess said. "It is a very great honor to be received here today in the interests of creating a peace between our two nations, and thereby finally putting an end to the abominable bloodshed between our peoples."

The Applause Squad started up again as Arianna paused. People picked up on the cue faster this time. Outside of the wizards who stood on the floor beneath the raised stage, the applause was still polite and halfhearted.

I waited until it began to die before I released the door. It closed with a quiet boom precisely in the moment of silence between the end of the applause and the duchess's next statement.

Nearly a thousand faces turned my way.

Silence fell. I could suddenly hear the little waterfall and the occasional twitter of a bird.

I stared hard at Arianna and said, my voice carrying clearly, "I want the girl, vampire."

She met my gaze with polite serenity for a moment. Then the hint of a smile touched her face, bringing with it a shadow of mockery. It made my blood boil, and I heard my knuckles pop as they clenched harder at my staff.

"Wizard Dresden!" Cristos said in sharp rebuke.

"This is neither the time nor the place for more of your warmongering idiocy."

I was so impressed with his authority that I raised my voice and said, louder, "Give back the child you took from her family, Arianna Ortega, kidnapper and thief, or face me under the provisions of the Code Duello."

Murmurs ran through the assembly like a rumble of thunder.

"Wizard Dresden!" Cristos cried, aghast. "This is an ambassador of an Accorded nation, promised safe conduct while she is here on a mission of peace. This is not *done*!" He looked around the room and pointed a finger at several grey-cloaked wizards standing not too far from me. "Wardens! Escort this man from the chamber!"

I shot a glance at them. They were all old guard, all dangerous, all tough, and they really didn't like me. Six sets of eyes with all the mercy and pity of a gun's mouth locked onto me.

I heard Molly gulp.

I looked back at them and said, in English, "You sure you want it to be like this, fellas?"

It must have come out sounding more threatening than I thought it had, because half a dozen White Council hard cases stopped walking. They traded looks with one another.

I turned from them back to the stage, and addressed the vampire. "Well, thief?"

Arianna turned to Cristos and gave him a rather sad and gentle smile. "I'm sorry about this disruption, Wizard Cristos. I'm not sure what this is about, but it's quite clear that Wizard Dresden feels that he has been badly wronged by my people. Bear in mind that whether justly held or not, his feelings contributed to this war's beginning."

"I apologize for this outrageous behavior," Wizard Cristos said.

"Not at all," Arianna assured him. "I, too, have suffered personal loss in this conflict. It's always difficult to control the emotions arising from such things—particularly for the very young. That's just one of the problems we'll need to overcome if we are to break the cycle of violence between your folk and mine. The veterans of wars suffer horrible mental and emotional scars, vampires and wizards alike. I take no offense at Wizard Dresden's words or actions, and do not hold him responsible for them." She turned to me and said, her voice compassionate, "I can sincerely say that I understand exactly how much pain you're in right now, Wizard Dresden."

I had to force myself not to raise my blasting rod and burn that false empathy off of the duchess's face. I gripped my gear with both hands, to make sure they weren't going to try anything without consulting me.

"We can never regain the loved ones this war has taken from us," she continued. "All we can do is end the fighting—before even more of our loved ones get hurt. I'm here to avert any more needless deaths, Dresden. Surely you can see exactly why I would do such a thing."

Boy, did I. It wasn't enough for her simply to kill me. She wanted to defeat me utterly first, to have her cake and eat it, too. If she brought the fighting to a close this way, she would garner massive credibility in the supernatural community—and if she did it while simultaneously sticking it to me, it would only be that much more elegant a victory.

She smiled at me again, with that same tiny shading of mockery so faint that no one who wasn't looking for it could possibly have seen it. It was just enough to make sure that I could see the malice behind it, to make sure that I damned well knew she was rubbing it in my face in front of the entire White Council. She'd probably practiced it in a mirror.

"I'm giving you a chance," I said, my voice harsh. "Return the child and it ends. We're quits. Make me take her from you and I'll play hardball."

She put long, elegant fingers to her chest, as if confused. "I don't know why you're so upset with me, or what I have to do with this child, sir," Arianna said. "But I understand your outrage. And I wish that I could help you."

Someone stepped up close to my side, a little in front of me. She was a young woman, not particularly tall, with curling brown hair and a heart-shaped face that was appealing and likable, if not beautiful. Her eyes were steady and hard.

"Harry," said Anastasia Luccio, captain of the Wardens, "don't do this. Please."

I clenched my jaw and spoke in a heated whisper. "Ana, if you *knew* what she'd done."

"You are *not* going to restart the war and tarnish whatever honor the White Council has left by attacking an ambassador visiting under a pledge of safe conduct," she said evenly. "You're strong, Dresden. But you aren't that strong. If you try it, there are at least thirty wizards here who could take you alone. Working together, they wouldn't just beat you. They'd swat you down like a bug—and then you'd be imprisoned until they decided what to do with you, three or four months from now."

My belly and chest felt like they were on fire. I looked past Anastasia to Duchess Arianna again.

She was watching me—hell, probably listening to me, too, vampire hearing being what it was. Her smile was a scalpel drawn slowly over my skin.

Anastasia put her hand on my arm—very gently, not firmly. She was making a request. "Harry, please."

Behind me, Molly added, "This won't help Maggie, boss."

I wanted to scream. I wanted to fight.

On the stage one of the hooded figures of the Senior Council reached up and drew back his hood. My old mentor, Ebenezar McCoy, was a stocky old man with broad hands and scarred knuckles, bald except for a faint fringe of pale white hairs. His blunt, strong features were smooth and unreadable, but he met my gaze and gave me a very small, very precise nod. The message was clear. I could practically hear the old man's voice growling, *Trust me, Hoss. Go with her.*

I felt my lip lift up from my teeth in a silent snarl.

Then I turned and stalked from the chamber, my work boots thumping heavily on the floor, my staff clenched in my hand. Anastasia walked with me, her hand still on my arm, making it clear that I was being escorted from the room, even if she'd used a gentler persuasion than Cristos would have preferred.

The Wardens closed the door behind me with a soft, solid boom, cutting me off from the assembled might of the White Council.

Chapter

Eight

"Hey," said one of the young Wardens outside the ostentatiatory. "Hey, Harry. What's up, man?"

I owed Carlos Ramirez more than a quick shake of my head, but I couldn't give it to him. I didn't want to talk at all, because I wasn't sure I could keep it from turning into furious shouting. I heard Molly turn quickly to him and say, "Not now. There's a problem, we're working on it, and I promise to call you if there's something you can do to help."

"But—" he said, taking a few steps after us.

"Warden," Luccio said firmly. "Remain at your post."

He must have obeyed. We kept on walking and he didn't follow us.

Luccio marched me down a tunnel I had never seen before, took a few turns into the darker hallways lit only by light she called to hang in the air around us, and then opened a door into a warm, firelit room. It looked like a den. There was a large fireplace crackling, several candles lit, and a lot of comfortable furniture scattered around in solitary nooks and in groups, so that one could have as much or as little conversational company as one wished. There was also a bar. A very large, very well-stocked bar.

"Oh," Molly said, as she came in behind me. "Cozy."

Anastasia let go of my arm and marched straight to the bar. She got down a bottle of black glass and poured amber fluid into three shot glasses. She brought them to a nearby table, gestured for us to sit, and then put all three glasses in the middle of the table, leaving it to us to choose which we would drink—two centuries of Warden-level paranoia tends to sink into your bones.

I sat down at the table. I took a glass and downed it. The liquor left a scouring heat in my chest as it went down, and I wanted it.

Anastasia took hers and made it vanish without twitching an eyelash. Molly looked at her glass, took a polite sip, and said, to the other woman's amused glance, "Somebody should be the designated . . . not driver, but sober person."

"Harry," Anastasia said, turning to me. "What you did today was dangerous."

"I could take the bitch," I growled.

"There's no way for us to know how old Arianna is," she contradicted, "because humanity hasn't had a written language for that long. Do you understand what I'm saying?"

I pushed my empty glass away with my fingers and said, "I could take the prehistoric bitch." I looked around the room for a moment and said, "What is this place?"

Anastasia leaned back in her chair and spread her hands, palms up. "Welcome to the Worry Room."

"Worry Room, huh."

She quirked an eyebrow. "Didn't you see the bar?"

Molly giggled, and suppressed it. "Sorry."

Anastasia's voice turned faintly ironic. "It's a place where we crusty old Wardens can go when we're sick of the softhearted wizards who are so lily-livered that they want us to permit wayward children with enough talent to go warlock to live instead of executing them. Like your apprentice, here. I guarantee you some drinks were poured in this room and bitter words said about how we would regret it after her trial."

I grunted. "Were you pouring, drinking, or talking?"

She shrugged. "If not for her, then for plenty of others. I was here when Morgan drank himself into a stupor after your trial, Harry."

"No wonder it feels so cozy."

She smiled tightly. "It's likely the most private and secure room in the complex."

"Paranoia Central is only *likely* free of spies? You guys are getting sloppy."

"Dammit, Harry." Luccio shook her head. "You've done the Warden job for a while. Or most of it. You still think that the Wardens never have a reason for acting as . . . decisively as they sometimes do?"

I sighed. Life is never simple. I had railed against the Wardens for years for killing children, young men and women who had gone warlock, lost control of their magical talents and their minds by indulging in black magic. Then I had seen the results of a few warlocks on a spree. They were ugly. Ugly, ugly, ugly. "You've got good reason," I said. "Doesn't mean I have to like it. Doesn't make it right."

"Not everyone is so far over the edge they can't come back," Molly added softly. "Sometimes people just . . . just get lost. They just need someone to show them how to come back."

"Yes. And in the time it takes to make that distinction, a lot of innocent people have died, Miss Carpenter,"

Anastasia said, her tone frank and gentle. "The human population has expanded with unthinkable speed in the past two centuries. More and more wizard-level talents are being born. Every time one of them goes warlock, we have less and less time to confront the problem—and nowhere near enough help."

"Prevention," I said. "Find them early and they don't *go* warlock."

"Resources." She sighed. We'd had this talk before. "If the entire Council did nothing but Warden duty, full-time, it still wouldn't be enough."

"Education," I said. "Use the Paranet. Get the smaller talents to help identify the gifted."

She smiled at me and said, "I'm still building support for it. It's a good idea, Harry. It might even work. The problem is making some of the others in the Council understand it. They see it only as a security risk, especially after Peabody. But it's a good idea. Its time will come—eventually."

I grunted. I was quiet for a moment, and then I said, "Familiar argument, huh? Give me some routine. Calm me down. Is that it?"

"Anxiety, anger, and agitation cloud the mind. That's why the Worry Room is here." She smiled faintly. "I'm well aware of what it looks like when a wizard has been pushed to the brink." She poured the two of us another shot and said, "So why don't you tell me how the prehistoric bitch did it to you?"

I took the glass without drinking. "She took a little girl."

"Vampires take a lot of children," Anastasia said. "What makes this one so special?"

I said nothing. Silence reigned. I looked up and met her eyes.

Anastasia and I had seen each other for a while. She knew me better than most. She studied my face for maybe half a second, and then took a deep breath. "Harry," she said, "don't say anything about this to anyone you don't trust with your life."

I gave her a small, bitter smile and nodded. Knowledge was power. Anyone who knew Maggie was my daughter might use her for leverage against me. Anastasia wouldn't, not for any reason—but others on the White Council would. Oh, they'd probably use softer gloves than Arianna had: I could just see being offered money to help support Maggie, give her access to nice schools, a privileged upbringing, and everything a father could want for his child—so that the offer could be withdrawn if I didn't play ball. After all, these were the *good* guys.

But it could get worse. I literally shuddered to think what Nicodemus might do with the knowledge—or, joyous thought, Mab. (Yes, *that* Mab. Take it from me: The stories don't do her justice.) I'd met some other real gems out there as well, and none of them had reasons to like me. On the other hand, I thought with a shiver, Arianna was the devil I *didn't* know.

Regardless, it wouldn't be helpful to let knowledge of Maggie become general. I had never planned on making an open case of her blood relation to me before the Council. It wouldn't win sympathy—only interest. The fewer people who knew I was Maggie's father, the safer she would be.

And yes.

I am aware of the irony.

I kept looking at Anastasia and asked, "Can I count on you?"

She put her hands flat on the table and looked down

at them for a slow five count, considering her words before she answered. "I am not what I was in a fight, Harry."

I ground my teeth. "So you'll sit here where it's safe."

For the first time since I'd arrived in Edinburgh, Anastasia Luccio's dark eyes flashed with real anger, and I suddenly remembered that this woman had been the captain of the Wardens for decades. The air between us grew literally physically hotter. "Think carefully," she said in a very quiet voice, "before you call me a coward."

Since the stern, iron-haired captain had been magically relocated to the body of a college grad student, her powers had diminished significantly—but her savvy and experience hadn't. I wouldn't care to fight Luccio, regardless of our relative strengths. And, hell, it wasn't as if I hadn't seen her fight more than once since then.

The anger inside me wanted to spill out onto her. But she deserved better than that from me. I stuffed it back down and lifted the fingers of one hand in a gesture of mute apology. Anastasia Luccio might be many things, but she was no coward—and she was born and raised in a day and age where such an accusation might literally require a duel to be refuted.

No, thank you.

She nodded, mollified, and some of the tension went out of her. "I was going to say that I would be of most use to you here—gathering intelligence, asking questions, and digging up resources for you to use. Of course you should fight—but you can't do that until you find the girl, and some of our own people will have an interest in making sure you don't disrupt the peace process. If I am working from here, I can circumvent them."

I glanced down at my hands, suddenly embarrassed. She was thinking more clearly than I was. "I didn't even think . . . Yeah. I'm sorry, Ana."

She inclined her head. "It's nothing."

"It was unnecessary." I scratched at my head. "You think you can sandbag the Merlin?"

She lifted both eyebrows.

"Hell's bells, I'm shocked he didn't rip off his hood and start screaming at me. Maybe challenge *me*, right there. No way he's going to sit on his ass when he can stick it to me inste—" I broke off speaking as I noticed that Molly's eyes had gone very wide. I turned to look behind me.

A painting on the wall had just finished sliding to one side, revealing a doorway hidden behind it. The door swung open soundlessly, and a wizard who was the solemn, movie-poster version of old Merlin himself came into the Worry Room.

Arthur Langtry was one of the oldest and the single most powerful wizard on the White Council. His hair and beard were long, all snowy white with threads of silver, and perfectly groomed. His eyes were winter sky blue and alert, his features long, solemn, and noble.

The Merlin of the White Council was dressed in simple white robes. What I could think of only as a gunslinger's belt of white leather hung at his hips. It looked like it had been designed after tactical gear made for Special Forces operators, but in an insignificant flash of insight I realized that, if anything, the opposite was likely to be true. Multiple vials, probably potions, rode in individual leather cases. The leather-wrapped handle of an anemic rod or a stubby wand poked out of a holster. Several pouches were fastened closed, and looked as though they would contain bits and pieces of the standard wizarding gear I habitually carried with me when I was working. He also bore a long, white staff, a simple wooden pole made of an unfamiliar wood.

I stared at him for a moment. Then I said, "The peace talks are over?"

"Of course not," the Merlin said. "Goodness, Dresden. We aren't going to allow the entire Senior Council to stand on a stage within reach of a vampire's claws. Are you mad?"

I blinked at him.

"Wizard McCoy was the only actual Senior Council member on the stage," he said, and then grimaced. "Aside from Cristos, of course, who is unaware of the security measure. The envoy might well be an assassin."

I worked my jaw a few times and said, "So. You left him up there by himself while you played it safe."

The Merlin shrugged. "One of us had to be there to handle any questions. It was McCoy's idea, Dresden. He is an irritating, arrogant, and formidable man."

I scowled and mentally flogged my brain for slacking, forcing myself to see past my emotionally driven hostile response. "You don't trust the vampires," I said slowly. "You aren't drinking the Kool-Aid in this peace conference."

Langtry looked at me patiently. Then he looked at Luccio.

"Jonestown," she provided. "The mass suicide last century."

He frowned at that and then nodded. "Ah, I see the metaphor. No, Dresden, we are not willing to simply accept them at their word—but a great many people on the Council do not concur. Cristos has garnered an enormous number of supporters who very much want to embrace the terms of peace."

"If you don't want to call off the war," I said, "then why the hell did you stop me, Captain Luccio? I could have fixed it for you right there."

"You wouldn't have," Langtry said calmly. "You would have been knocked senseless and thrown in a hole." A faint smile touched his lips as he spoke the words. "Granted, a pleasant notion, but not a practical one."

Next to me, Molly put her elbows on the table and propped up her chin in her hands, staring at the Merlin thoughtfully.

My brain kept chugging. *I think I can, I think I can.* When it got to the top of the hill, my eyes widened. "You aren't planning to smoke the peace pipe. You're expecting an attack."

He looked at me blandly, and rested one hand on the hilt of his combat wand as if by pure coincidence. "Egad. What gave it away, Dresden?"

I started to say something hot in reply, Merlin or no Merlin, but Anastasia put a hand on my wrist. "Our sources," she said, overriding my incipient insult, "have reported a great deal of activity in the Red Court camp. They're mobilizing."

I looked back and forth between them. "You figure they're trying a Trojan horse?"

"Or some variant thereof," Langtry replied.

"So we're getting ready for it," Anastasia said. "As well as preparing the heaviest counterattack we've thrown at them yet."

"Um," Molly said, "what if they're serious about making peace?"

Everyone looked at her, and my apprentice visibly wilted beneath the Merlin's gaze.

"It might happen," she said.

Langtry smiled faintly. "The leopard cannot change his spots, Miss Carpenter. Sheep can befriend a hungry wolf only briefly. The Red Court is all savagery and crocodile tears. If they make peace, it is only because they need the time to replenish themselves before fighting anew."

"Really old things get set in their ways," I confirmed to Molly, my tone including Langtry as a matter of course. "Always hope for the best and prepare for the worst."

Molly chewed her lip thoughtfully and nodded.

Langtry eyed me and said, "Need I explain why I have explained, Dresden?"

"Maybe you'd better," I said. "I mean, you didn't use illustrations or anything, Professor."

Langtry inhaled, briefly closed his eyes, and then looked away from me.

"Um?" Molly said, frowning.

"We want the Red Court to attack, if that is their intention," I told her. "We want the Red Court to think their trick is working. We want them to be overconfident. Then when they hit us, we hit them back so hard and fast that they don't know it's coming until it's over."

"No," Langtry said. "So they never *knew* it was coming. Period. We will no longer wage a war with that filth, cold, hot, or otherwise. We're going to destroy them, root and branch." He lifted his chin slightly as his voice turned to frost. "We're going to exterminate them."

Silence followed. The fire crackled cheerfully.

I felt my hands clench into fists. "But you need them to expose themselves first. And that," I whispered, "is why you're going to ask me to lay off Duchess Arianna."

"Don't be absurd," Langtry said in a calm, quiet voice. "I am not asking you. I am *ordering* you to desist, Warden Dresden."

"And let the child die," I said.

"In all probability the child is already dead, or else turned," Langtry said. "And even if she still survives, we must face a cold truth: Uncounted *billions* now living and yet to be born will be saved if we stop the Red Court from feeding on humanity *ever again*." His voice became even colder. "No one life, innocent or not, is worth more than that."

I said nothing for several long, silent seconds.

Then I stood up. I faced the Merlin for a moment. I could feel the obdurate, adamant will that drove the man, and made his power the greatest well of mortal magic on the face of the earth.

"You've got it backward, you know," I told him quietly. "No life is worth more than that? No, Merlin. No life is worth less."

His expression never changed. But his fingers tightened slightly on his staff. His cold blue eyes touched lightly upon Molly, and then returned to me.

The threat was plain to see.

I leaned over close to his ear and whispered, "Go ahead, Arthur. Try it." Then I straightened slowly away, letting every emotion and every thought drain out of my expression. The tension in the air was thick. No one moved. I could see Molly trembling where she sat.

I nodded slowly at the Merlin.

Then I said in a quiet, clear voice, "Grasshopper."

Molly stood up immediately.

I kept myself between the girl and Langtry as we

walked to the door. He didn't offer any challenge, but his eyes were arctic and absolute. Behind him, Luccio gave me a single, tiny, conspiratorial nod.

Hell's bells. She'd known who she would be working against all along.

Molly and I left Edinburgh behind and headed back home to Chicago.

Chapter

Nine

I watched out for trouble all the way back to Chicago, but it didn't show up.

The trip from Edinburgh would be a difficult one if limited by strictly physical means of transport. Wizards and jet planes go together like tornados and trailer parks, and with similarly disastrous results. Boats are probably the surest means of modern transport available to us, but it's a bit of a ride from Scotland to Chicago.

So we do what a good wizard always does when the odds are stacked up against us: We cheat.

The Nevernever, the spirit world, exists alongside our own, sort of like an alternate dimension, but it isn't shaped the same way as the mortal world. The Nevernever touches upon places in the mortal world that have something in common with it, a resonance of energies. So, if point A is a dark and spooky place in the Nevernever, it touches upon a dark and spooky place in the real world—let's say, the stacks at the University of Chicago. But the space five feet away from point A in the Nevernever, point B, is only dark and sad, not really scary. Maybe point B attaches to a cemetery in Seattle.

If you're a wizard, you could then start at the stacks at UC, open a doorway into the Nevernever, walk five feet, open another doorway back to the real world, and emerge into the cemetery in Seattle. Total linear distance walked, five or six feet. Total distance traveled, better than seventeen hundred *miles*.

Neat, huh?

Granted, it's almost never as little as five feet you walk in the Nevernever, and that stroll just might introduce you to some gargantuan, tentacular horror so hideous that it drives you insane just by looking at it. The Nevernever is a scary place. You don't want to go exploring without a whole lot of planning and backup, but if you know the safe paths—the Ways—then you can get a lot of traveling done nice and quick, and with a minimum incidence of spontaneous insanity.

Once upon a time, I would have refused even to enter the Nevernever except in the direst of emergencies. Now, the idea wasn't much more stressful to me than the thought of hitting a bus station. Things change.

We were back in Chicago before lunchtime, emerging from the Nevernever into an alley behind a big old building that used to be a slaughterhouse. I'd parked the *Blue Beetle*, my beat-up old Volkswagen Bug, nearby. We went back to my apartment.

Susan and Martin were waiting. About two minutes after we got back, there was a knock at the door, and I opened it to find both half vampires standing on my doorstep. Martin carried a leather valise on a sling over his shoulder.

"Who is the girl?" Martin asked, his eyes calm and focused past me, on Molly.

"It's nice to see you again, too, man," I said. "And don't mention it. I save people's lives all the time."

Susan smiled at me, giving Molly the Female Once-Over—a process by which one woman creates a detailed profile of another woman based upon about a million subtle details of clothing, jewelry, makeup, and body type, and then decides how much of a social threat she might be. Men have a parallel process, but it's binary: *Does he have beer? If yes, will he share with me?*

"Harry," Susan said, kissing me on the cheek. I felt like a pine tree in cougar country. I'd just have to hope territorial scoring of my bark wasn't next. "Who is this?"

"My apprentice, Molly Carpenter," I said. "Grasshopper, this is Susan Rodriguez. That's Marvin someone-or-other."

"Martin," he corrected me, unruffled, as he entered, "can she be trusted?"

"Every bit as much as you trust me," I said.

"Well." Martin's voice couldn't have been any drier, but he tried. "Thank goodness for that."

"I know who they are, Harry," Molly said quietly. "They're from the Fellowship of St. Giles, right? Vampire hunters?"

"Close enough," Susan said, standing right next to me, well inside my personal space perimeter. It was an intimate distance. She touched my arm for a moment with fever-hot fingers, but never looked away from Molly. "An apprentice wizard? Really? What's it like?"

Molly shrugged, averting her eyes, frowning slightly. "A lot of reading, a lot of boring practice, with occasional flashes of pure terror."

Susan looked from Molly to me and seemed to come to some sort of conclusion. She drifted out of my personal space again. "Did you speak to the Council?"

"A bit," I said. "The duchess was at headquarters. Spoke to her, too."

Susan drew in a sharp breath. "What? She hasn't left Mexico in more than a hundred and eighty years."

"Call Guinness. She broke her streak."

"Good God," she said. "What was she doing there?"

"Being compassionate and understanding and forgiving me for challenging her to a duel in front of about a thousand fellow wizards."

Martin made a choking sound. Susan's eyes looked a little wide.

"I wanted a piece of her right there," I said, "but she was operating under a pledge of safe conduct. Council intelligence says there's all kinds of vampire activity starting up. I've got feelers out for any other word, but it will take a little time."

"We already knew about the mobilization," Susan said. "The Fellowship warned the Council three days ago."

"Nice of the Council to inform everybody, I guess. But I'll get whatever else the Council knows in the next few hours," I said. "You guys turn up anything?"

"Sort of," Susan said. "Come on."

We went to the seating around the coffee table, and Martin plopped the valise down onto its surface. He drew out a manila folder and passed it to me.

"Out of nearly a petabyte of information—" he began.

"Petawhat?" I asked.

"One quadrillion bytes," he clarified. Helpfully.

Susan rolled her eyes and said, "Several libraries' worth of information."

"Oh. Okay."

Martin cleared his throat and continued as if he hadn't been interrupted. "We retrieved fewer than three hundred files. Most of them were inventory records."

I opened the folder and found several sheets of printer paper covered with lists, and several more that consisted of photographs of any number of objects accompanied by identification numbers.

"The objects in this file," Susan said, "were all categorized as metacapacitors."

I grunted, paging through the photos more slowly. A stone knife. An ancient, notched sword. A soot-stained brick. An urn covered in odd, vaguely unsettling abstract designs. "Yeah. Can't be sure without physically examining it, but this stuff looks like ritual gear."

I frowned and started cross-referencing numbers on the lists. "And according to this, they were all checked out of a secure holding facility in Nevada and shipped as a lot. . . ." I glanced up at Susan. "When was Maggie taken, exactly?"

"A little less than twenty-four hours before I called you."

I frowned at the timing. "They shipped it the same day Maggie was taken."

"Yes," she said. "About three hours after the kidnapping."

"Shipped where?"

"That's the question," she said. "Assuming it's connected with Maggie at all."

"Odds are that it isn't," Martin said.

"Yeah. Your time would be better employed running down all those other leads we have, Marvin." I spared him a glower, and went back to studying the pages. "If I can figure out what this gear is used for, maybe I can rule it out. For all I know it's meant for a rain dance." I tapped the pages on my knee thoughtfully. "I'll do that first. While I do, Molly, I want you to go talk with Father Forthill, personally—we have to assume the phones aren't safe. Forthill has some contacts down south. Tell him I'd like to know if any of them have reported anything unusual. Take Mouse to watch your back."

"I can look after myself, Harry. It's still daylight."

"Your weapons, grasshopper," I said in my Yoda voice. "You will not need them."

She frowned at me in annoyance and said, "You know, I believe it *is* possible to reference something other than *Star Wars*, boss."

I narrowed my eyes in Muppetly wisdom. "That is why you fail."

"That doesn't even . . . Augh. It's easier just to do it." She stood up and held out her hand. I tossed her the keys to the *Blue Beetle*. "Come on, Mouse."

Mouse rose from his position in the kitchen and shambled to Molly's side.

"Hold up a second, kid. Susan," I said. "Something about this is making the back of my neck itch. The bad guys knew where to find us last night. They must have some kind of tail on one of us, and we don't need to walk around with a target painted on our backs. Maybe you and Martin could go see if you can catch our shadow."

"They'll see us and pull a fade as soon as we leave the apartment," Martin said.

"Oh!" Molly said abruptly, her eyes brightening. "Right!"

I went out to get the mail and walk the dog around the little backyard while Molly, Susan, and Martin, under cover of one of Molly's first-class veils, slipped out of the apartment. I gave Mouse five minutes, then called him and went back down into the apartment.

Molly had beaten me back inside, after walking Susan

and Martin out of the view of any observers who had a line of sight to my apartment's door. "How was that?" she asked. She tried for casual, but by now I knew her well enough to spot when my answer mattered.

"Smooth," I said. "Did me proud."

She nodded, but there was a little bit too much energy in it to be offhand agreement. Hell's bells, I remembered what she was feeling: wanting, so badly, to prove my talent, my discipline, my skill—myself—to a teacher. It took me nearly a decade for my hindsight to come into focus, and to realize how inexperienced, how foolish, and how lucky I had been to survive my apprenticeship with both eyes and all my fingers intact.

I wasn't too worried about sending the kid on a solo mission. It was pretty tame, and Forthill liked her. Molly wasn't much in a fight, but she could avoid the hell out of them if she had an instant's warning—which was where Mouse came in. Very little escaped the big dog's solemn notice. If hostility loomed, Mouse would warn her, and hey-presto, they would both be gone.

She'd be fine.

"Don't take too long," I said quietly. "Eyes open. Play it safe."

She beamed, her face alight. "You aren't the boss of me."

I could all but taste the pride she felt at making her talents useful to my cause. "The hell I'm not," I told her. "Do it or I dock you a year's pay."

"You know you don't pay me anything, right?"

"Curses," I said. "Foiled again."

She flashed me another smile and hurried out, bouncing eagerly up the steps. Mouse followed close on her heels, his ears cocked alertly up, his demeanor serious.

He grabbed his leather lead from the little table by the door as he went by. Molly had forgotten it, but there were leash laws in town. I suspected that Mouse didn't care about the law. My theory was that he insisted on his lead because people were more inclined to feel comfortable and friendly toward a huge dog when he was "safely restrained."

Unlike me, he's a people person. Canine. Whatever.

I waited until the Beetle had started and pulled out to close the door. Then I picked up Martin's printed pages, tugged aside the rug that covered the trapdoor in the living room floor, and descended into my laboratory.

"My laboratory," I said, experimentally, drawing out each syllable. "Why is it that saying it like that always makes me want to follow it with 'mwoo-hah-hah-hah-hahhhhhh'?"

"You were overexposed to Hammer films as a child?" chirped a cheerful voice from below.

I got to the bottom of the stepladder, murmured a word, and swept my hand in a broad gesture. A dozen candles flickered to life.

My lab wasn't fancy. It was a concrete box, the building's subbasement. Someone probably had neglected to backfill it with gravel and earth when the house was built. Tables and shelves lined the walls, covered in wizardly bric-a-brac. A long table ran down the middle of the room, almost entirely occupied by a scale model of downtown Chicago made of pewter, right down to the streetlights and trees.

My apprentice had a workstation at a tiny desk between two of the tables. Though she had continued to add more and more of her own notes, tools, and materials as her training continued, somehow she had kept the same amount of space open. Everything was neatly organized and sparkling clean. The division between Molly's work area and the rest of the room was as sharp and obvious as the lines on a map.

I'd upgraded my summoning circle, which was set in the concrete floor at the far end of the little room, a five-foot hoop of braided copper, silver, and iron that had set me back three grand when I ordered it from a svartalf silversmith. The materials weren't all that expensive, but it took serious compensation to convince a svartalf to work with iron.

Each metal strand in the circle's braid was inscribed with sigils and runes in formulae that harnessed and controlled magical energies to a far greater degree than any simple circle. Each strand had its own string of symbols, work so tiny and precise that only svartalves and maybe Intel could have pulled it off. Flickers of light, like static discharge but more liquid, slithered around each strand of metal, red light, blue, and green dancing and intertwining in continuous spirals.

I'm still young for a wizard—but once in a while, I can make something that's fairly cool.

One shelf was different from all the others in the room. It was a simple wooden plank. Volcanic mounds of melted candle wax capped either end. In the center of the shelf was a human skull, surrounded by paperback romance novels. As I watched, orange flickering light kindled in the skull's empty eye sockets, then swiveled to focus on me. "Too many Hammer films," Bob the Skull repeated. "Or, possibly, one too many nights at the *Rocky Horror Picture Show*."

"Janet, Brad, Rocky, ugh," I said dutifully. I went to

the shelf, picked the skull up off of it ("Wheee!" said Bob), and then carried it over to a mostly clean space on one of the worktables. I set the skull down on top of a stack of notebooks, and then put Martin's manila folder down in front of him.

"Need your take on something," I said. I opened up the folder and started laying out the photographs Martin had given me.

Bob regarded them for a moment, and asked, "What are we looking at, here?"

"Metacapacitors," I said.

"That's weird. 'Cause they look like a bunch of ritual objects."

"Yeah. I figure *metacapacitor* is code language for *ritual object.*"

Bob studied the pictures and muttered to himself under his breath. He isn't actually a talking skull—he's a spirit of intellect who happens to reside inside a specially enchanted skull. He's been assisting wizards since the Dark Ages, and if he hasn't forgotten more than I ever knew about the wide world of magic, it's only because he doesn't forget anything, ever.

"They're traveling in a single group. I need to get a ballpark estimate on what they might be used for."

"Tough to tell from two-dimensional images," Bob said. "I start getting confused when there are any fewer than four dimensions." He rattled the skull's teeth together a few times, thoughtfully. "Is there anything else? Descriptions or anything?"

I opened the folder. "Just the inventory list." I put my finger on the picture of the stone knife and read, "'Flint blade.'" I touched an old brick with crumbling edges. "'Brick.'"

"Well, *that's* just blindingly useful," Bob muttered.

I grunted. "It's possible that this is just miscellaneous junk. If you don't think it has a specific purpose, then—"

"I didn't say that," Bob interrupted sourly. "Jeez, Harry. Ye of little faith."

"Can you tell me anything or not?"

"I can tell you that you're teetering on the edge of sanity, sahib."

I blinked at that. "What?"

Bob didn't look up from the pictures. "Your aura is all screwed up. It's like looking at an exploding paint factory. Crazy people get that way."

I grunted and considered Bob's words for a moment. Then I shrugged. "I'm too close to this case, maybe."

"You need some time in a quiet place, boss. Unkink your brain's do. Mellow your vibe."

"Thank you, Doctor Fraud," I said. "I'll take that under advisement. Can you tell me anything about those objects or what?"

"Not without getting to examine them," Bob said.

I grunted. "Super. Another bad inning for the wizard gumshoe."

"Sorry," he said. "But all I can tell you from here is the trigger."

I frowned. "What do you mean?"

"Oh, those are objects of dark, dangerous magic," Bob said. "I mean, obviously. Look at the angles. Nothing is proportional and balanced. They're meant for something destructive, disruptive, deadly."

I grunted. "That tracks. Rumor has it that the war is going to rev up again soon." I ran my fingers tiredly through my hair. "What did you say the trigger was, again?"

"For something this dark?" Bob asked. "Only one thing'll do."

I felt myself freeze. My coffeeless gorge began to rise.

"Human sacrifice," the skull chirped brightly. "The slaughter of an innocent."

Chapter
Ten

I leaned on a table with my eyes closed.

The Red Court was preparing a destructive act of high black magic.

The ritual, whatever it was, required a human sacrifice to succeed.

In my head, I watched a movie of Maggie being bled out like a slaughtered sheep within a ritual circle, surrounded by an army of vampires beneath a nightmare sky.

There was a hideous elegance in it. In a single stroke my daughter would die, and her death would be used to lash out against the Council. It was bald guesswork, but it fit what I'd seen of the duchess. She could inflict the maximum amount of personal agony on me and launch a sorcerous attack simultaneously. Revenge and war would both be served—all while she smiled and smiled and offered promises of peace and understanding, protected from me by the same idiots she was plotting to destroy.

I could try to warn them, but few would listen. Ebenezar, maybe, and Anastasia, and some of the young Wardens—but even if they listened and believed, they would still have to convince others. The freaking Council never does anything quickly, and I had a bad feeling that *tempus* was *fugit*ing furiously.

So. I'd just have to do it myself.

But to do that, I needed information.

I looked at my summoning circle again and took a slow, deep breath. There were things I could do. Horrible things. There were beings I could call up, malicious mavens and entities of wicked wisdom who might make the unknowable as plain as daylight.

If I did, there would be a terrible price.

I tore my eyes from the circle and shook my head. I wasn't that desperate.

Yet.

Someone knocked loudly on my apartment door.

I went upstairs, closed the lab, and picked up my blasting rod. I carried it to the door and looked out the peephole. Murphy stood outside, her hands in her coat pockets, her shoulders hunched.

"Couldn't use the phone," she said when I opened the door. She stepped in and I closed it behind her.

"Yeah, we figure the Red Court might be tapping them."

She shook her head. "I don't know about that, Harry. But Internal Affairs has got mine wired."

I blinked at her. "Those IA idiots? Again? Can't Rudolph just let it rest?" Rudolph the Brown-nosed Cop-cop, as he was affectionately known at SI, had managed to kiss enough ass to escape SI and get reassigned to IA. He seemed to hold a grudge against his former coworkers, irrationally blaming them for his (now concluded) exile among the proles of SI.

"Apparently not," Murphy said. "He's making quite a name for himself over there."

"Murph, you're a good cop. I'm sure that—"

She slashed a hand at the air and shook her head. "That's not important right now. Listen. Okay?"

I frowned and nodded at her.

"There's a full-scale investigation going into the bombing of your office building," Murphy said. "Rudolph talked to the lead FBI agent and the local lead detective in charge of the case and convinced them that you're a suspicious character and good perpetrator material."

I groaned. "Forensics will bear them out. The explosives were on my floor, some of them in the walls of my office."

Murphy pushed her hair back with one hand. The bags beneath her eyes had grown visibly darker. "They're going to bring you in and question you in the next couple of hours. They'll probably hold you for the full twenty-four. More if they can find a charge to stick you with."

"I don't have time for that," I said.

"Then you've got to get scarce," Murphy said. "And I've got to go. Neither of us will be helped if we're seen together."

"Son of a bitch," I snarled. "I am going to throw Rudolph halfway across Lake Michigan and see if the slimy little turd floats."

"I'll bring the lead weights," Murphy said. She drew the amulet I'd made to let her past my apartment's magical defenses from her shirt and showed it to me. "Hopefully I won't be able to find you. Get in touch with me when you need my help, huh?"

"Murph," I said. "If the authorities are getting set to come down on me . . . you can't be around."

Her eyebrows climbed a tiny fraction. It was a danger signal. "Excuse me?" she said politely.

"It's already going to look bad enough, we've worked together so much. If you're actually abetting me now . . . they won't let you keep your badge. You know they won't. And they might do even more than that. You could wind up in jail."

The subliminal angry tension in her abruptly vanished. "God, Dresden. You are a simp."

I blinked at her.

"If I go with you," she said, "I could wind up in the ground. That didn't seem to worry you."

"Well," I said. "I . . ."

"I choose my battles, Dresden. Not you." She looked up at me calmly. "Let me put this in terms that will get through your skull: My friend is going to save a child from monsters. I'm going with him. That's what friends do, Harry."

I nodded and was silent for several seconds. Then I said, "I know you, Karrin. For you, dying in a good fight would not be a terrible end. You've known it was possible, and you've prepared yourself for it." I took a deep breath. "But . . . if they took your shield away . . . I know what your job means to you. You'd die by inches. I don't think I could handle watching that happen."

"So you get to choose to shut me out? What I want doesn't count?"

"I don't know," I said. "Maybe."

"And you're the one who decides?"

I thought about it for a moment. Then I said, "No."

She nodded. "Good answer." She touched her fingertips to the shape of her amulet under her T-shirt. "Call."

"I will. Maybe by messenger, but I will."

"It's occurred to me that someone who wanted to make you suffer might start pulling the trigger on your friends. How do I verify the message?"

I shook my head. The more I thought about it, the more I was sure that even here, in my own home, I couldn't be too careful about being overheard. My apartment was blanketed in protective magic, but there were plenty of people (and not-people) who were stronger, more experienced, or wilier than me. "If I have to send a messenger, I'll make sure you know who it's from."

Murphy watched me answer. Then she glanced slowly around the room, as if looking for an unseen observer, and nodded her understanding. "All right. Don't stay here long, Harry."

"Yeah," I said. "Don't worry about me, Murph."

She made a face. "I'm not worried about just you. You've got at least one gun stashed here, and I'm betting there's more illegal material in the lab. If they like you for a suspect, they'll get a warrant. And the FBI, as far as I know, doesn't have any amulets to get them in here alive."

I groaned aloud. Murph was right. I had a couple of illegal weapons in my apartment. The Swords were still in the lab, too. Plus some miscellaneous material that the government probably wouldn't want me owning, including depleted uranium dust, for when the answer to "Who you gonna call?" turns out to be "Harry Dresden."

The wards that protected my apartment were going to be an issue as well. They wouldn't do anything if someone walked up and knocked on the door, or even if they fiddled with the doorknob—but anyone who tried to force the door open was in for a shock. About seventy thousand volts of shock, in fact, thanks to the defenses I'd put in place around my door. The lightning was savage, but it was only the first layer of the defense. It hadn't been so terribly long since an army of zombies tore their way into my living room, and I wasn't going to repeat the experience.

But my wards wouldn't have any way of differentiating between a zombie or a crazed vampire or a misguided FBI agent. They simply reacted to someone forcing his way inside. I'd have to deactivate the wards before someone got hurt. Then I'd have to remove any suspect gear from the house.

Hell's bells. Like I didn't have enough on my mind. I rubbed my thumb against the spot between my eyebrows where the headache was forming. "I did not need this on top of everything else. Which is why she did it."

"Why who did what?"

"Duchess Arianna of the Red Court," I said. I filled Murphy in on my day.

"That's out of character, isn't it?" Murphy asked. "I mean, for them to do something this obtrusive? Blowing up a building?"

"They did similar things several times during the war," I said. "She was making a statement. Blowing up my place of business right in front of God and everybody, the same way the wizards took out her husband's command post in Honduras. Plus she's diverting my attention and energy, yanking more potential support out from under me."

Murphy shook her head. "She's so clever she's making a mistake."

"Yeah?"

"Yeah. If she was all that smart, she would have blown you to pieces in your office."

I nodded. "Yeah. That's the most practical way."

"So why didn't she?"

"Figure she wants to inflict the maximum amount of pain she can before she gets rid of me."

Murphy lifted her eyebrows. "For vengeance? That's . . . kind of like a bad movie script, isn't it?" She put on a faint British accent. "No, Mr. Dresden. I expect you to die."

I grunted. Murphy had a point. Duchess Arianna almost couldn't have been the sort to enjoy indulging her sadistic side at the expense of practicality. You don't survive millennia as a vampire without being deadly cold-blooded.

Which meant . . .

"There's something else at work here," I said. "Some other game going on."

Murphy nodded. "How sure are you that Susan is being straight with you?"

"Pretty sure," I said. It sounded a little hollow, even to me.

Murphy's mouth twisted up into a bitter curl. "That's what I thought. You loved her. Makes it easy to manipulate you."

"Susan wouldn't do that," I said.

"I hope not," Murphy replied. "But . . . she's been gone awhile, Harry. Fighting a war, from the sounds of it. That's enough to change anyone, and not for the better."

I shook my head slowly and said, "Not Susan."

Murphy shrugged. "Harry . . . I've got a bad feeling that . . ." She scrunched up her nose, choosing her words. "I've got a bad feeling that the wheels are about to come off."

"What do you mean?"

She shrugged. "Just . . . the building blowing up is all over the news. You can't find an anchor talking about anything else. People are screaming about terrorists. The whole situation is gaining more attention from higher up in the government than anything else I've ever seen. You say that most of the White Council has been effectively placed under the control of this Cristos person. Now the upper ranks of the Red Court are getting involved, too, and from what you tell me everyone is reaching for their guns." She spread her hands. "It's . . . it's like the Cuban missile crisis. Everyone's at the edge."

Hell's bells. Murphy was right. The supernatural world *was* standing at the edge—and it was one hell of a long way down to the war of annihilation at the bottom.

I took a slow breath, thinking. Then I said, "I don't care about that."

Murphy's golden eyebrows went up.

"I'm not responsible for everyone else in the world, Murph. I'm going to find a little girl and take her somewhere safe. That's all. The rest of the world can manage without me."

"What if that's the last straw, Harry? The little girl. What will you do then?"

I growled as a column of pure rage rose up my spine and made my voice rough. "I *will* make Maggie safe. If the world burns because of that, then so be it. Me and the kid will roast some marshmallows."

Murphy watched me thoughtfully for several empty seconds. Then she said, very gently, "You're a good man, Harry."

I swallowed and bowed my head, made humble by the tone of her voice and the expression on her face, more than the words themselves.

"Not always rational," she said, smiling. "But you're the best kind of crazy."

"Thank you, Karrin."

She reached out and squeezed my arm once. "I should go. Call me."

"I will."

She left a moment later and I began sanitizing my apartment for government scrutiny. It would take me a little precious time, but being locked in a cage would take even more. I was still tucking away the last of my contraband when there was a knock at the door. I froze. After a moment, the knock was repeated.

"Harry Dresden!" called a man's voice. "This is Special Agent Tilly of the Federal Bureau of Investigation. I have a warrant to search this property and detain its occupants for questioning regarding last night's explosion. If you do not open this door, we will be forced to break it down."

Crap.

Chapter

Eleven

I tore the rug from the trapdoor again. I'd packed almost all of my questionable materials into a large nylon gym bag. I slung it over my shoulder, grabbed my duster, staff, and blasting rod, and nearly killed myself trying to go down the ladder too quickly. I stopped a couple of steps from the bottom and reached up to close the trapdoor again. There was a pair of simple bolts on the lower side of the door, so that I or the grasshopper could signal the other that something delicate was in progress, and distractions might be dangerous. I locked the door firmly.

"What's going on?" blurted Bob from his shelf.

"Bob, I need the wards down *now*."

"Why don't you just—"

"Because they'll come back up five minutes after I've used the disarming spell. I need them *down*. Get off your bony ass and do it!"

"But that will knock them out for at least a week—"

"I *know*. Go *do* it, and hurry! You have my permission to leave the skull for that purpose."

"Aye-aye, O captain, my captain," Bob said sourly. A small cloud of orange sparkling light flowed out of the skull's eye sockets and rushed upstairs through the cracks at the edge of the trapdoor.

I immediately started dumping things into my bag. I was making a mess doing it, too, but there was no help for that.

Less than half a minute later, Bob returned and flowed back into the skull again. "There're a bunch of guys in suits and uniforms knocking on the door, Harry."

"I know."

"Why?" he asked. "What's going on?"

"Trouble," I said. "What do I have in here that's illegal?"

"Do I look like an attorney? These ain't law books I'm surrounded by."

There was a heavy slam of impact from upstairs. Whoever was up there was trying a ram on the door. Good luck with that, boys. I'd had my door knocked down before. I had installed a heavy metal security door that nothing short of explosives was going to overcome.

"Where's the ghost dust?" I asked.

"One shelf over, two up, cigar tin in a brown cardboard box," Bob said promptly.

"Thanks," I said. "That section of rhino horn?"

"Under the shelf to your left, plastic storage bin."

So it went, with Bob's flawless memory speeding the process. I wound up stuffing the bag full. Then I tore the Paranet map off the wall and added it to the bag, and tossed the directory of contact numbers for its members in next to it. The last thing I needed was the FBI deciding that I was the hub of a network of terrorist cells.

Bob's skull went in, too. I zipped the bag closed, leaving just enough opening for Bob to see out. Last, I took the two Swords (at least one of which had been used in murders in the Chicago area), slipped them through some straps on the side of the bag, and then hurriedly duct-taped them into place, just to be sure I wouldn't lose them. Then I drew on my duster and slung the bag's strap over my shoulder with a grunt. The thing was heavy.

Bangs and bumps continued upstairs. There was a sudden, sharp cracking sound. I winced. The door and its frame might be industrial-strength, but the house they were attached to was a wooden antique from the previous turn of the century. It sounded like something had begun to give.

"I told you," Bob said. "You should have found out what was on the other side from here long before now."

"And I told *you*," I replied, "that the last thing I wanted to do was thin the barrier between my own home and the bloody Nevernever by going through it and then attracting the attention of whatever hungry boogity-boo was on the other side."

"And you were wrong," Bob said smugly. "And I told you so."

There was a tremendous crash upstairs, and someone shouted, "FBI!" at the same time someone else was shouting, "Chicago PD!"

An instant later, someone let out a startled curse and a gun went off.

"What was that?" screamed a rather high-pitched voice.

"A cat," said Agent Tilly's voice, dripping with disdain. "You opened fire on a freaking cat. And missed."

Mister. My heart pounded in my chest. I'd forgotten all about him. But, true to his nature, Mister seemed to have taken care of his own daring escape.

There were chuckles from several voices.

"It isn't funny," snapped the other voice. It was Rudolph, all right. "This guy is dangerous."

"Clear," called a voice from another room—which meant my bedroom and bathroom, since it was the only other room available. "Nothing in here."

"Dammit," Rudolph said. "He's here somewhere. Are you sure your men spotted him through the window?"

"They saw someone moving around in here not five minutes ago. Doesn't mean it was him." There was a pause and then Agent Tilly said, "Or, gee. Maybe he's down in the subbasement under that trapdoor over there."

"You still have men in place at the windows?" Rudolph asked.

"Yes," Tilly said wearily. He raised his voice a bit, as if speaking to someone on the far side of a large room. "This place is buttoned up. There's nowhere for him to go. Let's just hope he shows himself and gives himself up quietly. We'll be sure to respect all his rights and everything, and if he cooperates, this could be over pretty quickly."

I paused. I had some choices to make.

I could still do as Tilly suggested. In the long run, it was obviously the best choice for me. I'd be questioned and cleared by anyone reasonable (i.e., not Rudolph). I could even point them at the duchess's business interests and turn them loose to become a thorn in her side. After that, I would be back to the status quo of wary cooperation with the authorities—but that process would take precious time. A couple of days at the very least.

I didn't have that kind of time.

Agent Tilly struck me as someone not entirely unreasonable. But if I approached him now, protesting my innocence, and then vanished, I'd be up for resisting arrest at the very least. Even if everything else in this mess panned out in my favor, that could get me jail time, which I wished to avoid. Besides. There wasn't anything Tilly could do for Maggie.

And, I had to admit it, I was *angry*. This was my home, dammit. You don't just break down the door of a man's home on the say-so of a snake like Rudolph. I had plenty of anger already stored up, but hearing those voices in my living room added another large lump to the mound. I doubted my ability to remain polite for very long.

So instead of stopping to talk, I turned to the summoning circle, stepped into it, summoned up my will, and whispered, "*Aparturum.*"

I waved my staff from left to right, infusing the tool with my will, and reality rolled up along it like a scroll. Soft green light began to emanate from the empty air in front of me in a rectangular area seven feet tall and half as wide—a doorway between my apartment and the Nevernever. I had no idea what was on the other side.

The bolts to the trapdoor began to rattle. I heard someone call for a saw. The door wasn't closely fitted. They'd be able to slip a saw blade through the crack and slice those two bolts in seconds.

I gathered up my power into a defensive barrier around me, running it through my shield bracelet, and gritted my teeth. My heart pounded against my chest. It was entirely possible that walking through that doorway between worlds would take me to the bottom of a lake of molten lava, or over the edge of a rushing waterfall. There was no way to know until I actually stepped into it.

"I told you so!" Bob chortled.

An electric engine buzzed above me and then abruptly died. Someone made puzzled sounds. Then a slender steel blade slipped through the crack in the door and someone started cutting through the bolts by hand.

I stepped out of the real world and into the Nevernever.

I was braced for whatever would happen. Freezing cold. Searing heat. Crushing depth of water—even utter vacuum. The sphere of force around me was airtight, and would keep me alive even in someplace like outer space, at least for a few moments.

I emerged into the Nevernever, my shields at full strength, my blasting rod ready to unleash hell, as the invisible sphere of force around me slammed into—

—a rather lovely bed of daisies.

My shields mashed them flat. The entire bed, in its little white planter, immediately resembled a pressed-flower collection.

I looked around slowly, my body tight and ready, my senses focused.

I was in a garden.

It looked like an Italian number. Only a minority of the shrubs and flowers were planted in raised beds. The others had been laid out to give the impression that they had grown naturally into the space they occupied. Grassy paths wound through the irregularly shaped garden, twisting and turning this way and that. A hummingbird the size of a silver dollar darted down and tucked its beak into a particularly bright flower, and then vanished again. A bee buzzed by—just a regular old bumblebee, not some giant mutant monster thing.

Don't laugh. I've seen them over there.

I adjusted the shielding spell to allow air to pass through it and took a suspicious, cautious sniff. It might look like a nice place, but for all I knew the atmosphere was laced with chlorine gas.

It smelled like autumn sunshine, where the days might be balmy but the nights could carry a heavy nip. Letting the air in meant that sound had an easier time getting past my shield. Birds chirped lazily. Somewhere nearby, there was running water.

Bob started tittering. "Look out! Look out for the vicious megasquirrel, boss!" he said, hardly able to speak clearly. "My gosh! That ficus is about to molest you!"

I glowered down at the skull and returned to watching my surroundings for a moment more. Then I carefully lowered the shields. They burned a hell of a lot of energy. If I tried to hold them up for more than a few moments, I'd find myself too weary to function.

Nothing happened.

It was just a sleepy afternoon in a very pleasant, pretty garden.

"You should have seen your face," Bob said, still twitching with muffled laughter. "Like you were going to face an angry dragon or something."

"Shut up," I told him quietly. "This is the Nevernever. And it's way too easy."

"Not every place in the spirit world is a nightmare factory, Harry," Bob scolded me. "It's a universe of balance. For every place of darkness, there is also one of light."

I turned another slow circle, checking for threats, before I took my staff and waved it from left to right again, shutting the gateway back to my laboratory. Then I returned to cautiously scanning the area.

"Stars and stones, Harry," Bob said merrily. "I guess wearing that grey cloak for so long rubbed off on you. Paranoid much?"

I glowered and never stopped scanning. "Way. Too. Easy."

Five minutes later, nothing had happened. It's difficult to stay properly intimidated and paranoid when there is no evident threat and when the surroundings are so generally peaceful.

"Okay," I said, finally. "Maybe you're right. Either way, we need to get moving. Hopefully we can find somewhere one of us recognizes that can get us back to the Ways."

"You want to leave a trail of bread crumbs or something?" Bob asked.

"That's what you're for," I said. "Remember how to get back here."

"Check," he said. "Which way are we going?"

There were three paths. One wandered among high grasses and soaring trees. Another was pebbled and ran uphill, with plenty of large rocks figuring in the landscaping. The third had greenish cobblestones, and led through a field of nice low flowers that left lots of visibility around us. I went with option three, and started down the cobbled path.

After twenty or thirty paces, I started to get uneasy. There was no reason for it that I could see. It was pure instinct.

"Bob?" I asked after a moment. "What kinds of flowers are these?"

"Primroses," the skull replied instantly.

I stopped in my tracks. "Oh. Crap."

The earth shook.

The ground heaved around my feet, and along the primrose path ahead of me, the walking stones writhed and lifted up out of the soil. They proved to be the gently rounded crowns of segments of exoskeleton. Said segments belonged to the unthinkably large green centipede that had just begun shaking its way loose from the soil as we spoke. I watched in sickly fascination as the creature lifted its head from the soil, fifty feet away from us, and turned to look our way. Its mandibles clacked together several times, reminding me of an enormous set of shears. They were large enough to cut me in half at the waist.

I looked behind us and saw another fifty or sixty feet of the path ripping free, and looked down to see that the walking stone I stood upon was also part of the creature, albeit the last to unplant itself.

I fought to keep my balance as the stone ripped free, but I wound up being dumped into a bed of primroses while the enormous centipede's head slithered left and right and rolled toward me at a truly alarming rate.

Its enormous eyes glittered brightly, and slime dripped from its hungrily snapping jaws. Its hundreds of legs each dug into the ground to propel its weight forward, their tips like tent stakes, biting the earth. It sounded almost like a freaking locomotive.

I looked from the centipede down to the skull. "I told *you* so!" I screamed. "Way! Too! Easy!"

Chapter
Twelve

Yeah.

This was not what I'd had in mind when I got out of bed that morning.

The damned thing *should* have been slow. By every law of physics, by every right, a centipede that big should have been *slow*. Dinosauric. Elephantine.

But this was the Nevernever. You didn't play by the same rules here. Physics were sort of a guideline, and a very loose and elastic guideline at that. Here, the mind and heart had more sway than the material, and the big bug was *fast*. That enormous, predatory head shot at me like the engine of some psychotic locomotive, its killer jaws spreading wide.

Fortunately for me, I was, just barely, faster.

I brought forth my left hand, holding it out palm forth in a gesture of command and denial, a universal pose meaning one thing: *Stop!* Intent was important in this place. As the jaws closed, I brought up my spherical shield to meet it, the energy humming through my bracelet's charms, which burst into shining light as the magic coursing through them shone through the ephemeral substance of mere material metals.

The jaws closed with a crunch and a crash, and my

bracelet flared even brighter. The shield exploded in more colors and shapes than a company of kaleidoscopes, and turned aside the beast's jaws—its strength, after all, was just one more bit of materially oriented power in an immaterial realm.

I brought my right hand out of my coat holding my blasting rod, and with a shouted word loosed a sledge-hammer of searing power. It dipped down and then curled up an instant before it hit, landing a sorcerous up-percut on what passed for the centipede's chin. It flung the creature's head several yards up, and its entire body rippled in agony.

Which, in retrospect, probably shouldn't have caught me quite as off guard as it did.

The ground beneath my feet heaved and bucked, and I went flying, my arms whirling in a useless windmill. I landed in a sprawl amid ranks of primroses, which immediately began to move, lashing out with tiny stem-tendrils lined with wickedly sharp little thorns. Even as I struggled back to my feet, tearing them away from my wrists and ankles, I noticed that the flowers around me had begun to blush a deep bloodred.

"You know what, Harry!" Bob called. "I don't think this is a garden at all!"

"Genius," I muttered, as the centipede recovered its balance and began reorienting itself to attack. Its body flowed forward, following the motion of its head. I decided that all those legs hitting the earth like posthole diggers in steady sequence made the giant bug sound less like a locomotive than a big piece of farm equipment churning by.

I ran at it, focusing my will beneath me, planted my staff on the earth, and swung my legs up in a pole vault-er's leap. I unleashed my will beneath and behind me as

I did, and flew over the thing's back as it continued surging forward. It let out a rumbling sound of displeasure as I went, the head twisting to follow me, forced to slow down enough to allow its own rearmost legs to get out of its way. It bought me only a few seconds.

Bigger doesn't mean better, especially in the Nevernever. One second was time enough to turn, focus another beam of fire into a far smaller area, and bring it down like an enormous cutting torch almost precisely across the middle of the big bug's body, an act of precision magic that I'd learned from Luccio, and which I was not at all confident I could have duplicated in the real world.

The beam, no bigger around than a couple of my fingers, sliced the creature in half as neatly and simply as if I'd used a paper cutter the size of a semi trailer.

It shrieked in pain, a brazen, bellowing sound that conveyed, even from such an alien thing, the depth of its physical agony. Its hindquarters just kept right on rolling forward, as if they hadn't noticed that the head was gone. The front half of the thing began to veer and waver wildly, its limited brain perhaps overloaded by the effort of sending nerve impulses to bits of its anatomy that no longer existed. It settled into a pattern of chasing its own retreating midsection, rolling in a great circle that crushed the ranks of primroses on either side of the trail.

"Booya!" I shouted in pure triumph, the adrenaline turning my manly baritone into a rather terrified-sounding shriek. "What have you got for fiery beam of death, huh? You got *nothing* for fiery beam of death! Might as well go back to Atari, bug-boy, 'cause you don't got game enough for me!"

It took me five or ten seconds to realize what was happening.

The wound I'd inflicted hadn't allowed for much bleeding, cauterizing even as it sliced—but even that little bit of bleeding stopped on both severed halves of the monster. The front half's wounded rear end suddenly rounded out. The second half's wounded front end shuddered and suddenly warped in place, and then with a wriggling motion, a new head began to writhe free of the severed stump.

Within seconds, both halves had focused on me, and then two of the freaking things rolled at me, jaws clashing and snapping, equally strong, equally as deadly as before. Only they were going to come rushing at me from multiple directions now.

"Wow," Bob said, in a perfectly calm, matter-of-fact, conversational tone. "That is incredibly unfair."

"Been that kind of day," I said. I swapped my blasting rod for my staff. The rod was great for pitching fire around, but I needed to pull off something more complicated than it was really meant to handle, and my wizard's staff was a great deal more versatile, meant for handling a broad range of possibilities. I called forth my will and laced it with the soulfire within me, then thrust the staff ahead and called, *"Fuego murus! Fuego vellum!"*

Energy rushed out of me, and silver-white fire rose up in a ring nearly sixty feet across, three feet thick, and three or four yards high. The roar of the flames seemed to be somehow intertwined with an odd tone that sounded like nothing so much as the voice of a great bell.

The centipedes (plural—Hell's bells, I needed to stop being so arrogant) rose up onto their rearmost limbs, trying to bridge the wall in a living arch, but they recoiled from the flames even more violently than when I'd slammed the original head with a cannonball of fire.

"Hey, neat working!" Bob said. "The soulfire is a nice touch."

The effort of managing that much energy caught up to me in a rush, and I found myself gasping and sweating. "Yeah," I said. "Thanks."

"Of course, now we're trapped," Bob noted. "And that wall is going to run out of juice soon. You can keep chopping them up for a while. Then they'll eat you."

"Nah," I said, panting. "We're in this together. We'll both get eaten."

"Ah," Bob said. "You'd better open a Way back to Chicago, then."

"Back to my apartment?" I demanded. "The FBI is there just waiting to slap cuffs onto me."

"Then I guess you shouldn't have become a terrorist, Harry!"

"Hey! I *never*—"

Bob raised his voice and shouted toward the centipedes, "I'm not with him!"

None of my options were good ones. Getting eaten by a supernaturally resilient centipede-demon would be an impediment to my rescue effort. Getting locked up by the FBI wouldn't be much better, but at least with the feds putting me in a cell, I'd have a chance to walk out of it—unlike the centipedes' stomach. Stomachs.

But I couldn't walk back into my apartment with a bag full of no-nos. I'd have to hide them before I got there—and that meant leaving the bag here. That wasn't exactly a brilliant idea, but I didn't have much in the way of a choice. I would have to take whatever precautions I could to hide the bag and hope that they were enough.

Earth magic isn't my forte. It is an extremely demanding discipline, physically speaking. You are, after all, talking about an awful lot of weight being moved around. Using magic doesn't mean you get to ignore physics. The energy for creating heat or motion comes from a different source, but it still has to interact with reality along the same lines as any other kind of energy. That means that affecting tons of earth takes an enormous amount of energy, and it's damned difficult—but not impossible. Ebenezar had insisted that I learn at least one very useful, if enormously taxing, spell with earth magic. It would be the effort of an entire day to use it in the real world. But here, in the Nevernever . . .

I lifted my staff, pointed it at the ground before me, and intoned in a deep, heavy monotone, *"Dispertius!"* I unleashed my will as I did, though I was already winded, and the earth and stone beneath my feet cracked open, a black gap opening like a stony mouth a few inches in front of my toes.

"Oh, no, no," Bob said. "You are *not* going to put me in—"

It was an enormous effort to my swiftly tiring body, but I pitched the bag, with the Swords, Bob, and all, into the hole. It vanished into the dark, along with Bob's scream of, "You'd better come back!"

The furious hissing of the enraged centipedes sliced through the air.

I pointed my staff at the hole again and intoned, *"Resarcius!"* More of my strength flooded out of me, and as quickly as that, the hole mended itself again, with the earth and stone that the bag and its contents displaced being dispersed into a wide area, resulting in little more than a very slight and difficult-to-see hump in the ground. The spell would make retrieval of the gear difficult for anyone who didn't know exactly where it was, and I had put it deep enough to hide it from anyone who wasn't specifically looking for it. I hoped.

Bob and the Swords were as safe as it was possible for me to make them, under the circumstances, and my wall of silver fire was steadily dwindling. It was time to get going while I still could.

My legs were shaking with fatigue and I leaned hard on my staff to keep from falling over. I needed one more effort of will to escape this prettily landscaped death trap, and after that—

The ring of fire had fallen low enough that one of the centipedes arched up into the air, forming a bridge of its own body, and flowed over it and onto the ground outside. Its multifaceted eyes fixed upon me and its jaws clashed in hungry anticipation.

I turned away, focused my thoughts and will, and with a slashing motion of my hand cut a tiny slice into the air, opening a narrow doorway, a mere crack, between the Nevernever and reality. Then I threw myself at it.

I had never gone through such a narrow opening before. I felt as if it were smashing me flat in some kind of spiritual trash compactor. It hurt, an instant of such savage agony that it seemed to stretch out into an hour, all while my thoughts were compressed into a single, impossibly dense whole, a psychic black hole where every dark and leaden emotion I'd ever felt seemed to suffuse and poison every thought and memory, adding an overwhelming heartache to the physical torment.

The instant passed, and I was through the narrow opening. I sensed a fraction of a second in which the centipede tried to follow, but the slit I'd opened between worlds had healed itself almost instantaneously.

I tumbled through about three feet of empty air,

banged my hip on the side of the worktable in my lab, and hit the concrete floor like a sack of exhausted bricks.

People started shouting and someone piled onto me, rolling me onto my chest and planting a knee in my spine as they hauled my arms around behind my back. There was a bunch of chatter to which I paid no heed. I hurt too much, and was too damned tired to care.

Honestly, the only thought in my mind at the time was a sense of great relief at being arrested. Now I could kick back and relax in a nice pair of handcuffs.

Or maybe a straitjacket, depending on how things went.

Chapter
Thirteen

They took me to the Chicago division of the Federal Bureau of Investigation on Roosevelt. A crowd of reporters was outside the place, and immediately started screaming questions and snapping pictures as I was taken from the car and half carried into the building by a couple of patrolmen. None of the feds said anything to the cameras, but Rudolph paused long enough to confirm that an investigation into the explosion was ongoing and that several "persons of interest" were being detained, and that the good people of Chicago had nothing to fear, yadda, yadda, yadda.

A slender little guy in a fed suit with fish white skin and ink black hair strolled by Rudolph, put an arm around the other man's shoulder in a comradely fashion, and almost hauled him off his feet and away from the reporters. Rudolph sputtered, but Slim gave him a hard look and Rudy subsided.

I remember stumbling through a checkpoint and an elevator and then being plopped down into a chair. Slim took the cuffs off my wrists. I promptly folded my arms on the table in front of me and put my head down. I don't know how long I was out, but when I came to, a rather stiff, dour-looking woman was shining a penlight into my eyes.

"No evidence of concussion," she said. "Normal response. I think he's just exhausted."

Slim stood at the door to the little room, which had a single conference table, several chairs, and a long mirror on the wall. Rudolph was standing there with him, a young-looking man in a suit more expensive than his pay grade, with dark, insanely neat hair and an anxious hunch to his shoulders.

"He's faking it," Rudolph insisted. "He wasn't out of our sight for more than a few minutes. How could he have worked himself to exhaustion in that time, huh? Without sweating? Not even really breathing hard? He's dirty. I know it. We shouldn't have given him an hour to come up with a story."

Slim eyed Rudy without any expression showing on his lean, pale face. Then he looked at me.

"I guess that makes you Good Cop," I said.

Slim rolled his eyes. "Thanks, Roz."

The woman took a stethoscope from around her neck, gave me a look full of disapproval, and left the room.

Slim came over to the table and sat down across from me. Rudolph moved around to stand behind me. It was a simple psychological ploy, but it worked. Rudolph's presence, out of my line of sight, was an irritant and a distraction.

"My name is Tilly," said Slim. "You can call me Agent Tilly or Agent or Tilly. Whatever you're most comfortable with."

"Okay, Slim," I said.

He inhaled and exhaled slowly. Then he said, "Why didn't you just answer the door, Mr. Dresden? It would have been a lot easier. For all of us."

"I didn't hear you," I said. "I was asleep down in the subbasement."

"Bullshit," said Rudolph.

Slim looked from me to Rudy and back. "Asleep, huh?"

"I'm a heavy sleeper," I said. "Keep a pad underneath one of the tables in the lab. Snooze down there sometimes. Nice and cool."

Slim studied me for another thoughtful minute. Then he said, "Nah, you weren't asleep down there. You weren't down there at all. There was no open space large enough to have hidden you in that subbasement. You were somewhere else."

"Where?" I asked him. "I mean, not like it's a big apartment. Living room, bedroom, bathroom, subbasement. You found me on the floor in the subbasement, which only has one entrance. Where else do you think I was? You think I just appeared out of thin air?"

Slim narrowed his eyes. Then he shook his head and said, "I don't know. Seen a lot of tricks. Saw a guy make the Statue of Liberty disappear once."

I spread my hands. "You think I did it with mirrors or something?"

"Could be," he said. "I don't have a good explanation for how you showed up all of a sudden, Dresden. I get grumpy when I don't have good explanations for things. Then I go digging until I come up with something."

I grinned at him. I couldn't help it. "I was asleep in my lab. Woke up when you guys started twisting my arms. You think I came out of a secret compartment so well hidden that nobody found it in a full sweep of the room? Or maybe I appeared out of thin air. Which of those stories do you think will make more sense to the judge in the civil suit I bring against the CPD and the Bureau? Yours or mine?"

Slim's expression turned sour.

Rudolph abruptly appeared to my right and slammed a fist down on the table. "Tell us why you blew up the building, Dresden!"

I burst out laughing. I couldn't help it. I didn't have a whole lot of energy, but I laughed until my stomach was shaking.

"I'm sorry," I said a moment later. "I'm sorry. It was just so . . . ahhhh." I shook my head and tried to get myself under control.

"Rudolph," said Slim. "Get out."

"You can't order me out. I am a duly appointed representative of the CPD and a member of this task force."

"You're useless, unprofessional, and impeding this deposition," Slim said, his tone flat. He turned his dark eyes to Rudolph and said, "Get. Out."

Slim had a hell of a glare. Some men do. They can look at you and tell you, without saying a word, that they are perfectly capable of doing violence and willing to demonstrate it. That look doesn't convey any particular, single emotion, nor anything that can be easily put into words. Slim didn't need any words. He stared at Rudolph with some faint shadow of old Death himself in his eyes, and did nothing else.

Rudolph flinched. He muttered something about filing a complaint against the FBI and left the room.

Agent Tilly turned back to me. His expression softened, briefly, into something almost resembling a smile, and he said, "Did you do it?"

I met his eyes for a second and said, "No."

Tilly pursed his lips. Then he nodded his head several times and said, "Okay."

I lifted my eyebrows. "Just like that?"

"I know when people lie," he said simply.

"And that's why this is a deposition, not an interrogation?"

"It's a deposition because Rudolph lied his ass off when he fingered you to my boss," Tilly said. "Now I've seen you for myself. And bomber doesn't fit on you."

"Why not?"

"Your apartment is one big pile of disorganized clutter. Disorganized bomb makers don't have much of a life expectancy. My turn. Why is someone trying to tag you for the office building?"

"Politics, I think," I said. "Karrin Murphy has pissed off a lot of money by wrecking some of their shadier enterprises. Money leans on politicians. I get some spillover because she's the one who hired me as a consultant on some of it."

"Fucking Chicago," Tilly said, with real contempt in his voice. "The government in the whole state is about as corrupt as they get."

"Amen," I said.

"I read your file. Says you were looked at by my office before. Says four agents vanished a few days later." He pursed his lips. "You've been suspected of kidnapping, murder, and at least two cases of arson, one of which was a public building."

"It wasn't my fault," I said. "That building thing."

"You lead an interesting life, Dresden."

"Not really. Just a wild weekend now and then."

"To the contrary," Tilly said. "I'm very interested in you."

I sighed. "Man. You don't want to be."

Tilly considered that, a faint frown line appearing between his brows. "Do you know who blew up your office building?"

"No."

Tilly's expression might have been carved in stone. "Liar."

"If I tell you," I said, "you aren't going to believe me—and you're going to get me locked up in a psycho ward somewhere. So no. I don't know who blew up the building."

He nodded for a moment. Then he said, "What you are doing now could be construed as obstructing and interfering with an investigation. Depending on who was behind the bombing and why, it might even get bumped up to treason."

"In other words," I said, "you couldn't find anything in my apartment to incriminate me or give you an excuse to hold me. So now you're hoping to intimidate me into talking with you."

Agent Tilly leaned back in his chair and squinted at me. "I can hold you for twenty-four hours for no reason at all. And I can make them fairly unpleasant for you without coming close to violating any laws."

"I wish you wouldn't do that," I said.

Tilly shrugged. "And I wish you'd tell me what you know about the explosion. But I guess neither of us is going to get what we want."

I propped my chin on my hand and thought about it for a moment. I gave it even odds that someone in the supernatural scene, probably the duchess, had pulled some strings to send Rudolph my way. If that was the case, maybe I could bounce this little hand grenade back to her.

"Off the record?" I asked Tilly.

He stood up, went out the door, and came back in a moment later, presumably after turning off any recording devices. He sat back down and looked at me.

"You're going to find out that the building was wired with explosives," I said. "On the fourth floor."

"And how do you know that?"

"Someone I trust saw some blueprint files that showed where the charges had been installed, presumably at the behest of the building's owners. I remember that a few years ago, there were crews tearing into the walls for a week or so. Said they were removing asbestos. The owners had hired them."

"Nuevo Verita, Inc., owns the building. As insurance scams go, this isn't a great one."

"It isn't about insurance," I said.

"Then what is it about?"

"Revenge."

Tilly tilted his head to one side and studied me intently. "You did something to this company?"

"I did something to someone far up the food chain in the corporate constellation that Nuevo Verita belongs to."

"And what was that?"

"Nothing illegal," I said. "You might look into the business affairs of a man calling himself Paolo Ortega. He was a professor of mythology in Brazil. He died several years ago."

"Ah," Tilly said. "His family is who is after you?"

"That's a reasonably accurate description. His wife in particular."

Tilly absorbed that, taking his time. The room was silent for several minutes.

Finally, Tilly looked up at me and said, "I have a great

deal of respect for Karrin Murphy. I called her while you were resting. She says she'll back you without reservation. Considering the source, that is a significant statement."

"Yeah," I said. "Considering the source, it is."

"Frankly, I'm not sure if I can do anything to help you. I'm not in charge of the investigation, and it's being directed by politicians. I can't promise that you won't be questioned again—though today's events should make it harder to get judicial approval to move against you."

"I'm not sure I understand your meaning," I said.

Tilly waved a hand toward the rest of the building. "As far as they're concerned, you're guilty, Dresden. They're already writing headlines and news text. Now it's just a matter of finding the evidence to support the conclusion they want."

"They," I said. "Not you."

Tilly said, "They're a bunch of assholes."

"And you aren't?"

"I'm a different kind of asshole."

"Heh," I said. "Am I free to go?"

He nodded. "But since they've got nothing remotely like evidence that you were the one to plant the explosives, they're going to be digging into you. Your personal life. Your past. Looking for things to use against you. They'll play dirty."

"Okay by me," I said. "I can play, too."

Tilly's eyes smiled. "Sounds like. Yeah." He offered me his hand. "Good luck."

I shook it. I felt the very, very faint tingle of someone with a slight magical talent. It probably augmented Tilly's ability to separate truth from fiction.

I got up and walked wearily toward the door.

"Hey," Tilly said, just before I opened it. "Off the record. Who did it?"

I stopped, looked at him again, and said, "Vampires."

His expression flickered with swiftly banished emotions: amusement, then realization, followed by doubt and yards and yards of rationalization.

"See," I said to him. "I told you that you wouldn't believe me."

Chapter

Fourteen

I came out of the doors of the FBI building to find a ring of paparazzi surrounding it, waiting with predatory patience to get more material for their stories. A couple of them saw me and hurried toward me, beginning to ask me questions, thrust microphones toward me, that sort of thing. I winced. I was still pretty tired, but it was going to play merry hell with their gear if I got too close to it.

I looked around for a way to get down the sidewalks without messing up anybody's equipment, and that was when they tried to kill me.

I'd been the target of a drive-by attempt once before. This one was considerably more professional than the first. There was no roar of engines to give me a warning, no wildly swerving vehicle. The only tip-off I had was a sudden prickling of the hairs on the back of my neck and a glimpse of a dark sedan's passenger window rolling down.

Then something hit me in the left side of my chest and hammered me down onto the stairs. Stunned, I realized that someone was shooting at me. I could have rolled down the stairs and into the news crowd, put them between myself and the shooter, but I had no way of knowing whether the shooter wanted me bad enough to fire through a crowd in hopes of getting me. So I curled into a defensive ball and felt two more heavy blows land against me: one of them on my ribs, the second on my left arm, which I'd raised to cover my head.

There was an exclamation from below, and then there were several people standing over me.

"Hey, buddy," said a potbellied cameraman in a hunting jacket. He offered me a hand to help me up. "Nasty fall, there. You still in one piece?"

I just stared at him for a second, the adrenaline coursing through me, and realized that the cameraman—all of the newsies, in fact—didn't even know what had just happened.

It made a creepy kind of sense. I hadn't heard anything. The assassin must have been using a suppressor. There hadn't been any flashes, so he must have done it right, aiming at me through the car window while sitting far enough back to make sure the barrel of his gun didn't poke out suspiciously—and that he never became a highly visible target. I had helped, too, by denying the onlookers the subtle clue of a dead body with little holes in the front of it and big ones in the back. No sound, no sight, and no victim. Why should they think that murder had just been attempted?

"Move!" I said, hauling myself up by the cameraman's paw. I struggled to get higher, to look over the crowd and get a plate off of the dark sedan. It didn't take much more than stepping around a couple of people and standing on tiptoe to get a view of the shooter's vehicle, cruising calmly away, without roaring engines, without crashing up onto the sidewalk or running red lights. It just vanished into the traffic like a shark disappearing into the depths. I never got a clear look at the plates.

"Dammit," I growled. Pain was starting to register on me now, especially in my arm. The protective spells I'd woven over my duster had held out against the bullets, but the leather had been pulled pretty tight over my skin and as a result it felt like someone had smashed a baseball bat into my forearm. The fingers of my left hand were tingling and refused to do more than twitch. I felt similar throbs from the other two hits, and ran my hands over the duster, just to be sure none of them had gone through without my noticing.

I found a bullet caught in the leather of my left sleeve. It hadn't penetrated more than maybe a quarter of an inch, but it was trapped in the leather and deformed from the impact. I pulled a handkerchief out of my pocket, wrapped the bullet in it, and put it back again, managing to do the whole thing unnoticed while about a dozen people looked at me like I was a lunatic.

From the street came a wheezy little *beep-beep!* The *Blue Beetle* came slowly down the street and stopped in front of the building. Molly was behind the wheel, waving at me frantically.

I hurried down to the street and got in before the mismatched color scheme of my car sent the obsessive-compulsive federal personnel in the building behind me into a conniption. As Molly pulled away, I buckled up, then got a sloppy kiss on the face from Mouse, who sat in the backseat, his tail going *thump-thump-thump* against the back of the driver's seat.

"Ick!" I told him. "My lips touched dog lips! Get me some mouthwash! Get me some iodine!"

His tail kept wagging and he smooched me again before settling down and looking content.

I sagged back into my seat and closed my eyes.

Maybe two minutes passed. "You're welcome," Molly

said abruptly, her tone frustrated. "No problem, Harry. Whatever I can do to help."

"Sorry, padawan," I said. "This has been a long day already."

"I came back from the church and saw a bunch of guys and cops were going in and out of your apartment. The door was broken down and the whole place looked like it had been ransacked." She shuddered and clenched the wheel. "God. I was sure you were dead or in trouble."

"You were about ninety percent right," I said. "Someone told the feds I was the one who blew up the office building. They wanted to talk to me."

Molly's eyes grew wide. "What about the Swords? We've got to tell my dad, right away, or—"

"Relax," I said. "I stashed them. They should be safe for now."

Molly puffed out a breath and subsided in relief. "You look terrible," she said, after a minute. "Did they beat you up or something?"

I swept my eyes left and right as we went on, searching. "Giant centipede."

"Oh," Molly said, drawing the word out, as though I had explained everything. "What are you looking for?"

I'd been scanning the traffic around us for a dark sedan. I'd found about thirty of them so far, being a master detective and all. "The car of the guy who just shot at me." I produced the bullet, a little copper-jacketed round more slender than my pinkie and a little under an inch long.

"What is that?" Molly asked.

"Two-twenty-three Remington," I said. "I think. Probably."

"What's that mean?"

"That it could have been almost anybody. It's the

round used in most NATO assault rifles. A lot of hunting rifles, too." A thought struck me and I frowned at her. "Hey. How did you know where to find me?"

"I let Mouse drive."

Thump, thump, thump.

I was tired. It took my brain a second to sort out the humor in her tone. "It isn't funny when everyone does it, Molly. Not ready for the burden of constant wiseassery are you."

She grinned widely, evidently pleased at having scored the point on me. "I used a tracking spell and the hair you gave me in case I ever needed to find you."

Of course she had. "Oh, right. Well-done."

"Um," she said. "I'm not sure where we're driving. As far as I know, your apartment is still crawling with guys."

"Priorities, grasshopper. First things first."

She eyed me. "Burger King, huh?"

"I'm starving," I said. "Then back to the apartment. They should be gone by the time we get there, and it's the only place where I'm sure Susan and Martin will be trying to make contact."

She frowned. "But . . . the wards are down. It's not safe there anymore. Is it?"

"It never was," I said calmly. "If someone really wants to come kill you, it's hard to stop them. All you can do is make it expensive for them to try it, and hope that they decide the price is too high."

"Well, sure," Molly said. "But . . . without the wards, aren't you kind of having a super discount sale?"

Kid had a point. Anyone who ever wanted to take a whack at me had a peachy opportunity now. Attention, shoppers! Discount specials on Harry Dresden's life.

Slightly used, no refunds, limit one per customer. Shop smart. Shop S-Mart.

I leaned my head against the window, closed my eyes, and said, "What'd Forthill tell you?"

"What he always says. That he couldn't make any promises, but that he'd do whatever he could to help. He said to call him back in a few hours and he'd see what he could get from his peeps."

"Pretty sure that Roman Catholic priests don't have peeps," I said gravely. "Too trendy and ephemeral. Like automobiles. And the printing press."

Molly didn't return fire against my comments, though I'd made them lightly. She was conflicted on the whole issue of the Church, which I thought was probably a fine state for her mind to be in. People who ask questions and think about their faith are the last ones to embrace dogma—and the last to abandon their path once they've set out on it. I felt fairly sure that the Almighty, whatever name tag He had on at the moment, could handle a few questions from people sincerely looking for answers. Hell, He might even like it.

"Harry," she said. "We could talk to my father."

"No," I said in a calm and final tone. "That isn't even on the table."

"Maybe it should be. Maybe he could help you find Maggie."

I felt a sharp stab of anger and pain go through me—a vivid memory. Michael Carpenter, Knight of the Sword and unflagging friend, had gotten his body torn and beaten to bits trying to help me with one of my cases. Bearing a Sword melded to one of the nails of the Crucifixion, given him by an archangel, he had been a bulwark against very real, very literal forces of evil in the world.

It was incredibly comforting to have him on your side. We'd waded into all kinds of ridiculously lethal situations together and come out of them again.

Except that last time.

He was retired now, and happy, walking only with the aid of a cane, out of the evil-smiting business and spending his time building houses and being with his family, the way he'd always wanted to. So long as he stayed retired, I gathered that he had a certain amount of immunity against the powers of supernatural evil. It would not surprise me at all if there were literally an angel standing over his shoulder at all times, ready to protect him and his family. Like the Secret Service, but with swords and wings and halos.

"No," I said again. "He's out of the fight. He deserves to be. But if I ask for his help, he'll give it, and he'll have chosen to accept the consequences. Only he can't protect himself or your family from them anymore."

Molly took a very deep breath and then nodded, her worried eyes focused on the road. "Right," she said. "Okay. It's just . . ."

"Yeah?"

"I'm used to him being there, I guess. Knowing that . . . if I need him, he's there to help. I guess I always had it in my head that if things ever went really, truly bad, he'd Show Up," she said, putting gentle emphasis on the last words.

I didn't answer her. My father had died when I was young, before I learned that there was anything stronger than he was. I'd been operating without that kind of support for my whole life. Molly was only now realizing that, in some ways, she was on her own.

I wondered if my daughter even knew that she had a

father, if she knew that there was someone who wanted, desperately, to Show Up.

"You get yourself an apartment and your plumbing goes bad, he'll still be there," I said quietly. "Some guy breaks your heart, he'll come over with ice cream. A lot of people never have a dad willing to do that stuff. Most of the time, it matters a hell of a lot more."

She blinked her eyes several times and nodded. "Yeah. But . . ."

I got what she didn't say. But when you need someone to break down the door and commence kicking ass, you *really* need it. And Michael couldn't do that for his daughter anymore.

"Tell you what, Molly," I said. "You ever need a rescue, I'll handle that part. Okay?"

She looked at me, her eyes blurred with tears, and nodded several times. She clasped my hand with hers and squeezed tight. Then she turned her face back to the road and pressed down on the accelerator.

We hit a drive-through and went on back to my apartment.

At the top of the stairs that led down to my door, I felt myself starting to get angry. They'd hammered the door flat. There were some scuff marks on it, but not much more than that. Tough door. But the wooden frame around it was shattered. There would be no way to get the door mounted again without extensive repairs that were probably beyond my skill level.

I stood there shaking with rage. It wasn't like I lived in an ivory tower or Bag End. It was just a dingy little hole in the ground. It wasn't much of a place, but it was the only home I had, and I was comfortable there.

It was my home.

And Rudolph and company had trashed it. I closed my eyes and took a deep breath, trying to calm down.

Molly touched my shoulder for a second. "It's not so bad. I know a good Carpenter."

I sighed and nodded. I already knew that when all this was over, Michael would be Showing Up for me.

"Just hope Mister will be back soon. Might have to board him somewhere until the door is fixed." I started down the stairs. "I just hope that—"

Mouse let out a sudden, deep growl.

I had my blasting rod out and my shield up in less than two seconds. Mouse is not an alarmist. I've never heard him growl outside the presence of danger of one kind or another. I checked to my right, and saw no Molly standing there. The grasshopper had vanished from view even more quickly than I'd readied my defenses.

I swallowed. I'd heard many variants on my dog's snarl. This one wasn't as threatening as it might have been—as it *would* be, in the presence of dark threats. His body posture was a balance of tension and relaxation, simple wariness rather than the fighting crouch he had exhibited before. He'd smelled something that he thought was extremely dangerous, but not necessarily something that had to be immediately attacked and destroyed.

Slowly, I went down the steps, shield at the ready, my left hand extended before me, my fingers in a warding gesture, my thumb, pinkie, and index fingers stiff and spread wide apart, center fingers folded. My right hand held the blasting rod extended before me, seething scarlet power boiling out from the carved runes and the tendril of bright flame at its tip, simultaneously ready to destroy and lighting my way. Mouse came down the stairs with me, his shoulder against my right hip. His growl was a steady tone, like the engine of a well-tuned car.

I came down the stairs and saw that there was a fire crackling in the fireplace. Between that and my blasting rod and the stray bits of afternoon sunlight, I could see fairly well.

The FBI could have done worse to my apartment, I supposed. Books had been taken off my bookshelves, but at least they had been stacked in piles, more or less, rather than tossed on the floor. They'd moved my furniture around, including taking the cushions off, but they'd put them back. Incorrectly, but they were back. Similarly, my kitchen had been dismantled with a kind of cursory courtesy, but not destroyed.

All of that was secondary in my mind, next to the pair of coffin-sized cocoons of what looked like green silk. One of the cocoons was stuck to my ceiling, the other to the wall beside the fireplace. Susan's face protruded from the second cocoon, sagging in something near unconsciousness, her dark hair hanging limply. On the ceiling, I could see only a man's mouth and part of his chin, but I was pretty sure it was Martin. They'd come back to my apartment, presumably after the feds left, and been captured.

"Mouse," I murmured. "You smell any cordite?"

The dog shook his head as if to shed it of water, and his tags jingled.

"Me neither," I said. So. Whatever had been done to them, it had happened fast, before an extremely quick Susan or an extremely paranoid Martin could employ a weapon.

One of my old recliners was faced away from the door. As I stepped across the threshold, it spun around (completely ignoring the fact that it was neither meant to spin nor mounted on any kind of mechanism that would make such a thing possible) and revealed, in firelight and shadow, an intruder and my cat.

She was tall and beyond beautiful—like most of the Sidhe are. Her skin was fair and flawless, her eyes enormous, slightly oblique orbs of emerald green. In fact, they almost mirrored Mister's eyes as he sat primly in the Sidhe woman's lap. Her lips were full and very red, and her long red hair, accented with streaks of pure white, spilled down in silken coils and waves over her dress of emerald green.

When she saw me she smiled, widely, and it revealed neatly pointed canine teeth, both dainty and predatory. "Ah," she said warmly. "Harry. It's been such a long time since we've spoken."

I shivered and kept my blasting rod trained on the Sidhe woman. She was a faerie, and I'd learned, from long experience, that the folk of Faerie, Summer and Winter alike, were not to be underestimated. Only a fool would trust them—but on the other hand, only a madman would offend them. They set great store by the forms of courtesy, etiquette, and the relationship of guest to host. One flouted the proper forms at peril of . . . rather extreme reactions from the Sidhe, the lords of Faerie.

So instead of opening up with fire and hoping I got in a sucker punch, I lowered my blasting rod, gave the Leanansidhe a precise, shallow bow without ever taking my eyes off of her, and said, "Indeed. It's been a while, Godmother."

Chapter
Fifteen

"**A**ren't you pleased with me?" the Leanansidhe said. She gestured with one manicured hand to the two cocoons, then went back to caressing Mister. "I came upon these brigands ransacking your little cave and . . . What is the word?" Her smile widened. "I apprehended them."

"I see," I said.

"As I understand mortal business," she said, "next there is a trial, followed by . . . What is the word mortal law uses for murder? Ah, an *execution*." Her red-gold brows furrowed briefly. "Or is it execution and *then* trial?" She shrugged. "La. It seems largely a matter of semantics in any case. Harry, would you prefer to be the judge, the jury, or the executioner?"

I . . . just stared.

The last time I'd seen my faerie godmother, she had been ranting and raving in a couple of distinct personalities and voices while half-entombed in a sheet of ice at the heart of the Winter Court. Since I was sixteen, she'd pursued me relentlessly whenever I crossed into the Nevernever, apparently determined to transform me into one of her hounds.

For crying out loud. Now she was all smiles and bubbles? Protecting my apartment? Offering to play court-room with me, as if I were a child and Martin and Susan were a pair of dolls?

"It isn't that I don't like to see you, Lea," I said. "But I can't help but wonder what it is you want."

"Merely to ensure the well-being of your spiritual self," she replied. "That is what a godmother is supposed to do, is it not?"

"I was sort of hoping your answer would be a bit more specific."

She let out a musical laugh that rang like distant church bells over snow. "Sweet child. Have you learned nothing of the fae?"

"Does anyone, ever?"

Her slender fingers stroked Mister's fur. "Do you think it so impossible?"

"Don't *you* think it is?"

"In what way is my opinion relevant to the truth?"

"Are we going to stand around here all day answering each other's questions with questions?"

Her smile widened. "Would you like that?"

I lifted a hand, capitulating.

She inclined her head to me, a gracious victor. Lea was better at that sort of wordplay than me, having had several centuries to practice.

Besides, losing to the guest with grace was a tradi-tional courtesy, as well.

"What I would like," I said, nodding toward the co-coons, "is for you to please release these two. They aren't robbers. They're guests. And this is, after all, my home."

"Of course, child," she said agreeably. "No harm done." She snapped her fingers and the cocoons seemed to sublimate into a fine green mist that quickly dispersed.

Susan fell limply from the wall, but I was waiting to catch her and lower her gently to the floor.

Martin plummeted from the ceiling and landed on a threadbare throw rug covering the concrete floor. Nobody was there to catch him, which was awful. Just awful.

I examined Susan quickly. She had no obvious wounds. She was breathing. She had a pulse. And that was pretty much the length and breadth of my medical knowledge. I checked Martin, too, but was disappointed. He was in the same condition as Susan.

I looked up at my godmother. Mister was sprawled in her lap on his back, luxuriating as she traced her long nails over his chest and tummy. His purr throbbed continuously through the room. "What did you do to them?"

"I lulled their predator spirit to sleep," she said calmly. "Poor lambs. They didn't realize how much strength they drew from it. Mayhap this will prove a useful lesson."

I frowned at that. "You mean . . . the vampire part of them?"

"Of course."

I sat there for a moment, stunned.

If the vampire infection within half vampires like Susan and Martin could be enchanted to sleep, then it was presumably possible to do other things to it as well. Suppress it, maybe permanently.

It might even be possible to destroy it.

I felt a door in my mind open upon a hope I had shut away a long time ago.

Maybe I could save them both.

"I . . ." I shook my head. "I searched for a way to . . . I spent more than a . . ." I shook my head harder. "I spent more than a *year* trying to find a way to . . ." I looked at my godmother. "How? How did you do it?"

She looked back at me, her lips curled into something that wasn't precisely a smile. "Oh, sweet child. Information of that sort is treasure indeed. What have you to trade for such a precious gem of knowledge?"

I clenched my teeth. "It's always about bargains with you, isn't it."

"Of course, child. But I always live up to my end. Hence, my protection of you."

"Protection?" I demanded. "You spent most of a couple of decades trying to turn me into a dog!"

"Only when you strayed out of the mortal world," she said, as if baffled at why I would be upset. "Child, we had a bargain. And you had not willingly provided your portion of it." She smiled widely at Mouse. "And dogs are so charming."

Mouse watched her with calm, wary eyes, his body motionless.

I frowned. "But . . . you sold my debt to Mab."

"Precisely. At an excellent price, I might add. So now, all that remains twixt thou and I is your mother's bargain. Unless you would prefer to enter another compact, of course . . ."

I shuddered. "No, thank you." I finally lowered my shields. The Leanansidhe beamed at me. "I saw you in Mab's tower," I said.

Something dark flickered through her emerald eyes, and she turned her face slightly away from me. "Indeed," she said quietly. "You saw what it means for my queen to heal an affliction."

"What affliction?"

"A madness had beset me," she whispered. "Robbed

me of myself. Treacherous gifts . . ." She shook her head. "I can think on it no more, lest it make me vulnerable once again. Suffice to say that I am much better now." She stroked a fingertip over an icy white streak in her hair. "The strength of my queen prevailed, and my mind is mine own."

"Ensuring the well-being of my spiritual self," I murmured. Then I blinked. "The garden, the one on the other side of this place . . . It's *yours*."

"Indeed, child," she said. "Did you not think it strange that in your turmoil-strewn time here none of your foes—not *one*—ever sought to enter from the other side? Never sent a spirit given form directly into your bed, your shower, your refrigerator? Never poured a basket of asps into your closet so that they sought refuge in your shoes, your boots, the pockets of your clothing?" She shook her head. "Sweet, sweet child. Had you walked much farther, you would have seen the mound of bones of all the things that have attempted to reach you, and which I have destroyed."

"Yeah, well. I nearly wound up there myself."

"La," she said, smiling. "My guardians were created to attack any intruder—including one that looked like you. We couldn't have some clever shapeshifter slipping by, now, could we?" She sighed. "You took a terrible toll on my primroses. Honestly, child, there *are* elements other than fire, you know. You really ought to diversify. Now I have two gaping maws to feed instead of one."

"I'll . . . be more careful next time," I said.

"I should appreciate such a thing." She studied me quietly. "It has been true for your entire lifetime, child. I have followed you in the spirit world. Created guardians and defenses 'pon the other side to ward your sleep, to stand sentinel over your home. And you still have only the beginnings of an idea of how many have tried." She smiled, showing her delicately pointed canine teeth again. "Tried, and failed."

Which also explained how she was *always* near at hand whenever I had entered the Nevernever. How she would be upon my trail in seconds whenever I went in.

Because she had been there, protecting me.

From everything but herself.

"Now, then," she said, her tone businesslike. "You left a considerable trove of equipment in my garden for safekeeping."

"It was an emergency."

"I had assumed that," she said. "I will, of course, safeguard it or return it, as you wish. And, should you perish, I will deliver it to an heir of your designation."

I let out a weary laugh. "You . . . Of course you will." I eyed Mouse. "What do you think, boy?"

Mouse looked at me, and then at Lea. Then he sat down—but still kept watching her carefully.

"Yeah," I said. "I think that, too."

The Leanansidhe smiled widely. "It is good that you have taken my lessons to heart, child. It is a cold and uncaring universe we live in. Only with strength of body and mind can you hope to control your own fate. Be wary of everyone. Even your protector."

I sat there for a moment, thinking.

My mother had prepared protection for me with considerable foresight. She had anticipated my eventually looking for and finding my half brother, Thomas. Had she prepared other things for me, as well? Things I hadn't yet guessed at?

How would I pass on a legacy to my child if I knew

that I wasn't going to be alive to see it happen? What kind of legacy did I have, other than a collection of magical gear that anyone could probably accumulate without help, in time?

My only real treasure was knowledge.

Ye gods and little fishes, but knowledge was a dangerous legacy. I imagined what might have happened if, at the age of fifteen, I had learned aspects of magic that had not come to me on their own until I was over thirty. It would have been like handing a child a cocked and loaded gun.

A safety mechanism was needed—something that would prevent the child from attaining said store of knowledge until she was mature enough to handle it wisely. Something simple, but telling, for a child. A *wizard* child.

I smiled. Something like being able to admit one's own ignorance. Expressed in the simplest possible form: asking a question. And, as I now knew, my mother had not been called "LeFay" for nothing.

"Godmother," I asked calmly. "Did my mother leave anything for you to give me when I was ready for it? A book? A map?"

Lea took a very slow, deep breath, her eyes luminous. "Well," she murmured. "Well, well, well."

"She did, didn't she?"

"Yes, indeed. But I was told to give you fair warning. It is a deadly legacy. If you accept it, you accept what comes with it."

"Which is?" I asked.

She shrugged a shoulder. "It varies from one individual to the next. Your mother lost the ability to sleep soundly. It might be worse for you. Or it might be nothing."

I thought about that for a moment, and then nodded. "I want it."

Lea never took her eyes off me. She lifted her empty palm, closed her fingers over it, and opened them again.

A small, gleaming ruby, bright as a drop of blood, carved in a pentagon, lay in her hand.

"It is the sum of her knowledge of the Ways," Lea said quietly. "Every path, every shortcut, every connection. She developed enough skill at searching them out that she was eventually able to predict them. Ways may change from decade to decade, but your mother knew where they were and where they would be. Very few of mine own kind can say as much." She narrowed her eyes. "That knowledge is the burden I hold in my hand, child. Mine own belief is that it will destroy thee. The choice must needs be thine."

I stared at the gem for a long moment, forcing myself to breathe slowly. All the Ways. The ability to travel around the world without concern for geography. Knowledge like that could have won the war with the Red Court almost before it began. Whoever possessed that knowledge could regard laws with utter impunity, avoid retribution from mortal authorities or supernatural nations alike. Go anywhere. Escape from damned near anything. Gather more information than anyone else possibly could.

Hell's bells. That gleaming little gem was a subtle strength that had the potential to be as potent as any I had seen. Such *power*.

Such temptation.

I wondered if I'd be able to handle it. I am not a saint.

At the same time, I had never seen a tool so obviously

intended to help a man Show Up for his little girl. No matter where she was, I could go to her. Go to her and get away clean.

Maggie.

I reached out and took the gem from my godmother's hand.

Chapter

Sixteen

"Harry," Molly called from up in the living room, "I think they're waking up."

I grunted and lifted my pentacle necklace to examine it. The little pentagonal ruby had been quite obviously cut for this particular piece of jewelry. Or it had been before I'd been forced to use the necklace as a silver bullet. My little pentacle, the five-pointed star within a circle, had been warped by the extremes of stress I'd subjected it to. I'd been straightening it out with the set of jeweler's tools I used to update Little Chicago.

The jewel abruptly snapped into the center of the pentacle as if into a socket. I shook the necklace several times, and the gem stayed put. But there was no point in taking chances. I turned it over and smeared the whole back with a big blob of adhesive. It might not look pretty from the front after it had dried, but I was pressed for time.

"That'll do, pig," I muttered to myself. I looked up to Bob's shelf, where Mister was sprawling, using a couple of paperbacks for pillows while he amused himself dragging his claws through the mounded candle wax. I reached up to rub his ears with my fingertips, setting him to purring, and promised myself I would get Bob back soon. For the time being, he was, like the Swords, too valuable and too dangerous to leave unguarded. In Lea's bloodthirsty garden, they were probably safer than they had been in my apartment in the first place.

I left my mother's amulet and the glittering ruby sitting on my worktable so that the glue could dry, and padded up the stepladder.

I had hefted Susan up onto the sofa and fetched a pillow for her head, and a blanket. Molly had managed to roll Martin onto a strip of camping foam, and given him a pillow and a blanket, too. Mouse had settled down on the floor near Martin to sleep. Even though his eyes were closed and he was snoring slightly, his ears twitched at every sound.

While I had been in the lab, Molly had been cleaning up. She probably knew where all the dishes went better than I did. Or she was reorganizing them completely. Either way, I was sure that the next time I just wanted to fry one egg, I wouldn't be able to find the little skillet until after I had already used the big skillet and cleaned it off.

I hunkered down next to Susan, and as I did she stirred and muttered softly. Then she jerked in a swift breath through her nose, her eyes suddenly opening wide, as if she were panicked.

"Easy," I said at once. "Susan. It's Harry. You're safe."

It seemed to take several seconds for my words to sink in. Then she relaxed again, blinked a few times, and turned her head toward me.

"What happened to me?" she asked.

"You were mistaken for an intruder," I said. "You were hit with a form of magic that made you sleep."

She frowned tiredly. "Oh. I was dreaming. . . ."

"Yeah?"

"I was dreaming that the curse was gone. That I was human." She shook her head with a bitter little smile. "I thought I was done having that one. Martin?"

"Here," Martin slurred. "I'm all right."

"But maybe not for long," I said. "The apartment's wards are down. We're naked here."

"Well," Martin said in an acidic voice. "I think we learned our lesson about where that leads."

Susan rolled her eyes, but the look she gave me, a little hint of a smile and a level stare with her dark eyes, was positively smoldering.

Yeah. That had been pretty good.

"Did you guys find out about our tail?" I asked.

"Tails, as it turns out. Three different local investigative agencies," Martin supplied. "They were paid cash up front to follow us from the time we arrived. They all gave a different description of the woman who hired them. All of them were too beautiful to believe."

"Arianna?" I asked.

Martin grunted. "Probably. The oldest of them can wear any flesh mask they wish, and go abroad in daylight, hidden from the sun in the shadow of their own mask."

I lifted my eyebrows. *That* was news. I wasn't even sure the Wardens had that kind of information. Martin must have been a little groggy from his naptime.

"How long were we out?" Susan asked.

"I got here about five hours ago. Sun's down."

She closed her eyes for a moment, as if bracing herself for something, and nodded. "All right. Martin and I need to get moving."

"Where?" I asked.

"The airport," Martin said. "We should be able to be in Nevada by very late tonight or early tomorrow morning. Then we can move on the warehouse and look for more information."

"We discussed it, Harry," Susan said quietly. "You can't take a plane, and we're counting the minutes. A jet will get us there in about seven hours. The car will take two days. There's no time for that."

"Yeah, I can see your reasoning," I said.

Martin stood up creakily and stretched. "Entering the facility may require a reconnaissance period. We'll have to determine its weaknesses, patrol pacing, and so on before we—"

I interrupted him by slapping a piece of notebook paper down on the coffee table. "The storage facility is set into the side of a stone hill. There are some portable units stored outside in a yard with a twelve-foot razor-wire fence. A road leads into the hill and down into what I presume to be caverns either created for storage space or appropriated after a mining operation closed." I pointed at the notebook paper, to different points on the sketch, as I mentioned each significant feature.

"There is a single watchtower with one guard armed with a long-barreled assault rifle with a big scope. There are two men and a dog walking a patrol around the perimeter fence with those little assault rifles—"

"Carbines," Molly said brightly, from the kitchen.

"—and fragmentation grenades. They aren't in a hurry. Takes them about twenty minutes; then they go inside for a drink and come back out. There are security cameras here, here, and here, and enough cars in the employee parking lot to make me think that the underground portion of the facility is probably pretty big, and probably has some kind of barracks for their security team."

I nodded. "That's about it on the surface, but there's

no way we can get inside to scout it out ahead of time. Looks pretty straightforward. We move up to it under a veil; I shut down the communications. We use a distraction to draw everyone's attention, and when the reinforcements come running out, we're in. Hopefully we can find a way to lock them outside. After that, it's just a matter of . . ."

I trailed off as I looked up to find Martin and Susan staring at me, their jaws kind of hanging limply.

"What?" I said.

"How . . ." Martin began.

"Where . . ." Susan said.

Molly burst out into a fit of giggles she didn't even try to hide.

"How do I know?" I reached over to the table and held up an old set of binoculars I'd left sitting there. "I went over to take a look. Took me about fifteen minutes, one way. I could bring you, if you want, but it's cool if you guys want to take the plane. I'll wait for you."

Martin stared hard at me.

"You . . ." Susan began, something like anger in her tone. Then she threw back her head and laughed. "You insufferable, arrogant pig," she said fondly. "I shouldn't have underestimated you. You don't always perform gracefully when everything is on the line—but you're always there, aren't you?"

"I hope so," I said quietly. I stood up again. "Better eat something. I've got some things finishing up in the lab that might help us. We'll go in one hour."

Chapter

Seventeen

We rolled out in fifty-five minutes.

The *Blue Beetle* was full, but we weren't going more than a half dozen blocks. The entry into the proper Way was in an alleyway behind a brownstone apartment building in a fairly typical Chicago neighborhood. It was getting late, so there wasn't much traffic, and Mouse ghosted along behind us, staying mostly in the shadows and easily keeping pace with the car.

Which speaks to my dog's mightiness, and not to my car's wimpiness. Seriously.

Molly pulled up to the mouth of the alley and stopped. She looked nervously around as we unloaded from the car. I gave Susan a hand out of the tiny backseat, and then held the door open as Mouse jumped up into the passenger seat.

I ruffled his ears and leaned down to speak to Molly. "Go get coffee or something. Give us about an hour, an hour and a half tops. We'll be back by then."

"What if you aren't?" Molly asked. She reached one hand over to Mouse in an unconscious gesture, burying her fingers in his fur. "What do I do then?"

"If we don't show up by then, go on back home to your folks' place. I'll contact you there."

"But what if—"

"Molly," I said firmly. "You can't plan for everything or you never get started in the first place. Get a move on. And don't take any lip from the dog. He's been uppity lately."

"Okay, Harry," she said, still unhappily. She pulled out into the street again, and Mouse turned his head to watch us as she drove away.

"Poor kid," Susan said. "She doesn't like being left behind."

I grunted. "That kid's got enough power to take all three of us down if she caught us off guard," I said. "Her strength isn't an issue."

"I'm not talking about that, obviously."

I grunted. "What do you mean?"

Susan frowned at me briefly, and then her eyebrows rose. "Dear God. You don't realize it."

"Realize what?"

She shook her head, one corner of her mouth crooked into the same smile I remembered so well. It made my heart twitch, if such a thing is possible. "Molly has it bad for you, Harry."

I frowned. "No, she doesn't. We settled that early on. Isn't happening."

Susan shrugged a shoulder. "Maybe *you* settled it, but she didn't. She's in love."

"Is not," I said, scowling. "She goes on dates and stuff."

"I said she was in love. Not dead." Her expression went neutral. "Or half-dead." She stared after the vanished car for a moment and said, "Can I share something with you that I've learned in the past few years?"

"I guess."

She turned to me, her expression sober. "Life is too short, Harry. And there's nowhere near enough joy in it. If you find it, grab it. Before it's gone."

It cost Susan something to say that. She hid it well, but not as well as I knew her. Giving breath to those thoughts had caused her very real pain. I was going to disagree again, but hesitated. Then I said, "I never stopped loving you. Never wanted you to be gone."

She turned a little away from me, letting her hair fall across her face as a curtain. Then she swallowed thickly and said, her voice trembling slightly, "Same here. Doesn't mean we get to be together."

"No," I said. "I guess not."

She suddenly balled her fists and straightened her spine. "I can't do this. Not right now. We've got to focus. I . . ." She shook her head and started walking. She went to the end of the block, to stand there taking deep, slow breaths.

I glanced at Martin, who stood leaning against the wall of a building, his expression, of course, bland.

"What?" I snapped at him.

"You think what you're feeling about your daughter is rage, Dresden. It isn't." He jerked his chin at Susan. "That is. She knew the Mendozas, the foster parents, and loved them like family. She walked into their house and found them. She found their children. The vampires had quite literally torn them limb from limb. One of the Mendozas' four children was three years old. Two were near Maggie's age."

I said nothing. My imagination showed me terrible pictures.

"It took us half an hour to find all the pieces," Martin continued calmly. "We had to put them back together like a jigsaw puzzle. And the whole time, the blood thirst was driving us both mad. Despite the fact that she knew those people. Despite her terror for her daughter. Imagine that for a moment. Imagine Susan standing there, filled with the urge to rip into the bloody limb with her teeth, even though she knew that little dismembered leg might have been her daughter's. Picture that."

At that point, I didn't think I could avoid it.

"It was only when the puzzle was finished that we realized that Maggie had been taken," Martin continued, his words steady and polite. "She's barely holding on. If she loses control, people are going to die. She might be one of them." Martin's eyes went hard and absolutely cold. "So I would take it as a fucking courtesy if you wouldn't torture her by stirring up her emotions five minutes before we kick down the door of a high-security facility."

I looked over my shoulder at Susan. She was still facing away from us, but she was in the act of briskly pulling her hair back into a tail.

"I didn't know," I said.

"In this situation, your emotions are liabilities," Martin said. "They won't help Rodriguez. They won't help the little girl. I suggest you postpone indulging them until this is all over."

"Until what is all over?" Susan asked, returning.

"Uh, the trip," I said, turning to lead them into the alley. "It won't take us long—about thirty seconds of walking down a level hallway. But it's dark and you have to hold your breath and nose the whole way."

"Why?" Susan asked.

"It's full of methane gas and carbon monoxide, among others. If you use a light source, you run the risk of setting off an explosion."

Susan's eyebrows rose. "What about your amulet?"

I shook my head. "The light from that is actually . . . Glah, it's more complicated than you need to know. Suffice it to say that I feel there would be a very, very small possibility that it might make the atmosphere explode. Like those static electricity warnings at the gas stations. Why take the chance?"

"Ah," Susan said. "You want us to walk blind through a tunnel filled with poisonous gases that could explode at the smallest spark."

"Yeah."

"And . . . you're sure this is a good idea?"

"It's a terrible idea," I said. "But it's the fastest way to the storage facility." I lifted my fingertips to touch the red stone on my amulet as I neared the location of the Way. It was an old, bricked-over doorway into the ground level of the apartment building.

A voice with no apparent source began to speak quietly—a woman's voice, throaty and calm. My mother's voice. She died shortly after my birth, but I was certain, as sure as I had been of anything in my life: It was her voice. It made me feel warm, listening to it, like an old, favorite piece of music that you haven't heard for years.

"The hallway on the other side is full of dangerous levels of methane and carbon monoxide, among other gases. The mixture appears to be volatile, and in the other side you can never be sure exactly which energies might or might not trigger an explosion. Forty-two walking steps to the far end, which opens on a ridge outside Corwin, Nevada." There was a moment of silence, and then the same voice began to speak again, panting, shaking, and out of breath. "Notation: The hallway is not entirely abandoned. Something tried to grab me as

I came through." She coughed several times. "Notation *secundus*: Don't wear a dress the next time you need to go to Corwin, dummy. Some farmer's going to get a show."

"Maybe it was a grue," I murmured, smiling.

"What did you say?" Susan asked.

"Nothing," I said. "Never mind." I put a hand on the doorway and immediately felt a kind of yielding elasticity beneath my fingertips. The separation between the world of flesh and spirit was weak here. I took a deep breath, laid out a fairly mild effort of will, and murmured, *"Aparturum."*

A circle of blackness began to expand from the center of my palm beneath my hand, rapidly swelling, overlaying the wall itself. I didn't let it get too big. The gate would close on its own, eventually, but smaller gates closed more quickly, and I didn't want some poor fool going through it.

Present company excluded, of course.

I glanced back to Susan and Martin. "Susan, grab on to my coat. Martin, you grab hers. Take a deep breath and let's get this done fast and quiet."

I turned to the Way, took a deep breath, and then strode forward.

Mom's gem hadn't mentioned that it was flipping *hot* in there. When I'd stepped into the hallway on the first trip, I felt like I was inside about three saunas, nested together like those Russian dolls. I found the right-hand wall and started walking, counting my steps. I made them a bit shorter than normal, and nailed the length of Mom's stride more accurately this time. I hit the Way out at forty-three.

Another effort of will and a whispered word, and I

opened that gate as well, emerging into a cold mountain wind, and late twilight. Susan and Martin came out with me, and we all spent a moment letting out our pent-up breaths. We were in desert mountains, covered with tough, stringy plants and quick, quiet beasts. The gate behind me, another circle, stood in the air in front of what looked like the entrance to an old mine that had been bricked over a long time ago.

"Which way?" Martin said.

"Half mile this way," I said, and set out overland.

It was an awfully good hidey-hole, I had to admit. We were out so far in the desert hills that the commute to nowhere was a long one. The facilities had been cut into a granite shelf at the end of a box canyon. There was a single road in, and the floor of the canyon was wide and flat and empty of any significant features, like friendly rocks that one might try to take cover behind. The walls of the canyon had been blasted sheer. No one was coming down that way without a hundred yards of rope or a helicopter.

Or a wizard.

"All right," I said. The night was growing cold. My breath steamed in the air as I spoke. "Take these. Drink half of 'em. Save the rest." I passed out test tubes filled with light blue liquid to Martin and Susan.

"What is it?" Susan asked.

"A parachute," I said. "Technically a flight potion but I watered it down. It should get us to the valley floor safely."

Martin eyed his tube, and then me.

"Harry," Susan began. "The last time I drank one of your potions, it became . . . awkward."

I rolled my eyes. "Drop into a roll at the end." Then I drank away half of my potion and stepped off the edge of the cliff.

Flight is a difficult thing for a wizard to pull off. Everyone's magic works a little differently, and that means that, when it comes to flying, the only way to manage it is by trial and error. And, since flying generally means moving very quickly, a long way above the ground, would-be aeromancers tended to cut their careers (and lives) short at the first error.

Flying is hard—but *falling* is easy.

I dropped down, accelerating for a second, then maintaining a pace of somewhere around fifteen miles an hour. It didn't take long to hit the desert floor, and I dropped into a roll to spread out the impact energy. I stood up, dusting myself off. Susan and Martin landed nearby and also rose.

"Nice," Susan said. She bounced up in the air experimentally, and smiled when her descent was slowed. "Very cool. Then we drink more to climb out?"

"Should make that slope a piece of cake," I said. "But we'll need to move fast. Potion will last us maybe twenty minutes."

Susan nodded, adjusting the straps on the small pack she wore. "Got it."

"Get close to me," I said. "I can't veil all three of us unless we're all within arm's reach."

They did, and after a few seconds of focus and concentration, I brought up a veil around us that should hide us from view and disperse our heat signature as well. It wouldn't be perfect. We'd still show up on a night-vision scope, to one degree or another. I was counting on the fact that men guarding a building that isolated could not possibly deal with problems on a regular basis.

They'd have a very comfortable, reliable routine, which was exactly the sort of thing to take the edge off a sentry's wariness. That's just human nature.

I beckoned, and the three of us began approaching the facility. There was no fluttering from shadow to shadow, or camouflage face paint. The veiling spell took care of that. We just walked over the uneven ground and focused on staying close together. That part may have been more fun if Martin weren't there.

We got to within thirty yards of the fence, and I paused. I lifted my staff, pointed it at the first sentry camera, and whispered, "*Hexus.*"

I wasn't used to holding something as demanding as a veil in one hand while performing another working with the other—even such an easy spell as a technology hex. For a second, I thought I'd lose the veil, but then it stabilized again. The lights on the camera had gone out.

We moved around the perimeter while I hexed the other two cameras into useless junk, but just as I'd taken down camera number three, Susan gripped my arm and pointed. The foot patrol was moving by on their sweep.

"The dog will get our scent," Susan said.

Martin drew a short pistol from beneath his jacket, and screwed a silencer to its end.

"No," I half growled. I fished in the pocket of my duster and found the second potion I'd made while preparing for the trip. It was in a delicate, round globe of glass about as thick as a piece of paper. I flipped the globe toward the path of the oncoming dog and heard it break with a little crackle.

The two patrolmen and the dog went by the area where I'd left my surprise, and the dog snuffled the new scent with thorough interest. At a jerk of the lead, the dog hurried to catch up to the guards, and all three of them went by without so much as glancing at us.

"Dog'll have his senses of smell and hearing back in the morning," I murmured. "These guys are just doing a job. We aren't going to kill them for that."

Martin looked nonplussed. He kept the pistol in his hand.

We circled around to where the fence met the canyon wall, opposite the large parking lot. Susan got out a pair of wire cutters. She opened them and prepared to cut through when Martin snatched her wrist, preventing her from touching the fence. "Electricity," he whispered. "Dresden."

I grunted. Now that he'd pointed it out, I thought I could feel it, too—the almost inaudible hum of current on the move, making the hairs on my arms stand up. Hexing something with a microchip in it is simple. Impeding the flow of electricity through a conductive material is considerably more difficult. I pitched my best hex at the wiring where it connected to a power line and was rewarded with the sudden scent of burned rubber. Martin reached out and touched the fence with the back of his hand. No electricity burned him.

"All right," Susan whispered, as she began clipping us a way in, cutting a wire only when the gusting wind reached a crescendo and covered the sound of the clippers at work, then waiting for the next gust. "Where's that distraction?"

I winked at her, lifted my blasting rod, thrust it between links of fence in front of us, and aimed carefully. Then I checked the tower guard, to be sure he was looking away, and whispered, *"Fuego, fuego, fuego, fuego."*

Tiny spheres of sullen red light flickered out across the compound and into the parking lot opposite. My aim had been good. The little spheres hissed and melted their way through the rear quarter panel of several vehicles and burned on into the fuel tanks beneath.

The results were predictable. A gas tank explosion isn't as loud as an actual bomb going off, but when you're standing a few yards away from it, it could be hard to tell. There were several hollow booming sounds, and light blazed up from the cars that had been hit as flames roared up and consumed them.

The guard in the tower started screaming into a radio, but apparently could get no reply. No surprise. The second camera had been positioned atop his tower, and the hex that took it out probably got his radio, too. While he was busy, Susan, Martin, and I slipped through the opening in the fence and made our way into the shadows at the base of one of the portable storage units.

A car, parked between two flaming vehicles, went up with another whump of ignition, and it got even brighter. A few seconds later, red lights started to flash at several points around the facility, and a warning klaxon began to sound. The giant metal door to the interior of the facility began to roll upward, just like a garage door.

The two patrollers and their temporarily handicapable German shepherd came running out first, and were followed, in a moment, by nearly a dozen other guys in the same uniforms, or at least in portions of them. It looked like some of them had hopped out of bed and tossed on whatever they could reach. Several were dragging fire extinguishers, as if they were going to be useful against fires that large. Good luck with that, boys.

The moment the last of them was past our position

and staring agog at the burning automobiles, I hurried forward, putting everything I had into the veil, trusting that Martin and Susan would stay close. They did. We went through the big garage door and down a long ramp into the facility.

"Go ahead," Martin said. He hurried to a control panel on the wall and whipped out some kind of multitool. "I'll shut the door."

"As long as we can get it open on the way out," I muttered.

"Yes, Dresden," Martin said crisply. "I'd been doing this for sixty years before you were born."

"Better drop the invisibility thing, Harry," Susan said. "What we're looking for might be on a computer, so . . ."

"So I'll hold off on the magic until we know. Got it."

We went deeper into the facility. The caves ran very deep back into the stone, and we'd gone down maybe a hundred yards after moving about four hundred yards forward on a spiraling ramp. The air grew colder, to the ambient underground average.

More than that, though, it gained a definite spiritual chill. Malevolent energy hovered around us, slow and thick like half-frozen honey. There was a gloating, miserly quality to it, bringing to my mind images of old Smaug lying in covetous slumber upon his bed of treasure. That, then, was the reason the Red Court had hidden its dark treasures here. Ambient energy like this wasn't directly dangerous to anyone—but with only the mildest of efforts it would protect and preserve the magical implements jealously against the passing of time.

The ramp opened up into a larger area that reminded me of the interior corridors of a sports stadium. Three doors faced us. One was hanging slightly open, and read, QUARTERS. The other was shut and read, ADMINISTRATION.

The last, a large steel vault door, was labeled, STORAGE. A concrete loading dock with its edges painted in yellow and black caution stripes stretched before us, doubtless at just the right height to make use of the large transport van parked nearby.

Oh, and there were two guards standing in front of the vault door with some hostile-looking black shotguns.

Susan didn't hesitate. She blurred forward with nearly supernatural speed, and one of the guards was down before he realized he was in a fight. The other had already spun toward me with his weapon and opened fire. In his rush to shoot, he hadn't aimed. People make a big thing about shotguns hitting absolutely everything you point them at, but it ain't so. It still takes considerable skill to use a shotgun well under pressure, and in his panic the guard didn't have it. Pellets buzzed around me like angry wasps as I took three swift steps to my left and threw myself through the open barracks door, carrying me out of his line of fire.

From outside, there was a crack of something hard, maybe the butt of a gun hitting a skull, and Susan said, "Clear."

I came out of the emptied barracks nonchalantly. The two guards lay unconscious at Susan's feet. "God, I'm good," I said.

Susan nodded, and tossed both guns away from the unconscious men. "Best distraction ever."

I went to her and eyed the door. "How we getting through that?"

"We aren't," she said. She produced a small kit of locksmith tools and went to the administration door, ignoring the vault completely. "We don't need their treasures. We just need the receipts."

I'd learned a little bit about how to tickle a lock, but Susan had obviously learned more. Enough so that she took one look at the lock, pulled a lock gun from her kit, and went through it damned near as fast as if she'd had a key. She swung the door open and said, "Wait here. And don't break anything."

I put my hands behind my back and tried to look righteous. A smile lit her face, fast and fierce, and she vanished into the office.

I walked over to the barracks. My guns had been riding with the rest of my contraband when it got buried in Lea's garden, and I didn't like going unarmed on general principles. Magic is pretty damned cool when things get rowdy, but there are times when there's no replacing a firearm. They are excellent, if specialized, tools.

Two seconds of looking around showed me a couple of possibilities, and I picked up a big semiautomatic and a couple of loaded clips. I tucked them into a pocket of the duster. Then I picked up the assault rifle from its rack and found that two spare magazines were being held in this socklike device that went over the rifle's stock.

Rifles weren't my forte, but I knew enough to check the chamber and see that no round was in it. I made sure the safety was on and slung the assault rifle over my shoulder on its nylon-weave strap. Then I went back over to administration and waited outside.

Susan was cursing in streaks of blue and purple and vermilion inside. She appeared a moment later and spat, "Nothing. Someone was here first. They erased everything related to the shipment less than three hours ago."

"What about the paper copy?" I asked.

"Harry," Susan said. "Have you ever heard of the paperless office?"

"Yeah," I said. "It's like Bigfoot. Someone says he knows someone who saw him, but you don't ever actually see him yourself." I paused. "Though I suppose I actually *have* seen Bigfoot, and he seems like a decent guy, but the metaphor still stands. Remember who owns this place. You think someone like the duchess is a computer whiz? Trust me. You get to be over a couple of hundred years old, you get copies of everything in triplicate."

Susan arched an eyebrow and nodded. "Okay. Come on, then."

We went in and ransacked the office. There were plenty of files, but we had the identification number of the shipment of magical artifacts (000937, if it matters), and it was possible to flick through them very rapidly. We came up all zeroes, again. Whoever had covered up the back trail had done it well.

"Dammit," Susan said quietly. Her voice shook.

"Easy," I said. "Easy. We aren't out of options yet."

"This was the only lead we had," she said.

I touched her arm briefly and said, "Trust me."

She smiled at me a little. I could see the strain in her eyes.

"Come on," I said. "Let's get out of here before the cavalry arrives. Oh, here." I passed her the assault rifle.

"That's thoughtful of you," she said, smiling more widely. Her hands went over the weapon, checking the chamber as I had, only a lot more smoothly and quickly. "I didn't get you anything."

I turned and eyed the moving van, then went back to its cargo doors. "Here. Open this door for me?"

She got out her tools and did it in less time than it took to say it.

There were several long boxes in the van, standing vertically, and I realized after a moment that they were garment boxes. I opened one up and . . .

And found a long, mantled cloak made from some kind of white and green feathers, hanging from a little crossbar in the top of the garment box. It was heavy, easily weighing more than fifty pounds. I found a stick studded with chips of razor-sharp obsidian in there, too, its handle carved with pictographs. I couldn't read this particular form of writing very well, but I recognized it—and recognized that it was no ancient artifact, either. It had been carved in the past few decades.

"This is Mayan ceremonial costume," I murmured, frowning. "Why is it loaded up on the next truck out . . . ?"

The answer jumped at me. I turned to Susan and we traded a look that conveyed her comprehension as well. She went to the front of the van and popped it open. She started grabbing things, shoving them into a nylon gym bag that she had apparently found in the truck.

"What did you get?" I asked.

"Later, no time," she said.

We hurried back up the ramp to Martin.

The big door looked like it was having a tug-of-war with itself. It would shudder and groan and try to rise, and then Martin would do something with a pair of wires in the dismantled control panel and it would slam down again. I saw guards trying to stick their guns beneath the door for a quick shot, but they wound up being driven back by Martin's silenced pistol.

"Finally," Martin said as we came up to him. "They're about to get through."

"Damn," I said. "I figured they'd be firefighting longer than that." I looked around the barren tunnel. I was tired and shaking. If I were fresh, I would have no trouble with the idea of slugging it out with a bunch of guys with machine guns—provided they were all in front of me. But I was tired, and then some. The slightest wavering in concentration, and a shield would become porous and flexible. I'd be likely to take a bunch of bullets. The duster might handle most of them, but not forever, and I wasn't wearing it over my head.

"Plan B," I said. "Okay, right. We need a plan B. If we only had a wheelbarrow, that would be something."

Susan let out a puff of laughter, and then I turned to her, my eyes alight.

"We have a great big truck," Susan said.

"Then why didn't you list that among our assets?" I said, in a bad British accent. "Go!"

Susan vanished back down the tunnel, moving scary-fast.

"Martin," I said. "Get behind me!"

He did, as I lifted my left arm and brought up a purely physical shield, and within five or six seconds, the door had lifted two feet off the ground and a couple of prone shooters opened up on the first thing they saw—me.

I held the shield against the bullets as the door continued to rise, and they exploded into concentric circles of light spread across the front of the shield's otherwise invisible surface. The strain of holding the shield grew as more of the guards opened fire. I saw one poor fellow take a ricochet in the belly and go down, but I didn't have the time or the attention to spare to feel sorry for him. I ground my teeth and hung on to the shield as the guards kept a constant pressure on it.

Then there was a roar of large engines and Susan

drove the cargo truck forward like some kind of berserk bison, charging the group of guards blocking the road out.

Men screamed and sprinted, trying to avoid the truck. They made it. I didn't need Martin to tell me to move, as the truck slammed into a turn, throwing its rear end in a deadly, skidding arch. We both sprinted for it in the confusion and flung ourselves up into the cargo compartment, which Susan had thoughtfully left open.

One of the more alert guards tried the same trick, but Martin saw him coming, aimed the little pistol, and shot him in the leg. The man screamed and fell down as the truck picked up speed. Susan stomped the pedal flat, and metal and razor wire screamed as she drove through a section of the fencing and out onto the open valley floor. She immediately turned it toward our escape point, and the truck began to bounce and rattle as it raced away from the facility.

After that, it was simple.

We went back to our ascension point, drank our watered-down flying potions, and bounded up the rocky face of the valley wall like mountain goats. Or possibly squirrels. Either way, it made the eighty-degree incline feel about as difficult to handle as a long stairway.

"Harry," Susan said, panting, as we reached the top. "Would you burn that truck for me?"

"My pleasure," I said, and dealt with the cargo truck the same way I had the cars in the parking lot. Thirty seconds later, it huffed out its own explosion, and Susan stood there nodding.

"Okay," she said. "Good. Hopefully that makes it harder for them to do whatever they're going to do."

"What did you find?" Martin asked.

"Mayan ceremonial gear," I said. "Not focus items,

but the other stuff. The props. They were on the truck to be shipped out next."

Susan rustled in the nylon bag and held up a sheet of paper. "Bill of lading," she said. "Shipment number 000938. The next outgoing package after the original shipment, and it was initiated two days after the focus items went out."

Martin narrowed his eyes, thinking. "If it was going to the same place as the first shipment . . ."

"It means that we can make a pretty good guess that wherever it's going, it's within two days' drive," I said. "That gives the vampires time enough to get the first shipment, realize that some things got left out, and call in a second shipment to bring in the missing articles."

Martin nodded. "So? Where are they?"

Susan was going through the contents of the bag she'd appropriated. "Mexico," she said. She held up a U.S. passport, presumably falsified, since most people don't tote their passports around in manila envelopes, along with a wallet full of new-looking Mexican cash. "They were planning on taking those cloaks and things to Mexico."

I grunted and started walking back to the Way. Martin and Susan fell in behind me.

"Harry? Will destroying that gear ruin what they're doing?"

"It'll inconvenience them," I said quietly. "Not much more than that. The actual magic doesn't need the costumes. It's the people performing it who need them. So any replacement sixty-pound cloak of parrot feathers will do—and if they want it badly enough, they can do the ritual even without replacing them."

"They'll know who was here," Martin said. "Too many men saw us. Interior cameras might have gotten something, too."

"Good," I said. "I want them to know. I want them to know that their safe places aren't safe."

Susan made a growling sound that seemed to indicate agreement.

Even Martin's mouth turned up into a chilly little smile. "So other than somewhat discomfiting the sleep of some of the Red Court, what did we actually accomplish here?"

"We know where they're going to do their ritual," Susan said.

I nodded. "Mexico."

"Well," Martin said. "I suppose it's a start."

Chapter

Eighteen

Mrs. Spunkelcrief was a fantastic landlady. She lived on the ground floor of the old house. She rarely left her home, was mostly deaf, and generally didn't poke her nose into my business as long as my rent check came in—which it pretty much always did, these days, on time or a bit early.

A small army of crazy-strong zombies had assaulted my home without waking her up, probably because they'd had the grace to do it after her bedtime, which was just after sundown. But I guess the visit from the cops and the FBI had been even louder than that, because as Molly pulled the *Blue Beetle* into the little gravel parking lot, I saw her coming up the stairs from my apartment, one at a time, leaning heavily on her cane. She wore a soft blue nightgown and a shawl to ward against the October chill in the night, and her bright blue eyes flicked around alertly.

"There you are," she said irritably. "I've been calling your house all evening, Harry."

"Sorry, Mrs. S," I said. "I've been out."

I don't think she could make out the words very well, but she wasn't stupid. "Obviously you've been out," she said. "What happened to your nice new door? It's wide-open! If we get another one of those freak thunderstorms, the rain will pour right in and we'll have mold climbing up the walls before you can say Jack Robinson."

I spread my hands and talked as loudly as I could without actually shouting. "There was a mix-up with the police."

"No," she said, "the lease is quite clear. You are responsible for any damages inflicted on the apartment while you are a tenant."

I sighed and nodded. "I'll fix it tomorrow."

"Oh, not so much sorrow as surprise, Harry. You're a good boy, generally." She peered from me to Molly, Susan, and Martin. "Most of the time. And you help out so when the weather is bad."

I smiled at her in what I hoped was an apologetic fashion. "I'll take care of the door, ma'am."

"Good," she said. "I thought you would. I'll come check in a few days." Mouse emerged from the darkness, not even breathing very hard from running to keep up with the Beetle. He immediately went over to Mrs. Spunkelcrief, sat, and offered her his right paw to shake. She was so tiny and the dog so large that she hardly had to bend down to grip his paw. She beamed broadly at Mouse, shook, and then patted his head fondly. "You can tell a lot about a man from how he treats his dog," she said.

Mouse walked over to me, sat down panting happily, and leaned his shoulders against my hip affectionately, all but knocking me down.

Mrs. Spunkelcrief nodded, satisfied, and turned to walk away. Then she paused, muttered something to herself, and turned back around again. She dug into her robe's pocket and produced a white envelope. "I almost forgot. This was lying on your stairs, boy."

I took it from her with a polite nod. "Thank you, ma'am."

"Welcome." She shivered and wrapped her shawl a little more tightly around her. "What is the world coming to? People breaking down doors."

I shot a glance at Molly, who nodded and immediately went to Mrs. Spunkelcrief's side, offering an arm for support. My landlady beamed up at her, saying, "Bless you, child. My cane arm got tired on the way down." Molly began helping her back up the little ramp to her apartment's front door.

Mouse immediately went to the bottom of the stairs, his nose questing. Then he turned back to me, tail fanning the air gently. No surprises lurked in my apartment. I went on down into it, waving the candles and fireplace to life with a murmur and a gesture, tearing open the envelope as I went to the fireplace to open it.

Inside was a piece of folded paper and another, smaller envelope, upon which was written, in Luccio's flowing writing, *READ ME FIRST*. I did:

> *If you are receiving this letter, it is because someone has rendered me unable to contact you. You must presume that I have been taken out of play entirely.*
>
> *The bearer of this note is the person I trust the most among every Warden stationed at Edinburgh. I cannot know the particulars of my neutralization, but you can trust his description implicitly, and I have found his judgment to be uncommonly sound in subjective matters.*
>
> *Good luck, Harry.*
>
> *-A-*

I stared at the note for a moment. Then I unfolded the second piece of paper, very slowly. This one was written in blocky letters so precise that they almost resembled a printed font, rather than handwriting:

Hullo, Dresden.

Luccio wanted me to bring this note to you in the event something happened to her. No idea what her note says, but I'm to give you whatever information I can.

I'm afraid it isn't good news. The Council seems to have gone quite mad.

After your appearance at Cristos's grandstand, a number of ugly things happened. Several young Wardens were caught debating amongst themselves about whether or not they should simply destroy the duchess in Edinburgh to ensure that the war continued—after all, they reasoned, the vampires wouldn't be suing for peace if they could still fight. On Cristos's orders, they were arrested and detained by older members of the Council, none of whom were Wardens, in order to Prevent Them from Destabilizing Diplomatic Deliberations.

Ramirez heard about what had happened and I suspect you can guess that his Spanish-by-way-of-America reaction was more passionate than rational. He and a few friends, only one of whom had any real intelligence, hammered their way into the wing where the Wardens were being detained—at which point every single one

of them (except for the genius, naturally) was captured and similarly imprisoned.

It's quiet desperation here. No one can seem to locate anyone on the Senior Council except Cristos, who is quite busily trying to Save Us from Ourselves by sucking up to Duchess Arianna. The Wardens' chain of command is a smashing disaster at the moment. Captain Luccio went to Cristos to demand the release of her people and is, at this time, missing, as are perhaps forty percent of the seniormost Wardens.

She asked me to tell you, Dresden, that you should not return to Edinburgh under any circumstances until the Senior Council sorts this mess out. She isn't sure what would happen to you.

She also wanted me to tell you that you were On Your Own.

I will send dispatches to you as events unfold—assuming I don't Vanish, too.

"Steed"

PS—Why, yes, I can in fact capitalize any words I desire. The language is English. I am English. Therefore mine is the opinion which matters, colonial heathen.

I read over the letter again, more slowly. Then I sat down on the fireplace mantel and swallowed hard.

"Steed" was an appellation I'd stuck on Warden Chandler, who was a fixture of security in Edinburgh, one of the White Council's home guards, and, once I had thought upon it, one of the guys who I'd always seen operating near Anastasia and in positions of trust: Standing as the sole sentinel at a post that normally required half a dozen. Brewing the Wardens and their captain their tea.

He and I had been the only ones present at the conversation where I'd tacked that nickname on him, thanks to the natty suit and bowler he'd been wearing, and the umbrella he'd accessorized—or maybe it was accessorised, in England—with, so the signature itself served as his bona fides. The flippant tone was very like Chandler, as well. I also knew Anastasia's handwriting, and besides, the paper on which her letter was written was scented with one of the very gentle, very subtle perfumes she preferred.

The message was as legitimate as it was likely to get, under the circumstances.

Which meant we were in real trouble.

The White Council carried a fearsome reputation not simply because of its capability of engaging in direct action against an enemy, but because it wielded a great deal of economic power. I mean, it doesn't take a genius to get rich after two hundred and fifty years of compounded interest and open trading. There was an entire brigade of economic warriors for the White Council who constantly sought ways to protect the Council's investments against hostile economic interests sponsored by other long-lived beings, like vampires. Money like that could buy a lot of influence. Not only that, but the Council could make the world a miserable place for someone who had earned their displeasure, in about a million ways, without ever throwing magic directly at someone. There were people in the Council who could play dirty with the most fiendish minds in history.

Taken as a whole, it seemed like a colossus, an institution as fixed and unmoving as a vast and ancient tree, filled with life, with strength, its roots sunk deep into the earth, a survivor of the worst storms the world had offered it.

But all of it, the power, the money, the influence, revolved around a critical core concept—every member of the White Council acted in concert. Or at least, that was the face that was supposed to be presented to the outside world. And it was mostly true. We might squabble and double-deal one another in peacetime, but when there was an enemy at hand we closed ranks. Hell, they'd even done that with me, and most of the Council thought that I was the next-best thing to Darth Vader. But at the end of the day, I think a lot of them secretly liked the idea of having Vader on the team when the monsters showed up. They didn't love me, never would, and I didn't need them to love me to fight beside them. When things got hairy, the Council moved together.

Except now we weren't doing it.

I looked at the folded letter in my hands and had the sudden, instinctive impression that I was watching an enormous tree begin to fall. Slowly at first, made to seem so by its sheer size—but falling nonetheless, to the ruin of anything sheltered beneath its boughs.

I was pretty tired, which probably explained why I didn't have any particular emotional reaction to that line of thought. It should have scared the hell out of me for a laundry list of reasons. But it didn't.

Susan came over to stand near me. "Harry. What is it?"

I stared at the fire. "The White Council can't help us find Maggie," I said quietly. "There are things happening. They'll be of no use to us."

After all they had wrongly inflicted upon me, after all

the times I had risked my neck for them, when I needed them, truly *needed* their help, they were not there.

I watched my hands crush the letters and envelopes without telling them to do it. I threw them into the fire and glowered as they burned. I didn't notice that the fire in the fireplace had risen to triple its normal height until the blue-white brightness of the flames made me shade my eyes against them. Turning my face slightly away was like twisting the spigot of a gas heater—the fire immediately died back down to normal size.

Control, moron, I warned myself. *Control. You're a loaded gun.*

No one spoke. Martin had settled down on one of the sofas and was cleaning his little pistol on the coffee table. Molly stood at the wood-burning stove, stirring a pot of something.

Susan sat down next to me, not quite touching, and folded her hands in her lap. "What do we have left?"

"Persons," I said quietly.

"I don't understand," Susan said.

"As a whole, people suck," I replied. "But a person can be extraordinary. I appealed to the Council. I told them what Arianna was doing. I went to that group of people looking for help. You saw what happened. So . . . next I talk to individuals."

"Who?" she asked me quietly.

"Persons who can help."

I felt her dark eyes on me, serious and deep. "Some of them aren't very nice, I think."

"Very few of them, in fact," I said.

She swallowed. "I don't want you to endanger yourself. This situation wasn't of your making. If there's a price to be paid, I should be the one to pay it."

"Doesn't work like that," I said.

"He's right," Martin confirmed. "For example: You paid the price for his failure to sufficiently discourage you from investigating the Red Court."

"I made my choice," Susan said.

"But not an informed one," I said quietly. "You made assumptions you shouldn't have, because you didn't have enough information. I could have given it to you, but I didn't. And that situation wasn't of your making."

She shook her head, her expression resigned. "There's no point in all of us fighting to hold the blame stick, I guess."

Martin began to run a cleaning patch through his pistol's barrel on a short ramrod and spoke in the tone of a man repeating a mantra. "Stay on mission."

Susan nodded. "Stay on mission. Where do we start, Harry?"

"Not we," I said, "me. I'm going down to the lab while you four stay up here and watch for trouble. Make sure you warn me when it shows up."

"When it shows up?" Susan asked.

"Been that kind of day."

Molly turned from the stove, her expression worried. "What are you going to do, boss?"

I felt as if my insides were all cloying black smoke, but I summoned up enough spirit to wink at Molly. "I gotta make a few long-distance calls."

Chapter

Nineteen

I went to my lab and started cleaning off my summoning circle. I'd knocked a few things onto it in the course of sweeping up anything incriminating. The FBI or Rudolph had added a bit to the mess. I pushed everything away from the circle and then swept it thoroughly with a broom. When you use a circle as a part of ritual magic, its integrity is paramount. Any object that falls across it or breaks its plane would collapse the circle's energy. Dust and other small particles wouldn't collapse a circle, but they did degrade its efficiency.

After I was done sweeping, I got a new shop cloth and a bottle of cleaning alcohol and wiped it down as thoroughly as if I were planning to perform surgery upon it. It took me about twenty minutes.

Once that was done, I opened an old cigar box on one shelf that was full of river rocks. All but one of them were decoys, camouflage. I pawed through it until I found the smooth piece of fire-rounded obsidian, and took it out of the box.

I went to the circle and sat in it, folding my legs in front of me. I touched the circle with a mild effort of will, and it snapped to life in a sudden curtain of gossamer energy. The circle would help contain and shape the magic I was about to work.

I put the black stone down on the floor in front of me, took a deep breath, straightened my back, and then began to draw in my will. I remained like that, relaxed, breathing deeply and slowly as I formed the spell in my head. This one was a fairly delicate working, and probably would have been beyond my skill before I had begun teaching Molly how to control her own power. Now, though, it was merely annoyingly difficult.

Once the energy was formed in my mind, I took a deep breath and whispered, "*Voce, voco, vocius.*" I waited a few seconds and then repeated myself. "*Voce, voco, vocius.*"

That went on for a couple of minutes, while I sat there doing my impression of a Roman telephone. I was just starting to wonder whether or not the damned rock was going to work when the lab around me vanished, replaced by an inky darkness. The circle's energy field became visible, a pale blue light in the shape of a cylinder, stretching from the floor up into the infinite overhead space. Its light did not make my surroundings visible, as if the glow from the circle simply had nothing to reflect from.

"Uh," I said, and my voice echoed strangely. "Hello?"

"Hold on to your horses," said a grumpy, distant voice. "I'm coming."

A moment later, there was a flash of light and a cylinder like my own appeared, directly in front of me. Ebenezar sat in it, legs folded the same way mine were. A black stone that was a twin to my own sat in front of him. Ebenezar looked tired. His hair was mussed, his eyes sunken. He was wearing only a pair of pajama bottoms, and I was surprised at how much muscle tone he had kept, despite his age. Of course, he'd spent the last few centuries mostly working on his farm. That would put muscle on anyone.

"Hoss," he said by way of greeting. "Where are you?"

"My place," I said.

"Situation?"

"My wards are down. I've got backup but I don't want to stay here for long. The police and FBI have gotten involved and the Reds have swung at me twice in the past two days. Where are you?"

Ebenezar grunted. "Best if I don't say. The Merlin is preparing his counterstrike, and we're trying to find out how much they already know about it."

"When you say 'we,' I assume you mean the Grey Council."

The Grey Council was the appellation that had stuck to our little rogue organization inside the White Council itself. It consisted of people who could see lightning, hear thunder, and admit to themselves that wizards everywhere were increasingly in danger of being exterminated or enslaved by other interests—such as the Vampire Courts or the Black Council.

The Black Council was mostly a hypothetical organization. It consisted of a lot of mysterious figures in black robes with delusions of Ringwraith-hood. They liked to call up the deadly dangerous demons from outside of reality, the Outsiders, and to infiltrate and corrupt every supernatural nation they could get to. Their motivations were mysterious, but they'd been causing trouble for the Council and everyone else for quite a while. I had encountered members of their team, but I had no hard proof of their existence, and neither did anyone else.

Cautionary rumors of their presence had been met

with derision and accusations of paranoia by most of the White Council until last year, when a Black Council agent had killed more than sixty wizards and infiltrated the Edinburgh facility so thoroughly that more than 95 percent of the staff and security team had gotten their brains redecorated to one degree or another. Even the Senior Council members had been influenced.

The traitor had been stopped, if just barely, and at a heavy cost. And after that, the Council as a whole believed that there *might be* a faceless, nameless organization running amok in the world—and that any number of them could actually be members of the White Council itself, operating in disguise.

Paranoia and mistrust. They had been steadily growing within the White Council, whose leader, the Merlin, still refused to admit that the Black Council was real, for fear that our own people would start going over to the bad guys out of fear or ambition. His decision had actually had the opposite effect on the frightened, nervous wizards of the White Council. Instead of throwing the clear light of truth on the situation, the Merlin had made it that much more murky and shadowy, made it easier for fear to prey upon his fellow wizards' thoughts.

Enter the Grey Council, which consisted of me and Ebenezar and unspecified others, organized in cells in order to prevent either one of the other Councils from finding out about us and wiping out all of us at once. We were the ones who were trying to be sane in an insane time. The whole affair could backlash on us spectacularly, but I guess some people just aren't any good at watching bad things happen. They have to do something about it.

"Yes," Ebenezar said. "That is who I mean."

"I need the Grey Council to help me," I said.

"Hoss . . . we're all sitting under the sword of Damocles waiting for it to fall. The events unfolding in Edinburgh right now could mean the end of organized, restrained wizardry. The end of the Laws of Magic. It could drive us back to the chaos of an earlier age, unleash a fresh wave of warlock-driven monsters and faux demigods upon mankind."

"For some reason, sir, I always feel a little more comfortable when I'm sitting under that sword. Must be all the practice."

Ebenezar scowled. "Hoss . . ."

"I need information," I said, my voice hard. "There's a little girl out there. Someone knows something about where she is. And I know that the Council could dig something up. The White Council already shut the door in my face." I thrust out my jaw. "What about the Grey?"

Ebenezar sighed, and his tired face looked more tired. "What you're doing is good and right. But it ain't smart. And it's a lesson you haven't learned yet."

"What lesson?"

"Sometimes, Hoss," he said very gently, "you lose. Sometimes the darkness takes everyone. Sometimes the monster escapes to kill again another day." He shook his head and looked down. "Sometimes, Hoss, the innocent little ones are murdered. And there's not one goddamned thing you can do about it."

"Leave her to die," I snarled. "That's what you want me to do?"

"I want you to help save millions or billions of little girls, boy," he said, his own voice dropping into a hard, hard growl. "Not throw them away for the sake of one."

"I am *not* going to leave this alone," I snapped. "She—"

Ebenezar made a gesture with his right hand and my

voice box just stopped working. My lips moved. I could inhale and exhale freely—but I couldn't talk.

His dark eyes flashed with anger, an expression I had seldom seen upon his face. "Dammit, boy, you're smarter than this. Don't you see what you're doing? You're giving Arianna exactly what she wants. You're dancing like a puppet on her strings. Reacting in precisely the way she wants you to react, and it *will* get you killed.

"I told you long ago that being a real wizard means sacrifice. It means knowing things no one else does," he said, still growling. "I told you that it meant that you might have to act upon what you knew, and knew to be right, even though the whole world set its hand against you. Or that you might have to do horrible, necessary things. Do you remember that?"

I did. Vividly. I remembered the smell of the campfire we'd been sitting beside at the time. I nodded.

"Here's where you find out who you are," he said, his voice harsh and flat. "There's a lot of work to do, and no time to do it, let alone waste it arguing with you over something you should know by now." He closed his eyes for a moment and took a deep breath, as if bringing himself back under control. "Meet me at the Toronto safe house in twelve hours." He spoke in a voice of absolute authority, something I'd heard from him only a handful of times in my life. He expected his order to be obeyed.

I turned my head from him. In the edge of my vision, I saw him scowl again, reach down, and pick up his own black stone—and suddenly I was sitting on the floor of my lab again.

I picked up my sending stone wearily and slipped it into my pocket. Then I just lay back on the floor, breaking the circle as I did, and stared up at the ceiling for a little while. I turned my head to my left, and spotted the extra-thick green three-ring binder where I stored all my files on entities I could summon from the Nevernever.

No.

I looked away from the book. When you call things up for information, you've got to pay their price. It's always different. It's never been pleasant.

And the thought frightened me.

This would be the time those beings had been waiting for. When my need was so dire that I might agree to almost anything if it meant saving the child. For her, I might make a deal I would never consider otherwise.

I might even call upon—

I stopped myself from so much as *thinking* the name of the Queen of Air and Darkness, for fear that she might somehow detect it and take action. She had been offering me temptation passively and patiently for years. I had wondered, sometimes, why she didn't make more of an effort to sell me on her offer. She certainly could have done so, had she wished.

Now I understood. She had known that in time, sooner or later, there would come a day when I would be more needful than cautious. There was no reason for her to dance about crafting sweet temptations and sending them out to ensnare me. Not when all she had to do was wait awhile. It was a cold, logical approach—and that was very much in her style.

But there were other beings I could question, in the light blue binder sitting on top of the green one—beings of less power and knowledge, with correspondingly lower prices. It seemed unlikely that I would get anything so specific from them, but you never knew.

I reached for the blue book, rose, and set about calling creatures into my lab to answer a few questions.

* * *

After three hours of conjuring and summoning, I came up with absolutely nothing. I had spoken with nature spirits in the shape of a trio of tiny screech owls, and with messenger spirits, the couriers between the various realms within the Nevernever. None of them knew anything. I plucked a couple of particularly nosy ghosts who lived around Chicago out of the spirit world, and summoned servants of the Tylwyth Teg, with whose king I was on good terms. I asked spirits of water what they and their kin had seen regarding Maggie, and stared into the flickering lights of creatures of sentient flame, whose thoughts were revealed in the images quivering inside them.

One of the fire spirits showed me an image that lasted for no more than three or four seconds—the face of the little girl in Susan's picture, pale and a little grubby and shivering with fear or cold, reaching out to warm her hands over the fluttering lights of a fire. In profile, she looked a lot like her mother, with her huge dark eyes and slender nose. She'd gotten something of my chin, I think, which gave her little face the impression of strength or stubbornness. She was much paler than Susan, too, more like her father than her mother that way.

But then the image was gone.

That was as close as I got.

I sat down on my stool after three hours of work and felt more exhausted than at any time I could easily recall. I'd gotten nothing that would tell me where she was, nothing that would tell me what was in store for her. Except for the single flicker of knowledge that Maggie was still alive, I'd gotten nothing.

But even that might be enough. She was still breathing.

Hang in there, kid. Dad's coming.

I sat there on the stool for a moment, wearily. Then I reached for a piece of paper, an old pencil, and wrote:

Ivy,
I need your help.
It's for a little girl who is being held by bad people.
Please contact me.
Harry Dresd—

Before I'd gotten finished writing my name, the phone rang.

I'd just made contact with the Archive, with the magically constructed catalog of every bit of knowledge mankind has ever written down. It resided in the head of a teenager, the sum of human learning in the hands of a girl who should have been going to ninth grade this year.

Knowledge is power, and a couple of years before, the Archive had proved it. As a child not much older than Maggie, she had pitted her magic against the skills of beings with centuries of experience, and come out, for the most part, ahead. She was an unwholesomely powerful child, and while she had always comported herself with the gravity of a woman of forty, I had seen flashes of the child supporting the vast burden of the Archive. I knew what would happen if that child ever decided to take control of how the Archive was administered. It would probably look a lot like that episode of *The Twilight Zone* with the monstrous little kid with superpowers.

The phone rang again. I shivered and answered it. We'd run a long line down into the laboratory, and the old rotary phone sat near Molly's desk, benefiting from being on the fringes of such a well-organized place. "Hello?"

"It's Kincaid," said a man's baritone. Kincaid was

Ivy's driver, bodyguard, cook, and all-around teddy bear. He was the single deadliest gunman I had ever had the terror of watching, and one of a relatively few number of people who I both disliked and trusted. He had once described the method he would use to kill me, if he had to, and I had to admit that he had an excellent chance of succeeding. He was tough, smart, skilled, and had a mercenary sense of honor—whoever held his contract was his charge, body and mind, and he never abrogated a contract once he had signed it.

"Dresden," I replied, "this line probably isn't clear."

"I know," Kincaid replied. "What do you want?"

"I need to find a child. She was taken by the Red Court a few days ago. We believe her to be somewhere in Mexico."

"Somewhere in Mexico?" Kincaid said, and I could hear his grin. "You tried walking around and yelling her name really loud yet?"

"I'm getting there," I said. "Look, does she know anything or not?"

Kincaid muffled the phone with something, probably his hand. I heard his low, buzzing voice as he asked a question. I might have heard a light soprano voice answering him.

Kincaid returned to the phone and said, "Ivy says she can't get involved. That the business you're on is deadly. She dares not unbalance it for fear of changing the outcome."

I made a growling sound. "Goddammit, Kincaid. She owes me one. Remind her who came and took her away from those fucking Denarian lunatics."

Kincaid's voice became quieter, more sober. "Believe me, she remembers, Dresden. But she isn't free to share her knowledge like you or me. When she says she can't tell you, she's being literal. She physically cannot let such information leave her head."

I slammed the heel of my hand into a wall and leaned on it, closing my eyes. "Tell her," I said, "that this is information I *must* have. If she can't help me, I'll be taking it up with other sources. The ones in my green notebook."

Kincaid spoke with someone again. This time I definitely heard Ivy's voice answering him.

"She can't tell you where the girl is," Kincaid said. There was a hint of steel in his voice, warning me not to push too hard. "But she says she can tell you someone who might."

"Any help would be greatly appreciated," I said, exhaling.

"She says to tell you that before you try the green book, there's something else you might consider. The last man you want to see might have useful information."

I understood what she was talking about at once and groaned. "Dammit," I muttered. "Dammit."

I dialed another number. A receptionist asked me how she could direct my call.

"This is Harry Dresden," I said quietly. "Put me through to Mr. Marcone's personal line, please."

Chapter
Twenty

"I don't like it," Molly said, scowling. "You sure you don't want me to go in there with you? He's got people."

"Definitely not," I said calmly. "I don't want you showing up on his radar."

"I'd like to see him try something," Molly said, clenching one hand into a fist and thumping the *Blue Beetle*'s steering wheel for emphasis. "I'd eat him for breakfast."

"No, Molly," I said in a firm tone of voice. "You wouldn't. Marcone might be vanilla mortal, but he's dangerous. Most men have limits. He doesn't. Never forget that."

"If he's so dangerous, why are you talking to him?"

"Because he also has rules," I said. "And besides. I just had to see him here. Keep your eyes open for a third party interfering. I'll worry about Marcone. Okay?"

"Okay," Molly said, nodding, her eyes intent. In a spectacular bid for the Do as I Say, Not as I Do Award, she took a long pull from an energy drink in a can the size of a milk carton. "Okay."

I got out of the *Blue Beetle* and walked into my meeting with Gentleman Johnnie Marcone, the undisputed gang lord of Chicago.

Burger King had just opened its dining area, but it was already half-full. I ignored Marcone upon coming in and got in line. A sausage biscuit and cup of coffee later, I went to the back corner where Marcone sat and his retinue stood.

Hendricks was there, of course, in an extra-large suit and a red-haired buzz cut. Maybe he'd been working out, because he looked like he'd put on a few more pounds. If he got any bigger, he'd need a building permit. Miss Gard stood a little apart from Hendricks, covering the angles the big man couldn't. She was just as blond and athletic and Amazonian as ever, her suit and tie muting her curves without reducing her appeal.

Marcone sat in the booth as if at a boardroom table. He wore a silk suit probably worth more than my car, and sat with his elbows on the table, his fingertips pressed together into a steeple. He looked like a man in his mature prime, neat and precise from his haircut to his polished leather shoes. He watched me come over to the table and slide my plastic tray into place before me. I dumped four or five packets of sugar into my coffee and stirred it with a little stick. "You're not eating?"

He looked at his watch, and then at me. He had pale green eyes the color of old bills, but less personal. His stare was unsettling, and he met my eyes without concern. We had already taken the measure of each other's souls. It was why I knew precisely how dangerous the man sitting across the table from me could be, and why I insisted upon treating him in as cavalier a fashion as possible. One doesn't show dangerous predators weakness or fear. It makes them hungry.

I savored a bite of the biscuit, which was only a reminder of how good a real homemade biscuit and sausage was, but for the sake of my audience, I made sounds of enjoyment as I chewed and swallowed. "You sure?" I slurped some more coffee. "You're missing out on ambrosia, here."

"Dresden," Marcone said, "this is aggravating. Even for you."

"Yeah," I said, smiling, and took another bite of sausage.

Hendricks made a growling sound.

I finished chewing and said, "You sure about that, big guy?"

"Hendricks," Marcone said.

Hendricks subsided.

I nodded. Then I said, "You have information I want."

"Undoubtedly," Marcone said. "What information are you after, and what do you offer for it?"

"I'm not here to trade baseball cards with you, Marcone," I said.

"And I am not a charity organization, Dresden," he replied. "I take it this has something to do with your office building exploding." He shook his head in a gesture of faint regret.

"Right," I said. "You're all broken up over the destruction."

"I didn't order it. I made no money on it. I failed to profit financially or politically from its destruction. And you survived. It was a complete waste."

Hendricks made another growling sound that might have been gorilla for a laugh.

"Maybe it's got something to do with the building. How much do you know about its owners?"

Marcone's smile was a wintry thing. "That they are

a part of the organization whose servitors have been attempting to intrude upon my business."

I lifted an eyebrow. "Someone's muscling in on your territory?"

"Briefly," Marcone said, "but incessantly."

"Then we might have a common problem."

Marcone looked at me as though I were a rather slow child. "Yes. Hence this meeting."

I grunted and finished the biscuit. "The Red Court is on the move. Trouble is being stirred up between them and the Council. My interest in the matter is an eight-year-old girl. The Reds took her from her home. I believe that they're holding her somewhere in Mexico. I need to know where."

Marcone's stare went on for several seconds before he said, "Somewhere. In Mexico. That's as specific as you can be?"

"It's as much as I know," I said.

"For what purpose was she brought there?"

"Why does it matter?"

"If she was taken to be used as a sexual object, she would be in a different place than if she was going to be used as slave labor or harvested as an organ donor."

I clenched my teeth and looked away briefly, treated to a number of delightful images by his words.

Marcone's eyes narrowed. "Who is she to you, Dresden?"

"My client's kid," I said, struggling to keep my voice level and calm. "I think they're going to use her in some sort of sacrificial ritual."

"Then that narrows things considerably," Marcone said. "As I understand the process, rituals such as the one you mention need to happen at a place of power." He glanced up at Miss Gard, who nodded and immediately left the restaurant, heading for her car. "I suspect I can narrow it down even further for you, Dresden. Let's talk price."

"I'm going to use the information to put a major hurting on the people trying to take your territory away from you, Marcone," I said. "That's more than payment enough."

"And if I do not agree?" Marcone asked.

"Then we throw down, right here, and after I toss your attack dogs over the top of the Sears building, I hurt you until you give me the information anyway."

That cold smile returned. "Is that how you think it would happen?"

I shrugged a shoulder and kept my expression bland. "I think there's only one way to find out." I leaned forward a little and pitched my voice in a conspiratorial murmur. "But just between you and me, I don't think the terrain favors you here."

He stared across his steepled fingers at me for a time. Then he said, "It certainly doesn't favor me in the manner I would prefer." He laid his hands flat on the table and leaned back slightly. "There's no sense in making a confrontation out of this. And I have never yet regretted it when I allowed you to rid me of an enemy."

"I didn't do it as a favor to you."

He shrugged. "Your motivations are immaterial. The results are what matter."

"Just remember that you're on my list, Marcone. Soon as I get done with all the other evils in this town, you won't be the lesser of them anymore."

Marcone stared at me with half-lidded eyes and said, "Eek."

"You think it's funny?"

"I am not unduly concerned by dead men, Dresden."

I bristled. "Is that a threat?"

"Hardly. One day, probably soon, you'll get yourself killed thanks to that set of irrational compulsions you call a conscience, long before my name tops your list. I needn't lift a finger." He shrugged. "Giving you information seems an excellent way to accelerate that process. It will also tax the resources of my enemies." Marcone mused for a moment, and then said, "And . . . I believe I have no objection to contributing against any organization which would victimize children so."

I glowered at him. Partly because he was probably right, and partly because he'd once again shown the flash of humanity that prevented me from lumping him in with every other evil, hungry, predatory thing lurking in the wild world. For his own reasons, Marcone would go to extreme lengths to help and protect children. In Chicago, any adult was fair game for his businesses. Any child was off-limits. Rumor had it that he had vanished every single one of his employees who had ever crossed that line.

Gard reappeared, frowning, and walked over to our table.

Marcone glanced at her. "Well?"

Gard hesitated and then said, "He won't speak of it over the line. He says that you have incurred no debt with him for asking the question. He will only speak to Dresden. Personally."

Marcone lifted his eyebrows. "Interesting."

"I thought so," Gard said.

"Ahem," I said. "Who wants to meet me?"

"My . . . employer," Gard said. "Donar Vadderung, CEO of Monoc Securities."

Chapter

Twenty-one

Gard and I went to Oslo.

It sounds like it would be a long trip, but it's a hell of a lot faster when you don't have to worry about boarding, clearing security, going through customs, or actually moving a linear distance.

Gard opened a Way into the Nevernever down near the zoo, simply cutting at the fabric of reality with a rune-etched dagger. The Way took us on a short hike through a dark wood of dead trees, and ended when we emerged in what she said was Iceland. It sure as hell was cold enough. A second Way took us across the surface of a frozen lake, to stop before the roots of a vast old tree whose trunk could have contained my apartment with room to spare for a garage.

From there, we emerged into what seemed like a cold, damp basement, and I found myself face-to-face with two dozen men wearing body armor and pointing sleek-looking high-tech assault rifles at the end of my nose.

I did absolutely nothing. Carefully.

One of the men with guns said something, a short phrase in a language I didn't understand. Gard answered in what I presumed to be the same tongue, and gestured to me.

The leader of the guards eyed us both suspiciously for a moment, then said something quietly and all the rifles stopped pointing at me. Two guards returned to stand on either side of a doorway. Two more took up a station facing Gard and me, evidently cautious about getting more company through the same Way we'd just used. The rest returned to a couple of card tables and a few sleeping cots.

Gard shook her head and muttered, "Einherjar. Give them a little sip of renewed mortality, and four thousand years of discipline go right out the window."

"I recognize some of these guys," I said. I nodded toward a trio playing cards. "Those three. They were some of the mercenaries Marcone brought to that party in the Raith Deeps."

Gard glanced at the three and then rolled her eyes. "Yes. And?"

"And they're just available for hire?" I asked.

"If you can afford them," Gard said, smiling so that her teeth showed. "Though be warned that prices may vary. This way, Dresden."

I followed her out into a hallway and past several rooms filled with enough weaponry to win a minor war in a century of one's choice. Racks of ash-wood spears stood side by side with old bolt-action Mausers, which stood next to modern assault rifles. Katana-style swords shared a room with flintlocks and Maxim guns. One shelving unit housed an evolutionary progression of grenades, from powder-filled crockery with ignitable fuses to the most modern miniature flash-bang grenades. Judging from the variety of the place's contents, it was like looking at a museum—but from the quantities present, it could only be an armory.

We got to an elevator whose walls were a simple metal grid, so that we could see out of them as we went up. I stopped counting after seeing seven floors of similarly equipped armories go by.

"Guess your boss believes in being prepared," I said.

Gard smiled. "It's one of his things, yes."

"It's a little extreme, isn't it?"

She looked at me with an arched brow. Then she said, "One can have only as much preparation as he has foresight."

I considered that for a moment, and decided that as cryptic statements went, it was all kinds of bad.

The elevator kept going up and up and up. Brief views of various floors went by. One floor looked like an enormous gym and was filled with sweating men and women working out. Another looked like an expensive legal office. Another was all done in antiseptic white, bathed with just a bit too much light, and smelled of disinfectant. Another was lit by candles and the murmuring of voices chanting. Still another was obviously some kind of enormous chemical laboratory. Still another level was filled with cells whose occupants could not be seen as anything other than shadowy presences. And so on.

I shook my head. "Hell's bells. It's like some kind of demented theme park."

"The difference being that nothing you see here is meant to entertain," Gard said. "And don't bother asking questions. I won't answer them. Ah, we've reached the ground floor."

The elevator continued to rise up through an enormous atrium that housed ten or twelve stories of what looked like high-end corporate offices. Each floor was open to the atrium, and between the plants, decorative trees, the waterfall, and all the windows plus the skylights far above, the entire building looked like a single, massive garden. The sounds of office activity and equipment, birds, and the flowing waterfall all blended together into an active whole that formed a white noise bustling with life, variety, and movement. We soared up through the atrium and our open-sided elevator vanished into a short tunnel.

A moment later, the door opened on a rather novel reception area.

It had all the things such offices always did: a prominent desk, several seats in a waiting area, a coffee machine, and a table laden with magazines. In this office, however, all of those materials were made of stainless steel. So were the floors. So were the walls. As was the ceiling. Even the lamps and the coffeepot were made of stainless steel. The magazines alone stood out as shapeless, soft-looking blobs of garish color.

The logo for Monoc Securities stood out upon one wall, in bas-relief, and somehow reminded me more of a crest upon a shield than a corporate marketing symbol: a thick, round circle bisected by a straight vertical line emerging from either side of the circle. It might have been a simplified, abstract representation of an eye being cut from its socket by some kind of blade—I have some of that symbol written in scar tissue on my own face, where a cut had run down from eyebrow to cheekbone but had barely missed my eye. It might have been simple abstract symbology, representing the female and the male with round and straight shapes, suggesting wholeness and balance. Or, heck, it could have been overlaid Greek lettering, omega and iota on top of each other. Omega-iota. The last detail? The final detail? Maybe it meant something more like "every last little thing."

Or maybe it combined all of those things: the blind eye that sees all.

Yeah. That felt right.

Two women sat behind the big desk at computer monitors consisting of small clouds of very fine mist, wherein were contained all the drifting images and letters of the company cyber-reality, floating like the wispiest of illusions. Sufficiently advanced technology, I suppose.

The women themselves were, apparently, identical twins. Both had raven dark hair cut in close-fitting caps, and it matched the exact shade of their identical black suits. Both had dark eyes that sparkled with intensity and intelligence. They were both pale and their features were remarkable, if not precisely beautiful. They would stand out in any crowd, and not in an unpleasant way, either—but they would never be mistaken for cover models.

The twins rose as the elevator doors opened, and their eyes looked very intent and very black as they stared at us. I've looked down the barrel of a gun before. This was like looking down four of them at once. They stood there, inhumanly motionless. Both wore headsets, but only one of them murmured into hers.

I started to step out of the elevator, but Gard put out a cautionary hand. "Don't, until you're approved," she said. "They'll kill you. Maybe me, too."

"Like their receptionists tough in these parts, huh?"

"It would be wiser not to joke," she said quietly. "They don't miss anything—and they never forget."

The receptionist who had spoken into her mike flexed

one hand slowly closed and open. Her nails peeled up little silver curls from the stainless-steel desk.

I thought about making a manicure joke . . . and decided not to. Go, go, Gadget wisdom.

"Do you do oranges, too?" asked my mouth, without checking in with the rest of me. "What about sharpening table knives and scissors and lawn tools? My landlady's lawn mower blade could use a hand job from a girl like y—"

"*Dresden,*" Gard hissed, her eyes both furious and wide with near-panic.

Both of the receptionists were focused on me intently now. The one who had remained silent shifted her weight, as though preparing to take a step.

"Come on, Sigrun," I said to my companion. "I'm trying to be diplomatic. The wisdom of my ass is well-known. If I didn't lip off to them, after shooting my mouth off to faerie queens and Vampire Courts—plural, *Courts*—demigods and demon lords, they might get their feelings hurt."

Gard eyed me for a moment more, before her uncertain blue eyes gained a gleam of devil-may-care defiance. It looked a lot more natural on her than fear. "Perhaps your insults and insolence are not the valued commodities you believe them to be."

"Heh," I said. "Good one."

The chatty twin tilted her head slightly to one side for a moment, then said, "Right away, sir." She pointed her fingernail at me. "You are to enter the office through the doors behind me." She aimed her nail at Gard next. "You are to accompany him and make introductions."

Gard nodded shortly and then tilted her head in a "come along" sort of gesture. We walked out of the elevator and past the twins to the door behind them. They turned their heads as I went by, tracking my every movement. It was downright creepy.

On the other side of the door was a long hallway, also made of stainless steel. There were multiple ports or hatches of some kind in a row along the walls, all closed. They were about the size of dinner plates. I got a feeling that any visitors who tried the hors d'oeuvres served up from those plates would not be asking for the recipe later in the evening.

At the end of the hall was another set of steel doors, which gave way soundlessly before us, revealing another room done all in stainless steel, holding only a massive desk behind which was seated a man.

Donar Vadderung sat with his chin propped on the heel of his hand, squinting at a holographic computer display, and the first thing my instincts did was warn me that he was very, very dangerous.

He wasn't all that imposing to look at. A man in good shape, maybe in his early fifties. Lean and spare, in the way of long-distance runners, but too heavy in the shoulders and arms for that to be all he did. His hair was long for a man, and just a bit shaggy. It was the color of a furious thundercloud, and his eye was ice blue. A black cloth patch over the other eye combined with a vertical scar similar to my own made me think that I'd been right about the corporate logo. He kept a short, neat beard. He was a striking-looking rogue, particularly with the eye patch, and looked like the sort of person who might have served thirty years of a triple life sentence and managed to talk the parole board into setting him free— probably to their eventual regret.

"Sigrun," he said, his tone polite.

Gard went down to one knee and bowed her head. There was no hesitation whatsoever to the woman's movements—the gesture was not simply a technicality she had to observe. She *believed* that Vadderung merited such obeisance.

"My lord," Gard said, "I've brought the wizard, as you commanded."

"Well done," the grey-haired man said, and made a gesture to indicate that she should rise. I don't think she saw it, with her head bowed like that, but she reacted to it anyway, and stood up. Maybe they'd just had a few hundred years to practice.

"My lord, may I present Harry Dresden, wizard and Warden of the White Council of wizards?"

I nodded to Vadderung.

"Wizard, this is Donar Vadderung, CEO of Monoc Secur—"

"I think I've got a pretty good idea what he's in charge of," I said quietly.

The old man's mouth turned faintly up at the corners when I spoke. He gestured to a steel chair across the desk from him. "Please. Sit down."

I pointed at the holographic display. "You sure you want to put that at risk? If I stand too close to it . . ."

Vadderung turned his face up to the ceiling and barked out a laugh of genuine amusement. "I'll take my chances."

"Suits me," I said. I walked over to the desk and sat down in the steel chair across from Vadderung's. It didn't have a cushion or anything, but it was surprisingly comfortable nonetheless.

"Coffee?" he asked me. "Something to eat?"

I paused for a breath to think before answering. Duties such as this involved the obligations and responsibilities of guest to host and vice versa. If Vadderung was who I thought he was, he had been known, from time to time, to go forth and test people on how well they upheld that particular tradition—with generous rewards for the faithful, and hideous demises for the miserly, callous, or cruel.

In the supernatural world, such obligations and limits seem to be of vital importance to the overwhelming number of supernatural beings. I'm not sure why. Maybe it has something to do with the thresholds of protective energy that form around a home.

"Only if it isn't too much trouble," I said.

"And something to eat," Vadderung told Gard.

She bowed her head and said, "My lord." Then she padded out.

Though the big man hadn't stood up, I realized that he *was* big. Damned near a giant, really. Standing, he'd have more than a couple inches on me, and his shoulders made mine look about as wide as the spine of a book. He rested his chin on the heel of his hand again and studied me with his bright blue eye.

"Well," he said. "I take it you believe you know who I am."

"I've got a few guesses," I said. "I think they're good ones. Sigrun was kind of a tip-off. But honestly, that's got nothing to do with why I'm here today."

The blue eye wrinkled at the corners. "Doesn't it?"

I frowned at him and tilted my head. "How so?"

He lifted a hand palm up as he explained. "Someone with enough foresight might, for example, arrange to be in a position to assist a hotheaded young wizard of the White Council one day. Perhaps who I am is directly responsible for why I am here."

"Yeah. I guess that could be it," I said. "It's technically possible that your motives for assisting me are altruistic. On the other hand, it's also technically possible that you are speaking with a forked tongue, and that all you're really trying to do is find some way to take advantage of me when I'm under pressure." I shrugged. "No offense intended, but there's kind of a shortage of altruism out there."

"So cynical for one so young." He looked me up and down. "But you would be. You would be."

"I've got questions," I said. "Granted, they aren't as profound as 'Who am I?' or 'Why am I here?' but they're a lot more important to me at the moment."

Vadderung nodded. "You're looking for your daughter."

I felt my body go rigid. "How . . . ?"

He smiled rather wolfishly. "I know things, Dresden. And if I don't know something, I can find out. Like yourself, it is what I do."

I stared at the man for most of a minute. Then I said, "Do you know where she is?"

"No," he said in a quiet, firm voice. "But I know where she will be."

I looked down at my hands. "What's it going to cost me to find out?"

"Chichén Itzá," Vadderung said.

I jerked my head up in surprise. I stared at the man for a moment. "I—"

"Don't understand?" Vadderung asked. "It isn't complicated. I'm on your side, boy."

I raked my fingers back through my hair, thinking. "Why there?"

"The Red King and his inner circle, the Lords of Outer Night, have got some big juju to brew up. They need a site of power to do it. For this, they'll use Chichén Itzá."

"Why there?"

"They're enacting a sacrifice. Like in the old days." A snarl of anger touched his voice, and made it suddenly frightening. "They're preparing a bloodline curse."

"A what?"

"Death magic," he said, "focused upon the blood-line. From the sacrifice, the child, to her brothers, sisters, and parents. From the parents to their brothers, sisters, and parents, and so on. Spreading up the family tree until there's no one left."

A chill hit my guts. "I've . . . never even heard of death magic on that kind of scale. The energy required for that . . . It's enormous." I stopped for a moment and then said, "And it's *stupid*. Susan was an only child, and she's already lost her parents. Same with me . . ."

Vadderung arched an eyebrow at me. "Is it? They like to be thorough, those old monsters."

I smoothed my expression over, trying not to give away anything. This spell they were doing would kill me, if they pulled it off. It could also kill my only family, my half brother, Thomas. "How does it work?" I asked him, my voice subdued.

"It tears out the heart," Vadderung said. "Rips it to bits on the way out, too. Sound familiar?"

"Hell's bells," I said quietly. It had been years since I had even thought about Victor Sells or his victims. They had featured in my nightmares for quite a while until I upgraded.

Vadderung leaned toward me, his blue eye very bright. "It's all connected, Dresden. The whole game. And you're only now beginning to learn who the players are." He settled back into his seat, letting silence add emphasis to his statement before he continued. "The sorcerer who used the spell in Chicago before didn't have strength enough to make it spread past the initial target. The Red Court does. No one has used Power on this scale in more than a millennium."

"And they're pointing it at *me*?"

"They say you can know a man by his enemies, Dresden." He smiled, and laughter lurked beneath his next words, never quite surfacing. "You defy beings that should cow you into silence. You resist forces that are inevitable for no more reason than that you believe they should be resisted. You bow your head to neither demons nor angels, and you put yourself in harm's way to defend those who cannot defend themselves." He nodded slowly. "I think I like you."

I arched an eyebrow and studied him for a moment. "Then help me."

Vadderung pursed his lips in thought. "In that, you may be disappointed. I am . . . not what I was. My children are scattered around the world. Most of them have forgotten our purpose. Once the Jotuns retreated . . ." He shook his head. "What you must understand is that you face beings such as I in this battle."

I frowned. "You mean . . . gods?"

"Mostly retired gods, at any rate," Vadderung said. "Once, entire civilizations bowed to them. Now they are venerated by only a handful, the power of their blood spread out among thousands of offspring. But in the Lords of Outer Night, even the remnants of that power are more than you can face as you are."

"I've heard that one before," I said.

Vadderung just looked at me. Then he said, "Let me help you understand."

And a force like a hundred anvils smashed me out of the chair and to the floor.

I found myself on my back, gasping like a landed fish. I struggled to move, to push myself up, but I couldn't so much as lift my arms from the ground. I brought my will into focus, with the idea of using it to deflect some of that force from me and—

—and suddenly, sharply felt my will directly in contention with another. The power that held me down was not earth magic, as I had assumed it to be. It was the simple, raw, brute application of the will of Donar Vadderung, Thunder's Father, the Father and King of the Aesir. Father Odin's will held me pinned to the floor, and I could no more escape it or force it away than could an insect stop a shoe from descending.

In the instant that realization came to me, the force vanished, evaporating as if it had never been. I lay on the floor gasping.

"It is within my capabilities to kill you, young wizard," Vadderung said quietly. "I could wish you dead. Especially here, at the center of my power on Midgard." He got up, came around the desk, and offered me his hand. I took it. He pulled me to my feet, steady as a rock. "You will be at the center of their power. There will be a dozen of them, each nearly as strong as I am." He put a hand on my shoulder briefly. "You are bold, clever, and from time to time lucky. All of those are excellent qualities to have in battles like yours. But against power such as this you cannot prevail as you are. Even if you are able to challenge the Red King at Chichén Itzá, you will be crushed down as you were a moment ago. You'll be able to do nothing but watch as your daughter dies."

He stared at me in silence for a time. Then the door

to his office opened, and one of the receptionists leaned in. "Sir," she said, "you have a lunch appointment in five minutes."

"Indeed," Vadderung said. "Thank you, M."

She nodded and retreated again.

Vadderung turned back to me, as Gard returned to the room, carrying a covered tray. She set it down on the big steel desk and stepped back, unobtrusively.

"You've defied fate, Dresden," Vadderung said. "You've stood up to foes much larger than you. For that, you have my respect."

"Do you think I could swap in the respect for—I dunno—half a dozen Valkyries, a receptionist, and a couple of platoons of dead heroes?"

Vadderung laughed again. He had a hearty laugh, like Santa Claus must have had when he was young and playing football. "I couldn't do without my receptionists, I'm afraid." He sobered. "And those others . . . would be less strong at the center of the Red King's power." He shook his head. "Like it or not, this is a mortal matter. It must be settled by mortals."

"You're not going to help," I said quietly.

He went to a steel closet and opened the door, removing an overcoat. He slipped into it, and then walked over to me again. "I've been in this game for a long, long time, boy. How do you know I haven't given you exactly what you need?"

Vadderung took the lid off the covered tray, nodded to me pleasantly, and left.

I looked at the tray. A cup of tea steamed there, three empty paper packets of sugar beside it. The tea smelled like peppermint, a favorite. Next to the cup of tea was a little plate with two cake doughnuts on it, both of them covered in thick white frosting and unmarred by sprinkles or any other edible decorations.

I looked up in time to see Vadderung walk by, trailed by the pair of receptionists, and saw them all simply vanish, presumably into a Way.

"Well?" Gard asked me. "Are you ready to go?"

"Just a minute," I said.

I sat back down. And I drank the tea and ate the doughnuts, thoughtfully.

Chapter

Twenty-two

I needed sleep.

I rode back to my place with Molly in the mid-morning. Mouse came padding up the stairs from the apartment as we got out of the car, his alert, wary stance relaxing into the usual waving of a doggy tail and enthusiastic sniffs and nudges of greeting. I shambled on into my apartment calmly. All was obviously well.

Susan and Martin were both inside, both busy, as Mister looked on from his lordly peak atop the highest bookshelf. Susan had been shaking out all the rugs and carpets that cover the floor of my living room, and was now rolling them back into place, probably not in the same order as they had been before. She picked up one end of a sofa with a couple of fingers of one hand to get an edge into place.

Martin was alphabetizing my bookshelves.

They used to kill men for sacrilege like that.

I suppressed my twitches as best I could, and told myself that they thought they were helping.

"Success," Susan said. "Or at least a little of it. Our people found out exactly who is tailing us up here."

"Yeah?" I asked. "Who?"

"The Eebs," she said.

Molly came in and frowned severely at what they were doing. Granted, the place was kind of a mess after the FBI and cops got done, but still. She was probably as used to the place as I was. "Sounds like the Scoobies, only less distinctive."

Martin shook his head. "Esteban and Esmerelda Batiste," he clarified. "One of the husband-wife teams the Red Court uses for fieldwork."

"One of?" I asked.

"Couples traveling together attract less attention," Susan said. "They're often given the benefit of the doubt in any kind of judgment call made by various officers of the law. It smooths things out a little more than they would be otherwise."

"Hence you and Martin," I said.

"Yes," said Martin. "Obviously."

"Esteban and Esmerelda are notorious," Susan said. "They're unorthodox, difficult to predict, which is saying something when you're talking about vampires. They'll throw away their personnel, too, if that is what it takes to get results. Personally, I think it's because they have some kind of gruesome variation of love for each other. Makes them more emotional."

"They have complementary insanities," Martin said. "Don't dignify it with anything more."

"The one you said got away, Harry?" Susan said. "Esteban, probably. He rabbits early and often, which probably explains why he's still alive. Esmerelda would have been the spotter on top of a nearby building—also the one who probably triggered the explosives."

"Gotta figure they're behind the hit outside the FBI building, too," I said. "Tinted windows on the car. Shooter was way back inside the backseat, away from the window."

"Maybe, sure," Susan said. "They'll suit up in all-over coverage and head out in the daytime if they think it's really necessary."

I grunted. "So Esteban and Esmerelda . . ."

"Eebs," Susan said firmly.

"So the Eebs aren't really fighters. They're planners. Fair to say?"

"Very much so," said Martin. There might have been a faint note of approval in his voice.

I nodded. "So they and their vampire gang were supposed to follow you, only when they saw you heading into the data center, they were forced to do more than shadow you. They tried to protect the data. All rational."

Susan began to frown and then nodded at me.

"Of course," Martin said. "Difficult to predict but never stupid."

"So why," I said, "if they were here operating under orders from the duchess to foil your efforts, would they take the trouble to try an assassination on *me*?"

Martin opened his mouth, and then closed it again, frowning.

"I mean, Arianna wants to see me suffer, right? Thank God for clichéd mind-sets, by the way. I can't do that if I'm dead. I go early, it cheats her of the fun."

"There's division in the ranks of the Red Court," Susan murmured. "It's the only thing that would explain it. Countervailing interests—and at the summit of their hierarchy, too."

"Or," Martin said, "it was not the"—he sighed— "Eebs . . . who made the attempt."

"But I haven't seen any of the other people who want to kill me lately," I said. "I saw the Eebs just the other night. They're the simplest explanation."

Martin tilted his head slightly in allowance. "But remember that what you have is a theory. Not a fact. You are not blessed with a shortage of foes, Dresden."

"Um, Harry?" Molly asked.

I turned to her.

"I don't know if I'm supposed to jump in with this kind of thing or not, but . . . if there's some sort of internal schism going on inside the Red Court . . . what if the kidnapping and so on is . . . like a cover for something else she's doing, inside her court? I mean, maybe it isn't all about you. Or at least, not *only* about you."

I stared at her blankly for a moment. "But for that to be true," I said, "I would have to not be the center of the universe."

Molly rolled her eyes.

"Good thought, grasshopper," I said. "Something to keep in mind. Maybe we're the diversion."

"Does it matter?" Susan asked. "I mean, as far as our interests go?"

I shrugged. "We'll have to see, I guess."

She grimaced. "If the Eebs are working for a different faction than Arianna, then there goes our only lead. I was hoping I could convince them to tell us where Maggie was being held."

"Worth a try in any case," Martin said. "If we can catch them."

"We could do that," I said. "Or we could make sure we've got Chichén Itzá staked out and grab her when the Reds bring her there for their über-magic shindig."

Susan whirled to face me, her eyes wide. "What?"

"They're pulling off their big ceremony at Chichén Itzá," I said. I met Susan's eyes and nodded. "I found her. She'll be there. And we'll go get her."

Susan let out a fiercely joyful cry and pounced upon me clear from the other side of the room. The impact drove my back up against one of the bookshelves. Susan's legs twined around my waist and her mouth found mine.

Her lips were fever-hot and sweet, and when they touched mine silent fire spread out into my body and briefly consumed all thought. My arms closed around her—around Susan, so warm and real and . . . and so very, very *here*. My heart lurched into double time, and I started to feel a little dizzy.

Mouse's growl rolled through the room, sudden and deep in his chest.

"Rodriguez," Martin barked, his voice tense.

Susan's lips lifted from mine, and when she opened her eyes, they were solid black, all the way across—just like a Red vampire's. My lips and tongue still tingled at the touch of her mouth, a very faint echo of the insidious venom of one of the Reds. Bright red tattoos showed on her face, her neck, and winding down one arm. She stared at me for a moment, dazed, then blinked slowly and looked over her shoulder at Martin.

"You're close," he said, in a very quiet, very soothing voice. "You need to back down. You need to take some time to breathe."

Something like rage filled Susan's face for an instant. Then she shuddered, glancing from Martin to me and back, and then began disentangling herself from me.

"Sun's out, and it's warm," Martin said, taking her elbow gently. "Come on. We'll get some sun and walk and sort things out."

"Sun," Susan said, her voice still low and husky with arousal. "Right, some sun."

Martin shot me a look that he probably hoped would kill me, and then he and Susan left the apartment and walked up into the morning's light.

Molly waited until they were well away from the front door and said, "Well. That was stupid of you both."

I looked over my shoulder at her and frowned.

"Call it like I see it," my apprentice said quietly. "You know she has trouble controlling her emotions, her instincts. She shouldn't have been all over you. And you shouldn't have kissed her back." Her mouth tightened. "Someone could have gotten hurt."

I rubbed at my still-tingling lips for a moment and suppressed a flash of anger. "Molly . . ."

"I get it," she said. "I do. Look. You care about her, okay. Maybe even loved her. Maybe she loved you. But it can't be like that anymore." She spread her hands and said, "As messed up as that is, it's still the reality you have to live with. You can't ignore it. You get close to her, and there's no way for it to come out good, boss."

I stared hard at her, all the rage inside me coming out in my voice, despite the fact that I tried to hold it in. "Be careful, Molly."

Molly blanched and looked away. But she folded her arms and stood her ground. "I'm saying this because I care, Harry."

"You care about Susan?" I asked. "You don't even know her."

"Not Susan," she said. "You."

I took a step toward her. "You don't know a goddamned thing about me and Susan, Molly."

"I know that you already blame yourself for what happened to her," she said, spitting out the words. "Think about what it'll be like for her if she gets lost in a kiss with you and realizes, later, that she ripped your throat open and drank your blood and turned herself into a monster. Is that how you want your story, Susan and Harry, to end?"

The words made me want to start screaming. I don't know what kept me from lashing out at the girl.

Other than the fact that she would never believe me capable of such a thing.

And she was right. That might have something to do with it.

So I took a deep breath and closed my eyes and fought down the rage again. I was getting tired of that.

When I spoke, a moment later, my voice sounded raw. "Study with a wizard has made you manipulative."

She sniffed a couple of times, and I opened my eyes to see her crying silently. "N-no," she said. "That was my mom."

I made a sound of acknowledgment and nodded.

She looked at me, and made no move to wipe the tears from her face. "You look awful."

"I found out some things," I said.

She bit her lip. "It's bad. Isn't it."

I nodded. I said, "Real bad. We're . . ." I shook my head. "Without the Council's support, I don't see how it can be done."

"There's a way," she said. "There's always a way."

"That's . . . sort of the problem," I said. I looked at the hopelessly organized bookshelf nearest me. "I . . . think I'd like to be by myself for a while," I said.

Molly looked at me, her posture that of someone being careful, as if they're concerned that any move might shatter a delicate object. "You're sure?"

Mouse made a little whining noise in his throat.

"I'm not going to do anything desperate," I told her. *Not yet, anyway.* "I just need some time."

"Okay," she said. "Come on, Mouse."

Mouse watched me worriedly, but padded out of the apartment and up the stairs with Molly.

I went to my shower, started it up, stripped, and got under the cold water. I just stood there with it sheeting over me for a while and tried to think.

Mostly, I thought about how good Susan's mouth had felt. I waited for the cold water to sluice that particular thought down to a bearable level. Then I thought about Vadderung's warning about the Red Court.

I've taken on some tough customers in my time. But none of them had been godlike beings—or the remnants of them, or whatever the Lords of Outer Night and the Red King were. You couldn't challenge something like that in a direct confrontation and win. I might have powers, sure. Hell, on a good day I'd go along with someone who said that I was one of the top twenty or thirty wizards on the planet, in terms of sheer magical muscle. And my finesse and skill continued to improve. Give me a couple of hundred years and I might be one of the top two or three wizards on the planet.

Of course, if Marcone was right, I'd never make it that high. And the boss predator of the concrete jungle was not stupid. In fact, I'd say that there was an excellent chance I wouldn't live another two or three days.

I couldn't challenge the masters of the Red Court and win.

But they had my little girl.

I know. It shouldn't matter that she was my little girl in particular. I should have been just as outraged that *any* little girl was trapped in such monstrous hands. But it did matter. Maggie was my child, and it mattered a whole hell of a lot.

I stood in the shower until the cold water had muted away all the hormones, all the emotion, all the mindless power of blood calling to blood. After thinking about it for a while, I decided that three courses lay open to me.

The enemy was strong. So I could show up with more muscle on my side. I could round up every friend, every ally, every shady character who owed me a solid. Enough assistance could turn the tide of any battle—and I had no illusions that it *would* be a battle of epic proportions.

The problem was that the only people who would show up to that kind of desperate fight were my friends. And my friends would die. I would literally be using them to shield myself against the crushing power of the Red King and his court, and I had no illusions of what such a struggle would cost. My friends would die. Most of them. Hell, probably all of them, and me with them. Maybe I could get to the kid and get out, while my friends gave their lives to make it possible. But after that, then what? Spend my life running with Maggie? Always looking over my shoulder, never stopping in one place for longer than a few days?

The second thing I could do was to change the confrontation into something else. Find some way to sneak up close enough to grab the girl and vanish, skipping the whole doomed-struggle part of option one. That plan wouldn't require me to get my friends killed.

Of course, to pull it off, I'd have to find some way to get more clever and sneakier than beings with millennia of practice and experience at just such acts of infiltration and treachery. You didn't survive for as long as they had among a nation of predators without being awfully smart and careful. I doubted it would be as simple as bopping a couple of guards over the head, then donning their uniforms and sneaking in with my friends the Cowardly Lion and the Tin Woodsman.

(I had cast myself as the Scarecrow in that one. If I only had a brain, I'd be able to come up with a better plan.)

So, the stand-up fight with an all-star team was a bad idea. It probably wouldn't work.

The sneaky smash-and-grab at the heart of Red Court power was a bad idea. It probably wouldn't work, either.

And that left option three. Which was unthinkable. Or had been, a few days ago. Before I knew I was a father.

My career as a wizard has been . . . very active. I've smacked a lot of awfully powerful things in the kisser. I've mostly gotten away with it, though I bear the scars, physical and otherwise, of the times I didn't. A lot of the major players looked at me and saw potential for one kind of mayhem or another.

Some of them had offered me power.

A *lot* of power.

I mean, if I went out, right now, and gathered together everything I could—regardless of the price tag attached to it—it would change the game. It would make me more than just a hotshot young wizard. It would give my power an intensity, a depth, a scope I could hardly imagine. It would give me the chance to call upon new allies to fight beside me. It would place an almost unlimited number of new weapons at my disposal, open up options that could never otherwise exist.

But what about after?

I wouldn't have to go on the run with Maggie to protect her from the monsters.

I'd be one.

Maybe not that day. Maybe not that week. But one day before too long, the things I had taken into me would change me. And I probably wouldn't mind, even if I bothered to notice it happening. That was the nature of such power. You didn't feel it changing you.

There is no sensation to warn you when your soul turns black.

Option three shared one commonality with options one and two: I wouldn't survive it. Not as the man I was. The one who tried to make the world a little brighter or more stable. The one who tried to help, and who sometimes screwed things up. The one who believed in things like family, like responsibility, like love.

But Maggie might survive it. If I did it right—only to be orphaned again, in one way or another.

I felt so tired.

Maybe there isn't a way, whispered a voice in the back of my head.

I snapped the water off and reached for a towel. "Screw that kind of thinking, Dresden," I ordered myself. "There's a way through this. There's a way. You've just got to find it."

I dried myself off and stared intently at my stark, scarred, unshaven face in the mirror. It didn't look like the kind of face a child would love. Kid would probably start crying when she got a good look at me.

But it might be the kind of face that belonged to a man who could pull her safely out of a mob of bloodthirsty beasts. It was too early to throw in the towel.

I had no idea what I was going to do.

I just knew that I couldn't give up.

Chapter

Twenty-three

I called Murphy's cell phone.

"Murphy here."

"Heya, Murph. How you doing?"

"This line isn't—"

"I know," I said. "I know. Mine either. Hello, FBI guys. Don't you get bored doing this stuff all the time?"

Murphy snorted into the phone. "What's up?"

"I'm thinking about getting a broken-down doormat to go with my broken-down door and the broken frame around it," I said. "Thank you, FBI guys."

"Don't make demons of the Bureau," Murphy said. "They aren't much more inept than anyone else. There's only so much they can do when they're given bad intelligence."

"What about your place?" I asked.

"They came, they searched, they left. Rawlins and Stallings and a dozen other guys from SI were here assisting. The Bureau dusted and took out my trash after they were done."

I barked out a laugh. "The boys at SI got away with that?"

Murphy sounded decidedly smug. "They were there at the request of the new agent in charge."

"Tilly?"

"You met him, huh?"

"Did, and glad to. Spoke well of you."

"He's an *aikidoka*," Murphy said. "I've been to his dojo a few times to teach some practical application classes. He's come out to Dough Joe's to teach forms and some formal weapons classes."

"Oh, right. He's the guy who taught you staff fighting?"

"That's him. We started off in the same class, many moons ago."

I grunted. "Shame to meet him this way."

"The Bureau generally aren't a bad bunch. This is all about Rudolph. Or whoever is giving Rudolph his marching orders."

A thought struck me, and I went silent for a moment.

"Harry? You still there?"

"Yeah, sorry. Was just about to head out for a steak sandwich. Interested?"

"Sure. Twenty?"

"Twenty."

Murphy hung up and I said, to the still-open line, "Hey, if you've got someone watching my place, could you call the cops if anyone tries to steal my *Star Wars* poster? It's an original." Then I vindictively hung up on the FBI. It made my inner child happy.

Twenty minutes later, I walked into McAnally's.

It was too early for it to be properly crowded, and Murphy and I sat down at a corner table, the one farthest from the windows, and therefore from laser microphones, in case our federal pursuers had doubled up on their paranoia meds.

I began without preamble. "Who said Rudolph was

getting his orders from his direct superiors? Or from any-one in Chicago at all?"

She frowned and thought about it for a moment. I waited it out patiently. "You don't really think that," she said. "Do you?"

"I think it's worth looking at. He looked shaky when I saw him."

"Yeah," Murphy said thoughtfully. "At my place, too."

I filled her in on the details of what she'd missed, at my apartment and the FBI building, and by the time I was done she was nodding confidently. "Go on."

"We both know that ladder climbers like Rudolph don't usually get nervous, rushed, and pressured when they're operating with official sanction. They have too much fun swaggering around beating people over the head with their authority club."

"Don't know if all of them do that," she said, "but I know damned well that Rudolph does."

"Yeah. But this time, he was edgy, impatient. Desperate." I told her about his behavior in general, and specifically at my place and in the interrogation room downtown. "Tilly said that Rudolph had lied his ass off to point the FBI at me."

"And you believe that?" Murphy asked.

"Don't you?"

She shrugged. "Point. But that doesn't mean he's being used as some kind of agent."

"I think it does," I said. "He's not operating with the full authority of his superiors. Someone else has got to be pushing him—someone who scared him enough to make him nervous and hasty."

"Maybe that works," Murphy said. "Why would he do it?"

"Someone wanted to make sure I wasn't involved in the search for Maggie. So, maybe they sent Rudolph after me. Then, when Tilly turns me loose, they take things to the next level and try to whack me outside the FBI building."

Murphy's blue eyes were cold at the mention of the assassination attempt. "Could they have gotten someone into position that fast?"

I tried to work it through in my head. "After Tilly sent Rudolph out of the room, it didn't take long for me to get out. Ten minutes, fifteen at the most. Time enough to call in his failure, and for his handler to send in a hit, you think?"

Murphy thought about it herself and then shook her head slowly. "Only if they were very, very close, and moved like greased lightning. But . . . Harry, that hit was too calm, too smooth for something thrown together at the last possible moment."

I frowned, and we both clammed up as Mac came over to our table and put a pair of brown bottles down. He was a spare man, bald, and had been ever since I knew him, dressed in dark clothes and a spotless white apron. We both murmured thanks, and he withdrew again.

"Okay," she said, and took a pull from the bottle. "Maybe Rudolph's handler had already put the assassin in place as a contingency measure, in case you got loose despite Rudolph's efforts."

I shook my head. "It makes more sense if the assassin was already there, positioned to remove *Rudolph*, once he had served his purpose. Whoever his handler was, they would need a safety measure in place, a link they could cut out of the chain so that nothing would lead back to them. Only once Rudy calls them and tells them he isn't able to keep me locked up, they have the shooter switch targets."

Which meant . . . I had taken three bullets meant for Rudolph.

"Harry?" Murphy asked. "Why are you laughing?"

"I heard a joke yesterday," I said. "I just got it."

She frowned at me. "You need some rest. You look like hell. And you're obviously tired enough to have gotten the giggles."

"Wizards don't giggle," I said, hardly able to speak. "This is cackling."

She eyed me askance and sipped her beer. She waited until I had laughed myself out before speaking again. "You find out about Maggie yet?"

"Sort of," I said, abruptly sobered. "I think I know where she will be in the next few days." I gave her what we had learned about the duchess's intentions, leaving out the parts where I committed a bunch of crimes like theft, trespassing, and vandalism. "So right now," I concluded, "everyone's checking their contacts in Mexico while I'm talking to you."

"Susan?" she asked.

"And Father Forthill," I said. "Between them, they should be able to find out what's going on at Chichén Itzá."

Murphy nodded and asked, casually, "How's she holding up?"

I took another pull from the bottle and said, "She thinks Molly has the hots for me."

Murphy snorted. "Wow. She must have used her vampire superpowers to have worked that one out."

I blinked at Murphy.

She stared at me for a second and then rolled her

eyes. "Oh, come *on*, Harry. Really? Are you really that clueless?"

"Uh," I said, still blinking. "Apparently."

Murphy smirked down at her beer and said, "It's always staggering to run into one of your blind spots. You don't have many of them, but when you do they're a mile wide." She shook her head. "You didn't really answer my question, you know."

I nodded. "Susan's a wreck. Maybe more so because of the whole vampire thing."

"I don't know, Harry. From what you've said, I don't think you'd need to look any further than the whole mommy thing."

"Could be," I said. "Either way, she's sort of fraying at the edges."

"Like you," Murphy said.

I scowled at her. "What?"

She lifted an eyebrow and looked frankly at me.

I started to get angry with her, but stopped to force myself to think. "Am I?"

She nodded slowly. "Did you notice that you've been tapping your left toe on the ground for the past five minutes?"

I frowned at her, and then down at my foot, which was tapping rapidly, to the point that my calf muscles were growing tired. "I . . . No."

"I'm your friend, Harry," she said quietly. "And I'm telling you that you aren't too stable yourself right now."

"Monsters are going to murder my child sometime soon, Murph. Maybe tonight, maybe tomorrow night. Soon. I don't have time for sanity."

Murphy nodded slowly, then sighed like someone setting down an unpleasant burden. "So. Chichén Itzá."

"Looks like."

"Cool. When do we hit them?"

I shook my head. "We can't go all *Wild Bunch* on these people. They'll flatten us."

She frowned. "But the White Council . . ."

"Won't be joining us," I said. I couldn't keep a bit of the snarl out of my voice. "And to answer your question . . . we're not sure when the ritual is supposed to take place. I've got to come up with more information."

"Rudolph," Murphy said thoughtfully.

"Rudolph. Someone who is a part of this, probably someone from the Red Court, is leaning on him. I plan on finding that someone and then poking him in the nose until he coughs up something I can use."

"I think I'd like to talk to Rudolph, too. We'll start from our ends and work toward the middle again, then?"

"Sounds like a plan." I waved at Mac and pantomimed holding a sandwich in front of me and taking a bite. He nodded, and glanced at Murphy. "You want a steak sandwich, too?"

"I thought you didn't have time to be sane."

"I don't," I said. "I don't have time to be hungry, either."

Chapter

Twenty-four

"**H**ow does a police detective afford a place like this?" Molly asked.

We were sitting in the *Blue Beetle* on a quiet residential street in Crestwood. It was late afternoon, with a heavy overcast. The houses on the street were large ones. Rudolph's place, whose address I'd gotten from Murphy, was the smallest house on the block—but it was on the block. It backed right up to the Cook County Forest Preserve, too, and between the old forest and the mature trees it gave the whole area a sheltered, pastoral quality.

"He doesn't," I said quietly.

"You mean he's dirty?" Molly asked.

"Maybe," I said. "Or maybe his family has money. Or maybe he managed to mortgage himself to the eyeballs. People get real stupid when it comes to buying homes. Pay an extra quarter of a million dollars for a place because it's in the right neighborhood. Buy houses they damned well know they can't afford to make the payments on." I shook my head. "They should make you take some kind of iota-of-common-sense quiz before you make an offer."

"Maybe it isn't stupid," Molly said. "Everybody

wants home to mean something. Maybe the extra money they pay creates that additional meaning for them."

I grimaced. "I'd rather have my extra meaning come from the ancient burial ground under the swimming pool or from knowing that I built it with my own hands or something."

"Not everyone puts as low a value on the material as you do, boss," Molly said. "For them, maybe the extra material value represented by a higher price tag *is* significant."

I grunted. "It's still stupid."

"From your perspective," Molly said. "It's really all about perspective, isn't it."

"And from the perspective of those in need, that extra quarter of a million bucks your material person spent on the prestige addition for his house looks like an awful lot of lifesaving food and medicine that could have existed if the jerk with the big house in the suburbs hadn't blown it all to artificially inflate his sociogeographic penis."

"Heh," Molly said. "And their house is much nicer than your house."

"And that," I said.

Mouse grumbled quietly in his sleep from the backseat, and I turned to reach back and rub his ears until he settled down again.

Molly sat quietly for almost a minute before she said, "What else do we do?"

"Other than sit tight and watch?" I asked. "This is a stakeout, Molly. It's what you do on a stakeout."

"Stakeouts suck," Molly said, puffing out a breath that blew a few strands of hair out of her eyes. "How come Murphy isn't doing this part? How come we aren't doing magic stuff?"

"Murphy is keeping track of Rudolph at work," I said. "I'm watching his home. If his handler wanted him dead, this would be a logical place to bushwhack him."

"And we're not doing magic because . . . ?"

"What do you suggest we do?"

"Tracking spells for Rudolph and Maggie," she said promptly.

"You got any of Rudolph's blood? Hair? Fingernail clippings?"

"No," she said.

"So, no tracking spell for him," I said.

"But what about Maggie?" she said. "I know you don't have any hair or anything from her, but you pulled a tracking spell for me using my mother's blood, right? Couldn't you use your blood for that?"

I kept my breathing steady, and prevented the flash of frustration I felt from coming out in my voice. "First thing I tried. Right after I got off the phone with Susan when this all started."

Molly frowned. "Why didn't it work?"

"I don't know," I said. "Maybe it's because there's something more than simple blood relation involved. Maybe there has to be a bond, a sense of family between the parent and child, that the tracking spell uses to amplify its effects. Maybe the Red Court is using some kind of magic that conceals or jams tracking spells—God knows, they would have been forced to come up with some kind of countermeasure during the war." I shook my head wearily. "Or maybe it was simple distance. I've never tracked anything more than a couple of hundred linear miles away. I've heard of tracking spells that worked over a couple of thousand miles, but not from anyone who had actually done it. Gimme some credit, grasshopper. Of course I tried that. I wouldn't have spent half a day summoning my contacts if I hadn't."

"Oh," Molly said. She looked troubled. "Yeah. Sorry."

I sighed and tipped my head back and closed my eyes. "No problem. Sorry, kid. I'm just tense."

"Just a little," she said. "Um. Should we be sitting out here in broad daylight? I mean, we're not hiding the car or anything."

"Yeah," I said. "We want to be visible."

"Why?"

"I'm gonna close my eyes," I told her. "Just for a bit. Stay alert, okay?"

She gave me a look, but said, "Okay."

I closed my eyes, but about half a second after I had, Molly nudged me and said, "Wake up, Harry. We have company."

I opened them again and found that the grey late afternoon had settled into the murk of early evening. I looked up into the rearview mirror and spotted a white sports car coming to a halt as it parked on the street behind us. The running lights went off as the driver got out.

"Took him long enough," I muttered.

Molly frowned at me. "What do you mean?"

"Asked him to meet me here. Didn't know where to find him."

Molly peered through the back window, and even Mouse lifted his head to look around. "Oh," Molly said, understanding, as Mouse's tail thumped hesitantly against the back of my seat.

I got out of the car and walked to meet my half brother, the vampire.

Thomas and I were a study in contrasts. I was better

than six and a half feet tall and built lean. He was a hair
under six feet, and looked like a fitness model. My hair
was a muddy brown color, generally cut very short on
the sides and in back, a little longer on top. It tended
to stick up any which way within a few minutes of being
ordered by a comb. Thomas's hair was black, naturally
wavy, and fell to touch his shoulders. I wore jeans, a
T-shirt, and my big black leather duster. Thomas was
wearing custom-fitted pants made from white leather, a
white silk shirt, and a coarser silk jacket, also in white,
decorated with elaborate brocade. He had the kind of
face that belonged on billboards. Mine belonged on
wanted posters.

We had the same contour of chin, and our eyes resembled each other's unmistakably in shape, if not in
color. Mom gave them to us.

Thomas and I had finally met as adults. He'd been
right there next to me in some of the worst places I'd
ever walked. He saved my life more than once. I'd returned the favor. But that had been when he decided to
fight against his Hunger, the vampiric nature native to
the vampires of the White Court. He'd spent years maintaining control of his darker urges, integrating with Chicago's society, and generally trying to act like a human
being. We'd had to keep our kinship a secret. The Council would have used him to get at the White Court if
they knew. Ditto for the vampires getting at the Council
through me.

Then something bad happened to him, and he
stopped trying to be human. I might have seen him for a
total of two, even three minutes since he'd been knocked
off the life-force-nibbling wagon and started taking big
hearty bites again.

Thomas swaggered up to me as if we'd been talking

just yesterday, looked me up and down, and said, "You need an image consultant, stat, little brother."

I said, "Guess what. You're an uncle."

Thomas let his head fall back as he barked out a little laugh. "What? No, hardly, unless one of Father's by-blows actually survived. Which essentially just doesn't happen among—"

He stopped talking in midsentence and his eyes widened.

"Yeah," I said.

"Oh," he said, still wide-eyed, apparently locked into motionlessness by surprise. It was a little creepy. Human beings still look like human beings when they're standing still. Thomas's pale skin and bright blue eyes went *still*, like a statue. *"Oh."*

I nodded. "Say 'oilcan.'"

Thomas blinked. "What?"

"You get to be the Tin Woodsman."

"What?"

"Never mind, not important." I sighed. "Look, without going into too many details: I have an eight-year-old daughter. Susan never told me. Duchess Arianna of the Red Court took her."

"Um," said Thomas. "If I'd known that, maybe I would have been here sooner."

"Couldn't say anything on the phone. The FBI and the cops are involved, having been made into roadblocks to slow me down." I tilted my head down the street. "The cop who lives in that house at the end of the street has been coerced into helping whoever is trying to stop me. I'm here hoping to nab either his handler or his cleaner and grab every bit of information I can."

Thomas looked at me and said, "I'm an uncle."

I ran the palm of my hand over my face.

"Sorry," he said. "I just thought this was going to be another chat, with you all worried that the evil White Court had been abusing me. I need to take a moment."

"Make it a short moment," I said. "We're on the clock."

Thomas nodded several times and seemed to draw himself back into order. "Okay, so you're looking for . . . What's her name?"

"Maggie."

My brother paused for a couple of heartbeats, and bowed his head briefly. "That's a good name."

"Susan thought so."

"So you're looking for Maggie," he said. "And you need my help?"

"I don't know the exact date, but I know she's going to be brought to Chichén Itzá. Probably tonight, tomorrow night at the latest."

"Why?" Thomas asked. He then added, "And how does this have anything to do with me?"

"They're using her in a bloodline curse," I said. "When they sacrifice her, the curse kills her brothers and sisters, then her parents, then *their* brothers and sisters and so on."

"Wait. Maggie has *brothers and sisters*? Since when have you *ever* gotten *that* busy?"

"No, dammit!" I half shouted in frustration. "That's just an illustration for how the bloodline curse works."

His eyebrows shot up. "Oh, crap. You're saying that it's going to kill *me*, too."

"Yes, that is *exactly* what I'm freaking saying, you tool."

"Um," Thomas said, "I'm against that." His eyes widened again. "Wait. What about the other Raiths? Are they in any danger through me?"

I shook my head. "I don't know."

"Empty night," he muttered. "Okay. You know where she's going to be. You want me to saddle up and help you get Maggie back, like we did with Molly?"

"Not unless there's no other choice. I don't think we would survive a direct assault on the Red King and his retinue on their home turf."

"Well, maybe you and I couldn't, naturally. But with the Council behind y—"

"Way behind me," I interrupted, my voice harsh with anger. "So far behind me you wouldn't know they were there at all."

My brother's deep blue eyes flashed with an angry fire. "Those assholes."

"Seconded, motion carried," I agreed.

"So what do you think we should do?"

"I need information," I said. "Get me whatever you can. Any activity at Chichén Itzá or a nearby Red stronghold, sightings of a little girl surrounded by Reds, anything. There's got to be something, somewhere that will show us a chink in their armor. If we find out where they're holding her, we can hit the place. If I can learn something about the defensive magic around the site, maybe I can poke a hole in it so that we can just grab the girl and go. Otherwise . . ."

"Yeah," Thomas said. "Otherwise we have to take them on at Chichén Itzá. Which would suck."

"It's a couple of miles beyond suck."

Thomas frowned. "What about asking Lara for help? She can command a lot of firepower from the other Houses of the White Court."

"Why would she help me?" I asked.

"Self-preservation. She's big on that."

I grunted. "I'm not sure if the rest of your family is in any danger."

"You aren't sure they aren't, either," Thomas said. "And anyway, if you don't know, Lara won't."

"Don't be too sure," I said. "No. If I go to her with this, she'll assume it's a ploy motivated by desperation."

Thomas folded his arms. "A lame ploy, at that. But you're missing another angle."

"Oh?"

Thomas lowered his arms and then brought them up to frame his own torso the way Vanna White presents the letters on *Wheel of Fortune*. "Incontestably, I'm in danger. She'll want to protect me."

I looked at him skeptically.

Thomas shrugged. "I play for the team now, Harry. And everyone knows it. If she lets something bad happen to me when I ask for her help, it's going to make a lot of people upset. And not in the helpful, 'I sure don't want to mess with her' kind of way."

"For that to work as leverage, the stakes would have to be known to the rest of the Court," I said. "They'd have to know why you were in danger from a blood-line curse aimed at me. Then they'd all know about our blood relation. Not just Lara."

Thomas frowned over that for a moment. Then he shrugged. "Still. It might be worth the effort to approach her. She's a resourceful woman, my sister." His expression smoothed over into neutrality. "Quite gifted when it comes to removing obstacles. She could probably help you."

Normally I slap down suggestions like that without a second thought. This time . . .

I had the second thought.

Lara probably knew the Red Court as well as anyone. She'd been operating arm in arm with them, to one degree or another, for years. She was the power behind the throne of the White Court, which prided itself on its skills of espionage, manipulation, and other forms of indirect strength. If anyone was likely to know something about the Reds, it was Lara Raith.

The clock just kept on ticking. Maggie was running out of time. She couldn't afford for me to be squeamish.

"I would prefer not to," I said quietly. "I need you to find out whatever you can, man."

"What happens if I can't find it?"

"If that happens . . ." I shook my head. "If I do nothing, my little girl is going to die. And so is my brother. I can't live with that."

Thomas nodded. "I'll see what I can do."

"Don't see it. *Do* it."

It came out harsh enough that my brother flinched, though it was a subtle motion. "Okay," he said. "Let's—"

His head whipped around toward Rudolph's house.

"What?" I asked.

He held up a hand for silence, turning to focus intently. "Breaking glass," he murmured. "A lot of it."

"Harry!" Molly called.

I turned to see the Beetle's passenger door swing open. Molly emerged, hanging on to Mouse's collar with both hands. The big dog was focused on Rudolph's house as well, and his chest bubbled with the deep, tearing snarl I'd heard only a handful of times, and always when supernatural predators were nearby.

"Someone's there for Rudolph," I said, and launched myself forward. "Let's go!"

Chapter

Twenty-five

I looked like a cool guy leading the charge for about a second and a half, and then my brother and my dog left me and Molly eating their dust. If I hadn't been a regular runner, Molly would have done the same, albeit more gradually. By the time I had covered half the distance, Thomas and Mouse had already bounded around to the back, one around either side of Rudolph's house.

"Get gone, grasshopper!" I called, and even as we ran forward Molly vanished behind her best veil. It took us another quarter of a minute to cover the distance, and I went around the side of the house Thomas had taken. I pounded around the back corner to see that a large glass sliding door leading from a wooden deck into the house had been shattered. I could hear a big, thumping beat, as if from a subwoofer, pounding away inside the house.

I took the stairs up to the deck in a single jumping stride, and barely avoided a sudden explosion of glass, wood, drywall, and siding that came hurling toward me. I had an instant to realize that the projectile that had just come through the wall was my brother, and then something huge and black and swift came crashing through the same wall, expanding the hole to five times its original size.

The whatever-it-was stood within a step or two, and I was already sprinting. I kept doing it. I slapped one hand down and vaulted the railing on the far side of the deck. I barely jerked my hand from the rail before the thing smashed it to kindling with one huge, blindingly fast talon. That deep beat grew louder and faster as I landed, and I realized with a shock that I could hear the thing's rising heart rate as clearly as if it had been pounding on a drum.

I was kidding myself if I thought I could run from something that fast. I had a step or two on the creature, but it reclaimed them within half a dozen strides and swiped at my head with terrible speed and power.

I whirled desperately, drawing my blasting rod and letting out a burst of flame, but I stumbled and fell during the spin. The fire hammered into the creature, and for all the good it did me I might as well have hit it with a rubber chicken.

I thought I was done for—until Mouse emerged from the house onto the back deck, bathed in a faint nimbus of blue light. He took a single, bounding, thirty-yard leap that ended at the attacking creature's enormous, malformed shoulders. Mouse's claws dug into the thing's hide, and his massive jaws closed on the back of its thick, almost indistinguishable neck.

The creature arched up in pain, but it never made a sound. It tripped over me, too distracted to actually attack, but the impact of so much mass and power sent up flares of agony from my ribs and from one thigh.

Mouse rode the creature down into the dirt, tearing and worrying it, his claws digging furrows in the flesh of its back. His snarls reverberated in the evening air, and each shake and twist of his body seemed to send up little puffs of glowing blue mist from his fur.

Mouse had the thing dead to rights, but nobody seemed to have told the creature that. It twisted lithely, bouncing up from the ground as if made of rubber, seized Mouse's tail, and swung the huge dog in a single, complete arc. Mouse hit the ground like a two-hundred-pound sledgehammer, drawing a high-pitched sound of pain from him.

I didn't think. I lifted my blasting rod again, filling it with my will and with all the soulfire I could shove in, screaming, "Get off my dog!"

White fire slammed out of the rod and drew a line on the creature from hip to skull, digging into flesh and setting it ablaze. Once again, it convulsed in silent agony, and the boom-box beat of its heart ratcheted up even higher. It fell, unable to hold on to Mouse, and writhed upon the ground.

I tried to get up, but my injured leg wouldn't support me, and the sudden surge of weariness that overtook me made my arms collapse, too. I lay there, panting and helpless to move. Mouse staggered slowly to his feet, his head hanging, his tongue dangling loosely from his mouth. Behind me, I heard a groan and twisted awkwardly to see Thomas sit up, one shoulder hanging at a malformed angle. His clothes had been ripped to shreds, there was a piece of metal protruding from his abdomen, just next to his belly button, and half his face was covered in a sheet of blood a little too pale to belong to a human.

"Thomas!" I shouted. Or tried to shout. The acoustics were odd in this tunnel within which I was suddenly sprawled. "Get up, man!"

He gave me a blank, concussed stare.

The creature's movements had slowed. I turned to

see it beginning to relax, its body shuddering, the drumbeat of its heart steadying, and I got a better look at it than I had before.

It was huge, easily the size of a full-grown bull, and it carried a stench with it that was similar in potency. Or maybe that was because I had just overcooked it. Its body was odd, seemingly able to move on two legs or four with equal efficiency. Its flesh was a spongy blackness, much like the true skin of a Red vampire, and its head was shaped like something mixing the features of a human being, a jaguar, and maybe a crocodile or wild boar. It was pitch-black everywhere, including its eyes, its tongue, and its mouth.

And, despite the punishment I had just dealt out, it was getting up again.

"Thomas!" I shouted. Or wheezed.

The creature shook its head and its dead-black eyes focused on me. It started toward me, pausing briefly to swat my stunned dog out of its path. Mouse landed in a tumble, seemingly struggling to find his balance but unable to do so.

I lifted my blasting rod again as it came on, but I didn't have enough juice left in me to make the rod do anything but smoke faintly.

And then a stone sailed in from nowhere and struck the creature on the snout.

"Hey!" called Molly's voice. "Hey, Captain Asphalt! Hey, tar baby! Over here!"

The creature and I turned to see Molly standing maybe twenty yards away, in plain sight. She flung another rock, and it bounced off the creature's broad chest. Its heartbeat began to accelerate and grow louder again.

"Let's go, gorgeous!" Molly called. "You and me!"

She turned sideways to the thing, rolled her hips, and made an exaggerated motion of swatting herself on the ass. "Come get some!"

The thing tensed and then rushed forward, covering the ground with astonishing speed.

Molly vanished.

The creature smashed into the earth where she'd been standing, with its huge talons balled into furious fists, slamming them eight inches into the earth.

There was a peal of mocking laughter, and another rock bounced off of the thing, this time from the left. Furious, it whirled to rush Molly again—and again, she vanished completely. Once more it struck at empty ground. Once more, Molly got its attention with a rock and a few taunts, only to vanish from sight as it came at her.

Each time, she was a little closer to the creature, unable to match its raw speed. And each time, she led it a little farther away from the three of us. A couple of times, she even shouted, *"Toro, toro! Olé!"*

"Thomas!" I called. *"Get up!"*

My brother blinked his eyes several times, each time a little more quickly. Then he swiped a hand at the bloodied side of his face, shook his head violently to get the blood out of his eyes, and looked down at the section of metal bar sticking out of his stomach. He clenched it with his hand, grimaced, and drew it slowly out, revealing a six-inch triangle that must have been a corner brace in the wall he'd gone through. He dropped it on the ground, groaning in pain, and his eyes rolled briefly back into his head.

I saw his other nature coming over him. His skin grew paler, and almost seemed to take on its own glow. His breathing stabilized immediately, and the cut along his hairline where he'd been bleeding began to close.

He opened his eyes, and their color had changed from a deep, contented blue to a hungry, metallic silver.

He got up smoothly and glanced at me. "You bleeding?"

"Nah," I said. "I'm good."

A few feet away, Mouse got to his feet and shook himself, his tags jingling. Molly had gotten as far as the street again, and there was an enormous crashing sound.

"This time, we do it smart," Thomas said. He turned to Mouse instead of me. "I'm going to go in first and get its attention. Go for its strings. I think you'll have to hit two limbs to really cripple it."

Mouse woofed, evidently an affirmative, let out a grumbling growl, and once more very faint, very pale blue light gathered around him.

Thomas nodded, and picked up a section of ruined deck that had scattered around where he landed. He shouldered a corner post, a section of four-by-four about a yard and a half long, and said, "Don't sweat, Harry. We'll be back for you in a minute."

"Go, Team Dresden," I wheezed.

The two of them took off, zero to cheetah speed in about a second. Then they were out of sight. I heard Thomas let out a high-pitched cry that was a pretty darn good Bruce Lee impersonation, and there was a thunder crack of wood striking something hard.

An instant later, Mouse let out his battle roar. There was a flicker of strobing colors of light as Molly pitched a bit of dazzling magic at the creature. It wouldn't hurt the thing, but the kid could make eye-searing light in every color imaginable burst from empty air, accompanied by a variety of sounds if she so chose. She called it her One-woman Rave spell, and during the last Independence Day, she had used it to throw up a fireworks display from her parents' backyard so impressive that evidently it had caused traffic problems on the expressway.

It was hard to lie there twisted halfway around at the waist, to see only the occasional flash of light or to hear the thumps and snarls of combat. I tried my leg again and had no luck. So I just settled down and concentrated on not blacking out or breathing too hard. The creature had definitely cracked at least one of my ribs.

That was when I noticed the two sets of glowing red eyes staring at me from the forest, staring with the unmistakable fixation of a predator, and coming slowly, steadily, silently closer.

I suddenly realized that everyone around who might have helped me was sort of distracted at the moment.

"Oh," I breathed. "Oh, crap."

Chapter

Twenty-six

The eyes rushed toward me, and something dark and strong struck me across the jaw. I was already close to losing consciousness. The blow was enough to ring my bells thoroughly.

I was aware of being picked up and tossed over someone's shoulder. Then there was a lot of rapid, sickening motion. It went on long enough for me to throw up. I didn't have enough energy to aim at my abductor.

A subjective eternity later, I was thrown to the ground. I lay still, hoping to fool my captor into thinking I was barely conscious and weak as a kitten. Which should be easy, since I was. I've never really had much ambition as a performer.

"We don't like it," said a woman's voice. "Its Power smells foul."

"We must be patient," replied a man's voice. "It could be a great asset."

"It is listening to us," the woman said.

"We know that," replied the man.

I heard soft footsteps, cushioned by pine needles, and the woman spoke again, more slowly and lower. She sounded . . . hungry. "Poor thing. So battered. We should give it a kiss and let it sleep. It would be merciful. And He would be pleased with us."

"No, our love. He would be satisfied with us. There is a difference."

"Have we not come to understand this simple fact?" she shot back, acid in her voice. "Never will He name us to the Circle, no matter how many prizes we bring into the Court. We are interlopers. We are not of the first Maya."

"Many things can change in the span of eternity, our love. We will be patient."

"You mean that He might fall?" She let out a rather disconcerting giggle. "Then why aren't we currying favor with Arianna?"

"We shall not even consider it," he replied, his voice hard. "Should we even think of it too often, He might know. He might act. Do we understand?"

"We do," she said, her tone petulant.

Then someone grabbed my shoulder in iron-strong fingers and flipped me onto my back. The dark shapes of trees spun above me, nothing more than black outlines against the lights of Chicago reflecting from the overcast.

There was barely enough light to let me see the pale, delicate features of a tiny woman no larger than a child. Seriously, she might have been four-foot-six, though her proportions seemed identical to those of any adult. She had very pale skin with a light dusting of freckles, and looked as if she might be nineteen years old. Her hair was light brown and very straight. Her eyes were extremely odd-looking. One was pale icy blue, the other deep, dark green, and I had an immediate instinct that whatever creature lurking behind those mismatched eyes was not a rational being.

She was wearing a gown with long, flowing sleeves,

and some kind of sleeveless robe and corset over that. She was barefoot, though. I knew because I could feel her cold little foot when she planted it on my chest and leaned over to peer down at me.

"We're too late. Look, it's starting to go bad."

"Nonsense," said the male voice. "It's a perfectly appropriate specimen. Mortal wizards are supposed to be worn and tough, our love."

I looked up and saw the other speaker. He was perhaps five-foot-six, with a short brush of red hair, a black beard, and skin that looked darkened and bronzed by the sun. He wore black silk clothing, and looked like he'd just come from a dress rehearsal of *Hamlet*.

"Aha," I said. "You must be Esteban and Esmerelda. I've heard about you."

"We are *famous*," hissed the little woman, beaming up at the man.

He gave her a stern look, sighed, and said, "Aye, we are. Here to stop you from allowing Arianna to proceed with her design."

I blinked. "What?"

Esmerelda leaned closer. Her hair brushed my nose and lips. "Are its ears broken? If the ears are defective, can we detach them and send them back?"

"Peace, our love," Esteban said. He hunkered down on his heels and eyed me. "It isn't its fault. It doesn't even realize how Arianna is manipulating it."

"What are you talking about?" I said. "Look, folks, no one wants to stop Arianna more than me."

Esteban waved a vague hand. "Yes, yes. It feels it must rescue its spawn. It will try to take her back, from the very heart of His realm. Placing it at the center of vast moving powers where it might tip balances any number of ways."

"It hardly looks large enough." Esmerelda sniffed. "It's just a ragged, dirty creature."

Esteban shrugged. "We know, by now, that the outside hardly matters. What lies within is what holds importance. Would you agree, ragged wizard?"

I licked my lips. I really didn't feel up to bantering with a couple of insane vampires, but it was probably my best course of action. Anything that lives long enough tends to lose track of passing time rather easily, on the minute-to-minute scale. After a few thousand years have gone by, an hour doesn't really rate. If my brother and company were successful in their fight, they would realize I was gone within a few minutes—and I didn't think the Eebs had carried me far enough away to let them evade Mouse. As far as I can tell, Mouse can follow a scent trail from space.

Talk to them. Stall.

"That depends upon the nature of the subject and observer," I said. "But if you are using the metaphor in its simplest form, then yes. The true nature of any given being supersedes its outer appearance in terms of importance." I tried a smile. "This is quite pleasant treatment, by the way," I said. "I had expected something entirely different."

"We wanted to eat you and kill you. Or kill you, then eat you," Esmerelda said, smiling back. Hers was a lot crazier-looking than mine. I hoped. "And might still."

"Obviously you had something else in mind, though," I said. "Apparently you wish to talk. I'm more than willing to listen."

"Excellent," Esteban said. "We are pleased that you can address the matter rationally."

"To which matter do you refer, specifically?"

"The matter of your involvement with Arianna's

plan," Esteban said. "We wish you to discontinue your participation."

"That . . . could be problematic. Since if she does what she intends to do, it's going to kill me, along with the child's mother."

The two vampires traded a long, silent glance, their facial expressions shifting subtly. I got the impression that a lot of communication got done.

Esteban turned back to me. "How did you learn of this, ragged wizard?"

"It's what I do," I said.

"Oooo," said Esmerelda. She slid her body on top of mine, straddling my hips with hers. She was so tiny that I could hardly feel her weight on me. She smelled . . . wrong. Like formaldehyde and mildew. "It is arrogant. We *adore* arrogance. It's so sweet to watch arrogant little things succumb. Do you like our pretty eyes, ragged wizard? Which color do you like more? Look closely and carefully."

You don't look vampires in the eyes. Everyone knows that one. Even so, I'd had a couple of encounters with the stare of one of the Red Court and never had a problem shutting them out. It wasn't even particularly difficult.

But evidently, those vampires had been noobs.

Ice blue and deep sea green swirled in my vision, and it was only at the very last instant that I realized what was happening, slamming closed the vaults of my mind, leaving only the hard, fortified places to attack, a castle of idea and memory, ready to withstand an assault.

"Stop that, please," I said quietly a moment later. "The conversation isn't getting anywhere like this."

The little vampire pursed her lips, her head tilted as if she were deciding whether to be upset or amused. She went with amused. She giggled and wriggled her hips around a little. "Lovely, lovely, lovely. We are well pleased."

"You do have options," Esteban said. If he was put out by Esmerelda's behavior, it didn't show. Hell, he hadn't even seemed to notice.

"By all means," I said. "Enumerate them."

"I suppose the simplest means to solve our problem would be for you to take your own life," he said. "If you are dead, Arianna has no reason to harm your spawn."

"Aside from the being-dead part, there are some minor problems with that idea."

"By all means," Esteban said, "enumerate them."

"What confirmation would I have that the child was safe and returned to her mother? What security would I have to make me believe that Arianna might not do the same thing a month from now?"

"A contract could be drafted," Esteban said. "Witnessed and signed, arbitrated by one of the neutral parties of the Accords. For security, we suppose we could ask our Lord if He would give his Word upon it that your mate and spawn were free of the cycle of vengeance."

"A possibility worth consideration," I said. "Though the part where I die seems to be something of a flaw."

"Understandably," Esteban said. "We might also offer you an alternative to death."

The roll of Esmerelda's hips became slower, more sensuous. I've been abused by Red Court vampires in the past. I still have nightmares sometimes. But the pretty-seeming girl atop me had that feminine mystique that defies description and definition. Being so close to her was making me nauseous, but my body was reacting to her with uncomfortable intensity.

"Alternative," she said in a breathy little voice. "In

this day, that means fashionable. And we do so love showing little mortals how to be fashionable."

"You would make me like you," I said quietly.

Esmerelda nodded, slowly, her mouth drawing up into a lazy, sensual smile, her hips still circling maddeningly against mine. Her fangs were showing.

"It would offer you several advantages," Esteban said. "Even should Arianna complete the vengeance rite, the transformation of your blood would insulate you against it. And, of course, you would not be killed, captured, or tortured to death, as the White Council will be over the next six months or so."

"It certainly bears consideration as well," I said. "Very practical. Are there any other paths you think feasible?"

"One more," Esteban said. "Gift your spawn to our Lord, the Red King."

If I'd had the strength to take a swing at him, I would have. So it was probably a good thing that I didn't. "And what would that accomplish?"

"He would then take possession of the spawn. She would, in fact, be under his protection, until such time as He deemed her unfit, unworthy, or unneeding of such care."

Esmerelda nodded rapidly. "She would be his. He does so dote on his little pets. We think it quite endearing." She opened her mouth in a little O, like a schoolgirl caught in the midst of a whispered conference about forbidden subjects. "Oh, *my*, would Arianna be upset. She would howl for *centuries*."

"We could provide chattel in exchange to sweeten the deal, Dresden," Esteban said. "We would be willing to go as high as seven young women. You could select them from our stock or from their natural habitat, and we would see to their preparation and disposition."

I thought about it for a long moment and rubbed lightly at my chin. Then I said, "These are all very rational suggestions. But I feel that I do not understand something. Why does the Red King not simply order Arianna to desist?"

Both of the Eebs drew in breaths of scandalized surprise. "Because of her *mate*, Dresden," said Esteban.

"Slain by the wizard of the black stick," said Esmerelda. "A blood debt."

"Sacred blood."

"Holy blood."

Esteban shook his head. "Not even our Lord can interfere in the collection of a blood debt. It is Arianna's right."

Esmerelda nodded. "As it was Bianca's to collect from you, in the opening days of the war. Though many wished that she would not have done what she did, it was her right, even as a very, very young member of the Court. As her progenitor, Arianna's mate took up that debt. As Arianna now has done herself." She looked at Esteban and beamed. "We are so happy with the ragged wizard. It is so civil and pleasant. Completely unlike those other wizards. Might we keep it for our own?"

"Business, our love," Esteban chided. "Business first."

Esmerelda thrust out her lower lip—and abruptly turned, all motion ceasing, to focus intently in one direction.

"What is it, our love?" Esteban asked quietly.

"The Ik'k'uox," she said in a distant, puzzled voice. "It is in pain. It flees. It . . ." She opened her eyes very wide, and suddenly they flooded in solid black, just as the creature's had been. "Oh! It cheated!" Her face turned down to mine, and she bared her fangs, "It cheated! It brought a demon of its own! A mountain ice demon from the Land of Dreams!"

"If you don't exercise them, they're impossible," I said, philosophically.

"The constable," Esteban said. "Did it kill the constable?"

Esmerelda returned to staring at nothing for a moment and then said, "No. It was attacked only seconds after entering his home." She shivered and looked up at Esteban. "The ragged wizard's demon comes this way, and swiftly."

Esteban sighed. "We had hoped to work out something civilized. This is your last chance, ragged wizard. What say you to my offer?"

"Go fuck yourself," I said.

Esteban's eyes went black and flat. "Kill him."

Esmerelda's body tightened in what looked like a sexual fervor, and she leaned down, teeth bared, letting out a low sound filled to the brim with erotic and physical need.

During the last few moments, the fingers of my right hand had undone the clasp on my mother's amulet. As the little vampire leaned into me, she met the silver pentacle necklace, the symbol of what I believed. A five-pointed star, representing the four elements and the spirit, bound within a circle of mortal control, will, and compassion. I'm not a Wiccan. I'm not big on churches of any kind, despite the fact that I've spoken, face-to-face, with an archangel of the Almighty.

But there were some things I believed in. Some things I had faith in. And faith isn't about perfect attendance to services, or how much money you put on the little plate. It isn't about going skyclad to the Holy Rites, or meditating each day upon the divine.

Faith is about what you do. It's about aspiring to be better and nobler and kinder than you are. It's about making sacrifices for the good of others—even when there's not going to be anyone telling you what a hero you are.

Faith is a power of its own, and one even more elusive and difficult to define than magic. A symbol of faith, presented with genuine belief and sincerity, is the bane of many an otherworldly predator—and one of the creatures most strongly affected were vampires of the Red Court. I don't know how it works, or why. I don't know if some kind of powerful being or Being must get involved along the line. I never asked for one of them to do that—but if so, one of them was backing me up anyway.

The pentacle flared into brilliant silver light that struck Esmerelda like a six-foot wave, throwing her off of me and tearing the flesh mask she wore to shreds, revealing the creature inside it.

I twisted and presented the symbol to Esteban, but he had already backed several paces away, and it only forced him to lift his hand to shade his eyes as he continued retreating.

There was a hissing, serpentine sound from Esmerelda, and I saw a gaunt, black-skinned creature stand up out of the ruins of gown and flesh mask alike. It was just as small as she was, but its limbs were longer, by at least a third, than hers had seemed, long and scrawny. A flabby black belly sagged down, and its face would make one of those really ugly South American bats feel better about itself.

She opened her jaws, baring fangs and a long, writhing tongue that was pink with black spots. Her all-black eyes were ablaze with fury.

Shadows shifted as a pale blue light began to grow

nearer, and the woods suddenly rang out with Mouse's triumphant hunting howl. He had found my scent—or that of the vampires—and was closing in.

Esmerelda hissed again, and the sound was full of rage and hate.

"We mustn't!" Esteban snarled. He dashed around me with supernatural speed, giving the glowing pendant a wide berth. He seized the little vampire woman by the arm. They both stared at me for an instant with their cold, empty black eyes—and then there was the sound of a rushing wind and they were gone.

I sagged onto the ground gratefully. My racing heart began to slow, my fear to subside. My confusion as to what was happening remained, though. Maybe it was so tangled and impossible because I was so exhausted.

Yeah. Right.

Mouse let out a single loud bark and then the big dog was standing next to me, over me. He nudged me with his nose until I lifted a hand and scratched his ears a little.

Thomas and Molly arrived next. I was glad Thomas had let Mouse do the pursuit, while he came along more slowly so that my apprentice wouldn't be alone in the woods. His eyes were bright silver, his mouth set in a smug line, and there was broken glass shining in his hair. The left half of Molly's upper body was generously coated in green paint.

"Okay," I slurred. "I'm backward."

"What's that?" Molly asked, kneeling down next to me, her expression worried.

"Backward. 'M a detective. Supposed to find things out. I been working backward. The more I look at it, the more certain I am that I have no idea what's going on."

"Can you stand?" Thomas asked.

"Leg," I said. "Ribs. Might be broken. Can't take the weight."

"I'll carry him," Thomas said. "Find a phone."

"Okay."

My brother picked me up and carried me out of the woods. We went back to the car.

The car's *remains*.

I stared dully at the mess. It looked as though something had taken Thomas's white Jag and put it in a trash compactor with the *Blue Beetle*. The two cars, together, had been smashed down into a mass about four feet high. Liquids and fuel bled out onto the street below them.

Thomas gingerly put me down on my good leg as I stared at my car.

There was no way the Beetle was going to resurrect from this one. I found myself blinking tears out of my eyes. It wasn't an expensive car. It wasn't a sexy car. It was *my* car.

And it was gone.

"Dammit," I mumbled.

"Hmmm?" Thomas asked. He looked considerably less broken up than me.

"My staff was inna car." I sighed. "Takes weeks to make one of those."

"Lara's going to be annoyed with me," Thomas said. "That's the third one this year."

I rolled my eyes. "Yeah. I feel your pain. What happened with the big thing?"

"The fight?" Thomas shrugged. "Bullfighting tactics, for the most part. When it tried to focus on one, the other two would come at its back. Mouse did you rather proud."

The big dog wagged his tail cheerily.

"Paint?" I asked.

"Oh, the thing threw a five-gallon bucket of paint at her, either trying to kill her with it or so it could try to see her through the veil. Worked for about five seconds, too, but then she fixed it and was gone again. She did fairly well for someone so limited in offense," Thomas said. "Let me see if I can salvage anything from my trunk. Excuse me."

I just sat down on the street in front of the car, and Mouse came up to sit with me, offering a furry flank for support. The *Blue Beetle* was dead. I was too tired to cry much.

"I called a cab," Molly said, reappearing. "It will meet us two blocks down. Get him and I'll veil us until it arrives."

"Yeah," Thomas said, and picked me up again.

I don't remember being awake for the cab ride.

Chapter

Twenty-seven

Thomas supported most of my weight as my injured leg began to buckle, and settled me in one of the chairs in the living room.

"We can't be here long," he said. "Those two Reds know he's injured and exhausted. They'll be back, looking for an opening or trying to pick one of us off when we're vulnerable."

"Right, right," Molly said. "How is he?"

He crouched down in front of me and peered at me. His irises looked like polished chrome. "Still punchy."

"Shock?"

"Maybe. He's in a lot of pain."

I was? Oh. I was. That might explain the way I wasn't talking, I guessed.

"God," Molly said, her voice shaking. "I'll get some of his things."

"This isn't right," Thomas said. "Get Bob."

Molly sounded confused. "Get what?"

His expression flickered with surprise and then went neutral again. "Sorry. Lips disconnected from my brain. Get the Swords."

"They aren't here," Molly said, moving around. Her voice came from my bedroom. "He moved them. Hid them, along with his ghost dust and a bunch of other illegal things."

Thomas frowned at that and then nodded. "Okay. It'll have to do. Where do we take him?"

Molly appeared in my field of vision and knelt down to peer at me. She took one of my hands in hers. "Wherever is good, I guess."

Thomas took a slow breath. His silver eyes grew even brighter. It was creepy as hell and fascinating. "I was hoping you knew a good spot. I sure as hell can't take him to my place."

Molly's voice sharpened. "I don't even *have* a place," she said. "I still live at my parents' house."

"Less whining," Thomas said, his voice cool. "More telling me a place to take him where he won't be killed."

"I am—" Molly began. Then she closed her eyes for a second, and moderated her tone. "I am sorry. I'm just . . ." She glanced up at Thomas. "I'm just scared."

"I know," Thomas said through clenched teeth.

"Um," Molly said. She swallowed. "Why do your eyes do that?"

There was a lengthy pause before Thomas answered, "They aren't my eyes, Miss Carpenter. They're my demon's eyes. The better to see you with."

"Demon . . ." Molly said. She was staring. "You're hungry. Like, the vampire way."

"After a fight like that?" Thomas said. "I'm barely sane."

Both of them should have known better. Every time a wizard looks another person in the eyes, he runs the risk of triggering a deeper seeing, a voyeuristic peep through the windows of someone else's soul. You get a snapshot of the true nature of that person, and they get a peek back at you.

It was only the second time I'd ever seen a soulgaze happen to someone else. There was an instant where both of them locked their eyes on each other's. Molly's eyes widened suddenly, like a frightened doe's, and she jerked in a sharp breath. She stared at him with her chin twisting to one side, as if she were trying—and failing—to look away.

Thomas went unnaturally still, and though his eyes also widened, it reminded me more of a cat crouching down in anticipation, just before pouncing on its prey.

Molly's back arched slightly and a soft moan escaped her. Her eyes filled with tears.

"God," she said. "God. No. No, you're beautiful. God, you hurt so much, need so much. . . . Let me help you. . . ." She fumbled for his hand.

Thomas never moved as her fingers touched his. Not a muscle. His eyes closed very slowly.

"Miss Carpenter," he whispered, "do not touch me. Please."

"No, it's all right," Molly said. "It's all right. I'm here."

Thomas's hand moved too quickly to be seen. He caught her wrist in his pale fingers, and she let out a short gasp. He opened his eyes and focused on hers, and Molly began to breathe harder. The tips of her breasts showed against her shirt and her mouth opened with another soft moan.

I think I made a quiet sound of protest. Neither of them heard it.

He leaned closer, the motion feline and serpentine at the same time. Molly began trembling. She licked her lips and began to slowly lean forward, toward him. Their lips met, and her body quivered, tensed, and then went rigid. A breathless sound escaped her as her eyes rolled back in her head, and Thomas was suddenly pressed against her. Molly's hips rocked against his. Her hands came up and began clawing at his shirt, tearing the buttons from the silk so that her palms could flatten against his naked chest.

Mouse hit Thomas like a wrecking ball.

The big dog's charge tore my brother away from my apprentice and slammed him into the brick of the fireplace. Thomas let out a sudden snarl of pure, surprised rage, but Mouse had him by the throat before he could recover.

The big dog's jaws didn't snap closed—but the tips of his teeth sank into flesh, and he held Thomas there, a growl bubbling from his chest. My brother's hand flailed, reaching for the poker that hung beside the fireplace. Mouse took note of it and gave Thomas a warning shake, his teeth sinking a tiny bit deeper. My brother didn't quit reaching for the weapon, and I saw the tension gathering in the big dog's body.

I came rushing back into myself all at once and said, weakly, "Thomas."

He froze. Mouse cocked an ear toward me.

"Thomas," I croaked, "don't. He's protecting the girl."

Thomas let out a gasping, pained sound. Then I saw him grimace and force himself to relax, to surrender. His body slowly eased away from its fighting tension, and he held up both hands palms out, and lifted his chin a little higher.

"Okay," he rasped. "Okay. It's okay now."

"Show me your eyes," I said.

He did. They were a shade of pale, pale grey, with only flecks of reflective hunger dancing through them.

I grunted. "Mouse."

Mouse backed off slowly, gradually easing the pressure of his jaws, gently taking his teeth out of Thomas's throat. He took a pair of steps back and then sat down, head lowered to a fighting crouch that kept his own throat covered. He kept facing Thomas, made no sound, and didn't move. It looked odd and eerie on the big dog.

"Can't stay here," Thomas said. The bite wounds in his throat looked swollen, angry. Their edges were slightly blackened, as if the dog's teeth had been red-hot. "Not with her like that." He closed his eyes. "I didn't mean to. Sorry."

I looked at Molly, who was curled into a fetal position and shaking, still breathing hard.

"Get out," I said.

"How will you—"

"Thomas," I said, and my voice was slightly stronger, hot with anger. "You could have hurt Molly. You could have killed her. My only defense is down here babysitting you instead of standing guard. Get out. You're no good to me like this."

Mouse let out another warning growl.

"I'm sorry," Thomas said again. "I'm sorry."

Then he eased around Mouse and departed, his feet making little sound as he went up the stairs.

I sat there for a moment, hurting in practically every sense. My entire body tingled with unpleasant pinpricks, as though it had gone to sleep and was only now feeling the return of circulation. The soulfire. I must have pushed too much of it through me. Terror-adrenaline must have kept me rolling for a little while, but after that, I'd collapsed into pure passivity.

Terror on behalf of my brother and Molly had given me back my voice, my will, but it might not last. It hurt to sit upright. It hurt to breathe. Moving anything hurt, and *not* moving anything hurt.

So, I supposed, I might as well be moving.

I tried to get up, but my left leg wasn't having any of it, and I was lucky not to end up on the floor. Without being told, Mouse got up and hurried into my room. I heard some heavy thumping as he rustled around under my bed, which had required him to lift it onto his massive shoulders. He came out a moment later, carrying one of my crutches, left over from injuries past, in his teeth.

"Who's a good dog?" I said.

He wagged his tail at me and went back for the other one. Once I had them both, I was able to get up and gimp my way over to the kitchen. Tylenol 3 is good stuff, but it is also illegal stuff to have without a prescription if you aren't Canadian, so it was currently buried in my godmother's insane garden. I took a big dose of Tylenol the original, since I didn't have my Tylenol 3 or its lesser-known, short-lived cousin, Tylenol Two: The Pain Strikes Back.

I realized that I was telling Mouse all of this out loud as I thought it, which had the potential to become awkward if it should become a habit. Once that was done, and I'd drunk a third glass of water, I moved over to Molly and checked her pulse. It was steady. Her breathing had slowed. Her eyes were slightly open and unfocused.

I muttered under my breath. The damned girl was going to get herself killed. This was the second time she'd come very close to being fed upon by a vampire, though admittedly the first had been in a vicarious fashion. Still, it couldn't be good for her to be hit with it again. And if Thomas had actually begun to feed on her, there was no telling what it might do to her.

"Molly," I said. Then louder, "Molly!"

She drew in a sudden little breath and blinked up at me.

"You're smearing paint all over my rug," I said wearily.

She sat up, looking down at herself and at the green paint smeared all over her. She looked up at me again, dazed. "What just happened?"

"You soulgazed Thomas. You both lost perspective. He nearly ate you." I poked her with a crutch. "Mouse saved you. Get up."

"Right," she said. "Right." She stood up very slowly, wincing and rubbing at one wrist. "Um. Is . . . is Thomas all right?"

"Mouse nearly killed him," I said. "He's scared, ashamed, half out of his mind with hunger, and gone." I thumped her leg lightly with my crutch. "What were you thinking?"

Molly shook her head. "If you'd seen . . . I mean, if you'd seen him. Seen how lonely he was. Felt how much pain he was in, how *empty* he feels, Harry . . ." She teared up again. "I've never felt anything so horrible in my life. Or seen anyone braver."

"Apparently, you figured you'd help him out by letting him rip the life out of you."

She faced me for a moment, then flushed and looked away. "He . . . It doesn't get ripped out. It gets . . ." She blushed. "I think the only phrase that works is 'licked away.' Like licking the frosting off of a cake. Or . . . or the candy coating off of one of those lollipops."

"Except that as soon as you find out how many licks it takes him to get to your creamy center, you're dead," I said. "Or insane. Which is somewhat chilling to consider, given the things you can do. So I repeat." I thumped her leg with the tip of my crutch on each word. "What. Were. You. Thinking."

"It won't happen again," she said, but I saw her shiver as she said it.

I grunted skeptically, staring down at her.

Molly wasn't ready. Not for something like we were about to do. She had too much confidence and not nearly enough sound judgment.

It was frustrating. By the time I had been her age, I had finished my apprenticeship in private investigation and was opening my own business. And I had been living under the Doom of Damocles for the better part of a decade.

Of course, I had an experience advantage on Molly. I had made my first dark compact, with my old master Justin DuMorne, when I was ten or eleven, though I hadn't known what I was getting into at the time. I'd made a second one with the Leanansidhe when I was sixteen. And I'd wound up under round-the-clock observation from the paranoid Warden Morgan.

It had been a brief lifetime for me, at that point, but absolutely chock-full of lessons in the school of hard knocks. I had made plenty of dumb decisions of my own by then, and somehow managed to survive them.

But I also hadn't been dallying around in situations as hot as this one was. A troll under a bridge or an upset spirit or two was as bad as it got. It had prepared me for what I faced today.

Molly was facing it cold. She'd been burned once before, but it had taken me more than one attempt to learn that lesson.

She might not survive her next test.

She looked up at me and asked, "What?"

"We need to move," I said. "I met the Eebs while you

three were playing with the Ik'k' . . . with the Ik'koo-koo-kachoo . . ." I scrunched up my nose, trying to remember the name of the creature, and couldn't. "With the Ick," I said, "and they were charming in an entirely amoral, murderous sort of way. Thomas was right: They'll be after me, looking for an opening. We're going."

"Where?"

"St. Mary's," I said. "The Red Court can't walk on holy ground, and Susan knows I've used it as a fallback position before. She and Martin can catch up to me there. And I've got to get some rest."

She rose, nodding. "Okay. Okay, I'll get you a change of clothes, all right?"

"Call a cab first," I said. "And pack the Tylenol. And some of Mouse's food."

"Right. Okay."

I leaned on my crutches and stayed standing while she bustled around the room. I didn't want to risk sitting down again. The Tylenol had taken the worst edge off the pain, and my thoughts, though tired and sluggish, seemed to be firmly connected to my body again. I didn't want to risk relaxing into lassitude.

"Say that five times fast," I murmured, and tried. It was something to do that I couldn't screw up too badly.

A while later, Mouse made a whuffing sound from the top of the stairs outside, and Molly plodded up them wearily. "Cab's here, Harry," she called.

I got myself moving. Stairs on crutches isn't fun, but I'd done it before. I took my time, moving slowly and steadily.

"Look out!" she yelled.

A bottle smashed against the top interior wall of the stairwell, and its contents splashed all over the place, fire spreading over them as they did. Ye olde Molotov cocktail, still a formidable weapon even after a century of use. There's more to one of those things than simple burning fuel. Fire that hot sucks the oxygen out of the air around it, especially when it has a nice, dank stairway to use as a chimney. And you needn't get splattered by the spilling fuel to get burned. When a fire is hot enough, it'll burn exposed flesh from inches or feet away, turning the atmosphere around it into an oven.

I was only on the second or third step up from the bottom, but I staggered back before anything could get roasted—been there, done that, not going back. I tried to fall onto my uninjured side, figuring that it deserved a chance to join in the fun, too. I landed more or less the way I wanted to, and it hurt like hell, but at least I didn't faint. I screamed, though, a number of vitriolic curses, as fire roared above me, leaping from my little stairwell to the rest of the house, chewing into the old wood like a hungry, living thing.

"Harry!" Molly called from somewhere beyond the flames. "Harry!"

Mouse let out a heartsick-sounding bay, and I saw fire beginning to climb the sides of the house. The fire was starting from the outside. By the time it started setting off fire alarms, it would be too late to escape.

At this time of night, somewhere up above me, Mrs. Spunkelcrief was asleep and unaware of the danger. And on the second floor, my elderly neighbors, the Willoughbys, would be in similar straits, and all because they were unlucky enough to live in the same building as me.

I'd dropped one of my crutches up on the stairs and one end had caught on fire. There was no way I was pulling much in the way of magic out of my hat, not until I'd had food and some rest. Hell's bells, for that matter, I didn't know if I could *stand up* on my own.

But if I didn't do something, three innocent people—plus myself—were going to die in a fire.

"Come on, Harry," I said. "You aren't half-crippled. You're half-competent."

The fire roared higher, and I didn't believe myself for a second.

But I put my hands on the ground and began heaving myself upright. "Do or die, Dresden," I told myself fiercely, and firmly ignored the fear pounding in my chest. "Do or die."

The dying really did seem a lot more likely.

Chapter

Twenty-eight

I looked up at my apartment's ceiling, hobbling along on my crutch. I found the spot I thought would be the middle of Mrs. S's living room and noted that one of my old sofas was directly beneath it.

Using the crutch as a lever, I slipped one end of it behind one of my big old bookcases and heaved. The bookcase shuddered and then fell in a great crash of paperback novels and hardwood shelves, smashing down onto my couch. I grunted in satisfaction and climbed up onto the fallen bookcase, using its back as a ramp. I crawled painfully up to the end of the ramp, lifted my right hand, and triggered one of the rings I wore there.

They were magical tools, created to retain a little bit of kinetic energy every time I moved my arm, and when they were operating at capacity they packed one hell of a lot of energy—and I had freshly charged them up on the punching bag. When I cut loose with the ring, invisible force struck my ceiling, blowing completely through it and through the floor of the room above, tearing at faded carpeting the color of dried mustard.

I adjusted my aim a little and blew the entire charge out of the ring on the next finger, and another one after that, each one blasting the opening wider, until it was big enough that I thought I ought to fit through it.

I hooked the padded end of my crutch over the broken end of a thick floor joist and used it to haul myself up to my good leg. Then I tossed the crutch up through the hole and reached up to pull myself through.

Mister let out a harsh, worried meow, and I froze in place. My cat was still in my apartment.

I looked wildly around the room for him, and found him crouching in his usual favorite spot atop the highest bookshelf. His hair stood on end and every muscle on him seemed tight and strained.

I'd already tossed the crutch through. If I went back for him, I might not be able to stand once I'd made it back to the ramp. I had no idea how I'd hold him while climbing up, assuming I could do it at all. Mister weighs the next-best thing to thirty pounds. That's one hell of a handicap on a pull-up.

For that matter, if the fire spread as quickly as I thought it would, the extra time it took might mean that I wound up trapped with no exit. And there would be no one to help Mr. S and the Willoughbys.

I loved my cat. He was family.

But as I stared at him I knew that I couldn't help him.

"Unless you use your flipping *brain*, Harry," I snapped at myself. "Duh. Never quit. *Never* quit."

The sunken windows around my apartment were too small to be a means of escape for me, but Mister could clear them with ease. I took aim, used a single charge from my ring, and shattered the sunken window closest to the cat. Mister took the hint at once, and prowled down the tops of two bookcases. It was a five-foot leap from the top of the shelf to the window well, but Mister made it look casual. I felt myself grinning fiercely as he vanished through the broken window and into the cool air of the October night.

Stars and stones, at least I'd accomplished one positive thing that day.

I turned, reached up into the opening with my arms straight over my head, and hopped as hard as I could with one leg. It wasn't much of a leap, but it was enough to let me get my arms through and my elbows wedged against either side of the opening. My ribs were on fire as I kicked and wriggled my way up through the hole and hauled myself into Mrs. Spunkelcrief's living room.

It had last been decorated in the seventies, judging by the mustard yellow carpet and the olive green wallpaper, and it was full of furniture and knickknacks. I dragged myself all the way through the hole, knocking over a little display stand of collector's plates as I did. The room was dimly lit by the growing flames outside. I grabbed my crutch, climbed to my feet through screaming pain, and hobbled farther into the apartment.

I found Mrs. S in the apartment's one bedroom. She was sleeping mostly sitting up, propped on a pile of pillows. Her old television was on, sans volume, with subtitles appearing at the bottom of the screen. I gimped over to her and shook her gently.

She woke up with a start and slugged me with one tiny fist. I fell backward onto my ass, more out of pure surprise than anything else, and grimaced in pain—from the fall, not the punch. I shook it off and looked up again, to find the little old lady holding a little revolver, probably a .38. In her hands, it looked magnum-sized. She held it like she knew what she was doing, too, in two hands, peering down at me through the gun's sights.

"Mr. Dresden!" she said, her voice squeaky. "How dare you!"

"Fire!" I said. "Mrs. S, there's a fire! A fire!"

"Well, I won't fire if you just sit still," she said in a querulous tone. She took her left hand off the gun and reached for her phone. "I'm calling the police. You hold real still or I gotta shoot you. No bluff. This here is a grandfathered gun. Legal and proper."

I tried to point toward the bedroom door without moving my body, indicating it with my fingertips and tilts of my head.

"Are you on *drugs*, boy?" she said, punching numbers on the phone without looking. "You are acting like a crazy junkie. Coming into an old woman's . . ." She glanced past me, where there was some fairly bright light flickering wildly in the hallway outside the bedroom.

I kept wiggling my fingers and nodding toward it, desperately.

Mrs. S's eyes widened and her mouth dropped open. "Fire!" she said abruptly. "There's a fire right there!"

I nodded frantically.

She lowered the gun and started kicking her way clear of covers and pillows. She wore flannel pajamas, but grabbed at a blue robe in any case and hurried toward the door. "Come on, boy! There's a fire!"

I struggled desperately to my feet and started hobbling out. She turned to look at me, apparently surprised that she was moving faster than I was. You could hear the fire now, and smoke had begun to thicken the air.

I pointed up at the ceiling and shouted, "The Willoughbys! Willoughbys!"

She looked up. "Lord God almighty!" She turned and hurried down the hall, coming within ten feet of a wall that was already becoming a sheet of flame. She grabbed at something, cursed, then pulled her robe down over her hand and picked up something, using the material as an oven mitt. She hurried over to me with a ring of keys. "Come on! The front door's already going up! Out the back!"

We both hurried out the back door of the house and into its minuscule little yard, and I saw at once that the entire front side of the house was aflame.

The stairs up to the Willoughbys' place were already on fire.

I turned to her and shouted, "Ladder! Where's the ladder? I need to use the ladder!"

"No!" she shouted back. "You need to use the ladder!"

Good grief.

"Okay!" I shouted back, and gave her a thumbs-up.

She hustled back to the little storage shed in the backyard. She picked a key and unlocked it. I swung the door open and seized the metal extending ladder I used to put up and take down Christmas lights every year. I ditched my crutch and used the ladder itself to take some of the weight. I went as fast as I could, but it seemed to take forever to position the ladder under the Willoughbys' bedroom windows.

Mrs. Spunkelcrief handed me a loose brick from a little flower planter's wall and said, "Here. I can't climb this thing. My hip."

I took the brick and dropped it in my duster pocket. Then I started humping myself up the ladder, taking a grip with both hands, then hopping up with a painful little jump. Repeat, each time growing more painful, more difficult. I clenched my teeth over the screams.

And then there was a window in front of me.

I got the brick out of my pocket, hauled off, and shattered the window.

Black smoke bellowed out, catching me on the inhale. I started coughing viciously, my voice strangled as I tried to shout, "Mr. and Mrs. Willoughby! Fire! You've got to get out! Fire! Come to the window and down the ladder!"

I heard two people coughing and choking. They were trying to say, "Help!"

Something, maybe the little propane tank on Mrs. Spunkelcrief's grill, exploded with a noise like a dinosaur-sized watermelon hitting the ground. The concussion knocked Mrs. S down—and kicked the bottom of the ladder out from under me.

I fell. It was a horrible, helpless feeling, my body twisting uselessly as I tried to land well—but I'd had no warning at all, and it was a futile attempt. The small of my back hit the brick planter, and I achieved a new personal best for pain.

"Oh, God in Heaven," Mrs. Spunkelcrief said. She knelt beside me. "Harry?"

Somewhere, sirens had begun to wail. They wouldn't get there in time for the Willoughbys.

"Trapped," I choked out, as soon as I was able to breathe again. "They're up there, calling for help."

The fire roared louder and grew brighter.

Mrs. S stared up at the window. She grabbed the ladder and wrestled it all the way back up into position, though the effort left her panting. Then she tried to put a foot up on the first step. She grasped the ladder, began to shift her weight—and groaned as her leg buckled and she fell to the ground.

She screamed, agony in her quavering voice, "Oh, God in Heaven, help us!"

A young black man in a dark, knee-length coat hurdled the hedges at the back of the yard and bounded onto the ladder. He was built like a professional lineman, moved more quickly than a linebacker, and started up the ladder like it was a broad staircase. The planet's only Knight of the Cross flashed me a quick grin on the way up. "Dresden!"

"Sanya!" I howled. "Two! There're two of them in the bedroom!"

"*Da*, two!" he replied, his deep voice booming. The curving saber blade of *Esperacchius* rode at his hip and he managed it with thoughtless, instinctive skill as he went through the window. He was back a moment later, with Mrs. Willoughby draped over one shoulder, while he supported most of Mr. Willoughby's staggering body with the other.

Sanya went first, the old woman hanging limply over his shoulder, so that he could help Mr. Willoughby creep out the window and onto the ladder. They came down slowly and carefully, and as Sanya carefully laid the old woman out onto the grass, the first of the emergency response crews arrived.

"God in Heaven," Mrs. S said, weeping openly as she put her hand on Sanya's arm. "He must have sent you to us, son."

Sanya smiled at her as he helped Mr. Willoughby lower himself to the ground. Then he turned to my land-lady and said, his Russian accent less heavy than the last time I had seen him, "It was probably just a coincidence, ma'am."

"I don't believe in those," said Mrs. Spunkelcrief. "Bless you, son," she said, and hugged him hard. Her arms couldn't have gotten around half of him, but Sanya returned the hug gently for a moment.

"Ma'am," he said, "you should direct the medical technicians to come back here."

"Thank you, thank you," she said, releasing him.

"But now I have to go get those ambulance boys over here." She paused and gave me a smile. "And thank you, Harry. Such a good boy." Then she hurried away.

Mouse came racing around the side of the house where Mrs. S had just gone, and rushed to stand over me, lapping at my face. Molly wasn't far behind. She let out a little cry and threw her arms around my shoulders. "Oh, God, Harry!" She shouldered Mouse aside and squeezed tight for several seconds. She looked up and said, "Sanya? What are you doing here?"

"Hey, hey," I said. "Take it easy."

Molly eased up on her hug. "Sorry."

"Sanya," I said, nodding to him. "Thanks for your help."

"Part of the job, *da*?" he replied, grinning. "Glad to help."

"All the same," I said, my voice rough, "thank you. If anything had happened to them . . ."

"Oh, Harry," Molly said. She hugged me again.

"Easy, padawan, easy," I said quietly. "Think you should be careful."

She drew back with a frown. "Why?"

I took a slow breath and said, very quietly, "I can't feel my legs."

Chapter

Twenty-nine

It didn't take me long to talk Sanya and Molly out of taking me to the hospital. The Eebs, as it turned out, had shown up, pitched their firebomb from a moving car, and kept going, a modus operandi that was consistent with the earlier attempt on my life, except this time they'd been identified. Molly's description of the thrower was a dead ringer for Esteban.

I had to admit, the vampire couple had a very practical long-term approach to violence—striking at weakness and harassing the victim while exposing themselves to minimal risk. If I'd been a couple of steps higher up when that Molotov hit, I'd be dead, or covered in third-degree burns. Individually, their attempts might not enjoy a high success rate—but they needed to get it right only once.

It would be consistent with that practical, cold-blooded style to keep an eye on the hospitals in order to come finish me off—during surgery, for example, or while I was still in recovery afterward. Sanya, though, had EMT training of some kind. He calmly stole a backboard out of an open ambulance while its techs were seeing to the Willoughbys, and they loaded me onto it in a procedure that Sanya said would protect my spine. It seemed kind of "too little, too late" to me, but I was too tired to rib him over it.

I couldn't feel anything below the waist, but that apparently didn't mean that the rest of me got to stop hurting. I felt them carrying the board out, and when I opened my eyes it was only to see nearly a third of the building give way and crash down into the basement—into my apartment. The building was obviously a lost cause. The firemen were focusing on containing the blaze and preventing it from spreading to the nearby homes.

They loaded the backboard into the rental minivan Sanya had, by happy coincidence, been given at the airport when he arrived, at no additional fee, in order to substitute for the subcompact he'd reserved but couldn't have. As it drove away during the confusion and before the cops could lock everything down, I got to watch my home burn down through the back window of the van.

Even after we were several blocks away, I could see the smoke rising up in a black column. I wondered how much of that smoke was made of my books. My second-hand guitar. My clothes. My comfy old furniture. My bed. My blankets. My Mickey Mouse alarm clock. The equipment in my lab that I'd worked so hard to attain or create—the efforts of years of patient effort, endless hours of concentration and spellcraft.

Gone.

Fire is as destructive spiritually as it is materially, a purifying force that can devour and scatter magical energy. In a fire that large everything I'd ever built, including purely magical constructs, would be destroyed.

Dammit.

Dammit, but I hated vampires.

I'd had one hell of a day, all in all, but practically the only thing I had left to me was my pride. I didn't want anyone to see me crying. So I just kept quiet in the back of the van, while Mouse lay very close to me.

At some point, sorrow became sleep.

I woke up in the utility room at St. Mary of the Angels, where Father Forthill kept several spare folding cots and the bedding to go with them. I'd visited several times in the past. St. Mary's was a surprisingly stout bastion against supernatural villains of nearly any stripe. The ground beneath it was consecrated, as was every wall, door, floor, and window, blessed by prayers and stately rituals, Masses, and communions over and over through the decades, until that gentle, positive energy had permeated the ground and the very stone from which the church was built.

I felt safer, but only a little. Vampires might not be able to set foot on the holy ground, but they knew that, and someone like the Eebs would certainly take that into account. Hired human killers could be just as dangerous as vampires, if not more so, and the protective aura around the building couldn't make them blink an eye.

And, I supposed, they could always just set it on fire and burn it down around me if they really, *really* wanted to get me. I tried to imagine myself a century from now, still dodging vampires and getting my home burned to the ground on an irregular basis.

No way in hell was I gonna accept that. I'd have to deal with the Eeb problem.

And then I remembered my legs. I reached a hand down to touch my thigh.

I felt nothing. Absolutely nothing. It felt like touching the limb of someone else entirely. I tried to move my legs and nothing happened. Maybe I'd been too ambitious. I pulled at my blanket until I could see my toes. I tried wiggling them. I failed.

I could feel the backboard beneath me, and the band around my head that kept me from moving it to look around. I gave up on my legs with a sharp surge of frustration and lifted my eyes to the ceiling.

There was a piece of paper taped to it, directly over my head. Molly's handwriting in black marker was scrawled in large letters across it: *Harry. Don't try to get up, or move your neck or back. We're checking in on you several times an hour. Someone will be there soon.*

There was a candle burning nearby, on a folding table. It was the room's only light. I couldn't tell how long it had been burning, but it looked like a fairly long-lived candle, and it was nearly gone. I breathed in and out steadily, through my nose, and caught some half-remembered scents. Perfume of some kind, maybe? Or maybe just the scent of new leather, still barely tinged with the harsh aroma of tanning compounds and the gummy scent of dye. Plus I could smell the dusty old room. The church had only recently begun to use its heating system for the winter. I could smell the warm scent of singed dust that always emerges from the vents the first time anyone turns on a heater after it's been unneeded for a while.

I was glad that I wasn't cold. I wouldn't have been able to do anything about it, otherwise.

The candle guttered out and left me alone in the dark.

In my memories, a bloody old caricature of a man, his skin more liver spots than not, leered at me in mad satisfaction and whispered, "Die alone."

I shivered and shook the image away. Cassius was thoroughly dead. I knew that. An outcast member of the society of demented freaks known as the Knights of the Blackened Denarius, Cassius had thrown in with an insane necromancer in order to get a chance to even a score with me. He'd come within a hairbreadth of dissecting me. I was able to take him down in the end—and he'd uttered a death curse as he croaked. Such a curse, a spell uttered in the last instants of life, could have hideous effects upon its victim. His curse, for me to die alone, was pretty vague as such things went. It might not even have had enough power or focus to take.

Sure. Maybe it hadn't.

"Hello?" I said to the darkness. "Is anyone there?"

There wasn't.

Die alone.

"Stop that," I snapped out loud. "Control yourself, Dresden."

That sounded like good advice. So I started taking deep, steady, controlled breaths and tried to focus my thoughts. Focus. Forethought. Reason. Sound judgment. That was what was going to get me through this.

Fact one: My daughter was still in danger.

Fact two: I was hurt. Maybe badly. Maybe forever. Even the efficient resilience of a wizard's body had its limits, and a broken spine was quite likely beyond them.

Fact three: Susan and Martin could not get the girl out on their own.

Fact four: There wasn't a lot of help forthcoming. Maybe, with Sanya along, the suicidal mission could be considered only mostly suicidal. After all, the Knights of the Cross were a big deal. Three of them were, apparently, enough Knights to protect the whole world. For the past few years, the dark-skinned Russian had been covering all three positions, and apparently doing it well. Which made a vague amount of sense, I suppose—Sanya was the wielder of *Esperacchius*, the Sword of Hope. We needed hope right now. At least, I did.

Fact five: I had missed the rendezvous with Ebenezar many hours ago. I'd never intended to go, and there was nothing I could do about the fact that he was going to be upset—but my absence had probably cost me the support of the Grey Council, such as it was.

Fact six: Sanya, Susan, Martin, and whatever other scanty help I could drum up couldn't get to Chichén Itzá without me—and I sure as hell couldn't get there in the shape I was in. According to the stored memories in my mother's jewel, the Way required a swim.

Fact seven: I was going to Show Up for my daughter, and to hell with what it would cost.

And there were only so many options open to me.

I took the least terrifying one. I closed my eyes, steadied my breathing, and began to picture a room in my mind. My now-ruined improved summoning circle was in the floor. Candles were lit at five equidistant points around it. The air smelled of sandalwood incense and burned wax. It took a few minutes to picture it all, in perfect detail, and to hold it in my mind, as rock solid to my imagination as the actual room the construct was replacing.

That took considerable energy and discipline.

Magic doesn't require props to function. That's a conceit that has been widely propitiated by the wizarding community over the centuries. It helped prove to frightened villagers, inquisitions, and whoever else might be worried that a person was clearly not a wizard. Otherwise he'd have all kinds of wizardly implements necessary to his craft.

Magic doesn't require the props, but magic is wrought by people, and people need them. Each prop has a symbolic as well as a practical reason for being a part of any spell. Simple stuff, lighting candles and the like, could be accomplished neatly in the mind, eventually becoming a task as easy and thoughtless as tying one's shoe.

Once you got into the complicated stuff, though, you had an enormous number of things to keep track of in your mind, envisioning flows of energy, their manipulation, and so on. If you have the real props, they serve as a sort of mnemonic device: You attach a certain image to the prop, in your head, and every time you see or touch that prop, the image is packaged along with it. Simple.

Except that I didn't have any props.

I was winging the whole thing. Pure imagination. Pure concentration.

Pure arrogance, really. But I was at a lower rock bottom than normal.

In my thoughts I lit the candles, walking slowly around the circle in a clockwise fashion—or deosil, as the fairy tales, Celtic songs, and certain strains of Wicca refer to it—gradually powering up the energy it required to operate. I realized that I had forgotten to make the floor out of anything specific, in my head, and the notional floor space, from horizon to horizon, suddenly became the linoleum from my first ratty Chicago apartment. Hideous stuff, green lines on a grey background, but simple to envision.

I imagined performing the spell without ever moving my body, envisioned every last detail, everything from the way the floor dug unpleasantly into my knees as I began to the slight clumsiness in the fingers of my left hand, which always seemed to be a little twitchy whenever I got nervous.

I closed the circle. I gathered the power. And then, when all was prepared, when I held absolutely everything in my imagination so vividly that it seemed more real than the room around me, I slid Power into my voice and called quietly, "*Uriel*, come forth."

For a second, I couldn't tell whether the soft white light had appeared only in my head or if it was actually in the room. Then I realized that it stabbed at my eyes painfully. It was real.

I kept the spell going in my head, easier now that it was a tableau. I just had to keep my concentration focused.

I squinted into the light and saw a tall young man there. He wore jeans and a T-shirt and a farmer's duck coat. His blond hair fell over his eyes, but they were blue and bright and guileless as he looked around the room. He stuck his hands into his coat pockets and nodded slowly. "I was wondering when I'd get this call."

"You know what's happening, then?" I asked.

"Yes, yes," he answered, with perhaps the slightest bit of impatience in his tone. He turned his gaze to me and frowned abruptly. He leaned forward slightly, peering at me.

I carefully fortified and maintained the image of the restraining magical circle in my imagination. When an entity was called forth, the circle was the only thing protecting the caller from its wrath.

"Please, Dresden," the archangel Uriel said. "It's a very nice circle, but you can't honestly think that it's any kind of obstacle to me."

"I like to play it safe," I said.

Uriel let out a most unangelic snort. Then he nodded his head and said, "Ah, I see."

"See what?"

He paused and said, "Why you called me, of course. Your back."

I grunted. It was more effort than usual. "How bad is it?"

"Broken," he said. "It's possible that, as a wizard, your body might be able to knit the ends back together over forty or fifty years. But there's no way to be sure."

"I need it to be better," I said. "Now."

"Then perhaps you shouldn't have climbed that ladder in your condition."

I let out a snarl and tried to turn toward him. I just sort of flopped a little. My body never left the surface of the backboard.

"Don't," Uriel said calmly. "It isn't worth getting upset over."

"Not upset?!" I demanded. "My little girl is going to die!"

"You made your choices," Uriel told me. "One of them led you here." He spread his hands. "That's a fair ball, son. Nothing to do now but play it out."

"But you could fix me if you wanted to."

"My wishes have nothing to do with it," he said calmly. "I could heal you if I were meant to do so. Free will must take precedence if it is to have meaning."

"You're talking philosophy," I said. "I'm telling you that a child is going to die."

Uriel's expression darkened for a moment. "And I am telling you that I am very limited in terms of what I can do to help you," he said. "Limited, in fact, to what I have already done."

"Yeah," I said. "Soulfire. Just about killed myself with that one. Thanks."

"No one is making you use it, Dresden. It's your choice."

"I played ball with you when you needed help," I said. "And this is how you repay me?"

Uriel rolled his eyes. "You tried to send me a *bill*."

"You want to set a price, feel free," I said. "I'll pay it. Whatever it takes."

The archangel watched me, his eyes calm and knowing and sad. "I know you will," he said quietly.

"Dammit," I said, my voice breaking. Tears started from my eyes. The colors and lines in my imagination began to blur. "Please."

Uriel seemed to shiver at the sound of the word. He turned his face from me, clearly uncomfortable. He was silent.

"Please," I said again. "You know who I am. You know I'd rather have my nails torn out than beg. And I am begging you. I am not strong enough to do this on my own."

Uriel listened, never quite looking at me, and then shook his head slowly. "I have already done what I can."

"But you've done nothing," I said.

"From your point of view, I suppose that's true." He stroked his chin with a thumb, frowning in thought. "Though . . . I suppose it isn't too much of an imbalance for you to know . . ."

My eyes were starting to cramp from looking to one side so fiercely without being able to move my head. I bit my lip and waited.

Uriel took a deep breath and looked as if he were considering his words with care. "Your daughter, Maggie, is alive and well. For now."

My heart skipped a beat.

My daughter.

He'd called her *my daughter.*

"I know you wanted Susan to be the woman you loved and remembered. Wanted to be able to trust her. But even if you weren't admitting it to yourself, you had to wonder, on some level. I don't blame you for it," he said. "Especially after those tracking spells failed. It's natural. But yes." He met my eyes. "Flesh of your flesh and bone of your bone. Your daughter."

"Why tell me that?" I asked him.

"Because I have done all that I can," he said. "From here, it is up to you. You are Maggie's only hope." He started to turn away, then paused and said, "Consider Vadderung's words carefully."

I blinked. "You know Od . . . Vadderung?"

"Of course. We're in similar fields of work, after all."

I exhaled wearily, and stopped even trying to hold the spell. "I don't understand."

Uriel nodded. "That's the difficult part of being mortal. Of having choice. Much is hidden from you." He sighed. "Love your child, Dresden. Everything else flows from there. A wise man said that," Uriel said. "Whatever you do, do it for love. If you keep to that, your path will never wander so far from the light that you can never return."

And as quickly as that, he was gone.

I lay in the darkness, shivering with weariness and the effort of the magic. I pictured Maggie in my head, in her little-girl dress with ribbons in her hair, like the picture.

"For you, little girl. Dad's coming."

It took me less than half a minute to restore the spell, and not much longer than that to build up the next wave of energy I would need. Until the last second, I wondered if I could actually go through with it. Then I saw a horrible image of Maggie in her dress being snatched up by a Red Court vampire, and my whole outraged being seemed to fuse into a singularity, a single white-hot pin-point of raw, unshakable will.

"Mab!" I called, my voice steady. "Mab, Queen of Air and Darkness, Queen of the Winter Court! Mab, I bid you come *forth*!"

Chapter

Thirty

The third repetition of her name hung ringing in the air, and deafening silence came after as I awaited the response.

When you trap something dangerous, there are certain fundamental precautions necessary to success. You've got to have good bait, something to draw your target in. You've got to have a good trap, something that works and works fast. And, once the target is in the trap, you've got to have a net or a cage strong enough to hold it.

Get any of those three elements wrong, and you probably won't succeed. Get two of them wrong, and you might be looking at a result far more disastrous than mere failure.

I went into this one knowing damned well that all I had was bait. Mab, for her own reasons, had wanted to suborn me into her service for years. I knew that calling her by her name and title would be enough to attract her interest. Though the mechanism of my improved summoning circle would have been a fine trap—if it still existed, I mean—the cage of my will had always been the weakest point in any such endeavor.

Bottom line, I could get the tiger to show up. Once

it was there, all I had was a really good chalk drawing of a pit on the sidewalk and "Nice kitty."

I wasn't going into it blind and ignorant, though. I was desperate, but not stupid. I figured I had the advantage of position. Mab couldn't kill a mortal. She could only make him desperately wish he was dead, instead of enduring her attentions. I didn't have a lot to lose. She couldn't make me any more useless to my daughter than I was already.

I waited, in perfect darkness, for the mistress of every wicked fairy in every dark tale humanity had ever whispered in the night to put in an appearance.

Mab didn't disappoint me.

Surprise me, yes. But she didn't disappoint.

Stars began to appear in front of my eyes.

I figured that was probably a really bad thing, for a moment. But they didn't spin around in lazy, dizzy motion like the kind of stars that mean your brain is smothering. They instead burned steady and cold and pure above me, five stars like jewels on the throat of Lady Night.

Seconds later, a cold wind touched my face, and I became conscious of a hard smoothness beneath me. I laid my hands carefully flat, but I didn't feel the cot and the backboard under me. Instead, my fingers touched only cold, even stone, a planar surface that seemed level beneath my entire body. I wriggled my foot and confirmed that there was stone beneath it there, too.

I stopped and realized that I could feel my foot. I could move it.

My whole body was there. And it was naked. I wavered between yelping at the cold suddenly being visited upon my ass, and yelling in joy that I could feel it at all.

I saw land to one side and scrambled to get off the cold slab beneath me, crouching down and hanging on to the edge of the slab for balance.

This wasn't reality, then. This was a dream, or a vision, or something that was otherwise in between the mortal world and the spiritual realm. That made sense. My physical body was still back in St. Mary's, lying still and breathing deeply, but my mind and my spirit were here.

Wherever "here" was.

My eyes adjusted to the darkness and I saw gentle mist and fog hanging in the air. Boiling clouds let a flash of moonlight in, and it played like a spotlight over the hilltop around me, and upon the ancient table of stone beside me. The moon's touch made deeply carved runes all around the table's edge dance with flickers of illumination, writing done in some language I did not know.

Then I understood. Mab had created this place for our meeting. It was known as the Valley of the Stone Table. It was a broad, bowl-shaped valley, I knew, though the mist hid most of it from me. In its exact center stood a mound maybe fifty feet across and twelve feet high at its center. Atop the mound stood the massive slab of stone, held up on four stumpy pillars. Other stones stood in a circle around it, some tumbled down, some broken, only one remaining in Stonehenge-like lintel. The stones all shed faint illumination in shades of blue and purple and deep, deep green. Cold colors.

Winter colors.

Yeah. It was after the equinox. So that tracked. The Table was in Winter's domain. It was an ancient conduit of power, transferred in the most primitive, atavistic fashion of all—in hot blood. There were grooves and whorls in the table's surface, coated with ancient stains, and it squatted on the hill, patient and hungry and immovable, like a snapping turtle waiting for warm, vital creatures to wander too close.

The blood spilled upon this table would carry the power of its life with it, and would flow into the well of power in the control of the Winter Queen.

A movement across the table from me drew my eye. A shadow seemed to simply congeal from the mist, forming itself into a slender, feminine shape draped in a cloak and cowl. Glittering green candle flames flickered in what looked like two eyes within the cowl's hood.

My throat went dry. It took me two tries to rasp, "Queen Mab?"

The form vanished. A low, feminine laugh drifted through the mist to my right. I turned to face it.

A furious cat squall erupted from the air six inches behind me and I nearly jumped out of my skin. I spun to find nothing there, and the woman's laugh echoed around the top of the misty mound, this time more amused.

"You're enjoying this, aren't you?" I said, my heart pounding in my throat. "You told me so, didn't you?"

Whispering voices hissed among the stones around me, none of them intelligible. I saw another flicker of mocking green eyes.

"Th-this is a limited-time offer," I said, trying to make my voice sound steady. "It's been forced by circumstance. If you don't get off your royal ass and jump on it, I'm walking."

"I warned you," said a calm voice behind me. "Never let her bring you here, my godchild."

I carefully kept myself from letting out a shriek. It

would have been unwizardly. Instead, I took a deep breath and turned to find the Leanansidhe standing a few feet away, covered in a cloak the color of the last seconds of twilight, the deep blue-purple fabric hiding her completely except for her pale face inside the hood. Her green cat eyes were wide and steady, her expression solemn.

"But I'm here," I said quietly.

She nodded.

Another shadow appeared beside her, green eyes burning. Queen Mab, I presumed, and noted that she was actually a couple of inches shorter than my godmother. Of course, especially in a place like this, Mab could be as gargantuan or Lilliputian as she chose.

Probably-Mab stepped closer, still covered in shadows despite the fact that she was nearer to me than my godmother was. Her eyes grew brighter.

"So many scars," said my godmother, and her voice had changed subtly, growing cold and precise. "Your scars are beautiful things. Within and without." The shadowed figure stepped behind one of the fallen stones and emerged from behind another on the opposite side of the circle. "Yes," said the cold voice coming from the Leanansidhe's lips. "I can work with this."

I shivered. Because it was really cold and I was naked, I'm sure. I looked from the dark figure to my godmother and back, and asked, "You're still using a translator?"

"For your sake," said the cold voice, as a shadowed figure stepped behind the next menhir and appeared atop another. Walking deosil, clockwise.

Mab was closing the circle around *me*.

"Wh-why for my sake?" I asked.

The cold voice laughed through the Leanansidhe's lips. "This conversation would quickly grow tedious if you kept falling to your knees, screaming in agony and clawing at your bleeding ears, my wizard."

"Yeah. But why?" I asked. "Why would your voice hurt me?"

"Because she is angry," answered the Leanansidhe in her natural voice. "Because her voice is a part of her power, and her rage is too great to be contained."

I swallowed. Mab had spoken a few words to me a couple of years back, and I'd reacted exactly as she described. I'd lost a few minutes of time during the episode her words had provoked as well. "Rage?" I asked. "About what?"

The shadowed figure let out a spitting hiss, another feline sound that made me flinch and cringe away from it as if from the lash of a whip. My godmother jerked sharply to one side. She straightened only slowly, and as she did I saw that a long, fine cut had been drawn across one of her cheeks. Blood welled up and dripped down slowly.

My godmother bowed her head to Mab, and the cold voice came from her mouth again. "It is not for my hand-maiden to judge or question me, nor to speak for me upon her own account."

Lea bowed her head to Mab again, and not a flicker of either anger or chagrin showed in her features. Again, Mab moved from one stone to another without crossing the space in between. It should have been getting easier to deal with due to repetition. It wasn't. Each time she did it I realized that she could just as easily have reappeared behind me with foul intentions, and there wouldn't be anything I could do about it.

"There are ancient proprieties to be honored," Mab's voice said, her tone measured and somehow formal.

"There are words which must be said. Rites which must be observed. Speak your desire, mortal man."

Now I really *was* shivering with the cold. I folded my arms and hunched in on myself. It didn't help. "Power," I said.

The shadowed figure froze in place and turned to stare at me. The burning green eyes tilted slightly, as if Mab had cocked her head to one side. "Tell me why."

I fought to keep my teeth from chattering. "My body is badly injured, but I must do battle with the Red Court."

"This you have done many a time."

"This time I'm fighting all of them," I said. "The Red King and his inner circle."

The fire of her eyes intensified. "Tell me why."

I swallowed and said, "They've taken my daughter."

The shadowed figure shuddered, and her disembodied voice breathed a sigh of pleasure. "Ahhh. Yes. Not for your own life. But for your child's. For love."

I nodded jerkily.

"So many terrible things are done for love," Mab's voice said. "For love will men mutilate themselves and murder rivals. For love will even a peaceful man go to war. For love, man will destroy himself, and that right willingly." She began walking in a physical circle now, though her movements were so touched with unexpected motions and alien grace that it almost seemed that there must be something else beneath the shrouding cloak. "You know my price, mortal. Speak it."

"You want me to become the Winter Knight," I whispered.

A laugh, both merry and cold, bubbled beneath her response. "Yes."

"I will," I said. "With a condition."

"Speak it."

"That before my service begins, you restore my body to health. That you grant me time enough to rescue my daughter and take her to safety, and strength and knowledge enough to succeed. And you give me your word that you will never command me to lift my hand against those I love."

The figure kept its eerie pace as she circled me again, and the temperature seemed to drop several degrees. "You ask me to risk my Knight in a place of dire peril, to no gain for my land and people. Why should I do this?"

I looked at her steadily for a moment. Then I shrugged. "If you don't want to do business, I'll go elsewhere. I could still call Lasciel's coin to me in a heartbeat—and Nicodemus and the Denarians would be more than happy to help me. I am also one of the only people alive who knows how to pull off Kemmler's Darkhallow. So if Nicky and the Nickelheads don't want to play, I can damned well get the power for myself—and the next time I call your name, I won't need to be nearly so polite."

Mab let out a mirthless laugh through my godmother's lips. "You are spoiled for choices, my wizard. What reason have you to select me over the others?"

I grimaced. "Please don't take this as an insult. But you're the least evil of my options."

The cold voice told me nothing about her reaction. "Explain."

"The Denarians would have me growing a goatee and gloating malevolently within a few years, if I didn't break and turn into some kind of murderous tardbeast first. And I'd have to kill a lot of people outright, if I wanted to use the Darkhallow." I swallowed. "But I'll do it. If I have no other way to get my child out of their hands, I'll do it."

Silence reigned for an unbroken minute on the mound.

"Yes," mused Mab's voice. "You will, won't you? And yes, you know that I do not kill indiscriminately, nor encourage my Knight to do so." She paused and murmured, "But you have proven willing to destroy yourself in the past. You won your last confrontation with my handmaiden in just such a fashion, by partaking of the death angel. What prevents you from taking a similar action to cheat me of my prize?"

"My word," I said quietly. "I know I can't bluff you. I won't suicide. I'm here to deal in good faith."

Mab's burning eyes stared at me for a long moment. Then she began to walk again, more slowly on this, her third traversing of the circle around me. "You must understand, wizard. Once you are my Knight, once this last quest of yours is complete, you are *mine*. You will destroy what I wish you to destroy. Kill whatsoever I wish you to kill. You will be mine, blood, bone, and breath. Do you understand this?"

I swallowed. "Yes."

She nodded slowly. Then she turned to stare at the Leanansidhe.

Lea bowed her head again, and snapped her fingers.

Six cloaked figures appeared out of the mists, small, misshapen things that might have been kobolds or gnomes or any of a half dozen other servitor races of the Sidhe. I couldn't tell because the cloaks had rendered them faceless, without identity.

But I knew the man they were carrying strapped to a plank.

Like me, he was naked. He had been shorter than me, but more athletic, heavier on muscle. But that had been years ago. Now he was a wasted shell of a human being, a charcoal sketch that had been smudged by an uncaring hand. His eyes were missing. Gone, but neatly gone, as if removed surgically. There were tattoos covering his entire face, particularly his sunken eyelids, all of them simply a word in different languages and styles of lettering: *traitor*. His mouth was partly open, and his teeth had been inscribed with whorls and Celtic design, then stained with something dark and brown, turning his mouth into living scrimshaw.

His entire body, in fact, was adorned with either tattoos or artistic, ritually applied scars. He was held to the plank with seven lengths of slender silken cord, but his emaciated limbs looked like they would never have the strength to overcome even those frail bonds.

He was weeping, sobbing softly, the sound of it more like an animal in horrible pain than anything human.

"Jesus," I said, and looked away from him.

"I am somewhat proud of this," Mab's cold voice said. "To be sure, the White Christ never suffered so long or so terribly as did this traitor. Three days on a tree. Hardly enough time for a prelude. When it came to visiting agony, the Romans were hobbyists."

The servitors slid the plank up onto the stone table, positioning Slate in its center. Then they bowed toward Mab and retreated in measured silence. For a moment, the only sounds were those of a cold, gentle wind and Slate's sobs.

"For a time, I was contented to torment him to the edge of sanity. Then I set out to see how far over the edge a mortal could go." Her eyes glittered merrily in the shadows. "A pity that so little was left. And yet, he is the Winter Knight, young wizard. The vessel of my power amidst mortals, and consort to the Queens of Winter. He betrayed me. See where it has taken him."

The thing that used to be Lloyd Slate made quiet, hopeless sounds.

I trembled, afraid.

The dark shape came closer, and a pale hand emerged from the folds of cloth. Something glittered coldly in the strange light and landed in the thick grass at my feet. I bent to take it up and found an ancient, ancient knife with a simple leaf-blade design, set into a wooden handle and wrapped with cord and leather. It was, I thought, made of bronze. Its double edge had a wickedly sharp shine to it, and its needle point looked hungry, somehow.

Energy surged through the little blade, power that was unfettered and wild, that mocked limits and scoffed at restraint. Not evil, as such—but hungry and filled with the desire to partake in its portion of the cycle of life and death. It thirsted for bloodshed.

"While Lloyd Slate lives and breathes, he is my Knight," said Mab's voice. "Take Medea's bodkin, wizard. Take his life's blood."

I stood there holding the knife and looking at Lloyd Slate. The last time I'd heard him speak, he had begged me to kill him. I didn't think he'd be capable of even that much now.

"If you would be my Knight, then this is the first death I desire of you," Mab said, her voice almost gentle. She faced me across the Stone Table. "Send his power back to me. And I will render it unto thee."

I stood in the cold wind, not moving.

What I did with the next moments would determine the course of the rest of my life.

"You know this man," Mab continued, her voice still gentle. "You saw his victims. He was a murderer. A rapist. A thief. A monster in mortal flesh. He has more than earned his death."

"That isn't for me to judge," I whispered quietly. Indeed not. I was tempted to hide behind that rationale, just for a moment—just until it was done. Lie to myself, tell myself that I was his lawful, rightful executioner.

But I wasn't.

I could have told myself that I was ending his pain. That I was putting him out of his hideous misery in an act of compassion. Necessarily an act of bloodshed, but it would be quick and clean. Nothing should suffer as much as Lloyd Slate had. I could have sold myself that story.

But I didn't.

I was a man seeking power. For good reasons, maybe. But I wasn't going to lie to myself or anyone else about my actions. If I killed him, I would be taking a life, something that was not mine to take. I would be committing deliberate, calculated murder.

It was the least evil path, I told myself. Whatever else I might have done would have turned me into a monster in truth. Because of Lloyd Slate, I knew that whatever Mab might say, she did not control her Knight completely. Slate had defied her power and influence.

And look where it got him, a little voice whispered inside my head.

The full, round moon emerged from behind the clouds and bathed the whole Valley of the Stone Table in clear, cold light. The runes upon the table and the menhirs blazed into glittering, cold light.

"Wizard," whispered Mab's appropriated voice, seemingly directly into my ear, "the time has come."

My heart began pounding very hard, and I felt sick to my stomach.

"Harry Blackstone Copperfield Dresden," Mab's voice said, almost lovingly. "Choose."

Chapter

Thirty-one

I stared at the broken man. It was easy enough to envision my own mutilated face, looking blindly up from the table's surface. I took one step toward the table. Then two. Then I was standing over Lloyd Slate's broken form.

If it was a fight, I wouldn't think twice. But this man was no threat to me. He was no threat to anyone anymore. I had no right to take his life, and it was pure, overwhelming, nihilistic arrogance to say otherwise. If I killed Slate, how long would it take for my turn to come? I could be looking at myself, months or years from now.

I couldn't, any more than I could cut my own throat.

I felt my hand drop back to my side, the knife too heavy to hold before me.

Mab suddenly stood at the opposite end of the Stone Table, facing me. Her right hand moved in a simple outward motion, and the mists over the Table suddenly thickened and swirled with color and light. For a few seconds, the image was hazy. Then it snapped into focus.

A little girl crouched in the corner of a bare stone room. There was hay scattered around, and a wool blanket that looked none too clean. She had dark hair that had been up in pigtails, but wasn't anymore. One of the little pink plastic clips had evidently been lost or stolen, and now she had only one pigtail. Her face was red from crying. She'd evidently been wiping her nose on the knees of her little pink overalls. Her shirt, white with yellow flowers and a big cartoon bumblebee on it, showed stains of dirt and worse. She crouched in the tiniest ball she could make of her body, as if hoping that if something should come for her, she might be overlooked.

Her big brown eyes were quietly terrified—and I could see something familiar in them. It took me a moment to realize they reminded me of my reflection in a mirror. Other features showed themselves to me, muted shapes that maturity would bring forth eventually. The same chin and jawline Thomas and I shared. The same mouth as her mother's. Susan's straight, shining black hair. Her hands and her feet looked a little too large for her, like a puppy's paws.

Dimly, as if from a great distance, I heard the cry of a Red Court vampire in its true form, and she flinched and started crying again, her entire body trembling in terror.

Maggie.

I remembered when Bianca and her minions had kept me prisoner.

I remembered the things they had done to me.

But it didn't look like they had harmed my child—yet.

"Yes," said Mab's cold voice, empty of emotion. The image began to slowly fade away. "It is a true seeing of your child, as she is even now. I give you my word. No tricks. No deceptions. This *is.*"

I looked through the translucent image to where Mab and my godmother waited. Lea's face was somber. Mab's eyes were narrowed to glowing green slits within her hooded cloak.

I faced them both for a moment. The cold wind

gusted over the hilltop and stirred the cloaks of the two Sidhe. I stared at them, at ancient eyes full of the knowledge of dark and wicked things. I knew that neither the child in the image nor the man on the table meant anything to them. I knew that if I went forward with Mab's bargain, I would probably end up on the table myself.

Of course, that was why Mab had shown me Maggie: to manipulate me.

No. There was a distinction in what she had done. She had shown me Maggie to make perfectly clear exactly what choice I was about to make. Certainly, it might influence my decision, but when a stark naked truth stares you in the face . . . shouldn't it?

I'm not sure it's possible to manipulate someone with candor and truth.

I think you call that enlightenment.

And as I stared at my daughter's fading image, my fear vanished.

If I wound up like Slate, if that was the price I had to pay to make my daughter safe, so be it.

If I was haunted for the rest of my life because Maggie needed me to make hard choices, so be it.

And if I had to die a horrible, lingering death so that my little girl could have a chance to live . . .

So be it.

I tightened my grip on the hideous weight of the ancient bronze knife.

I put one hand gently on Lloyd Slate's forehead to hold him still.

And then I cut his throat.

It was a quick, clean death, which made it no less lethal than if I'd hacked him up with an ax. Death is the great equalizer. It doesn't matter how you get there. Just when.

And why.

He never struggled. Just let out a breath that sounded like a sigh of relief and turned his head to one side as if going to sleep. It wasn't neat, but it wasn't a scene from a gorefest slasher movie, either. It looked more like the kind of mess you'd see in a kitchen when preparing a big bunch of steaks. Most of his blood ran into the carved indentions on the table and seemed to become quicksilver once there, running rapidly outward through the troughs and down the lettering carved in the sides and the legs. The blood made the letters reflect the eerie light around us, giving them a sort of flickering fire of their own. It was a terrible, beautiful sight. Power hummed through that blood; the letters, the stone, and the air around me were shaken by its silent potency.

I sensed the two Sidhe behind me, watching with calm, predatory eyes as the Knight who had betrayed his queens died. I knew when it was over. The two of them let out small sighs of . . . appreciation, I suppose. I couldn't think of any other phrase that fit. They recognized the significance of his death while in no way actually feeling any empathy for him. A life flowed from his broken body into the Stone Table, and they held the act in a respect akin to reverence.

I just stood there, blood dripping from the bronze knife in my hand onto the earth beneath my feet. I shivered in the cold and stared at the remains of the man I'd murdered, wondering what I was supposed to feel. Sadness? Not really. He'd been a son of a bitch of the first order, and I'd gladly have killed him in a straight-up fight if I had the chance. Remorse? None yet. I had done him a favor when I killed him. There was no getting him out of what he'd gotten himself into. Joy? No. None of that, either. Satisfaction? Precious little, except that it was over, the deed done, the dice finally cast.

Mostly? I just felt cold.

A minute or an hour later, the Leanansidhe lifted a hand and snapped her fingers. The cloaked servitors appeared from the mist as silently as they'd left, and gathered up what was left of Lloyd Slate. They lifted him in silence, carried him in silence, and vanished into the mist.

"There," I said quietly to Mab. "My part is done. Time for you to live up to yours."

"No, child," said Mab's voice through Lea's lips. "Your part is only begun. But fear not. I am Mab. The stars will rain from the sky before Mab fulfills not her word." She tilted her head slightly to one side, toward my godmother, and said, "I give thee this adviser for thy final quest, sir Knight. My handmaiden is among the most powerful beings in all of my Winter, second only to myself."

Lea's warmer, more languid voice came from her lips as she asked, "My queen, to what degree am I permitted to act?"

I thought I saw the fell light gleam on Mab's teeth as Lea's lips said, "You may indulge yourself."

Lea's mouth spread into a wide, dangerous smile of its own, and she bowed her head and upper body toward the Queen of Winter.

"And now, my Knight," Mab's voice said, as her body turned to face me exclusively. "We will see to the strength of your broken body. And I will make you mine."

I swallowed hard.

Mab lifted a hand, a dismissive gesture, and the Leanansidhe bowed to her.

"I am no longer needed here, child," Lea murmured. "I will be ready to go with thee whenever thou dost call."

My throat was almost too dry to get any words out. "I'll want the things I left with you, as soon as you can get them to me."

"Of course," she said. She bowed to me as well, and took several steps back into the mist, until it swallowed her whole.

And I was alone with Queen Mab.

"So," I said into the silence. "I guess there's . . . there's a ceremony of some kind to go through."

Mab stepped closer to me. She wasn't an enormous, imposing figure. She was considerably shorter than me. Slender. But she walked with such perfect confidence that the role of predator and prey was clear to both of us. I edged back from her. It was pure instinct, and I could no more stop from doing it than I could have stopped shivering against the cold.

"Going to be hard for us to exchange oaths if you can't talk, huh," I said. My voice sounded thin and shaky, even to me. "Um. Maybe it's paperwork or something."

Pale hands slipped up from the dark cloak and drew her hood back. She shook her head left and right, and pale, silken tresses, whiter than moonlight or Lloyd Slate's dead flesh, spilled forth.

My voice stopped working for a second. My bare thighs hit the Stone Table behind me, and I wound up sitting on it.

Mab kept pacing toward me, one slightly swaying step at a time. The cloak slid from her shoulders, down, down, down.

"Y-you, uh," I said, looking away. "You m-must be cold."

A throaty little laugh bubbled up out of her frozen-berry lips. Mab's voice, touched with anger, could cause physical damage to living flesh. Her voice filled with simmering desire . . . did other things.

And the cold was suddenly the least of my concerns.

Her mouth closed on mine, and I gave up even trying to speak. This wasn't a ceremony so much as a rite, and one as ancient as beasts and birds, earth and sky.

My memory gets shaky after the kiss.

I remember her body gleaming brightly above me, cold, soft, feminine perfection. I don't have the words to describe it. Inhuman beauty. Elfin grace. Animal sensuality. And when her body was atop mine, our breaths mingled, cold sweetness with human imperfection. I could feel the rhythm of her form, her breath, her heart. I could feel the stone of the table, the ancient hill of the mound, the very earth of the valley around us pulsing in time to Mab's rhythm. Clouds raced over the sky, and as she moved more quickly she grew brighter, and brighter, until I realized that the eerie luminescence around us all evening had been nothing but a dim, muffled reflection of Mab's loveliness, veiled for the sake of the mortal mind it could have unmade.

She did not veil it as her breathing mounted. And it burned me, it was so pure.

What we did wasn't sex, regardless of what it appeared to be. You can't have sex with a thunderstorm, an earthquake, a furious winter gale. You can't make love to a mountain, a lake of ice, a freezing wind.

For a few moments, I saw the breadth and depth of Mab's power—and for a fleeting instant, the barest, tiniest glimpse of her *purpose*, as well, as our entwined bodies thrashed toward completion. I was screaming. I had been for a while.

Then Mab's cry joined mine, our voices blending together. Her nails dug into my chest, chips of ice sliding beneath my skin. I saw her body drawn into an arch of pleasure, and then her green cat eyes opened and bored into—

Her mouth opened, and her voice hissed, *"MINE."*

Absolute truth made my body vibrate like the plucked string of a guitar, and I jerked into a brief, violent contortion.

Mab's hands slid down my ribs, and I could suddenly feel the fire of the cracked bones again, until those icy hands tightened as again she said, *"MINE."*

Again, my body bowed into a violent bow, every muscle trying to tear its way off of my bones.

Mab hissed in eagerness as her hands slid around my waist, covering the numb spot where my spine had probably been broken. I felt myself screaming and struggling, with no control whatsoever over my body.

Mab's feline eyes captured my own gaze, trapping my attention within their frozen beauty as again a jolt of terrible, sweet cold flowed out from her fingertips and she whispered, her voice a velvet caress, *". . . mine . . ."*

"Again!" screamed a voice I vaguely recognized.

Something cold and metallic pressed to my chest.

"Clear!" shouted the voice.

A lightning bolt hit my chest, an agonizing ribbon of silver power that bent my body into a bow. I started screaming, and before my hips had come down, I shouted, *"Hexus!"* spewing out power into the air.

Someone shouted and someone else cursed, and sparks exploded all around me, including from the lightbulb above, which seemed to overload and shatter into powder.

The room was dark and quiet for a few seconds.

"D-did we lose him?" asked a steady, elderly man's voice. Forthill.

"Oh, God," said Molly's quavering voice. "H-Harry?"

"I'm fine," I said. My throat felt raw. "What the hell are you doing to me?"

"Y-your heart stopped . . ." said a third voice, the familiar one.

I felt my chest and found nothing there, or around my neck. My fingers quested out and touched the bed and the backboard beneath me, and found my necklace there, the ruby still fixed in place by an ugly glob of rubber. I gripped the chain and slipped a little of my will into it, and cold blue light filled the room.

". . . so I did what any good mortician would," Butters continued. "Hit you with a bolt of lightning and tried to reanimate you." He held up two shock paddles, whose wires had evidently been melted right off them. They weren't attached to anything now. He was a wiry little guy in hospital scrubs with a shock of black hair, narrow shoulders, and a thin, restless body. He held up his hands and mimed employing the shock paddles. Then he said, in a goofy voice that was probably meant to sound hollow, "It's alive. Alliiiiiivve." After a beat he added, "You're welcome."

"Butters." I sighed. "Who called you into—" I stopped and said, "Molly. Never mind."

"Harry," she said. "We couldn't be sure how badly you were hurt, and if you couldn't feel, you couldn't know either, and I thought we needed a real doctor, but the only one I knew you trusted was Butters, so I got him instead—"

"Hey!" Butters said.

I pushed the straps off of my head and kicked irritably at the straps on my legs.

"Whoa, there, tiger!" Butters said. The little medical examiner threw himself across my legs. "Hold your horses, big guy! Easy, easy!"

Forthill and Molly meant well. They joined in and the three of them flattened me to the backboard again.

I snarled out a curse and then went limp. I sat there not resisting for a moment, until I thought they'd be listening. Then I said, "We don't have time for this. Get these straps off of me."

"Dresden, you might have a broken back," Butters said. "A pinched nerve, broken bones, damage to the organs in your lower abdomen—for God's sake, man, what were you thinking, not going to a hospital?"

"I was thinking that I didn't want to make an easy target of myself," I said. "I'm fine. I'm better."

"Good Lord, man!" sputtered Forthill. "Be reasonable. Your *heart* wasn't beating three minutes ago."

"Molly," I said, my voice hard. "Unfasten the straps. Do it now."

I heard her sniffle. But then she sat up and came up to where she could see my eyes. "Um. Harry. Are you still . . . you know. You?"

I blinked at her for a second, impressed. The grasshopper's insight was evidently serving her well.

"I'm me," I said, looking back at her eyes. That should be verification enough. If someone else had come back behind the wheel of my car, so much change to my insides and a look like that would certainly trigger a soul-gaze and reveal what had happened. "For now, at least."

Molly bit her lip. Then she said, "Okay. Okay, let him up."

Butters sat up from my legs and then stood scowling. "Wait a minute. This is just . . . This is all moving a little too fast for me."

The door behind him opened, and a heavyset man in street clothes lifted a gun and put two rounds into Butters's back from three feet away. The sheer sound of the shots was incredible, deafening.

Butters dropped like a slaughtered cow.

The gunman's eyes were tracking toward the rest of us before Butters hit the floor. I knew who he was looking for when his eyes swept over me and locked on.

He didn't talk, didn't bluster, didn't hesitate. A professional. There were plenty of them in Chicago. He raised the gun to aim at my head—while I lay there, strapped to a board from the hips down and unable to move. And, as I lifted my left wrist, I noted that my shield bracelet was gone. Of course. They must have removed it so that the defibrillator's charge wouldn't have gotten any ideas, just as they'd taken the metal necklace from around my throat, and the rings from my fingers.

They were being helpful.

Clearly, this was just not my day.

Chapter

Thirty-two

I was tied down, but my hands weren't. I flexed the fingers of my right hand into the mystic position of attack—holding them like a pretend gun—and snapped, *"Arctis!"*

The spell tore the heat from all around the gun and drew water from the air into an instant, thick coating of ice, heaviest around the weapon's hammer. The shooter twitched in reaction to the spell and pulled the trigger.

The encrusting ice held the hammer back and prevented it from falling.

The gunman blinked and tried to pull the trigger several more times, to no avail. Forthill hit him around the knees. Both men went down, and the gun came loose from the gunman's cold-numbed fingers as they hit the floor, and went spinning across the room. It struck a wall, cracked the ice around its hammer, and discharged harmlessly into the wall with another roar.

The gunman kicked Forthill in the face and the old priest fell back with a grunt of pain. Molly threw herself at him in pure rage, knocking him flat again, and began pounding her fists into him with elemental brutality and no technique whatsoever. The gunman threw an elbow that got her in the neck and knocked her back, then rose, his eyes searching the floor, until he spotted his weapon. He started for it.

I killed the light from the amulet. He tripped and fell in the sudden darkness. I heard him scuffling with the dazed Forthill.

Then there was a single bright flash of light that showed me the gunman arching up in pain. Then it was gone and there was the sound of something large falling to the floor. Several people were breathing heavily.

I got my fingers onto my amulet again and brought forth light into the room.

Forthill sat against one wall, holding his jaw, looking pale. Molly was in a crouch, one hand lifted as if she'd been about to do something with her magical talents, the way she should have at the first sound of the shots, if she'd been thinking clearly. The gunman lay on his side, and began to stir again.

Butters wheezed, "Clear," and touched both ends of the naked wires in his hands to the gunman's chest.

The wires ran back to the emergency defib unit. When they'd been melted off the paddles, it had left several strands of pure copper naked on the ends of both of them. The current did what current does, and the gunman bucked in agony for a second and sagged into immobility again.

"Jerk," Butters wheezed. He put a hand on the small of his back and said, "Ow. Ow, ow, ow, *OW!*"

"Butters!" Molly croaked, and hugged him.

"Urgckh," Butters said. "Ow." But he didn't look displeased at the hug.

"Grasshopper, don't strain him until we know how bad it is," I said. "Dammit." I started fumbling with the straps, getting them clear of my upper body so I could sit up and work on my legs. "Forthill? Are you all right?"

Father Forthill said something unintelligible and let out a groan of pain. Then he heaved himself to his feet and started helping me with the buckles. His jaw was purple and swollen on one side. He'd taken one hell of a hit and stayed conscious. Tough old guy, even though he looked so mild.

I got off the backboard, onto my feet, and picked up the gun.

"I'm all right," Butters said. "I think." His eyes went wide and he suddenly seemed to panic. "Oh, God, make sure I'm all right!" He started clawing at his shirt. "That maniac freaking shot me!"

He got the scrubs top off and turned around to show Molly his back. He was wearing an undershirt.

And on top of that, he was wearing a Kevlar vest. It was a light, underclothing garment, suitable only for protection against handguns—but the gunman had walked in with a nine-millimeter. He'd put both shots onto the centerline of Butters's lower back, and the vest had done its job. The rounds were still there, flattened and stuck in the ballistic weave.

"I'm hit, aren't I?" Butters stuttered. "I'm in shock. I can't feel it because I'm in shock. Right? Was it in the liver? Is the blood black? Call emergency services!"

"Butters," I said. "Look at me."

He did, his eyes wide.

"Polka," I said, "will never die."

He blinked at me. Then he nodded and started forcing himself to take slower, deeper breaths. "I'm all right?"

"The magic underwear worked," I said. "You're fine."

"Then why does my back hurt so much?"

"Somebody just hit it twice with a hammer moving about twelve hundred feet per second," I said.

"Oh," he said. He turned to look at Molly, who nodded at him and gave him an encouraging smile. Then he shuddered and closed his eyes in relief. "I don't think I'm temperamentally suited for the action thing."

"Yeah. Since when are you the guy in the bulletproof vest?" I asked him.

Butters nodded at Molly. "I put it on about ten seconds after she called me and said you needed help," he said. He fumbled a small case from his pocket and opened it. "See? I got chalk, and holy water, and garlic, too."

I smiled at him, but felt a little bit sick. The gunman had put Butters down for the simple reason that he had been blocking the shooter's line of sight to the room. If he'd been trying for Butters, the two shots to clear his sight line would have included a third shot to the back of Butters's head. Of course, if Butters hadn't been in the way, my head wouldn't have fared any better than his.

We're all so damned fragile.

Footsteps sounded outside the door, and I raised the gun to cover it, taking a grip with both hands, my feet centered. I was lining up the little green targeting dots when Sanya came through the door carrying a platter of sandwiches. He stopped abruptly and lifted both eyebrows, then beamed broadly. "Dresden! You are all right." He looked around the room for a moment, frowning, and said, "Did I miss something? Who is that?"

"I don't think there's anything broken," Butters told Forthill, "but you'd better get an X-ray, just to be sure. Mandibular fracture isn't anything to play around with."

The old priest nodded from his chair in the living quarters of the church's residents, and wrote something down on a little pad of paper. He showed it to Butters.

The little guy grinned. "You're welcome, Father."

Molly frowned and asked, "Should we take him to the emergency room?"

Forthill shook his head and wrote on his notepad: *Things to tell you first.*

Now I had a pair of guns I'd swiped from bad guys: the security guard's .40-caliber and the gunman's nine-millimeter. I was inspecting them both on the coffee table, familiarizing myself with their function, and wondering if I should be planning to file off the serial numbers or something. Mouse sat next to me, his flank against my leg and his serious brown eyes watching me handle the weapons.

"You found out something?" I asked Forthill.

In a way, he wrote back. *There are major movements afoot throughout South and Central America. The Red Court's upper echelon uses human servitors to interface with mortals. Many of these individuals have been sighted at airports in the past three days. All of them are bound for Mexico. Does Chichén Itzá have any significance to you?*

I grunted. Donar Vadderung's information seemed to have been solid, then. "Yeah, it does."

Forthill nodded and continued writing. *There is a priest in that area. He cannot help you with your fight, but he says he can offer you and your people sanctuary, care, and secure transportation from the area when you are finished.*

"It seems like begging for trouble to plan for our victorious departure before we know if we can get there in the first place," I said. "I can get us to the general area, but not into the ruins themselves. I need to know anything he can find out about the security the Red Court will be setting up in the area."

Forthill frowned at me for a moment. Then he wrote, *I'll ask him. But I'll need someone to talk for me.*

I nodded. "Molly, you're with the padre. Get a little sleep as soon as you can. Might not get a chance to before we move out, otherwise."

She frowned but nodded instead of trying to talk me out of it. It's nice how brushes with violent death can concentrate even the most stubbornly independent apprentice's better judgment.

Forthill held up a hand. Then he wrote, *First, I need to know how it is that you are back on your feet. Dr. Butters said that you would be too injured to get out of bed.*

"Magic," I said calmly, as if that should explain everything.

Forthill eyed me for a moment. Then wrote, *I hurt too much to argue with you. Will make the calls.*

"Thank you," I said quietly.

He nodded and wrote, *God go with you.*

"Thank you," I repeated.

"What about me?" Butters asked. There were equal measures of dread and excitement in his voice.

"Hopefully, we won't need any more of your help," I said. "Might be nice if you were standing by, though. Just in case."

"Right," Butters said, nodding. "What else?"

I clenched a hand and resisted the urge to tell him that he would be better off hiding under his bed. He knew that already. He was as frightened as a bunny in a forest full of bears, but he wanted to help. "I think Father Forthill has a car. Yes, Father?"

He started to write something, then scratched it out and held out his hand in a simple thumbs-up.

"Stay with them," I said. I slapped magazines into both guns, confident that I knew them well enough to be sure they'd go bang when I pulled the trigger. "Soon as Forthill is done, get him to an emergency room."

"Emergency room," Butters said. "Check."

Forthill frowned and wrote, *Are you certain we shouldn't turn our attacker over to the police?*

"Nothing in life is certain, Father," I said, rising. I stuck a gun in either pocket of my duster. "But if the police get involved, they're going to ask a lot of questions and take a long time trying to sort everything out. I can't spare that time."

You don't think this gunman will go to the authorities?

"And tell them what?" I asked. "That he got kidnapped off the street by a priest from St. Mary's? That we beat him up and took his illegal weapon away?" I shook my head. "He doesn't want the cops involved any more than we do. This was business to him. He'll make a deal to fess up to us if it means he gets to walk."

And we let a murderer go free?

"It's an imperfect world, Father," I said. "On the other hand, you don't hire professional killers to take out nice old ladies and puppy dogs. Most of the people this guy has an appointment with are underworld types—I guarantee it—mostly those who are going to turn state's evidence on their organization. Sooner or later one of them gets lucky, and no more hit man."

Live by the sword, die by the sword, Forthill wrote.

"Exactly."

He shook his head and winced as the motion caused him discomfort. *It will be hard to help a man like that.*

I snorted. "It's a noble sentiment, padre, but a guy like him doesn't want any help. Doesn't see any need for it." I shrugged. "Some men just enjoy killing."

He frowned severely, but didn't write down any response. Just then, someone rapped on the door, and Sanya opened it and poked his head in. "Dresden," the Knight said, "he's awake."

I rose, and Mouse rose with me. "Cool. Maybe get started on those calls, padre."

Forthill gave me another thumbs-up rather than nodding. I walked out, Mouse stolid at my back, and went to the utility closet with Sanya to talk to our . . . guest, I suppose.

The blocky hit man lay on the backboard, strapped down to it, and further secured in a cocoon of duct tape.

"Stand him up," I said.

Sanya did so, rather casually lifting the gunman, backboard and all, and leaning it back at a slight angle against the wall.

The gunman watched me with calm eyes. I picked up a wallet from the little folding card table we had set up and opened it. "Steven Douglas," I read from the license. "That you?"

"Stevie D," he said.

"Heard of you," I said. "You did Torelli a couple of years back."

He smiled, very slightly. "I don't know any Torelli."

"Yeah, I figured," I said.

"How is he?" Stevie D asked.

"Who?"

"The little guy."

"Fine," I said. "Wearing a vest."

Stevie D nodded. "Good."

I lifted an eyebrow. "Professional killer is happy he didn't kill someone?"

"Had nothing against him. Wasn't getting paid for him. Don't wanna do time for hitting the wrong guy. Isn't professional. But everything I heard about you said I shouldn't dick around waiting to get the shot off, so I had to get him out of the way."

"Stevie," I said, "this can go a couple of different

ways. The simplest is that you give me who hired you, and I let you go."

His eyes narrowed. "No cops?"

I gestured at his bound form with one hand. "Does it look like we want cops all over this? Spill and you're loose as fast as we can take the tape off."

He thought about it for a moment. Then he said, "Nah."

"No?"

He made a motion that might have been a shrug. "Did that for you, I might never work again. People get nervous when a contractor divulges personal information about their clients. I gotta think long-term."

I nodded. "I can respect that. Honoring a bargain and all."

He snorted softly.

"So we can go to option two. I'm going to go call Marcone. I'm going to tell him what happened. I'm going to ask him if he's interested in talking to you, Stevie. I'm sure he'll want to know who is purchasing hits in his territory, too. What impact will that have on your long-term productivity, do you think?"

Stevie's nerve cracked. He licked his lips. "Um," he said. "What's option three?"

Sanya stepped forward. He beamed at Stevie D, picked the backboard up off the floor without too much trouble, and in his lowest voice and thickest Russian accent said, "I pick up this board, break in half, and put both halves into incinerator."

Stevie D looked like a man who suddenly realizes he is sitting near a hornets' nest and is trying desperately not to run away screaming. He licked his lips again and said, "Half of what I hear about you says Marcone wants you dead, that you hate his guts. The other half says you work for him sometimes. Kill the people he thinks need killing."

"I wouldn't pay much attention to rumors if I were you, Stevie," I said.

"Which is it?" he asked.

"Find out," I said. "Don't tell me anything."

Sanya put him back down again. I stood facing him expectantly.

"Okay," he said, finally. "A broad."

"Woman, huh. Who?"

"No name. Paid cash."

"Describe her."

Stevie nodded. "Five-nine, long legs, brown eyes," he said. "Some muscle on her, weighed maybe one fifty. Long, dark hair. Had these tattoos on her face and neck."

My heart just about stopped in my chest.

I closed down every doorway and window in my head, to shut out the gale that was suddenly whipping up in my heart. I had to stay focused. I couldn't afford to let the sudden tide of emotion drown my ability to think clearly.

I reached into my pocket and drew out my own wallet. I'd kept a picture of Susan in there for so long that when I pulled it out some of the image's colors stuck to the plastic sleeve. I showed him the picture.

The hit man squinted and nodded. "Yeah," he said. "That's her."

Chapter
Thirty-three

"**G**ive me the details," I said quietly.

"She said you'd be here. Gave me twenty thousand up front, twenty more held in escrow until delivery was confirmed."

Mouse made a soft, uncomfortable noise that never quite became a whine. He sat watching my face intently.

"When?" I asked.

"Last night."

I stared at him for a moment. Then I tossed Stevie's wallet back onto the folding card table and said, "Cut him loose. Walk him to the door."

Sanya let out what seemed like a disappointed sigh. Then he produced a knife and began cutting Stevie free.

I walked down the hall, back toward the living area with my head bowed, thinking furiously.

Susan had hired a gunman to kill me. Why?

I stopped walking and leaned against a wall. Why would she hire someone to kill me? Or, hell, more to the point—why would she hire a *gunman* to kill me? Why not someone who stood a greater chance of success?

Granted, a gunman could kill even a wizard if he were taken by surprise. But pistols had to be fired at dangerously short ranges to be reliable, and Stevie D had a reputation as a brazen sidearm specialist. It meant that the wizard would have more time to see something bad coming, as opposed to being warned only when a high-powered rifle round hit his chest, and would have an easier time responding with hasty defensive magic. It was hardly an ideal approach.

If Susan wanted me dead, she wouldn't really need to contract it out. A pretext to get me alone and another one to put us very close to each other would just about do it. And I'd never see that one coming.

Something about this just wasn't right. I'd have called Stevie a liar, but I didn't think he was one. I was sure he believed what he was saying.

So. Either Stevie was lying and I was just too dim to pick up on it, or he was telling the truth. If he was lying, given what kind of hot water I could get him into, he was also an idiot. I didn't think he was one of those. If he was telling the truth, it meant . . .

It meant that either Susan really had hired someone to kill me, or else someone who could look like Susan had done business with Stevie D. If Susan had hired someone to kill me, why this guy, in particular? Why hire someone who didn't have better than even chances of pulling it off? That was more the kind of thing Esteban and Esmerelda would come up with.

That worked a lot better. Esmerelda's blue and green eyes could have made Stevie remember being hired by Mister Snuffleupagus, if that was what she wanted. But how would she have known where to find me? Had they somehow managed to tail Sanya back to the church from my apartment without being noticed by Mouse?

And just where the hell were Susan and Martin? They'd had more than enough time to get here. So why weren't they?

Someone was running a game on me. If I didn't start getting some answers to these questions, I had a bad feeling that it was going to turn around and bite me on the ass at the worst moment imaginable.

Right, then.

I guessed that meant it was time to go get some answers.

Paranoia is a survival trait when you run in my circles. It gives you something to do in your spare time, coming up with solutions to ridiculous problems that aren't ever going to happen. Except when one of them does, at which point you feel way too vindicated.

For instance, I had spent more than a couple of off hours trying to figure out how I might track someone through Chicago if I didn't have some kind of object or possession of theirs to use as a focus. Basic tracking magic is completely dependent upon having a sample of whoever it is you want to follow. Hair, blood, and nail clippings are the usual thing. But let's say you don't have any of those, and you still want to find someone. If you have a sample of something in their possession, a piece snipped from their clothing, the tag just torn out of their underwear, whatever, you can get them that way, too.

But let's say things are hectic and crazy and someone has just burned down your house and your lab and you still need to follow somebody.

That's when you need a good, clear photograph. And minions. Lots of minions. Preferably ones who don't demand exorbitant wages.

There's a Pizza 'Spress less than two blocks from St. Mary's. Sanya and I went straight there. I ordered.

"I do not see how this helps us," Sanya said, as I walked out from the little shop with four boxes of pizza.

"You're used to solving all your problems the simple way," I said. "Kick down the door, chop up everybody who looks fiendish, save everyone who looks like they might need it. Yeah?"

"It is not always that simple," Sanya said, rather stiffly. "And sometimes I use a gun."

"Which I applaud you for, very progressive," I said. "But the point is, you do your work directly. You pretty much know where you're going, or get shown the way, and after that it's just up to you to take care of business."

"Da," Sanya said as we walked. "I suppose."

"My work is sort of the same," I said. "Except that nobody ever points the way for me."

"You need to know where to go," Sanya said.

"Yes."

"And you are going to consult four large pizzas for guidance."

"Yes," I said.

The big man frowned for a moment. Then he said, "There is, I think, humor here which does not translate well from English into sanity."

"That's pretty rich coming from the agnostic Knight of the Cross with a holy Sword who takes his orders from an archangel," I said.

"Gabriel could be an alien being of some kind," Sanya said placidly. "It does not change the value of what I do—not to me and not to those whom I protect."

"Whom," I said, with as much Russian accent as I could fit into one word. "Someone's been practicing his English."

Sanya somehow managed to look down his nose at me, despite the fact that I was several inches taller. "I am only saying that I do not need the written code of a spiritual belief to act like a decent human being."

"You are way kookier than me, man," I said, turning into an alley. "And I talk to pizza."

I laid out the four pizza boxes on top of four adjacent trash cans, and glanced around to be sure no one was nearby. It was getting near to lunch break, and it wasn't the best time for what I was about to do, but it ought to work. I turned to look up and down the alley as best I could, drew a breath, and then remembered something.

"Hey, Sanya. Stick your fingers in your ears?"

The big Russian stared at me. "What?"

"Your fingers," I said, wiggling all of mine, "in your ears." I pointed to mine.

"I understand the words, obviously, as I am someone who has been practicing his English. Why?"

"Because I'm going to say something to the pizza and I don't want you to hear it."

Sanya gave the sky a single, long-suffering glance. Then he sighed and put his fingers in his ears.

I gave him a thumbs-up, turned away, cupped my hands around my mouth so that no one could lip-read, and began to murmur a name, over and over again, each utterance infused with my will.

I had to repeat the name only a dozen times or so before a shadow flickered overhead, and something the size of a hunting falcon dropped out of the sky, blurred wings humming, and hovered about two feet in front of me.

"*Bozhe moi!*" Sanya sputtered, and *Esperacchius* was halfway from its sheath by the time he finished speaking.

I couldn't stop myself from saying, "There's some real irony in your using that expression, O Knight of Maybe."

"Go ahead!" piped a shrill voice, like a Shakespearean actor on helium. "Draw your sword, knave, and we will *see* who bleeds to death from a thousand tiny cuts!"

Sanya stood there with his mouth open and his sword still partly in its sheath. "It is . . ." He shook his head as if someone had popped him in the nose. "It is . . . a *domovoi, da?*"

The little faerie in question stood nearly fifteen full inches in height, appearing as a slender, athletic youth with the blurring wings of a dragonfly standing out from his shoulders and a tuft of hair like lavender dandelion fluff. He was dressed in garments that looked like they'd been thugged from someone's old-school G.I. Joe doll, an olive-drab jumpsuit with the sleeves removed and holes cut through it for his wings. He wore a number of weapons about his person, most of them on nylon straps that looked like they'd been lifted from convention badges. He was carrying one letter opener shaped like a long sword at his side and two more, crossed over each other, on his back. I'd given him the letter opener set last Christmas, advising him to keep half of them stashed somewhere safe, as backup weapons.

"Domovoi?" the little faerie shrilled, furious. "Oh, no, you didn't!"

"Easy there, Major General," I said. "Sanya, this is Major General Toot-toot Minimus, the captain of my house guard. Toot, this is my boon companion Sanya, Knight of the Cross, who has faced danger at my side. He's okay."

The faerie quivered with outrage. "He's Russian! And he doesn't even know the difference between a *domovoi* and a *polevoi* when he sees one two feet away!" Toot-toot let out a blistering string of words in Russian, shaking a finger at the towering Knight.

Sanya listened in bemusement at first, but then blinked, slid his sword away, and held up both hands. He said something that sounded somber and very formal, and only then did Toot's ire seem to abate. He said one or two more harsh-sounding words toward Sanya, added a flick of his chin that screamed, *So there*, and turned back to me.

"Toot," I said. "How is it that you speak Russian?"

He blinked at me. "Harry," he said, as if the question made no sense at all, "you just *speak* it, don't you? I mean, come on." He gave me a formal bow and said, "How may I serve you, my liege?"

I peered at him a bit more closely. "Why is half your face painted blue?"

"Because we're Winter now, my liege!" Toot said. His eyes darted to the side and down several times. "And . . . say, that doesn't mean we have to eat the pizza cold, does it?"

"Of course not," I said.

Toot looked relieved. "Oh. Good. Um. What were we talking about?"

"I have a job for you," I said, "and for everyone you can get to help." I nodded at the pizza. "Standard rates."

"Very good, my liege," Toot said, saluting. His eyes slid down again. "Maybe someone ought to check the pizza. You know. For poison and things. It would look real bad if someone poisoned your vassals, you know."

I eyed him askance. Then I held up a finger and said, "All right. *One* piece. And after— Ack!"

Toot hit the pizza box like a great white shark taking a seal. He slammed into it, one bright sword slashing the top off of the box. Then he seized the largest piece and began devouring with a will.

Sanya and I both stood there, fascinated. It was like watching a man try to eat a pizza slice the size of a small car. Pieces flew up and were skewered on his blade. Sauce got everywhere, and it gave me a gruesome little flashback to the Stone Table.

"Harry?" Sanya asked. "Are you all right?"

"Will be soon," I said.

"This creature serves you?" Sanya asked.

"This one and about a hundred smaller ones. And five times that many part-timers I can call in once in a while." I thought about it. "It isn't so much that they serve me as that we have a business arrangement that we all like. They help me out from time to time. I furnish them with regular pizza."

"Which they . . . love," Sanya said.

Toot spun in a dizzy, delighted circle on one heel, and fell onto his back with perfectly unself-conscious enthusiasm, his tummy sticking out as far as it could. He lay there for a moment, making happy, gurgling sounds.

"Well," I said. "Yes."

Sanya's eyes danced, though his face was sober. "You are a drug dealer. To tiny faeries. Shame."

I snorted.

"What was that he said about Winter?" Sanya asked.

"Harry's the new Winter Knight!" Toot-toot burbled. "Which is fantastic! The old Winter Knight mostly just sat around getting tortured. He never went on adventures or *anything*." He paused and added, "Unless you count going crazy, I guess."

"Toot," I said. "I'm . . . kind of trying to keep the Winter Knight thing low-profile."

"Okay," Toot said. "Why?"

I glanced from the little faerie to Sanya. "Look, I; uh . . . It's personal, okay, and—"

"Because every creature in Faerie got to see the ceremony," Toot said proudly. "Mab made sure of it! It was reflected in all the streams and ponds and lakes and puddles and every little drop of water!"

I stared at the engorged faerie, at something of a loss

for words. "Um," I said. "Oh. How . . . very, very disturbing."

"Did it hurt when you kissed Mab?" Toot asked. "Because I always thought her lips looked so cold that they would burn. Like streetlamps in winter!" Toot sat up suddenly, his eyes wide. "Ooooooh. Did your *tongue* get stuck to her, like on that Christmastime show?"

"Okayyyyy," I said with forced cheer, clapping my hands. "Way, way too personal. Um. The job. I have a job for you."

Toot-toot leapt up to his feet. His stomach was already constricting back toward its normal size. "Yes, my liege!"

Where the hell did he put it all? I mean . . . it just wasn't *possible* for him to eat that much pizza and then . . . I shook my head. Now wasn't the time.

I produced my picture of Susan. "This human is somewhere in Chicago. I need your folk to find her. She's probably accompanied by a human man with blond hair, about the same size she is."

Toot took to his wings again and zoomed down to the picture. He picked it up and held it out at arm's length, studying it, and nodded once. "May I have this, my lord, to show the others?"

"Yeah," I said. "Be careful with it, though. I want it back."

"Yes, my liege!" Toot said. He brandished his sword with a flourish, sheathed it, and zipped straight up into the October sky.

Sanya stood looking steadily at me.

I coughed. I waited.

"So," he said. "Mab."

I grunted vaguely in reply.

"You hit that," Sanya said.

I did not look at him. My face felt red.

"You"—he scrunched up his nose, digging in his memory—"tapped that ass. Presumably, it was phat."

"Sanya!"

He let out a low, rolling laugh and shook his head. "I saw her once. Mab. Beautiful beyond words."

"Yeah," I said.

"And dangerous."

"Yes," I said, with emphasis.

"And you are now her champion," he said.

"Everybody's gotta be something, right?"

He nodded. "Joking about it. Good. You will need that sense of humor."

"Why do you say that?"

"Because she is cold, Dresden. She knows wicked secrets Time himself has forgotten. And if she chose you to be her Knight, she has a plan for you." He nodded slowly. "Laugh whenever you can. Keeps you from killing yourself when things are bad. That and vodka."

"That some kind of Russian saying?" I asked.

"Have you seen traditional folk dances?" Sanya asked. "Imagine them being done by someone with a bottle of vodka in them. Laughter abounds, and you survive another day." He shrugged. "Or break your neck. Either way, it is pain management."

His voice sounded almost merry, though the subject matter was grim as hell. If not more so.

I had expected him to try to talk me out of it. Or at least to berate me for being an idiot. He didn't do either. There was a calm acceptance of terrible things that was part and parcel of Sanya's personality. No matter how bad things got, I didn't think anything would ever truly faze him. He simply accepted the bad things that happened and soldiered on as best he could.

There was probably a lesson for me in there, some-where.

I was quiet for a while before I decided to trust him. "I get to save my girl first," I said. "That was the deal."

"Ah," he said. He seemed to mull it over and nod-ded. "That is reasonable."

"You really think that?"

He lifted both eyebrows. "The child is your blood— is she not?"

I nodded and said quietly, "She is."

He spread his hands, as if it were a self-evident fact that needed no further exploration. "As horrible fates go, that is a good one," he said. "Worthwhile. Save your little girl." He clapped me on the shoulder. "If you turn into a hideous monster and I am sent to slay you, I will remember this and make it as painless as I can, out of respect for you."

I knew he was joking. I just couldn't tell which part of it he was joking about. "Uh," I said. "Thanks."

"It is nothing," he said. We stood around quietly for another five minutes before he frowned, looking at the other pizza boxes, and asked, "Is there some purpose for the rest of th—"

A scene out of *The Birds* descended upon the alley. There was a rush of wing-beaten wind, and hundreds of tiny figures flashed down onto the pizza. Here and there I would spot one of the Pizza Lord's Guard, recogniz-able thanks to the orange plastic cases of the box knives they had strapped to their backs. The others went by in twinkles and flashes of color, muted by the daylight but beautiful all the same. There were a *lot* of the Little Folk involved. If I'd been doing this at night, it might have induced a seizure or something.

The Little Folk love pizza. They love it with a passion

so intense that it beggars the imagination. Watching a pizza being devoured was sort of like watching a plane coming apart in midair on those old WWII gun camera reels. Bits would fleck off here and there, and then suddenly in a rush, bits would go flying everywhere, each borne away by the individual fairie who had seized it.

It was over in less than three minutes.

Seriously. Where do they *put* it?

Toot came to hover before me and popped a little fistful of pizza into his mouth. He gulped it down and saluted.

"Well, Major General?" I asked.

"Found her, my liege," Toot reported. "She is a captive and in danger."

Sanya and I traded a look.

"Where?" I asked him.

Toot firmly held up the picture, still in one piece, and two strands of dark hair, each curled into its own coil of rope in his tiny hands. "Two hairs from her head, my liege. Or if it is your pleasure, I will guide you there."

Sanya drew his head back a little, impressed. "They found her? That quickly?"

"People underestimate the hell out of the Little Folk," I said calmly. "Within their limits, they're as good as or better than anything else I know for getting information—and there are a *lot* of them around Chicago who are willing to help me out occasionally."

"Hail the Pizza Lord!" Toot-toot shrilled.

"Hail the Pizza Lord!" answered a score of piping voices that came from no apparent source. The Little Folk can be all but invisible when they want to be.

"Major General Minimus, keep this up and I'm making you a full general," I said.

Toot froze. "Why? Is that bad? What did I do?"

"It's good, Toot. That's higher than a major general."

His eyes widened. "There's *higher*?"

"Oh, yeah, definitely. And you're on the fast track for the very top." I took the hairs from him and said, "We'll get the car. Lead us to her, Toot."

"Yes, sir!"

"Good," Sanya said, grinning. "Now we know where to go and have someone to rescue. This part I know how to do."

Chapter

Thirty-four

"Admittedly," Sanya said a few minutes later, "normally I do not storm headquarters buildings of the Federal Bureau of Investigation. And in broad daylight, too."

We were parked down the block from the FBI's Chicago office, where Toot had guided us, crouched on the dashboard and demanding to know why Sanya hadn't rented one of the cars that could fly instead of the poky old landbound minivan he had instead. Toot hadn't taken the answer that "cars like that are imaginary" seriously, either. He had muttered a few things in Russian that only made Sanya's smile wider.

"Damn," I said, staring at the building. "Toot? Was Martin with her?"

"The yellow-hair?" Toot sat on the dashboard facing us, waving his feet. "No, my liege."

I grunted. "I don't like that, either. Why wouldn't they have been taken together? Which floor is she on, Toot?"

"There," Toot said, pointing. I leaned over and hunkered down behind him so that I could look down the length of his little arm to the window he was pointing at.

"Fourth," I said. "That was where Tilly was talking to me."

Sanya reached down to produce a semiautomatic he'd hidden beneath the seat of the minivan and cycled a round into the chamber, his eyes glued to the outside mirror. "Company."

A bald, slightly overweight bum in a shabby overcoat and cast-off clothing shambled down the sidewalk with vacant eyes—but he was moving a little too purposefully toward us to be genuine. I was watching his hands with my shield bracelet ready to go, expecting him to pull a weapon out from beneath the big coat, and it wasn't until he was a few steps away that I realized it was Martin.

He stopped on the sidewalk next to the passenger window of the van and wobbled in place. He rapped on the glass and held out his hand as if begging a handout. I rolled down the window and asked him, "What happened?"

"The FBI did its legwork," he said. "They tracked our rental car back to my cover ID, got my picture, put it on TV. One of the detectives we shook down confirmed my presence and told them I'd been seen at your place, and they were waiting there when we came back to get you. Susan created a distraction so that I could get away."

"And you left her behind, huh?"

He shrugged. "Her identity is genuine, and while they know she arrived with me and was seen with me, they can't prove that she's done anything. I've been operating long enough that the Red Court has seen to it that I'm on multiple international lists of wanted terrorists. If I were caught, both of us would have been taken."

I grunted. "What did you find out?"

"The last of the Red King's inner circle arrived this

morning. They'll do the ceremony tonight," he said. "Midnight, or a little after, if our astronomer's assessment is solid."

"Crap."

Martin nodded. "How fast can you get us there?"

I touched a fingertip to my mother's gem and double-checked the way there. "This one doesn't have a direct route. Three hops, a couple of walks, one of them in bad terrain. Should take us ninety minutes, gets us to within five miles of Chichén Itzá."

Martin looked at me for a long moment. Then he said, "I can't help but find it somewhat convenient that you are suddenly able to provide that kind of fast transport to exactly the places we need to go."

"The Red Court had their goodies stashed near a confluence of ley lines," I said, "a point of ample magical power. Chichén Itzá is at another such confluence, only a lot bigger. Chicago is a crossroads, both physically and metaphysically. There are dozens of confluences either in the town or within twenty-five miles. The routes I know through the Nevernever mostly run from confluence to confluence, so Chicago's got a direct route to a lot of places."

Sanya made an interested sound. "Like the airports in Dallas or Atlanta. Or here. Travel nexuses."

"Exactly."

Martin nodded, though he didn't look like he particularly believed or disbelieved me. "That gives us a little more than nine hours," he said.

"The Church is trying to get us information about local security at Chichén Itzá. Meet me at St. Mary of the Angels." I handed him the change scrounged from my pockets. "Tell them Harry Dresden said you were no Stevie D. We'll leave from there."

"You . . ." He shook his head a little. "You got the Church to help you?"

"Hell, man. I got a Knight of the Cross driving me around."

Sanya snorted.

Martin studied Sanya with eyes that were a little wide. "I . . . see." A certain energy seemed to enter him as he nodded, and I knew exactly what he was feeling— the positive upswing in his emotions, an electricity that came with the sudden understanding that not only was death not certain, but that victory might actually be possible.

Hope is a force of nature. Don't let anyone tell you different.

Martin nodded. "What about Susan?"

"I'll get her out," I said.

Martin ducked his head in another nod. Then he took a deep breath and said simply, "Thank you." He turned and shambled away drunkenly, clutching his coins.

"Seems a decent fellow," Sanya said. His nostrils flared a little. "Half-vampire, you say? Fellowship of St. Giles?"

"Yeah. Like Susan." I watched Martin vanish into Chicago's lunchtime foot traffic and said, "I'm not sure I trust him."

"I would say the feeling is mutual," Sanya said. "When a man lives a life like Martin's, he learns not to trust anyone."

I grunted sourly. "Stop being reasonable. I enjoy disliking him."

Sanya chuckled and said, "So. What now?"

I took the guns out of my duster pockets and stowed them beneath the minivan's passenger seat. "You go back to St. Mary's. I go in and get Susan and meet you there."

Sanya lifted his eyebrows. "You get her from in there?"

"Sure."

He pursed his lips thoughtfully, then shrugged. "Okay. I suppose it is your funeral, *da?*"

I nodded firmly. *"Da."*

I walked into the building and through the metal detectors. They went beep. I stopped and dropped all the rings and the shield bracelet into a plastic tub, then tried again. They didn't fuss at me the second time. I got my stuff back and walked up to a station in the center of the floor that looked like an information desk. I produced one of my cards, the ones that called me a private investigator. I had only half a dozen of them left. The rest had been in my desk drawer at the office. "I need to speak to Agent Tilly about his current investigation."

The woman behind the desk nodded matter-of-factly, called Tilly's office, and asked if he'd see me. She nodded once and said, "Yes, sir," and smiled at me. "You'll need a visitor's badge. Here. Please make sure it is displayed at all times."

I took the badge and clipped it to my duster. "Thanks. I know the drill."

"Fourth floor," she said, and nodded at the person in line behind me.

I walked down to the elevators, rode them up to four, and walked to Tilly's office, which turned out to be right across the hall from the interrogation room. Tilly, small, dapper, and quick-looking, stood in the doorway, looking at a file in a manila folder. He let me see that there was a picture of Susan paper-clipped to the inside cover before he closed the file and tucked it under his arm.

"So," he said, "it's Mr. Known Associate. Just as well. I needed to talk to you again anyway."

"I'm a popular guy this week," I said.

"You're telling me," Tilly said. He folded his arms, frowning. "So. We got a car rented by a mystery man using a bogus identity, right outside a building that blows up. We got sworn testimony from two local snoops that this leggy looker named Susan Rodriguez was seen in his company. We got a pancaked Volkswagen Bug, belonging to Harry Dresden, and seventy thousand dollars' worth of property damage near the house of a local crooked IA cop who lied his ass off to point me at you. We got a file that says that Susan Rodriguez was at one point your girlfriend. Eyewitnesses that place both her and the mystery man at your apartment—which seemed to be a little too clean of anything that could implicate you. But before we could go back and take a real hard close look at it for trace evidence, it burns to the ground. Fire chief is still working on the investigation, but his first impression is arson." Tilly scratched his chin thoughtfully. "I don't know if you're current on investigative technique, but when there are this many connections between a relatively small number of people and events, it can sometimes be an indicator that they might be up to something nefarious."

"Nefarious, huh?" I asked.

Tilly nodded. "Good word, isn't it?" He scrunched up his nose. "Disappoints me, because my instincts said you were playing it level with me. Close to the chest, but level. I guess you can always run into someone better at lying than you are at catching them, huh."

"Probably," I said. "But you didn't. At least not with me."

He grunted. "Maybe. Maybe." He glanced back into his office. "What do you think?"

"I think you're playing with dynamite again, Tilly," said Murphy's voice.

"Murph," I said, relieved. I leaned around Tilly and waved at her. She looked at me and shook her head. "Dammit, Dresden. Can't you ever do anything quietly and in an orderly fashion?"

"No way," I said. "It's the only thing keeping Tilly here from deciding I'm some kind of bomb maker."

Murphy's mouth twitched up at one corner, briefly. She asked soberly, "Are you okay?"

"They burned down my house, Murph," I said. "Mister got out, but I don't know where he's at. I mean, I know that a lost cat isn't exactly a priority right now but"—I shrugged—"I guess I'm worried about him."

"If he misses his feeding," Murphy said wryly, "I'm more worried about *me*. Mister is the closest thing to a mountain lion for a few hundred miles. He'll be fine."

Tilly blinked and turned to Murphy. "Seriously?"

Murphy frowned at him. "What?"

"You still back him," Tilly said. "Despite all the flags he's setting off."

"Yeah," Murphy said.

Tilly exhaled slowly. Then he said, "All right, Dresden. Step into my office?"

I did. Tilly shut the door behind us.

"Okay," he said. "Tell me what's going on here."

"You don't want to know," Murphy said. She'd beaten me to it.

"That's funny," Tilly said. "I just checked in with my brain about an hour ago, and at that time, it told me that it *did* want to know."

Murphy exhaled and glanced at me.

I held up both hands. "I hardly know the guy. Your call."

Murphy nodded and asked Tilly, "How much do you know about the Black Cat case files?"

Tilly looked at her for a moment. Then he looked at his identification badge, clipped to his jacket. "Funny. For a second there, I thought someone must have changed it to say 'Mulder.'"

"I'm serious, Till," Murphy said.

His dark eyebrows climbed. "Um. They were the forerunner to Special Investigations, right? Sixties, seventies, I think. They got handed all the weirdo stuff. The files make some claims that make me believe several of those officers were having fun with all the wonderful new psychotropic drugs that were coming out back then."

"What if I told you they weren't stoned, Till?" Murphy asked.

Tilly frowned. "Is that what you're telling me?"

"They weren't stoned," Murphy said.

Tilly's frown deepened.

"SI handles all the same stuff the Black Cats did. It's just been made real clear to us that our reports had better not sound like a drug trip. So the reports provide an explanation. They don't provide much accuracy."

"You're . . . standing there, right in front of me, telling me that when Dresden told me it was vampires, he was being serious?"

"Completely," Murphy said.

Tilly folded his arms. "Jesus, Karrin."

"You think I'm lying to you?" she asked.

"You aren't," he said. "But that doesn't mean there are vampires running around out there. It just means that you believe it's true."

"Maybe I'm just gullible," Murphy suggested.

Tilly gave her a reproachful look. "Or maybe the pressure is getting to you and you aren't seeing things objectively. I mean—"

"If you make some comment even obliquely alluding to menstruation or menopause and its effect on my judgment," Murphy interrupted, "I will break your arm in eleven places."

Tilly pressed his lips together sourly. "Dammit, Murphy. Can you hear yourself? Vampires? For Christ's sake. What am I supposed to think?"

Murphy spread her hands. "I'm not sure. Harry, what's actually happening?"

I laid out the last couple of days, focusing on the events in Chicago and leaving out everything but the broadest picture of the White Council and the Red Court and their involvement.

"This vampire couple," Murphy said. "You think they're the ones who got to Rudolph?"

"Stands to reason. They could put pressure on him a lot of different ways. They wanted to remove him before he could squeal and sent their heavy to do it."

"I can't believe what I'm hearing here," Tilly said.

"So when are you moving?" Murphy asked me, ignoring him.

"Tonight."

"No one is moving anywhere until I get some answers," Tilly said. To his credit, he didn't stick any bravado into the sentence. He made it as a statement of simple fact.

"Don't know how many of those I can give you, man," I said, quietly. "There's not much time. And my little girl is in danger."

"This isn't a negotiation," Tilly said.

"Agent," I said, sighing, "there's still a little time.

I'm willing to talk with you." My voice hardened. "But not for long. Please believe me when I say that I can take Susan out of this building, with or without your cooperation."

"Harry," Murphy said, as if I'd just uttered something unthinkably rude for which I ought to be ashamed.

"Tick-tock, Murph," I answered. "If he pushes me, I can't afford to stand here and smile."

"Now I'm curious," Tilly said, bristling almost visibly. "I think I'd like to see you try that."

"Till," Murphy said in exactly the same voice. "Mother of God, boys, would it kill either of you to behave like adults? Please?"

I folded my arms, scowling. Tilly did the same. But we both shut up.

"Thank you," Murphy said. "Till . . . Do you remember that tape that was on the news a few years back? After the deaths at Special Investigations?"

"The werewolf thing?" Tilly asked. "Yeah. Blurry, badly lit, out of focus, and terrible effects. The creature didn't look anything like a werewolf. Only suddenly the tape mysteriously vanishes, so it can't be verified by anyone. Secondhand versions are probably on the Internet somewhere." He mused and said, "The actress they had playing you was pretty good, though."

"That wasn't an actress, Till," Murphy said quietly. "I was there. I saw it happen. The tape was genuine. You have my word."

Tilly frowned again. He ducked his head down slightly, dark eyes focused on his thoughts, as if he were reading from a report only he could see.

"Look, man," I said quietly. "Think about it like this. What if you'd never heard me say the word *vampire*? What if I'd said *drug cartel* or *terrorists* instead? And

I told you that this group of terrorists was financed by shady corporations and that one of them had blown the office building to prevent their illegal data from being stolen and exposed to the world? What if I had told you that because I'd pissed them off, a bunch of terrorists had taken my daughter? That they were going to cut her head off and put the video on the Internet? That Susan and the mystery man were spooks from an organization I was not at liberty to divulge, trying to help me find and recover the girl? Would it still sound crazy?"

Tilly cocked his head for a second. Then he said in a subdued voice, "It would sound like the plot of a cheesy novel." He shrugged. "But . . . the logic would hold up. I mean . . . they don't call those assholes 'extremists' for nothing."

"Okay," I said gently. "Then . . . maybe we can just pretend I said it was terrorists. And go from there. It's my daughter, man."

Tilly looked back and forth from me to Murphy. He said quietly, "Either you're both crazy—or I am— or you're telling me the truth." He shook his head. "And . . . I'm not sure which of the possibilities disturbs me more."

"You got a piece of paper?" I asked him.

Bemused, he opened his drawer and got out a pad.

I grabbed a pen and wrote on it:

Susan,
Tell him everything.
Harry

I tore off the page, folded the note, and said, "I guess Susan hasn't said much to you."

Tilly grunted. "Nothing, in fact. Literally nothing. Which is fairly hard-core, in my experience."

"She can be stubborn," I said. "Go give her this. You know I haven't seen her in hours. Get her story, off the record. See how well it matches up."

He took the note and looked at it. Then back at me.

"Hard to know who to trust," I said. "Talk to her. Try to take the story apart. See if it stands up."

He thought about it for a moment and said, "Keep him here, Murphy."

"Okay."

Tilly left.

There were two chairs, and neither looked comfortable. I settled down on the floor and closed my eyes.

"How bad is it?" she asked me.

"Pretty bad," I said quietly. "Um. I need to ask you a favor."

"Sure."

"If . . . Look. I have a will in a lockbox at the National Bank on Michigan. If something should happen to me . . . I'd appreciate it if you'd see to it. You're on the list of people who can open it. Listed as executor."

"Harry," she said.

"Granted, there's not much to have a will *about* at the moment," I said. "Everything was in my house or office, but . . . there are some intangibles and . . ." I felt my throat tighten, and cut short my request. "Take care of it for me?"

There was silence, and then Murphy moved and settled down next to me. Her hand squeezed mine. I squeezed back.

"Sure," she said.

"Thanks."

"There's . . . there's nothing in there about Maggie, obviously," I said. "But if I can't be there to . . . I want her in a good home. Somewhere safe."

"Hey, emo boy," she said, "time to take a gloom break. Right? You aren't dead yet, as far as I can tell."

I snorted quietly and opened my eyes, looking up at her.

"You'll take care of her yourself when this is done."

I shook my head slowly. "I . . . can't, Murph. Susan was right. All I can offer her is a life under siege. My enemies would use her. She's got to vanish. Go somewhere safe. Really safe. Not even I can know where she is." I swallowed on a choking sensation in my throat. "Father Forthill at St. Mary's can help. Mouse should go with her. He'll help protect her."

Murphy looked at me, troubled. "You aren't telling me something."

"It isn't important for now," I said. "If you could find Mister . . . Molly might like to have him around. Just so long as he's taken care of."

"Jesus, Harry," Murphy said.

"I'm not planning a suicide run, if that's what you're thinking," I said. "But there's a possibility that I won't come back from this. If that happens, I need someone I can trust to know my wishes and carry them out. In case I can't."

"I'll do it," Murphy said, and let out a short laugh. "For crying out loud, I'll do it, just so we can talk about something else."

I smiled, too, and Rudolph entered Tilly's office and found us both on the floor, grinning.

Everyone froze. No one looked certain of how to react.

"Well," Rudolph said quietly, "I always figured this

for what it was. But, boy, did you have everyone at your headquarters fooled, Murphy."

"Hi, Rudy," I said. "You've got a beautiful home."

Rudolph gnashed his teeth and drew an envelope out of his pocket. He flicked it to the floor near Murphy. "For you. A cease-and-desist order, specifying that you aren't allowed within two hundred yards of this case or anyone involved in the active investigation, until your competence and noncomplicity have been confirmed by a special tribunal of the Chicago Police Board. Also a written order from Lieutenant Stallings, specifying that you are to have nothing to do with the investigation into the explosion, and relieving you of duty forthwith if you do not comply." His eyes shifted to me. "You. I haven't forgotten you."

"Shame," I said. "I'd almost forgotten you, but you've ruined that. Walking into the room and all."

"This isn't over, Dresden."

I sighed. "Yeah. I've been having that kind of week."

Murphy opened the envelope and read over a pair of pages. Then she looked at Rudolph and said, "What did you tell them?"

"You have your orders, Sergeant," Rudolph said coldly. "Leave the building before I relieve you of your weapon and your shield."

"You mosquito-dicked weasel," she said, her voice coldly furious.

"That remark is going into my report for the tribunal, Murphy," Rudolph said. There was a vicious satisfaction in his voice. "And once they read the rest, you're done. With your record? They aren't paying you any more slack, bitch. You're gone."

Something dark and ugly stirred in my chest, and the sudden image of Rudolph pinned to the wall by a ton of crystalline ice popped into my brain.

"Bitch?" Murphy said, rising.

"Whoa," I said, drawing out the word as I came to my own feet, and speaking as much to myself as to the furious woman. "Murph, don't play his game here."

"Game?" Rudolph said. "You're a menace, Murphy, and a disgrace. You belong behind bars. Once you're out, it'll happen, too. You and this clown both."

"Clown?" I said, in the exact same tone Murphy had used.

And the lights went out.

There was a sudden hush all around us, as FBI headquarters was plunged into powerless darkness. After several seconds, the emergency lights still hadn't come on.

"Harry," Murphy said, her tone annoyed.

I felt the hairs on the back of my neck crawling around. I lowered my voice and said, "That wasn't me."

"Where are the emergency lights?" Rudolph said. "Th-they're supposed to turn on within seconds. Right?"

"Heh," I said into the darkness. "Heh, heh. Rudy, old buddy, do you remember the night we met?"

Tilly's office was adjacent to the elevator. And I distinctly heard the hunting scream of a Red Court vampire echoing around the elevator shaft.

It was followed by a chorus of screams, more than a score of individual hunting cries.

Lots of vampires in an enclosed space. That was bad.

The heavy, throbbing beat of a hideous heart underlay the screams, audible four stories up and through the wall. I shuddered.

Lots of vampires *and* the Ick in an enclosed space. That was worse.

"What is that?" Rudolph asked in a squeaky whisper.

I willed light into my amulet, prepared my shield bracelet, and drew my blasting rod out of my coat. Beside me, Murphy had already drawn her SIG. She tested the little flashlight on it, found it functional, and looked up at me with the serene expression and steady breathing that told me that she was controlling her fear. "What's the play?" she asked.

"Get Susan and get out," I said. "If I'm not here and she's not here, they've got no reason to attack."

"What is it?" Rudolph asked again. "What is that noise? Huh?"

Murphy leaned her head a bit toward Rudolph, questioning me with a quirked eyebrow.

"Dammit." I sighed. "You're right. We'll have to take him with us, too."

"Tell me!" Rudolph said, near panic. "You have to tell me what that is!"

"Do we tell him?" I asked.

"Sure."

Murphy and I turned toward the door, weapons raised, and spoke in offhanded stereo. "Terrorists."

Chapter
Thirty-five

By the time Murphy and I had moved into the hall, gunfire had erupted on the floors below us. It didn't sound like much—simple, staccato thumping sounds— but anyone who'd heard shots fired in earnest would never mistake them for anything else. I hoped that no- body was carrying rounds heavy enough to come up through the intervening floors and nail me. There just aren't any minor injuries to be had from something like that.

"Those screams," Murphy said. "Red Court, right?"

"Yeah. Where's Susan?"

"Interrogation room, that way." She nodded to the left, and I took the lead. I walked with my shoulder brushing the left-hand wall. Murph, after dragging the sputtering Rudolph out of the office, walked a step be- hind me and a pace to my right, so that she could shoot past me if she had to. We'd played this game before. If something bad came for us, I'd stand it off long enough to give her a clean shot.

That would be critical, buying her the extra second to place her shot. Vampires aren't immune to the dam- age bullets cause, but they can recover from anything but the most lethal hits, and they know it. A Red Court vampire would almost always be willing to charge a mortal gunman, knowing how difficult it is to really place a shot with lethal effect, especially with a howling monster rushing toward you. You needed a hit square in the head, severing the spine, or in their gut, rupturing the blood reservoir, to really put a Red Court vampire down—and they could generally recover, even from those wounds, with enough time and blood to feed upon.

Murphy knew exactly what she was shooting at and had proved that she could be steady enough to deal with a Red—but the other personnel in the building lacked her knowledge and experience.

The FBI was in for a real bad day.

We moved down the hall, quick and silent, and when a frightened-looking clerical type stumbled out of a break room doorway toward us, I nearly sent a blast of flame through him. Murphy had her badge hanging around her neck, and she instructed him to get back inside and barricade the door. He was clearly terrified, and responded without question to the tone of calm authority in Murph's voice.

"Maybe we should do that," Rudolph said. "Get in a room. Barricade the door."

"They've got a heavy with them," I said to Murphy as I took the lead again. "Big, strong, fast. Like the loup-garou. It's some kind of Mayan thing, an Ik-something-or-other."

Murphy cursed. "How do we kill it?"

"Not sure. But daylight seems a pretty good bet." We were passing down a hallway that had several offices with exterior windows. The light of the autumn afternoon, reduced by the occasional curtain, created a kind of murky twilight to move through, and one that my ambient blue wizard light did little to disperse.

Eerier than the lighting was the silence. No air ducts sighed. No elevators rattled. No phones rang. But twice I heard gunshots—the rapid *bang-bang-bang* of practically useless panic fire. Vampires shrieked out their hunting cries several different times. And the *thub-dub* of the Ick's bizarre heartbeat was steady, omnipresent—and slowly growing louder.

"Maybe we need a lot of mirrors or something," Murphy said. "Bring a bunch of daylight in."

"Way harder to do than it looks in the movies," I said. "I figure I'll just blow open a hole in the side of the building." I licked my lips. "Crud, uh. Which way is south? That'll be the best side to do it on."

"You're threatening to destroy a federal building!" Rudolph squeaked.

Gunshots sounded somewhere close—maybe on the third floor, directly below us. Maybe on the other side of the fourth floor, muffled by a lot of cubicle walls.

"Oh, God," Rudolph whimpered. "Oh, dear, sweet Jesus." He just started repeating that in a mindlessly frightened whisper.

"Aha," I said as we reached the interrogation room. "We have our Cowardly Lion. Cover me, Dorothy."

"Remind me to ask what the hell you're talking about later," Murphy said.

I started to open the door, but paused. Tilly was armed, presumably smart enough to be scared, and it probably wasn't the best idea in the world to just open the door of the room and scare him. So I moved as far as possible to one side, reached way over to the door, and knocked. In code, even. *Shave and a haircut.*

There was a lengthy pause and then someone knocked on the other side of the door. *Two bits.*

I twisted the knob and opened the door very, very slowly.

"Tilly?" I said in a hoarse whisper. "Susan?"

The interrogation room didn't have any windows, and it was completely dark inside. Tilly appeared in the doorway, holding up a hand to shield his eyes. "Dresden?"

"Yeah, obviously," I said. "Susan?"

"I'm here," she said from the darkness, her voice shaking with fear. "I'm cuffed to the chair. Harry, we've got to go."

"Working on it," I said quietly.

"You don't understand. That thing, that drumming sound. It's a devourer. You don't fight them. You run, and pray someone slower than you attracts its attention."

"Yeah. Already met the Ick," I said. "I'd rather not repeat the experience." I held out a hand to Tilly. "I need cuff keys."

Tilly hesitated, clearly torn between his sense of duty and order and the primal fear that had risen in the building. He shook his head, but it didn't seem like his heart was in it.

"Tilly," Murphy said. She turned to him, her expression ferociously determined, and said, "Trust me. Please just do it. People are going to die as long as these three are in the building."

He passed me the keys.

I took them over to Susan, who was sitting in the same chair I had during my chat with the feds. She wore her dark leather pants and a black T-shirt and looked oddly vulnerable just sitting there during a situation like this. I went to her and started unfastening the cuffs.

"Thank you," she said quietly. "I was getting a little worried there."

"They must have come in through the basement somehow," I said.

She nodded. "They'll work their way up, floor by floor. Kill everyone they can. It's how they operate. Remove the target and leave a message for everyone else."

Tilly shook his head as if dazed. "That's . . . What? That's how some of the cartels operate in Colombia, Venezuela, but . . ."

Susan gave him an impatient look and shook her head. "What have I been *telling* you for the last fifteen minutes?"

A vampire let out a hunting scream, one not interdicted by floors.

"They're here," Susan whispered as she rubbed at her newly freed wrists. "We have to move."

I stopped for a moment. Then I said quietly, "They'll just keep on killing until they find the target, floor by floor," I said.

Susan nodded tightly.

I bit my lip. "So, if we run . . . they'll keep going. All the way up."

Murphy turned her head to look at me, then jerked her eyes back out to the hallway, wary. "Fight?"

"We won't win," I said, certain. "Not here, on their timing. They've got all the advantages. But we can't just abandon all those people, either."

She took a deep breath and let it out slowly. "No, we can't," Murphy said. "So. What are we going to do?"

"Does anyone have an extra weapon?" Susan asked. No one said anything, and she nodded, turned to the heavy conference table, and flipped it over with one hand. She tore off a heavy steel leg as if it had been attached with a kindergartner's glue rather than high-grade steel bolts.

Tilly stared, his mouth open. Then he said, very quietly, "Ah."

Susan whirled the table leg once, testing its balance, and nodded. "It will do."

I grunted. Then I said, "Here's the plan. We're going to show ourselves to the vampires and the Ick. We're going to hit whoever they have out front with everything we have and squash them flat. That should make sure we have the attention of the entire strike team."

"Yes," Murphy said in a dry tone. "That's brilliant."

I made a face at her. "Once they're good and interested, you, Tilly, and Rudolph are going to split off from the rest of us and hit the nearest emergency exit. If it comes down to it, you probably have better odds of surviving a jump out the window than you do staying in here. You with me?"

Murphy frowned. "What about you?"

"Susan, me, and your stunt doubles are going to jump over into the Nevernever and try to draw the bad guys after us."

"Stunt doubles?" Murphy asked.

"We are?" Susan asked, alarmed.

"Sure. I need your mighty thews to protect me. You being superchick and all."

"Okay," Susan said, eyeing me as if she thought I was losing my mind—which, hey, I admit. Totally possible. "What's on the other side?"

"No clue," I said, and a touch to my mother's gem told me that she hadn't ever actually been in this building on her dimension-hopping jaunts. "We'll hope it isn't an ocean of acid or a patch of cloud five thousand feet above a big rock."

Susan's eyes widened slightly. And then she shot me a wolfish smile. "I love this plan."

"Thought you would," I said. "Meanwhile, you three get out. Does this place have an exterior fire escape?"

Rudolph just rocked back and forth, making soft moaning noises. Tilly still looked stunned at what he had just seen from Susan.

Murphy cuffed him lightly on the back of the head. "Hey. Barry."

Tilly shook his head and looked at her. "Fire escape. No."

"Find a stairwell, then," I told Murphy. "Go quiet and fast, in case some of them were too stupid to follow me."

Murphy nodded and gave Tilly's shoulder a little shake. "Hey. Tilly. You're in charge of Rudolph. All right? Keep him moving and out of any lines of fire."

The slender little man nodded, slowly at first, and then more rapidly as he seemed to take control of himself. "Okay. I'm his nanny. Got it."

Murphy gave him part of a grin and a firm nod.

"Right," I said. "Is this a great plan or what? I'm point; Murph, you've got my six; Susan, you ride drag."

"Got it," Susan said.

The faint, constant drumbeat of the Ick's throbbing heart got fractionally louder.

"Go," I said, and hit the hallways again. At my request, Tilly steered us toward the central staircase running parallel to the elevator shafts, because I figured it would make sense for most of the strike team to use the central stairwell, while the others were covered by maybe a single guard.

We ran into another handful of people who were hovering, uncertain of what to do, and who looked at me in a manner that suggested they would find my advice less than credible.

"Tilly," I said, half pleading.

Tilly nodded and started speaking in a calm, authoritative tone. "There's some kind of attack under way. Tammy, you and Joe and Mickey need to get to one of the offices with a window. You got that? A window. Take the curtains down, let the light in, barricade the door, and sit tight." He looked at me and said, "Help's on the way."

I swapped a look with Murphy, who nodded confidently at me. Tilly had gotten the supernatural shoved in his face pretty hard, but he'd rebounded with tremendous agility. Or maybe he'd simply cracked. I guessed we'd see eventually.

The federal personnel scurried to obey Tilly, running down the hall we'd just come from.

If we'd been about ten seconds slower, the vampire would have found them first instead of us.

I heard a scream, shrill and terrible, meant to send a jolt of terrorized surprise through the prey so that the vampire could close upon it. It really said something about the Red Court, that simple tactic. Animals would never have been startled into immobility that way. It takes a thinking mind, trying to reason its way to what was happening, to fall for a psychological ploy like that one.

And it probably said something about me that it completely failed to startle me. Or maybe it wasn't that big a deal. As the Scarecrow, I felt that I had amply proven that I didn't *have* much of a brain with which to be messed.

So instead of finding a helpless target waiting for him, the Red Court vampire found a field of adamant, invisible power as I brought my shield up. And while it might have supernatural strength, that didn't increase its mass. It bounced off my shield like any other body would if abruptly meeting someone's front bumper at fifty or sixty miles an hour.

There was a flash of blue light, and I released the shield with a little English on it, tossing the vampire to sprawl on the ground on the right-hand side of the hallway, squarely in Murphy's line of fire, and started moving forward again.

Murphy calmly put two bullets into the vampire's head, which made an unholy mess of the wall behind it. She put two more into its blood-gorged belly on the way by, and as Susan passed, I heard an ugly, moist sound of impact.

Tilly stood there staring for a second, frozen. Then Susan nudged him into motion again. The agent grabbed Rudolph and dragged him after Murphy and me.

We found the first human body several steps later, a glassy-eyed young woman covered in her own blood. Beyond her, a man in a suit lay sprawled on his face in death, and the corpses of two more women lay within a few feet of him.

There was the most furtive of sounds from a darkened supply closet near an intersection of hallways, its doorway gaping wide open. I didn't let on that I'd heard it.

"You know what?" I said quietly to no one in particular. "That makes me mad."

I turned with my blasting rod's runes blazing into sudden life and roared, *"Fuego!"*

A spear of white-hot fire erupted from the rod, blowing through the interior wall in a concussive chorus of shattering materials. I slewed it along the length of the closet at waist height, cutting through the wall like an enormous buzz saw.

A surprised scream of inhuman agony greeted my efforts, and I spun in place at once, bringing up the shield again. A second vampire bounded around the intersection ahead, running on all fours along the wall, and threw itself at me. At the same time, another of the rubbery black creatures exploded out of an air vent I would have sworn was too tiny to contain it, coming down from almost straight overhead.

I rebounded the first vamp from my shield, as I had only moments before, and Murphy's gun began to bark the instant it bounced off the wall and to the floor.

I couldn't get my shield up in time to stop the one plunging down from overhead.

It landed on me, a horrible, squishy weight, and with the crystalline perceptions of surging adrenaline I saw its jaws dropping open nightmarishly wide, unhinging like a snake's. Its fangs gleamed. Black claws on all four limbs were poised to rake, and its two-foot-long tongue lashed at me as well, seeking exposed skin in order to deliver its stupefying venom.

I went down to the floor on my face, hurriedly covering my head with my arms. The vampire raked at me furiously, but the defensive spells on my duster held and prevented its claws from scoring. The vampire shifted tactics quickly, tossing me over like a rodeo cowboy taking down a calf. The writhing, slimy tongue lashed at my face, now vulnerable.

Susan's hand closed on that tongue in midmotion, and with a twist of her wrist and shoulders, she ripped it out of the vampire's mouth. The vamp threw its head back and shrieked—and my ex-sweetie's improvised mace smashed its skull down into its torso.

The vampire in the closet, still out of sight, continued to wail its agony as I rose again and checked around me to make sure everyone was there. "Anyone hurt?"

"W-we're fine," Tilly said. For a guy who'd just had a couple of close encounters with imaginary creatures, he seemed to be fairly coherent. Rudolph had retreated to his happy place, and just kept on rocking, crying, and whispering. "What about you, Dresden?"

"Peachy."

Murphy turned toward the closet, her face grim, her gun in her hand. I shook my head at her. "No. Let it scream. It'll draw the others to us and away from anyone else."

Murphy looked at me for a moment, frowning gently, but nodded. "God, that's cold, Harry."

"I lost my warm fuzzies for the Reds a long time ago," I said. The wounded vampire just wouldn't shut up. Fire's tough on them. Their outer layer of skin is combustible. My attack had probably left it in two pieces, or otherwise pared down its body mass. It would be a smoldering lump of agony writhing on the floor, in so much pain that it could literally do nothing *but* scream.

And that suited me just fine.

"We aren't just standing here, are we?" Tilly asked.

A pair of particularly loud, simultaneous shrieks came through the vents and shafts, ululating over and under each other. They were particularly strident and piercing, and went on for longer than the others. A chorus of lesser shrieks wailed briefly in reply.

The Eebs, as generals, sending orders to the troops. It had to be, coordinating the raid and directing it toward the injured member of the team.

"Indeed we are not. All right, folks. Murph, Tilly, Rudolph, get scarce. Follow Murphy and do whatever the hell she tells you to do if you want to get out of this alive."

Murphy grimaced at that. "Be careful, Dresden."

"You too," I said. "See you at the church."

She gave me a sharp nod, beckoned Tilly, and the two of them started off down another hallway to one of the side stairwells. With any luck, the Eebs had just sent everyone they had running toward me. Even if Murphy and Tilly weren't lucky, I figured they'd probably have only a single sentry to deal with, at the most. I gave Murphy even odds of handling that. A 50 percent chance of survival wasn't real encouraging, but it was about 50 percent higher than if they'd stayed.

Susan watched them go and then looked at me. "You and Murphy never hooked up?"

"You're asking this now?" I demanded.

"Should I fix us both a nice cup of tea, in our copious free time?"

I rolled my eyes and shook my head. "No. We haven't."

"Why not?" she asked.

"A lot of reasons. Bad timing. Other relationships. You know." I took a long, deep breath and said, "Keep an eye out. I've got to pull off something hard here."

"Right," Susan said. She went back to watching the gloom, her club held ready.

I closed my eyes and summoned up my will. Time for some real razzle-dazzle stuff.

Illusions are a fascinating branch of magic. There are two basic ways to manage them. One, you can create an image and put it in someone else's head. There's no actual visible object there, but their brain tells them that it's there, big as life—a phantasm. It's walking real close to the borders of the Laws of Magic to go that way, but it could be very effective.

The second method is the creation of an actual visible object or creature—a kind of hologram. Those things are much harder to produce, because you have to pour a lot more energy into them, and while a phantasm uses a foe's own mind to create consistency within the illusion, you've got to do it the hard way with holomancy.

Murph's image was easy to fix in mind, as was Rudolph's, though I admit that I might have made him look a bit skinnier and slouchier than he might actually have been. My holomancy, my rules.

The hardest was Tilly. I kept getting the image of the actor from *The X-Files* confabulated with the actual Tilly, and the final result was kinda marginal. But I was in a rush.

I pictured the images with as much clarity as I could and sent my will, including a tiny bit of soulfire, into creating the mirages.

Soulfire isn't really a destructive force. It's sort of the opposite, actually. And while I used it in fights to enhance my offensive spells, it really shone when creating things.

I whispered, "*Lumen, camerus, factum!*" and released energy into the mental images. The holograms of Murphy, Tilly, and Rudolph shimmered into existence, so absolutely real-looking that even I thought they might have been solid matter.

"They're coming!" Susan said abruptly. She turned to me and practically jumped out of her shoes upon seeing the illusions. Then she waved a hand at Tilly's image, and it flickered straight through. She let out a low whistle and said, "Time to go?"

The thunder of the Ick's heart grew abruptly louder, a vibration I could feel through the soles of my shoes.

Vampires boiled out of the central stairwell, a sudden tide of flabby, rubbery black bodies and all-black eyes, of spotted pink tongues and gleaming fangs. At their center, in their flesh-masked forms, were Esteban and Esmerelda. And looming behind them was the Ick.

Susan and I turned and sprinted. The three illusions did the same thing, complete with the sounds of running footfalls and heavy breathing. With a group howl the vampires came after us.

I ran as hard as I could, drawing up more of my will. I should have been feeling some of the strain by now, but I wasn't. Go, go, Gadget Faustian bargain.

I gathered my will, shouted, *"Aparturum!"* and slashed at the air down the hallway with my right hand.

I'd used a lot of energy to open the Way, and it tore wide, a diagonal rip in the fabric of space, crooked and off center to the hallway. It hung there like some kind of oddly geometric cloud of mist, and I pointed at it, shouting wordlessly to Susan. She shouted something back, nodding, while behind us the vampires gained ground with every second.

We both screamed in a frenzy of wild fear and rampant adrenaline, and hit the Way moving at a dead run.

We plunged through—into empty air.

I let out a shriek as I fell, and figured I'd finally taken my last desperate gamble—but after less than a second, my flailing limbs hit solid stone and I dropped into a roll. I came back up to my feet and kept running through what appeared to be a spacious cavern of some kind, and Susan ran beside me.

We didn't run far. A wall loomed up out of the blackness and we barely stopped in time to keep from braining ourselves against it.

"Jesus," Susan said, panting. "Have you been working out?"

I turned, blasting rod in hand and ready, to wait for the first of the pursuing vampires to appear. There were shrieks and wails and the sound of scrabbling claws—but none of them emerged from the shadows.

Which . . . just couldn't have been good.

Susan and I stood there, a solid wall to our backs, unsure of what to do next. And then a soft green light began to rise.

It intensified slowly, coming from nowhere and everywhere at the same time, and within a few seconds I realized that we weren't in a cave. We were in a hall. A medieval dining hall, to be precise. I was staring at a double row of trestle tables that stretched down the length of the hall, easily better than a hundred yards, leaving an open aisle between them. Seated at the tables were . . . things.

There was a curious similarity among them, though no two of the creatures were the same. They were vaguely humanoid. They wore cloth and leather and armor, all of it inscribed with odd geometric shapes in colors that could only with difficulty be differentiated from black. Some of them were tall and emaciated, some squat and muscular, some medium-sized, and every combination in between. Some of the creatures had huge ears, or no ears, or odd, saggy chins. None of them carried the beauty of symmetry. Their similarity was in mismatchedness, each individual's body at aesthetic war with itself.

One thing was the same: They all had gleaming red eyes, and if ever a gang looked evil, these beings did.

They had one other thing in common. They were all armed with knives, swords, axes, and other, crueler implements of battle.

Susan and I had come in sprinting down the center aisle between the tables. We must have startled our hosts, who reacted only in time to catch the second batch of intruders to come through—and catch them they had.

Some of the largest of the beings, easily weighing half a ton themselves, had piled onto the Ick and held it pinned to the earth. Nearby, the mob of vampires were lumped more or less together, each one entangled in nets made out of some material that I can only describe as flexible barbed wire.

Only Esteban and Esmerelda stood on their feet, back-to-back, between the Ick and the netted minions. There was blood on the floor near them, and two of the native creatures were lying still upon the stone floor.

"Jesus," Susan whispered. "What are those things?"

"I . . ." I swallowed. "I think they're goblins."

"You think?"

"I've never seen one before," I replied. "But . . . they match the descriptions I've heard."

"Shouldn't we be able to handle, like, a million of them?"

I snorted. "You liked those movies, too, huh?"

Her reply was a smile, one touched with sadness.

"Yeah," I said. "I was thinking of you when I saw them, too." I shook my head. "And no. This is a case of folklore getting it wrong. These guys are killers. They're sneaky and they're smart and they're ruthless. Like ninjas. From Krypton. *Look what they did.*"

Susan stared at the downed Red Court strike team for a moment. I watched the wheels turn in her head as she processed what had happened to the vampires and the Ick, in a handful of seconds, in complete darkness and in *total silence.*

"Um. I guess we'd better make nice, then, huh?" Susan asked. She slipped her club around behind her back and put on her old reporter's smile, the one she used to disarm hostile interviewees.

And then I had a thought.

A horrible, horrible thought.

I turned slowly around. I looked at the wall I'd been standing against.

And then I looked up.

It wasn't a wall, exactly. It was a dais. A big one. Atop it sat a great stone throne.

And upon the throne sat a figure in black armor, covered from head to toe. He was huge, nine feet tall at least, and had a lean, athletic look to him despite the armor. His helm covered his head and veiled his face with darkness, and great, savagely pointed antlers rose up from the helmet, though whether they were adornment or appendage I couldn't say. Within the visor of that helmet was a pair of steady red eyes, eyes that matched the thousands of others in the hall.

He leaned forward, the Lord of the Goblins of Faerie, leader of the Wild Hunt, nightmare of story and legend and peer of the Queen of Air and Darkness, Mab herself.

"Well," murmured the Erlking. "Well, well, well. Isn't this *interesting*."

Chapter

Thirty-six

I stared up at the Erlking, and with my typical pithy brilliance said, "Uh-oh."

The Erlking chuckled, a deep sound. It echoed around the hall, resonating from the stone, amplified into subtle music. If I'd had any doubts that I was standing at the heart of the Erlking's power, that laugh and the way the hall had responded in harmony took care of them for me. "It seems, my kin, that we have guests."

More chuckles rose up from a thousand throats, and evil red eyes crinkled with amusement.

"I confess," the Erlking said, "that this is a . . . unique event. We are unaccustomed to visitors here. I trust you will be patient whilst I blow the dust from the old courtesies."

Again, the goblins laughed. The sound seemed to press directly against whatever nerve raised the hairs on my arms.

The Erlking rose, smooth and silent despite his armor and his mass, and descended from the dais. He walked around to loom over us, and I took note of the huge sword at his side, its pommel and hilt bristling with sharp metal protrusions that looked like thorns. He studied us for a moment and then did two things I hadn't really expected.

First, he took off his helmet. The horns were, evidently, fixed to the dark metal. I braced myself to view something horrible but . . . the Lord of Goblins was nothing like what I had expected.

Upon his face, the hideous asymmetries of the goblins of his hall were all reflected and somehow transformed. Though he, too, shared the irregular batch of features, upon him their fundamental repulsiveness was muted into a kind of roguish distinction. His crooked nose seemed something that might have been earned rather than gifted. Old, faint scars marred his face, but only added further grace notes to his appearance. Standing there before the Erlking, I felt as if I were looking at something handcrafted by a true master, perhaps carved from a piece of twisted driftwood, given its own odd beauty, and then patiently refined and polished into something made lovely by its sheer, unique singularity.

There was power in that face, too, in his simple presence. You could feel it in the air around him, the tension and focus of a pure predator, and one who rarely failed to bring down his prey.

The second thing he did was to bow with inhuman elegance, take Susan's hand, and bend to brush his lips across the backs of her fingers. She stared at him with wide eyes that were more startled than actually afraid, and she kept her smile going the whole time.

"Lady huntress," he said, "the scent of fresh blood hangs upon you. Well does it become your nature."

He looked at me and smiled, showing his teeth, which were white and straight and even, and I had to fight to keep from flinching from his gaze. The Erlking had a score to settle with me. I had better come up with a plan, and fast, or I was a dead man.

"And the new Knight of Winter," he continued. "I nearly had thee at Arctis Tor, when the ogres caught up to thee upon the slopes. Hadst thou departed but three-score heartbeats later . . ." He shook his head. "Thou art an intriguing quarry, Sir Knight."

I bowed to the Erlking in what I hoped was a respectful fashion. "I do thank thee for the compliment, O King," I said. "Though it is chance, not design, that brought me hither, I am humbled by thy generosity in accepting us into thine home as guests. Mine host."

The Erlking cocked his head slightly to one side, and then his mouth turned up into another amused smile. "Ah. Caught out by mine own words, 'twould seem. Courtesy is not a close companion unto me, so perhaps it is meet that in a duel of manners, thou wouldst have the advantage. And this hall honors cleverness and wisdom as much as strength."

A murmur of goblin voices ran through the hall at his words, because I'd just done something impossibly impudent. I'd dropped myself into the dinner hall of the greatest hunter of Faerie—practically thrown myself onto a plate with an apple in my mouth, in fact—and then used an idle slip of his tongue to claim the ancient rights of protection as his guest, thus obligating him, as host, to uphold those responsibilities to me.

I've said it before. The customs of host and guest are a Big Deal to these people. It's insane, but it's who they are.

I bowed my head to him respectfully, rather than saying anything like, *Gee, it's not often one of the fae gets outwitted by a lowly human*, which should be proof enough for anyone that I'm not entirely devoid of diplomatic skills. "I should not wish to intrude upon your hospitality any longer than is absolutely necessary, Lord of Hunters. With your goodwill, we will depart immediately and trouble you no more."

"Do not listen to it, O Erlking," called a woman's clear soprano. It was easy to recognize Esmerelda. "It speaks honeyed words with a poisoned tongue, full intent upon deceiving you."

The Erlking turned to regard the pair of vampires, still on their feet despite the efforts of the goblins who had initially attacked them. He studied them in complete silence for several seconds and then, after a glance at the fallen goblins near them, inclined his head. "Hunters of the Red Court, I bid ye continue. I listen. Pray tell me more."

"Wiley game indeed, this wizard kin," said Esteban. "It was well treed and out of tricks but for this shameful bid to escape the rightful conclusion of the hunt. With full intent did the wizard bring us here, into your demesne, intending to use you, O Erlking, to strike down his own foes."

"When hunting a fox, one must be wary not to follow it into the great bear's lair," the Erlking replied. "This is common sense for any hunter, by my reckoning."

"Well-spoken, Goblin King," Esmerelda said. "But by this action, the wizard seeks to draw you into the war betwixt its folk and ours, for we hunt it upon the express wishes of our lord and master, as part of our rightly declared war."

The Erlking's red eyes narrowed and flicked back over to me. I could hear a low and angry undertone to his next words. "I desire naught of any other being, save to pursue my hunts in accordance with the ancient traditions without interference. I tell thee this aright, Sir Knight. Should this hunter's words prove true, I will lay a harsh penalty upon thee and thine—one which the Powers will speak of in whispers of dread for a thousand years."

I swallowed. I thought about it. Then I lifted my chin and said calmly, "I give thee my word, as Knight of the Winter Court, that I had no such intention when coming here. It was chance that brought this chase to thy hall, O Erlking. I swear it upon my power."

The ancient fae stared hard at me for several more seconds, his nostrils flaring. Then he drew back his head slowly and nodded once. "So. I am given a riddle by my most thoughtful visitors," he said, his voice rumbling. He looked from the Eebs and company back to Susan and me. "What to do with you all. For I wish not to encourage visits such as this one." His mouth twisted in distaste. "Now I am reminded why I do not indulge in courtesy as do the Sidhe. Such matters delight them. I find that they pall swiftly."

A very large, very powerful-looking goblin near the front of the hall said, "My king, render blood judgment upon them all. They are intruders in your realm. Place their heads upon your gates as a warning to any who would follow."

A rumble of agreement ran through the crowd of goblins.

The Erlking seemed to muse on the idea for a moment.

"Or," I offered, "such an act might invite more interference. The express servants of the king of the Red Court would surely be missed should they not return. The White Council of wizards would, I assure you, have very strong feelings about my own disappearance. To say nothing, of course, of Mab's reaction. I'm still quite new, and she hasn't yet tired of me."

The Erlking waved a hand. "Nay, nay. The Knight caught my words fairly. Guests they are, Lord Ordulaka, and I will not cheapen my honor by betraying that ancient compact." He narrowed his eyes. "Mmmm. Guests they are. Perhaps I should treat them most courteously. Perhaps I should insist that you remain my guests, to be cared for and entertained, for the next century." He gave me a chilly little smile. "After all, you are all but the first visitors to my realm. I could understandably find it greatly insulting were you not to allow me the opportunity to honor you appropriately."

The Eebs looked at each other and then both bowed sinuously to the Erlking. "Generous host," Esteban said, "you honor us greatly. We should be pleased to stay as your guests for whatever length of time you feel appropriate."

"Harry," Susan hissed, tensing.

She didn't need to explain it to me. A delay of even a few hours might mean Maggie's death.

"Honored host," I said. "Such a path would be no less than your due, given the . . . unanticipated nature of our visit. But I would beg you only to consider my obligations to my Lady Mab. I pursue a quest that I may not lay aside, and which she has bidden me complete. It hinges upon things that occur in mortal time, and were you to insist upon your rights as host, it could compromise my own honor. Something I know that you, as mine host, would never wish to do."

The Erlking gave me a look that blended annoyance with amusement and said, "Few Winter Knights have had swords as swift as your tongue, boy. But I warn thee:

Name your Lady a third time and you will not like what follows."

I hadn't even thought of that. Hell's bells, he was right. Speaking Mab's name here, in the Nevernever, could indeed summon her. At which point not only would she be an intruder in another ruler's domain, perhaps vulnerable to his power or influence, but she would be extremely annoyed with one overtaxed wizard for having brought her. The clashing of such Powers in simple proximity could prove dangerous, even deadly.

I bowed my head again and said, "Of course, mine host."

A goblin about five feet tall, and so slender that it looked like a stiff wind might blow him down, appeared from the shadows and diffidently took the Erlking's helmet. He began to turn to carry it away, paused, and suggested, in a spidery, whispering, unpleasant voice, "We are all predators here, my lord. Let it be settled in a trial of blood."

The Erlking spread his hands, as if he felt the suggestion should have been self-evident to everyone present. "Of course, Rafforut. Again, thou hast given excellent service."

The wispy goblin bowed at the waist and retreated to the shadows, his mouth curling up in a small smile.

"Oh," I said. "Oh, crap."

"What?" Susan asked.

I turned to speak quietly to her in a whisper pitched to register only to her more-than-human hearing, and hoped that the goblins didn't hear even better than that. "The Erlking can't harm us, or allow us to come to harm while we are his guests. Ditto for the Reds. But since we have competing claims that must be settled, he *can* establish a trial by combat to see who is correct—or at least, most committed to his version of the story."

Susan's eyes widened as she understood. "If we won't fight for our side of the story, he decides against us and for the Eebs."

I nodded. "At which point he can declare that we have abused his hospitality," I said. "And he will be free to kill us, probably without repercussion."

"But you just said—"

"M— The Winter Queen doesn't feel a thing for me," I said. "She might be annoyed. But this time next week, she'll barely remember me."

"But the Council—"

"I said they would feel strongly about it," I said. "I never said they'd be upset."

Susan's eyes got a little wider.

"A trial of skill, then," the Erlking said. "A match. The Knight and the lady huntress versus two of your own, Red hunters. Choose which will stand for your side of the issue." He clapped his hands once, a sound like a small cannon going off. "Prepare the hall."

Goblins leapt to obey, and cleared the long trestle tables outward with great energy and efficiency. Others began to rip at the stone with their bare, black-nailed hands. They tore it like wet earth, swiftly gouging out a great ring in the floor, a trench six inches wide, almost that deep, and thirty or forty yards across.

"We're hardly armed properly for such a trial, mine host," I said. "Whilst the Red hunters are fully equipped for battle as they are."

The Erlking spread his hands again. "Ah, but they are armed with what they deemed necessary to them for the hunt. And a true hunter never leaves himself unprepared for what the world may bring to face him. Do you say, perhaps, that you are no hunter after all?"

"No," Susan said at once. "Of course not."

The Erlking looked at her and gave her a nod of approval. "I am glad you find yourselves appropriately armed." He glanced over at the Eebs, who were discussing matters in furious whispers, probably employing a nonstandard use of pronouns. "Sooth, boy, you were quick enough at wordplay that I would fain feed thee and send thee on thy way, had you come here unpursued. But I will not rouse the wrath of the Lords of Outer Night lightly. A war with them would be a waste of dozens of excellent hunting moons." He shrugged. "So. Prove yourselves worthy, and you may be on your way."

I cleared my throat. "And our . . . fellow visitors?"

The Erlking didn't smile or otherwise change his expression, but I suddenly got creeped out enough to have to fight to keep from stepping away from him. "My hall is fully furnished to receive all manner of outsiders. There are rooms in these caves filled with clever devices meant for the amusement of my kin, and lacking only the appropriate . . . participants."

"What happens if we lose?" Susan asked.

"If fortune is kind, you will have clean deaths in the trial. If not . . ." He shrugged. "Certain of my kin—Rafforut, for example—are most eager to give purpose to all the rooms of my hall. You would amuse them for as long as you could respond. Which might be a very, very long time."

Susan eyed the Erlking. Then she said, "Let's do it, then. I, too, have promises to keep."

He inclined his head to her. "As you wish, lady huntress. Sir Knight, lady, please enter the circle."

I started toward it and Susan walked beside me.

"How should we do it?" she asked.

"Fast and hard."

Her voice turned wry. "How did I know you'd want it like that?"

I let out a short bark of genuine laughter. "I thought I was supposed to be the one with one thing on his mind."

"Oh, when we were younger, certainly," she replied. "Now, though, our roles have reversed."

"Meaning you want it fast and hard, too?"

She gave me a sly and very heated look with her dark eyes from beneath her dark lashes. "Let's just say that there's something to be said for that, once in a while." She spun the table leg in a few circles. I watched. She stopped and glanced at me, arching an eyebrow inquisitively.

My godmother might have tipped me off to a cure, a way to free Susan of the creature that had devoured half of her being and thirsted for me, something the Fellowship of St. Giles had been trying—and failing—to do for hundreds of years. It was possible that, with a bit more work, I could make it happen for her, give her back control of her life.

But even if I did, we couldn't be together. Not now.

Mab was bad enough . . . and Hell's bells, I hadn't even *thought* about it, I'd been so busy, but Mab's understudy, Maeve, the Winter Lady, was arguably more psychotic than Mab herself. And she was unarguably pettier, more vicious, and more likely to want to play games with anyone close to me.

I wondered how long it would take me to lose myself. Weeks? Months? Neither Mab nor Maeve would want me to remain my own man. I wondered if, when I was what they wanted me to be, it would bother me to remember what I had been. What others had meant to me.

All I said was, "I miss you."

She looked down and away, blinking. Then she gave me a rather hesitant smile as a tear fell—as if it were something she hadn't done in a while, and was still remembering how to accomplish it. "I miss joking with you."

"How could you do it?" I asked quietly. "How could you not tell me about her?"

"By tearing out a piece of myself," she said quietly. "I know it was wrong. I knew it was wrong when I did it, and that . . . that I was going to regret it someday. But I had to keep her safe. I'm not asking you to forgive. Just . . . just understand."

I thought about that moment of stillness and choice at the Stone Table.

"Yeah," I said. I lifted a hand and touched her face with my fingertips. Then I leaned over to kiss her forehead. "I do understand."

She stepped closer and we hugged. She felt surprisingly slender and fragile in my arms. We stayed that way for a little while, both of us feeling the fear of what was coming. We tried to ignore the hundreds of red eyes watching us. We more or less succeeded.

Another cannon clap of sound echoed around the vast hall, and the Erlking said, "Red hunters. Let your chosen champions enter the circle or else forfeit the trial."

"Okay," I said. "The Eebs will be tough but they're doable. They rely on stealth tactics, and this is going to be as straight up as you can get. I'm going to hit them with something that should give you enough time to close. Take whichever one is on the left. Move too far to the right and you'll be in my line of fire, so don't. You smash one, I burn the other, and we go get some custom coffee mugs to memorialize the occasion later."

Susan said, "I stopped drinking coffee. You know, the caffeine."

I looked at her with mock disgust. "You heathen."

"Fine!" Esmerelda said from the far side of the circle.

She pointed a finger at one of the vampires trapped beneath the goblins' nets. "You. You do it." Impatiently, the tiny woman went to the trapped vampire, hideous and inhuman in its true form, and sliced through the odd material of the net with her nails, freeing the captive. Without ceremony, she pitched the vampire into the circle.

One of her foot soldiers? Okay. This might be easier than I'd thought.

Esteban appeared then, walking calmly forward.

The slowly accelerating *lub-dub* sound of the Devourer's unsettling heartbeat came with him. The Devourer loomed over Esteban, horrible and hungry-looking, and at a command from the vampire, it shambled forward into the circle, its all-black eyes staring at us with unnerving intensity. I might have been projecting or something, but it seemed to me that the Ick was spoiling for some payback.

"Oh, crap," Susan said in a very small voice.

"When the circle is closed," said the Erlking's deep baritone, "the trial begins. It will conclude when one party has been neutralized. Do the champions of the Red hunters stand ready?"

All of the vampires let out wailing shrieks, and even the Ick emitted a hissing burble, like an overfull teakettle.

"What are we going to do?" Susan whispered frantically.

I had no idea. "You take the scrub," my mouth said. "I'll handle the Devourer."

"Right," she said, her eyes wide. "Right."

The Erlking appeared, halfway between the two parties, standing outside the circle. "Sir Knight! Do you and the lady huntress stand ready?"

We both nodded sharply, though our eyes were fixed

upon our opponents, not the Erlking. I began drawing in my will, and power seethed in my belly and chest and became an odd pressure behind my eyes.

The Erlking drew his sword and held it high, and every goblin in the place began roaring. Fire licked up the blade of the sword, wreathing it in green flame, and then he dropped the sword, thrusting its tip into the trough in the stone the goblins had dug.

Green goblin fire flared up with a howl and clouds of foul smoke. It raced around the exterior of the circle in both directions, until the two tongues of flame met at the point opposite where they had begun.

Susan screamed. I screamed. The vampire screamed. The Ick . . . did that teakettle thing.

And then we all started trying to kill one another.

Chapter

Thirty-seven

Vampires and Icks are fast, but I'd dueled their like before. Like the apocryphal Loki, my previous opponents had learned that no matter how quick you are on your feet, you aren't faster than thought.

The spell I'd been holding ready lashed out before either of our opponents had moved more than a couple of feet, naked force howling out from my outstretched hand to seize not the Ick, but, in a sudden flash of inspiration, I directed it at the vampire beginning to bound along beside and a little behind it. Clearly, maybe even wisely, the vamp was hoping to stand in the Devourer's shadow when the hurt started flying.

I cried out, *"Forzare!"* and my raw will hammered the vampire down and at an oblique angle—directly in front of and beneath the feet of the Ick.

If you have no weapons with which to fight the enemy, find a way to make your enemy *be* your weapon. If you can pull it off, it makes you look amazing.

The vampire went under the Ick's feet with a wailing squeal and a crunchy-sounding splatter of vile fluids. The collision tripped up the massive hunting creature as its legs tangled with the vampire's rubbery, sinuous limbs, and the Ick came crashing to the ground, its unnatural drumbeat heart thudding loud and furious, swiping and smashing in fury at the entanglement without ever bothering to consider what it might be destroying.

Susan adjusted almost instantly to what had happened, and closed on the sprawling Ick with incredible speed. Her arm blurred as the Ick began recovering its balance, smashing her club straight down onto its skull and driving its head down to rebound from the floor.

The Ick took the hit like it was a love tap, slashing at Susan with its claws—but she had already bounded into the air, jerking her knees up to avoid the grabbing claws and flying clear over the Devourer to a roar of approval from the watching goblins. She landed in a baseball player's slide and shot forward over the gore-smeared stone, snapping one hand back to grab the throat of the downed vampire as she did.

The battered body came free of the Ick's limbs, minus a limb or two of its own, and thrashed weakly, slowing Susan's slide and stopping her forward motion a bare inch before her feet would have slid into the green flame surrounding the fighting ring.

The Ick whirled around as it staggered to its feet again, preparing to pursue her, when I lifted my blasting rod, snarled, *"Fuego,"* and hammered it with all the power I could shove through the magical focus. Blue-white fire, blindingly bright against the rather dim green flames of the Erlking's will, drew a group scream of surprise and discomfort from the gathered goblins. The fire struck the Ick and gouged a chunk of black, rubbery flesh the size of a watermelon out of the massive muscles of its back. Its head whipped back so sharply that the top of its head practically touched its own spine, and it lost its balance for another second or two, slipping on the gore the first vampire had provided as it turned toward me.

I dimly took note of Susan as this happened. The half-crushed, half-dismembered vampire flailed wildly with its remaining claws and fangs, putting up an insanely desperate, vicious fight in an attempt to hang on to its life.

Susan took a hard blow to the side of the head, and when she turned back, her lip was bloodied, her teeth bared in a snarl, and the dark swirls and points of her tattoos began to spread over her face like black ink dripped upon water. She dropped the improvised club, got both hands on the vampire's throat, and, with calm, precise strength, thrust its head into the green fire.

There was a bloody explosion as that fire devoured the vampire, and though its heat had seemed no greater than any campfire's, the temperature within that fire had to be something as hot as the sun. As the vampire's skull entered it, it simply disintegrated with a howl of vaporized liquids, spattering tiny bits of bone like shrapnel and covering Susan and the dying vampire both in an enormous, dark, foul-smelling cloud.

"Susan!" I shouted, and darted over to one side so that I wouldn't be loosing blasts of fire blindly into that cloud if I missed. I hit the Devourer, gouging out a small trough in one of its arms, missed with the third blast, and scored with a fourth, burning a scorch mark as wide as my thigh across its hip. The drumbeat of its heart was a huge, pounding rhythm by now, like the double bass drums of a speed-metal band. The hits seemed only to make it more furious, and it shifted into a controlled forward rush meant to crowd me into the outer ring of fire or else leave me unable to escape its grasping claws.

But either the blow on the noggin or one of the blasts I'd unleashed had slowed the Ick down. I sprinted for the angle on its approach, for the path that would let me evade the Devourer and its outstretched claws, and got clear of its attack, beating the monster out on footwork and keeping from being trapped against the circle's perimeter as it came at me.

I found a fierce smile spreading over my lips as I moved. I kept hurling blasts at its legs as I ran, attempting to slow it even more. I didn't hit with more than a quarter of them, I think, but the missed bolts of fire splashed against the Erlking's green fire in sizzling bursts of light. The adrenaline made my senses crystalline, bringing me every sight and sound with a cold purity, and I suddenly saw where the Devourer was weakest.

Though it was hard to tell with its alien movement, I realized that it was favoring one side ever so slightly. I darted in for a better look, nearly got my head ripped off by a flailing fist, and saw that the Ick's leg was wounded, low on the back of its thigh, where the black flesh was twisted and mangled. Had it been mortal skin and tissue, I would have thought it the result of a severe burn—as long as whatever had done the burning had been molten-metal hot and shaped like Mouse's teeth. The Foo dog had gotten to the Ick during its encounter with Thomas, with a wound that had threatened to cripple it. That was why it had been forced to withdraw. If it stayed and Mouse had managed another such strike, it would have been entirely immobilized.

"Good luck this time, big guy," I heard myself say. "You've got nowhere to run."

The part of my mind that was still mostly sane thought the statement was utterly crazy. Maybe stupid, too. The Ick was still chasing *me*, after all. If it hit me once with one of those enormous, clawed hands, it would liquefy the bones under whichever part of my body it hit. (With the possible exception of my head. I maintain that all evidence seems to point to the fact that someone did one of those adamantium upgrades on my skull when I wasn't looking.)

I was scrambling and blasting away for all I was worth, and I couldn't keep up a pace like that forever. I was scoring on the Ick, maybe slowing it even more, but I wasn't even close to killing it.

It all came down to a simple question: Was the Ick better at taking it than I was at dishing it out? If so, then I was living on borrowed time, and the continuing on-slaught of magic I threw at the thing amounted to an extremely high rate of interest.

Before I could find out, the fight changed.

The Ick made a painful-looking surge of effort, and got close enough to hit me. I barely got out of the way in time, almost fell, turned it into several spinning steps instead, and recovered my balance. The Ick turned to follow, and Susan burst out of the cloud of greasy smoke the instant it turned its back.

Her tattoos had flushed from black to a deep, deep crimson, and she moved with perfect grace and in per-fect silence. So when she gracefully, silently swung that steel table leg at the side of the Ick's knee joint—on its unmarred leg, no less—it took the monster entirely off guard.

There was a sharp, terrible crack, a sound that I would have associated only with falling timber or possibly small-caliber gunfire if I'd heard it somewhere else. The steel bar smashed the Ick's knee unnaturally inward, until it made an angle of nearly thirty degrees.

It bellowed in agony and one arm swept back toward its attacker. The Ick hit Susan, and though it had been off balance, startled, and falling when it did so, it still knocked her ten feet backward and to the ground. Her club bounced out of her hand with a chiming, metallic clang, and tumbled, ringing like a tinny gong, into the circling flames.

The heat within the green fires sliced off half the table leg as neatly as any high-temperature torch possibly could have done. The colors of the flame briefly striated with tendrils of amber, violet, and coppery red. The severed end rolled free of the fire, and its edge was glowing white-hot.

I noticed it in the periphery of my heightened vision.

Susan had landed on the ground with her back twisted at an impossible angle.

The Ick lurched toward me as I stood there, frozen in shock for the briefest of instants. It was more than enough time for the Devourer to close, rake at me with its claws, and bat me twenty feet across the circle, all at the same time.

Again, the spells on my coat withstood the brute power of the Ick's claws, but this hadn't been a glancing blow, or incidental damage collected when it had tripped over me. This was a full-on sledgehammer slam of the kind that had probably tossed the *Blue Beetle* onto Thomas's sports car du jour. It was exactly what I had dreaded, and as my body hit the ground, a kind of resolved calm washed over me, along with howls of goblin excitement.

I was a dead man. Simple as that. The only question was whether or not I would survive long enough to feel the pain that the shock of impact was delaying. And, of course, where to aim my death curse.

My limp arms and legs slowed my tumble and I wound up on my back with my hips twisted to one side as the Ick threw back its head and let out a burbling, teakettle scream. Its heart pounded like surreal thunder, and my body suddenly felt awash with cold, as if I'd landed in a pool of icy water. The Ick came at me, pain showing in its movements now. It howled and lifted both arms above its head, ready to smash them down onto my skull. I didn't have much time to use my death curse, said the little sane voice in my head.

And then another voice in my head, one far louder and more furious, screamed denial. My few glimpses of Maggie whirled through my mind, along with images of her death—or worse—at Arianna's hands. If I died here, there would be no one to take her out of darkness.

I had to try.

I thrust both fists at the Ick's least injured leg and let go with every energy ring I had left.

I guess from the outside it must have looked like one of those kung fu–type double fist strikes, though the only thing my actual fists were doing was collecting a new round of bruises and little scars. The energy released from the rings, though, kicked the Ick's leg so hard that it swept out parallel to the floor. The Ick toppled.

I rolled desperately, and escaped being crushed by its bulk by a hairbreadth. It landed in whistling agony.

And I suddenly saw a way to kill it that would never have been visible to me if I hadn't been flat on my back and looking up.

I raised the blasting rod to point at the ceiling above, deeply shadowed but still barely visible. It was a natural cavern roof. The floor might have been carved and polished smooth to host the Erlking's hall, but stalactites the size of city buses hung from the ceiling like some behemoth's grim teeth. I checked to be sure that Susan was on the far side of the circle, as far away as possible from what I was about to bring down.

Then I hurled my fear and rage at the base of a great

stone fang that was almost directly overhead, and put almost everything I had left into it.

Blue-white fire screamed through the blasting rod, so intense that the rune-carved implement itself exploded into a cloud of glowing splinters. It hit the far-above stalactite with a thunderous concussion. Beside me, the Ick rose up and reached for my skull with one enormous hand.

I threw up my hands, hissed, *"Aparturum,"* and, with the last of my will, ripped open the veil between the Erlking's hall and the material world, tearing open a circular opening maybe four feet across—and floating three feet off the ground and parallel to the floor, oriented so that its entry point was on its upper side. Then I curled up into a fetal position beneath that opening and tried to cover my head with my arms.

Tons and *tons* of stone tumbled down with slow, deadly grace. The Devourer's heartbeat redoubled its pace. Then there was an incredible noise, and the whole world was blotted away.

I lay there on my side for several moments, not daring to move. Stone fell for a while, maybe a couple of minutes, before the sounds of falling rocks slowly died away, like the pops from a pan of popcorn just before it starts to burn. Only, you know, rockier.

Only then did I allow myself to lift my head and look around.

I lay in a perfectly circular four-foot-across tomb that was maybe five feet deep. The sides of the tomb were perfectly smooth, though I could see from all the cracks and crevices that they were made from many mismatched pieces of rock, ranging from one the size of my fist to a boulder half as big as a car.

Above me, the open Way glowed slightly. All the stone that would have fallen on me had instead plunged through the open Way and back into the material world.

I took a deep breath and closed it again. I hoped that no one was hanging around wherever it was that Way emptied out. Maybe in the FBI cafeteria? No way to know, except to go through and look. I didn't want to face the collateral damage of something like that.

My sane brain pointed out that there was every chance that we weren't talking about falling stones at all. As matter from the spirit world, they would transform to simple ectoplasm when they reached the material world, unless ongoing energy was provided in order to preserve their solidity. I certainly hadn't been trying to pump any energy into the stones as they hit the Way. So odds were that I just dumped several dozen tons of slime onto a random spot in the FBI building—and slime that would evaporate within moments. It would grossly reduce the chances of inflicting injuries on some hapless FBI staffer.

I decided that my sanity and I could live with that.

I closed the Way with a wave of my hand and an effort of will, and slowly stood up. As I did, I realized that I felt a bit creaky, and that I was shaking with fatigue. But what I didn't feel was . . . pain.

I tried to dust myself off and get a good look at my injuries. I should have broken ribs. Ruptured organs. I should be bleeding all over the place.

But as far as I could tell, I didn't even have whiplash.

Was that Mab's power, running through me, wrapped around me? I didn't have any other explanation for it. Hell, when Susan and I had run from the FBI building, she had been the one to get winded first, while I felt no more need to breathe heavily than I would have had walking out to my mailbox. For that matter, I'd outrun the Devourer during this fight.

I thought I should probably feel disturbed by the sudden increase in my physical speed and toughness. But given what I'd had to pay for them, I couldn't feel anything but a certain sense of satisfaction. I would need every advantage I could get when I went to take Maggie away from the Red Court.

I looked up as the green fire of the fighting circle began to die away, and as it did the goblins of the hall erupted into an earsplitting, spine-chilling symphony of approving howls.

I climbed out of the hole, then over and around a couple of dump trucks' worth of rubble, and hurried over to Susan's side on the opposite end of the ring.

She lay limp and still. There were small cuts and bruises all over her. Her leather pants had hundreds of little holes in them—the shards of bone from the exploding vampire skull, I guessed. Her spine was bent and twisted. I couldn't tell how bad it was. I mean . . . Susan had always been fairly limber, and I had more reason to know than most. With her entire body limp like that, it was hard to say.

She was breathing, and her tattoos were still there, now bright scarlet. Her pulse was far too slow, and I wasn't sure it was steady. I leaned down and peeled back one eyelid.

Her eyes were black, all the way through.

I licked my lips. The tattoos were a warning indicator the Fellowship used. As Susan's vampire nature gained more influence over her actions, the tattoos appeared, solid black at first, but lightening to bright red as the vampire within gained more control. Susan wasn't conscious, but if she had been, she would have been insane with bloodlust. She'd nearly killed me the last time it had happened.

It was sort of what had started this whole mess, in fact.

Her body was covered in injuries of various sizes, and I thought I knew what was happening. It was instinctively drawing upon the vampire portion of her nature to restore her damaged flesh—but as she had not provided that nature with sustenance, it could offer her only limited assistance.

She needed blood.

But if she got it, woke up, and decided that she just had to have more . . . yikes.

Her breathing kept slowing. It caught for a moment, and I nearly panicked.

Then I shook my head, took my penknife from my duster's pocket, and opened a cut in my left palm, in an area where the old burn scars were thickest, and which still didn't have a lot of sensitivity.

I cupped my hand while I bled into my palm. Then, very carefully, I reached down and tipped my palm to carefully spill a few drops into Susan's mouth.

You would have thought I'd just run a current of electricity through her body. She quivered, went rigid, and then arched her back into a bow. Strange popping sounds came from her spine. Her empty black eyes opened and she gasped, then stared blindly, trying to find my hand again with her mouth, the way a suckling baby finds its meals. I held my hand over her mouth and let the blood trickle in slowly.

She surged in languid motion beneath my hand, savoring the blood as if it were chocolate, a massage, good sex, and a new car all rolled into one. Two minutes of slow, dreamy, arching motion later, her eyes suddenly focused on me and then narrowed. She snatched at my arm with her hands—and I drove my right fist into her face.

I didn't pull the punch, either. If her darker nature was allowed to continue, it would destroy her, killing me as a by-product of the process. Her head snapped back against the ground, and she blinked her eyes, stunned.

I stood up, took a few steps back, and stuffed my injured hand into my pocket. I was tired, and feeling shocky. My whole arm felt cold. I didn't stop falling back until I was sure I could shield in time to hold her off if she came at me.

I recognized it when Susan checked back in. Her breathing slowed, becoming controlled and steady. It took her four or five minutes of focus to push her darker self away from control, but eventually she did. She sat up slowly. She licked at her bloodstained lips and shuddered in slow ecstasy for a second before dashing her sleeve across her mouth and forcing herself to her feet. She looked around wildly, a terrible dread in her eyes—until she spotted me.

She stared at me for a moment, and then closed her eyes. She whispered, "Thank God."

I nodded to her and beckoned for her to stand at my side.

I waited until she reached me. Then we both turned to face the Erlking.

Off to one side, the members of the Red Court remained where they had been—save that Esteban and Esmerelda had been trapped in the goblins' nets as well. I had apparently been too intent on Susan to hear the sound of any struggle in the aftermath of the duel, but I could guess what had happened. As soon as the Ick had begun to falter, they must have made a run for it. This time, though, they hadn't had the advantage of showing up in a totally unexpected place, with the goblins intent upon their meals.

This time the goblins had taken them, probably before they had actually begun to flee. Both of the Eebs were staring at Susan and me with raw hatred written on their snarling faces.

The Erlking looked at the captured vampires for a moment, and smiled faintly. "Well fought," he said, his deep voice resonant.

We both bowed our heads slightly to him.

Then he lifted his hand and snapped his fingers, once. It echoed like the report of a firearm.

Screams went up from the entire helpless Red Court crew as several hundred violence-amped goblins fell on them in a wave. I watched for a moment in sickened fascination, but turned away.

I hate the Red Court. But there are limits.

The Erlking's kin had none.

"What about the Red King?" I asked him. "The Lords of Outer Night?"

His red eyes gleamed. "His Majesty's folk failed to prove their peaceful intentions. The trial established their deception to the satisfaction of law and custom. Let him howl his fury if he so wills it. Should he begin a war over this matter, all of Faerie will turn upon him in outrage. And his people will make fine hunting."

Beneath the screams of the Red Court—Esmerelda's were especially piercing—a ragged chuckle ran through the hall. The sound danced with its own echoes. It was like listening to the official sound track of Hell. A goblin wearing thick leather gloves appeared, holding what was left of Susan's club as if it were red-hot. The touch of iron and its alloys is an agony to the creatures of Faerie. Susan accepted the steel calmly, nodding to the gloved goblin.

"I presume, then," I said quietly, "that we are free to go?"

"If I did not release you now," the Erlking said, his tone almost genial, "how should I ever have the pleasure of hunting you myself some fine, bright evening?"

I hoped my gulp wasn't audible.

The Lord of the Hunt turned and gestured idly with one hand, and a Way shimmered into being behind us. The green light that had let us see began to darken rapidly. "May you enjoy good hunting of your own, Sir Knight, lady huntress. Please convey my greetings to the Winter Queen."

My sane brain fell asleep at the switch, and I said, "I will. It was a pleasure, Erl."

Maybe he didn't get it. He just tilted his head slightly, the way a dog does at a new sound.

We all bowed to one another politely, and Susan and I stepped through the Way, careful not to take our eyes off of our host, until the world shimmered and that hall of horrors was gone.

It was replaced with an enormous, rustic-style building that appeared to be filled from the basement to the ceiling with everything you might possibly need to shoot, catch, find, stalk, hook, clean, skin, cook, and eat pretty much anything that ran, slithered, hopped, or swam.

"What the hell?" Susan said, looking around in confusion.

"Heh," I said. "This is the Bass Pro in Bolingbrook, I think. Makes sense, I guess."

"I didn't mean that," she said, and pointed. "Look."

I followed her gaze to a large clock on the far wall of the big store.

It said that the time was currently nine thirty p.m.

Thirty minutes *after* our departure time.

"How can that be?" Susan demanded. "We were there for half an hour at the *most*. Look. My watch says it's *two*."

My heart began to beat faster. "Hell's bells, I didn't even think of it."

"Of what?"

I started walking. Susan ditched her club behind a shelf and followed me. We must have made a charming sight, both of us all scuffed up, torn, ragged, and wounded. A few late shoppers stared, but no one seemed willing to approach us.

"Time can pass at a different rate in the Nevernever than it does here," I said. "All those stories about people partying with the fae overnight and waking up in a new century? That's why it happens." The next link in the logic chain got forged, and I said, "Oh. Oh, *dammit*."

"What?" Susan said.

"It's a three-hour trip to Chichén Itzá," I said quietly. "We can't get there by midnight." Lead ingots began to pile up in my belly and on my shoulders and the back of my neck. I bowed my head, my mouth twisting bitterly. "We're too late."

Chapter

Thirty-eight

"**N**o," Susan said fiercely. "No. This isn't set up on Greenwich mean time, Harry. These creatures aren't performing their ceremony based on a clock. They're using the stars. We only know an approximate time. It could happen after midnight."

It could happen half an hour before *midnight*, I thought, but I didn't say that to Susan. Instead, I nodded. She was right. What she was saying just didn't *feel* right, but I knew, in my head, that she was on target. I forced myself to ignore that little whispering voice of defeat in my ear.

"Right," I said. "Keep going, maximum speed. We need to get back to St. Mary's and pick up everyone there."

Susan nodded and said, "Half an hour back if there's no traffic."

"And if you have a car," I said, "which we don't."

Susan's mouth twitched into a smile. "Good thing there's a whole parking lot full of them, then."

I opened the front door for Susan, followed her out onto the sidewalk, and nearly got run over by an emerald green stretch limousine, its tail fins, elongated hood, and shining chrome grille marking it as something created in the extravagant years subsequent to the Second World War. The limo screeched to a halt, and the driver, dressed in a no-nonsense black suit, got out and hurried around to the door nearest us. He was medium height, thin, young, and good-looking enough to be acting or modeling—so much so, in fact, that I decided immediately that he wasn't human.

Almost as soon as I had the thought, I suddenly saw the young Sidhe lord as he truly appeared—dressed in an emerald green tunic and tights, each with accents of deep violet. His sunny hair was bound back into a tight braid that fell past his waist, and his feline, cat-slitted amber eyes were piercing. He saw me staring and gave me a mocking little bow that only barely moved his head and chest, then opened the limo's door.

The Leanansidhe leaned over from the far side of the passenger compartment, an exasperated look on her face. "And here thou art at last, child. What madness possessed thee to pay a social call upon the Hunter? He has a *grudge* against thee. Know you not what that *means?*"

Susan tensed and took a step back from her. My godmother noticed it and favored her with a toothy smile. "Fear not, half child. I've no reason to restrain thee again—unless, of course, thou wouldst like to see where it leads." She glanced up at the night sky—mostly hidden behind all the light pollution—and said, "Granted, we would be forced to indulge such curiosity another time."

"Godmother," I said, staring. "What . . . a big car you have."

She shook a finger at me. "The better to take you

to the House of the Weeping Mother so that we may embark upon our quest, child. Glenmael, help them in, if you please. We race against time."

The young Sidhe gestured gallantly toward the rear of the limo and offered me a supporting arm.

I scowled at him (provoking another smiling bow of his head) and helped Susan into the car. I got in without help of my own, and in short order we found ourselves seated facing the rear of the vehicle and my godmother as the young Sidhe pulled out of the lot and headed for I-55.

"Ridiculous," Lea said, staring at me in disapproval. "You look utterly ridiculous."

I blinked at her and then down at myself. Okay, well, granted. I'd been smeared with ichor and then rolled around in dirt and debris and I had a bleeding cut on one hand, which does not for neatness make. My jeans were a wreck, my T-shirt was beyond repair and going to get cut up for rags, and even my duster looked dirty and strained. Susan wasn't in much better condition.

"I'm not going to a state dinner, Godmother," I said.

Her voice turned wry. "That depends upon who wins the battle, methinks." She looked me up and down and shook her head. "No. No, it won't do at all. My queen has a certain reputation to maintain, after all. Your first engagement as the Winter Knight calls for something a bit less . . . postapocalyptic." She studied Susan with a critical expression. "Mmmm. And your concubine cannot be allowed to bring any shame upon you and, by extension, upon the queen."

I sputtered.

Susan arched an eyebrow. "His *concubine*?"

"His lover, the mother of his child, yet to whom he is not wed? I believe the term applies, dear." She waved a hand. "Words. La. Let us see."

She rested a fingertip thoughtfully upon the end of her nose, staring at me. Then she said, "Let us begin with silk."

She murmured a word, passed her hand over me, and my clothes started writhing as if they'd been made out of a single, flat organism, and one that hadn't yet had the courtesy to expire. It was the damnedest feeling, and I hit my head on the roof of the limo as I jumped in surprise.

A few seconds later, clenching my head, I eyed my godmother and said, "I don't need any help."

"Harry," Susan said in a strangled voice. She was staring at me.

I looked down and found myself garbed in silken clothing. My shirt had become a billowing affair of deep grey silk, fitted close to my torso by a rather long vest of midnight black seeded in patterns of deep amethysts, green-blue opals, and pale, exquisite pearls. The tights were also made of silk, closely fit, and pure white, while the leather boots that came up to my knees were the same deep grey as the shirt.

I stared at me. Then at Susan.

"Wow," Susan said. "You . . . you really *do* have a fairy godmother."

"And I've never been able to indulge," Lea said, studying me absently. "This won't do." She waved her hand again. "Perhaps a bit more . . ."

My clothing writhed again, the sensation so odd and intrusive that I all but banged my head on the roof again.

We went through a dozen outfits in half as many minutes. A Victorian suit and coat, complete with tails, was nixed in favor of another silk outfit, this one inspired by imperial China. By then, Susan and Lea were actively engaged in the project, exchanging commentary with each other and ignoring absolutely every word that came out of my mouth. By the seventh outfit, I had given up trying to have any say whatsoever in how I was going to be dressed.

I was given outfits drawing inspiration from widely diverse cultures and periods of history. I lobbied for the return of my leather duster stridently, but Lea only shushed me and kept speaking to Susan.

"Which outfit is really going to get that bitch's goat?" Susan asked her.

Finally, Lea's mouth curled up into a smile, and she said, "Perfect."

My clothes writhed one more time and I found myself dressed in ornate Gothic armor of the style used in Western Europe in the fifteenth century. It was black and articulated, with decorated shoulder pauldrons and an absurdly ornate breastplate. Gold filigree was everywhere, and the thing looked like it should weigh six hundred pounds.

"Cortés wore armor in just this style," Lea murmured. She studied my head and said, "Though it needs . . ."

A weight suddenly enclosed my head. I sighed patiently and reached up to remove a conquistador's helmet decorated to match the armor. I put it down on the floor of the limo and said firmly, "I don't do hats."

"Poo," Lea said. "Arianna still hates the Europeans with a vengeance, you know. It was why she took a conquistador husband."

I blinked. "Ortega?"

"Of course, child," Lea said. "Love and hate are oft

difficult to distinguish between. She won Ortega's heart, changed him, wed him, and spent the centuries after breaking his heart over and over again. Calling for him and then sending him away. Giving in to him and then reversing her course. She said it kept her hatred fresh and hot."

"Explains why he was working in bloody Brazil," I said.

"Indeed. Hmmm." She flicked a hand and added a Roman-style cloak of dark grey to my armor-broadened shoulders, its ties fastened to the front of the breastplate. Another flick changed the style of my boots slightly. She added a deep hood to the cloak. Then she thoughtfully wrought all the gold on the armor into a spectrum that changed from natural gold to a green that deepened along the color gradient to blue and then purple the farther it went from my face, giving the gold filigree a cold, eerily surreal look. She added front panels to the cloak, so that it fell like some kind of robe in the front, belted to my waist with a sash of deep, dark purple. A final adjustment made the armor over my shoulders a bit wider and thicker, giving me that football shoulder-pad profile I remembered from Friday nights in high school.

I looked down at myself and said, "This is ridiculous. I look like the Games Workshop version of a Jedi Knight."

Susan and Lea blinked at me, then at each other.

"I want my duster back, dammit," I clarified.

"That old rag?" Lea said. "You have an image to maintain."

"And I'm gonna maintain it in my duster," I said stubbornly.

"Harry," Susan said. "She might have a practical point here."

I eyed her. Then my outfit. "Practical?"

"Appearances and first impressions are powerful things," she said. "Used correctly, they're weapons in their own right. I don't know about you, but I want every weapon I can get."

Lea murmured, "Indeed."

"Okay. I don't see why my image can't wear my duster. We need to be quick, too. This getup is going to be binding and heavier than hell."

Lea's mouth curled up at one corner. "Oh?"

I scowled at her. Then I shook my shoulders and twisted about a bit. There was a kind of springy flexibility to the base material of the armor that steel would never match. More to the point, now that I was actually moving about, I couldn't feel its weight. At all. I might as well have been wearing comfortable pajamas.

"No mortal could cut through it by strength of mundane arms," she said calmly. "It will shed blows from even such creatures as the vampires of the Red Court—for a time, at least. And it should help you to shield your mind against the wills of the Lords of Outer Night."

"Should?" I asked. "What do you mean, 'should'?"

"They are an ancient power, godchild," Lea replied, and gave me her cat's smile again. "I have not had the opportunity to match my new strength against theirs." She looked me up and down one more time and nodded, satisfied. "You look presentable. Now, child," she said, turning to Susan. "Let us see what we might do for you."

Susan handled the whole thing a lot better than I had.

I got distracted while they were working. I looked out the window and saw us blowing past a highway patrol car as if it were standing still instead of racing down the highway with its bulbs flashing and its siren wailing. We had to be doing triple digits to have left him eating our dust so quickly.

The patrolman didn't react to our passage, and I realized that Glenmael must be hiding the car behind some kind of veil. He was also, I noticed, weaving and darting through the traffic with entirely impossible skill, missing other motorists' bumpers and fenders by inches, with them apparently none the wiser. Not only that, but I couldn't feel the motion at all within the passenger compartment. By all rights, we should have been bouncing off the windows and the roof, but it didn't feel as if the car were moving at all.

Long story short: He got us to St. Mary's in less than fifteen minutes, and gave me several dozen new grey hairs in the process.

We pulled up and Glenmael was opening the door to the rear compartment at seemingly the same instant that the car's weight settled back against its parking brakes. I got out, the dark grey cowl covering my head. My shadow, on the sidewalk in front of me, looked friggin' huge and scary. Irrationally, it made me feel a little better.

I turned to help Susan out and felt my mouth drop open a little.

Her outfit was . . . um, freaking hot.

The golden headdress was the first thing I noticed. It was decorated with feathers, with jade carved with sigils and symbols like those I had seen on the stone table, and with flickering gems of arctic green and blue. For a second, I thought her vampire nature had begun to rise again, because her face was covered in what I mistook for tattoos. A second glance showed me that they were some kind of precisely drawn design, sort of like henna markings, but far more primitive and savage-looking in appearance. They were also done in a variety of colors of black and deep, dark red. The designs around her dark brown eyes made them stand out sharply.

Under that, she wore a shift of some material that looked like simple, soft buckskin, split on the sides for ease of movement, and her feet were wrapped in shoes made of similar material, also decorated with feathers. The moccasins and shift both were pure white, and made a sharp contrast against the dark richness of her skin, and displayed the smooth, tight muscles of her arms and legs tremendously well.

A belt of white leather had an empty holster for a handgun on one of her hips, with a frog for hanging a scabbard upon it on the other. And over all of that, she wore a mantled cloak of feathers, not too terribly unlike the ones we had seen in Nevada—but the colors were all in the rich, cool tones of the Winter Court: glacial blue, deep sea green, and twilight purple.

She looked at me and said, "I'm waiting for you to say something about a Vegas showgirl."

It took me a moment to reconnect my mouth to my brain. "You look amazing," I said.

Her smile was slow and hot, with her dark eyes on mine.

"Um," I said. "But . . . it doesn't look very practical."

Lea accepted Glenmael's hand and exited the limo. She leaned over and murmured something into Susan's ear.

Susan arched an eyebrow, but then said, "Okaaay . . ." She closed her eyes briefly, frowning.

And she vanished. Like, completely. Not behind a hard-to-pierce veil. Just *gone*.

My godmother laughed and said, "The same as before, but red, child."

"Okay," said Susan's voice from empty air, and suddenly she was back again, smiling broadly. "Wow."

"The cloak will hide you from the eyes and other senses as well, child," my godmother said. "And while you wear those shoes, your steps will leave no tracks nor make the smallest sound."

"Um, right," I said. "But I'd feel better if she had some Kevlar along or something. Just in case."

"Glenmael," said my godmother.

The chauffeur calmly drew a nine-millimeter, pointed it at Susan's temples from point-blank range, and squeezed the trigger. The gun barked.

Susan jerked her head to one side and staggered, clapping one hand to her ear. "Ow!" she snarled, rising and turning on the young Sidhe. "You son of a bitch, those things are loud. That *hurt.* I ought to kick your ass up between your ears for you."

In answer, the Sidhe bent with consummate grace and plucked something from the ground. He stood and showed it to Susan, and then to me.

It was a bullet. The nose was smashed in flat, until it vaguely resembled a small mushroom.

Our eyes got kind of wide.

Lea spread her hands and said calmly, "Faerie godmother."

I shook my head, stunned. It had taken me years to design, create, and improve my leather duster's defensive spells, and even then, the protection extended only as far as the actual leather. Lea had whipped up a whole-body protective enchantment in *minutes.*

I suddenly felt a bit more humble. It was probably good for me.

But then I tilted my head, frowning. The power involved in my godmother's gifts was incredible—but the universe just doesn't seem to be willing to give you something for nothing. That was as true in magic as it was in physics. I could, with years of effort, probably duplicate what Lea's gifts could do. The Sidhe worked with the same magic I did, though admittedly they seemed to have a very different sort of relationship. Still, that much power all in one spot meant that the energy cost for it was being paid elsewhere.

Like maybe in longevity.

"Godmother," I asked, "how long will these gifts endure?"

Her smile turned a little sad. "Ah, child. I am a faerie godmother, am I not? Such things are not meant to last."

"Don't tell me midnight," I said.

"Of course not. I am not part of Summer." She sniffed, rather scornfully. "Noon."

And that made more sense. My duster's spells lasted for months, and I thought I'd worked out how to make them run for more than a year the next time I laid them down. Lea's gifts involved the same kind of power output, created seemingly without toil—but they wouldn't last like the things I created would. My self-image recovered a little.

"Lea," I asked, "did you bring my bag?"

Glenmael opened the trunk and brought it over to me. The Swords in their scabbards were still strapped to the bag's side. I picked it up and nodded. "Thanks."

He bowed, smiling. I was tempted to tip him, just to see what would happen, but then I remembered that my wallet had been in my blue jeans, and was now, presumably, part of the new outfit. Maybe it would reappear at noon tomorrow—assuming I was alive to need it, I mean.

"I will wait here," Lea said. "When you are ready to travel to the first Way, Glenmael will take us there."

"Right," I said. "Let's go, princess."

"Of course, Sir Knight," Susan said, her eyes sparkling, and we went into the church.

Chapter

Thirty-nine

Sanya was guarding the door. He swung it open wide for us, and studied Susan with a grin of appreciation. "There are some days," he said, "when I just love this job."

"Come on," I said, walking past him. "We don't have much time."

Sanya literally clicked his heels together, took Susan's hand, and kissed the back of it gallantly, the big stupidhead. "You are beyond lovely, lady."

"Thank you," Susan said, smiling. "But we don't have much time."

I rolled my eyes and kept walking.

There was a quiet conversation going in the living room. It stopped as I came through the door. I paused there for a second, and looked around at everyone who was going to help me get my daughter back.

Molly was dressed in her battle coat, which consisted of a shirt of tightly woven metal links, fashioned by her mother out of titanium wire. The mail was then sandwiched between two long Kevlar vests. All of that was, in turn, fixed to one of several outer garments, and in this case she was wearing a medium brown fireman's coat. Her hair was braided tightly against the back of her head—and back to its natural honey brown color—and a hockey helmet sat on a table near her. She had half a dozen little focus items I'd shown her how to create, none of which were precisely intended for a fight. Her face was a little pale, and her blue eyes were earnest.

Mouse sat next to her, huge and stolid, and rose to his feet and padded over to give me a subdued greeting as I came in. I knelt down and roughed up his ears for a moment. He wagged his tail, but made no more display than that, and his serious brown eyes told me that he knew the situation was grave.

Next came Martin, dressed in simple black BDU pants, a long-sleeved black shirt, and a tactical vest, all of which could have been purchased from any military surplus or gun store. He was in the midst of cleaning and inspecting three sets of weapons: assault rifles, tactical shotguns, and heavy pistols. He wore a machete in a scabbard on his belt. A second such weapon rested in a nylon sheath on the table, next to a blade-sharpening tool kit. He never looked up at me, or stopped reassembling the pistol he'd finished cleaning.

A small chess set had been set up on the other end of the coffee table from Molly, next to Martin's war gear. My brother sat there, with Martin (and, once he had finished greeting me, Mouse) between himself and the girl. He was wearing expensive-looking silk pants and a leather vest, both white. A gun belt bearing a large-caliber handgun and a sword with an inward-curving blade, an old Spanish falcata, hung over the corner of the couch, casually discarded. He lay lazily back on the couch, his eyes mostly closed, watching the move of his opponent.

Murphy was decked out in black tactical gear much like Martin's, but more worn and better fitting. They don't generally make gear for people Murph's size, so she couldn't shop off the shelf very often. She did have her own vest of Kevlar and mail, which Charity had made for her for Christmas the previous year, in thanks for the occasions when Murphy had gone out on a limb for them, but Murph had just stuck the compound armor to her tac vest and been done. She wore her automatic on her hip, and her odd-looking, rectangular little submachine gun, the one that always made me think of a box of chocolates, was leaned against the wall nearby. Murph was hunched over the chessboard, her nose wrinkled as she thought, and moved one of her knights into a thicket of enemy pieces before she turned to me.

She took one look at me and burst out giggling.

That was enough to set off everyone in the room except Martin, who never seemed to realize that there were other people there. Molly's titters set off Thomas, and even Mouse dropped his jaws open in a doggy grin.

"Hah, hah, hah," I said, coming into the room, so that Susan and Sanya could join us. No one laughed at Susan's outfit. I felt that the injustice of that was somehow emblematic of the unfairness in my life, but I didn't have time to chase that thought down and feed it rhetoric until the lightbulb over my head lit up.

"Well," Murphy said, as the laughter died away, "I'm glad you got out all right. Went shopping after, did you?"

"Not so much," I said. "Okay, listen up, folks. Time is short. What else did we manage to find out about the site?"

Murphy told Thomas, "Mate in six," took a file folder from beneath her chair, and passed it to me.

"You wish," Thomas drawled lazily.

I eyed him and opened the folder. There were multiple pages inside, color aerial and satellite photos of the ruins.

"Good grief," I said. "How did you get these?"

"Internet," Murphy said calmly. "We've got an idea of where they're setting up and what security measures they'll need to take, but before we can talk about an approach, we need to know where we're going to arrive."

I stroked a thumb over my mother's gem and consulted the knowledge stored there. Then I went through the maps until I found one of the proper scale, picked up a pen from the table, and drew an X on the map. "Here. It's about five miles north of the pyramid."

Thomas whistled quietly.

"What?" I asked him. "You can't do five miles?"

"Five miles of sidewalk, sure," Thomas said. "Five miles of jungle is a bit different, Dresden."

"He's right," Martin said. "And at night, too."

Thomas spread his hands.

"Have done a little jungle," Sanya said, coming over to study the map. "How bad is the bush there?"

"Tougher than the lower Amazon, not as bad as Cambodia," Martin said calmly.

Sanya grunted. Thomas wrinkled his nose in distaste. I tried to pretend that Martin had given me some kind of tangible information, and idly wondered if Thomas and Sanya were doing the same thing as me.

"How long, Martin?" I asked him.

"Two hours, bare minimum. Could be more, depending."

I grunted. Then I said, "We'll see if Lea can't do something to help us along."

The room went still.

"Um," Murphy said. "Your psycho faerie godmother? That Lea?"

"Harry, you told me she was dangerous," Molly said.

"And I still have the scar to prove it," Thomas added.

"Yes," I said quietly. "She's powerful and by any reasonable standard she's insane and she's currently pointed in the direction of our enemy. So we're going to use her."

"We're using her, are we?" Sanya asked, grinning.

"He told us what Toot said about Mab, Harry," Molly said softly.

There was a long stretch of quiet.

"You made a deal," Murphy said.

"Yeah, I did. For Maggie, I did." I looked around the room. "I'm me until this is all over. That was part of the deal. But if there's anyone here who wants to bail on me and Susan, do it now. Otherwise, feel free to keep your mouth closed about the subject. My daughter doesn't have time for us to debate the ethics of a choice that isn't any of your goddamned business anyway."

I looked around the room and Sanya said, "I am going. Who else goes with us?"

Mouse sneezed.

"I figured that," I told him.

He wagged his tail.

"Me, obviously," Martin said.

Murphy nodded. Molly did, too. Then Thomas rolled his eyes.

"Good," I said. "Lea will probably have something to speed the trip," I said.

"She'd better," Thomas said. "Time's short."

"We will be there in time," Sanya said confidently.

I nodded. Then I said, "And I have a favor to ask two of you."

I put the bag down and pulled *Fidelacchius* from where I'd tied it. The ancient katana-style Sword had a smooth wooden handle that perfectly matched the wood of its sheath, so that when the weapon was sheathed it looked innocuous, appearing to be a slightly curved, sturdy stick of a good size to carry while walking. The blade was razor-sharp. I had dropped a plastic drinking straw across it as an experiment once. The rate of fall had been all the exquisite weapon had needed to slice the straw neatly in half.

"Karrin," I said, and held out the Sword.

Sanya's eyebrows climbed toward the roof.

"I've . . . been offered that Sword before, Harry," she said quietly. "Nothing's changed since then."

"I'm not asking you to take up the mantle of a Knight," I said quietly. "I want to entrust it to you for this night, for this purpose. This sword was made to fight darkness, and there's going to be plenty to go around. Take it up. Just until my girl is safe."

Murphy frowned. She looked at Sanya and said, "Can he do this?"

"Can you?" Sanya asked, looking at me.

"I was entrusted as the Sword's guardian," I said calmly. "Exactly what am I supposed to do with it if it is *not* my place to choose the Sword's bearer to the best of my ability?"

Sanya considered that for a moment, then shrugged. "Seems implicit to me. They gave you the power of choice when they entrusted you with the Swords. One of those things they seem to tell you without ever actually saying anything that sounds remotely related."

I nodded. "Murph. Used for the right reasons, in

good faith, the Sword is in no danger. You're the only one who can know if you're doing it for the right reasons. But I'm begging you. Take it. Help me save my daughter, Karrin. Please."

Murphy sighed. "You don't play fair, Harry."

"Not for one second," I said. "Not for something like this."

Murphy was quiet for a moment more. Then she stood up and walked to me. She took the Sword from my hand. There was an old cloth strap fixed to the sheath, so that the weapon could be carried over one shoulder or diagonally across the back. Murphy slipped the weapon on and said, "I'll carry it. If it seems right to me, I'll use it."

"That's all I can ask for," I said.

Then I picked up *Amoracchius*, a European long Sword with a crusader-style hilt and a simple wire-wrapped handle.

And I turned to Susan.

She stared at me and then shook her head slowly. "The last time I touched one of those things," she said, "it burned me so bad I could still feel it three months later."

"That was then," I said. "This is now. You're doing what you're doing because you love your daughter. If you stay focused on that, this Sword will never do you harm." I turned the hilt to her. "Put your hand on it."

Susan did so slowly, almost as if against her will. She hesitated at the last moment. Then her fingers closed on the blade's handle.

And that was all. Nothing happened.

"Swear to harm no innocents," I said quietly. "Swear to use it in good faith, to return your daughter safely home. Swear that you will safeguard the Sword and return it faithfully when that task is done. And I don't see any reason why you shouldn't be able to wield it."

She met my eyes and nodded. "I swear."

I nodded in reply and took my hands from the weapon. Susan drew it slightly from its sheath. Its edge gleamed, and its steel was polished as smooth and bright as a mirror. And when she moved to buckle it to her belt, the Sword fit there as if made for it.

My godmother was probably going to feel very smug about that.

"I hope that the Almighty will not feel slighted if I carry more, ah, innovative weaponry as well," Susan said. She crossed to the table, slid one of Martin's revolvers into her holster, and after a moment picked up the assault rifle.

Sanya stepped forward as well, and took the tactical shotgun with its collapsible shoulder stock. "If He exists, He has never given me any grief about it," he said cheerfully. "*Da.* This is going very well already."

Thomas barked out a laugh. "There are *seven* of us against the Red King and his thirteen most powerful nobles, and it's going well?"

Mouse sneezed.

"Eight," Thomas corrected himself. He rolled his eyes and said, "And the psycho death faerie makes it nine."

"It is like movie," Sanya said, nodding. "Dibs on Legolas."

"Are you kidding?" Thomas said. "I'm obviously Legolas. You're . . ." He squinted thoughtfully at Sanya and then at Martin. "Well. He's Boromir and you're clearly Aragorn."

"Martin is so dour, he is more like Gimli." Sanya

pointed at Susan. "Her sword is much more like Aragorn's."

"Aragorn wishes he looked that good," countered Thomas.

"What about Karrin?" Sanya asked.

"What—for Gimli?" Thomas mused. "She *is* fairly—"

"Finish that sentence, Raith, and we throw down," said Murphy in a calm, level voice.

"Tough," Thomas said, his expression aggrieved. "I was going to say 'tough.'"

Martin had gotten up during the discussion. He came over to me and studied the map I'd marked. Then he nodded. As the discussion went on—with Molly's sponsorship, Mouse was lobbying to claim Gimli on the basis of being the shortest, the stoutest, and the hairiest— Martin explained what they knew of the security measures around the ruins.

"That's why we're going in here," he said, pointing to the easternmost point of the ruins, where rows and rows and rows of great columns stood. Once, they had held up some kind of roof over a complex attached to the great temple. "Now," Martin continued, "the jungle has swallowed the eastern end of it. They're only using torchlight, so movement through the galleries should be possible. There will be considerable shadow to move through."

"Means they'll have guards there," I said.

"True. We'll have to silence them. It can be done. If we can move fully through the galleries, we'll be within two hundred feet of the base of the temple. That's where we think they'll be performing the ritual. In the temple."

"Plenty of temples got built on top of ley line confluences," I said, nodding. I studied the map. "A lot can happen in two hundred feet," I said. "Even moving fast."

Martin nodded. "Yes, it can. And, if our various intelligence sources are correct, there are more than a thousand individuals nearby."

"A thousand vampires?" I asked.

Martin shrugged. "Many. Many will be their personal guards. Others, the . . . highest-ranking servants, I suppose you would call them. They are like Susan and myself. There may also be mortal foot soldiers, there to keep the sacrifices in line."

"Sacrifices, plural?"

Martin nodded. "The ceremonies of the Red Court of old could last for days, with blood sacrifices made every few minutes. There might be a hundred or two hundred others chosen to die before the ritual."

I didn't shudder, but only by sheer force of will. "Yeah. Priming the pump." I nodded. "Probably they're doing it right now."

"Yes," Martin said.

"What we need," I said.

"A diversion," Martin said.

I nodded. "Get everyone looking in one direction. Then Susan, Lea, and I will hit the temple, get the kid. Then we all run for Father Forthill's sanctuary on holy ground."

"They'll catch us long before we can cover that distance."

"You ever tried chasing a faerie through the woods at night?" I asked wryly. "Trust me. If we can break contact, we can make it a few miles."

"Why not retreat directly to the spirit world?" Martin asked.

I shook my head. "No way. Creatures this old and powerful know all the tricks there, and they'll be familiar with the terrain on the other side that close to their strong places. I won't fight them on that ground unless there's no other choice. We head for the church." I pointed to the location of the church, in a small town only about two and a half miles from Chichén Itzá.

Martin smiled faintly. "Do you honestly think a parish chapel will withstand the might of the Red King?"

"I have to think that, Martin," I said. "Besides, I think a parish chapel with all three Swords defending it, along with two members of the White Council and an elder sorceress of the Winter Sidhe, will be a tough nut to crack. And all we have to do is make it until dawn. Then we're back in the jungle and gone."

Martin mused on that for a moment and said, "It might work."

"Yeah. It might," I said. "We need to move. Our ride is outside waiting."

"Right."

Martin looked at Susan and nodded. Then he put his fingers to his mouth and let out a piercing whistle. The good-natured discussion came to a halt and he said, "The car's outside."

"Let's go, people," I said quietly. "It's the big green car."

Everyone grew serious rather rapidly, and began gathering up their various forms of gear.

Susan went out first, to make sure there weren't any problems with Lea, and everyone filed out after her, Sanya last.

"Sanya," I said. "Who did I get cast as?"

"Sam," Sanya said.

I blinked at him. "Not . . . Oh, for crying out loud, it was perfectly obvious who I should have been."

Sanya shrugged. "It was no contest. They gave Gandalf to your godmother. You got Sam." He started to leave and then paused. "Harry. You have read the books as well, yes?"

"Sure," I said.

"Then you know that Sam was the true hero of the tale," Sanya said. "That he faced far greater and more terrible foes than he ever should have had to face, and did so with courage. That he went alone into a black and terrible land, stormed a dark fortress, and resisted the most terrible temptation of his world for the sake of the friend he loved. That in the end, it was his actions and his actions alone that made it possible for light to overcome darkness."

I thought about that for a second. Then I said, "Oh."

He clapped me on the shoulder and left.

He didn't mention the other part of the book. That following the heroes when they set out was the tenth member of their party. A broken creature who went through all the same dangers and trials, who had made a single bad choice and taken up a power he didn't understand—and who had become a demented, miserable, living nightmare because of it. In the end, he had been just as necessary to the overthrow of the darkness.

But he sure as hell didn't enjoy his part.

I shook my head and berated myself sharply. Here I was wasting time talking about a damned book. About a world of blacks and whites with precious little in the way of grey, where you could tell the good guys from the bad guys with about two seconds of effort.

And right now, I didn't give a damn about good and bad. I just wanted a little girl home safe.

It didn't matter which of them I was. As long as I got Maggie home.

I picked up my bag, left St. Mary's behind me, and stalked out to my wicked godmother's limo, pulling the soft hood of my dark cape up over my head.

If I was on the road to Hell, at least I was going in style.

Chapter

Forty

There was room for everyone in the back of the limo. I was pretty sure that there hadn't been the first time I'd ridden in it. But it had gotten several extra feet of seats along the walls, and everyone was sitting there being only a little bit crowded as Glenmael charged out to assault Chicago's streets.

"I still think we should try a frontal assault," Sanya argued.

"Suicidally stupid," Martin said, his voice scornful.

"Surprise tactic!" Sanya countered. "They will not expect it after a thousand years of never being challenged. Harry, what do you think?"

"Uh," I said.

And then Ebenezar's voice said, quite clearly and from no apparent source, "Damn your stubborn eyes, boy! Where have you been?"

I went rigid with surprise for a second. I looked around the interior of the limo, but no one had reacted, with the exception of my godmother. Lea sighed and rolled her eyes.

Right. The speaking stones. I'd stuck mine in the bag, but since I was holding it on my lap now, it was close enough to be warmed by the heat of my body to function. It was possible to send terse messages through the stones without first establishing a clear connection, as my mentor and I had done back toward the beginning of this mess.

"Damnation and hellfire, Hoss!" growled Ebenezar's voice. "Answer me!"

I looked from Sanya to my godmother. "Uh. I kind of have to take this call."

Sanya blinked at me. Thomas and Murphy exchanged a significant glance.

"Oh, shut up," I said crossly. "It's magic, okay?"

I closed my eyes and fumbled through the bag until I found the stone. I didn't really need to show up in my outlandish costume for this conversation, so I thought about my own physical body for a moment, concentrating on an image of my limbs and flesh and normal clothing forming around my thoughts.

"So help me, boy, if you don't—"

Ebenezar appeared in my mind's eye, wearing his usual clothing. He broke off suddenly as he looked at me and his face went pale. "Hoss? Are you all right?"

"Not really," I said. "I'm kind of in the middle of something here. What do you want?"

"Your absence from the conclave did not go over well," he responded, his voice sharp. "There are people in the Grey Council who think you aren't to be trusted. They're very, very wary of you. By missing the meeting, you told them that either you don't respect our work enough to bother showing up, or else that you don't have the wisdom and the fortitude to commit to the cause."

"I never saw the appeal of peer pressure," I said. "Sir, I'm finding a little girl. I'll come play Council politics after I get her home safe, if you want."

"We need you here."

"The kid needs me more. It's not as noble as trying to save the whole White Council from its own stupidity, I know. But by God, I *will* bring that child out safe."

Ebenezar's mostly bald pate flushed red. "Despite my orders to the contrary."

"We aren't an army. You aren't my superior officer. Sir."

"You arrogant *child*," he snapped. "Get your head out of your ass and get your eyes on the world around you or you're going to get yourself killed."

"With all due respect, sir, you can go to hell," I snarled. "You think I don't know how dangerous the world is? *Me?*"

"I think you're doing everything in your power to isolate yourself from the only people who can support you," he said. "You feel guilty about something. I get that, Hoss. You think you ain't fit for company because of what you've done." His scowl darkened still more. "In my time, I've done things that would curl your hair. Get over it. Think."

"After I get the girl out."

"Do you even know where she is?" Ebenezar demanded.

"Chichén Itzá," I said. "She's scheduled to be the centerpiece of one of the Red King's shindigs in the next couple of hours."

Ebenezar took a sharp breath, as if I'd poked him in the stomach with the end of a quarterstaff. "Chichén Itzá . . . That's a confluence. One of the biggest in the world. The Reds haven't used it in . . . Not since Cortés was there."

"Confluence, yeah," I said. "The Duchess Arianna is going to kill her and use the power to lay a curse on her bloodline—Susan and me."

Ebenezar began to speak and then blinked several times, as if the sun had just come out of a cloud and into his eyes. "Susan and . . ." He paused and asked, "Hoss?"

"I meant to tell you the last time we spoke," I said quietly. "But . . . the conversation wasn't exactly . . ." I took a deep breath. "She's my daughter by Susan Rodriguez."

"Oh," he said very quietly. His face looked grey. "Oh, Hoss."

"Her name's Maggie. She's eight. They took her a few days ago."

He bowed his head and shook it several times, saying nothing. Then he said, "You're sure?"

"Yeah."

"H-how long have you known?"

"Since a day or so after she was taken," I said. "Surprised the hell out of me."

Ebenezar nodded without looking up. Then he said, "You're her father and she needs you. And you want to be there for her."

"Not want to be there," I said quietly. "Going to be."

"Aye-aye," he said. "Don't go back to the Edinburgh facility. We think Arianna laced it with some kind of disease while she was there. So far there are sixty wizards down with it, and we're expecting more. No deaths yet, but whatever this bug is, it's putting them flat on their backs—including Injun Joe, so our best healer isn't able to work on the problem."

"Hell's bells," I said. "They aren't just starting back in on the war again. They're going to try to decapitate the Council in one blow."

Ebenezar grunted. "Aye. And without the Way nexus around Edinburgh, we're going to have a hell of a time with that counterstroke." He sighed. "Hoss, you got a damned big talent. Not real refined, but you've matured a lot in the past few years. Handle yourself better in a fight than most with a couple of centuries behind them. Wish you could be with us."

I wasn't sure how to feel about that. Ebenezar was generally considered the heavyweight champion of the wizarding world when it came to direct, face-to-face mayhem. And I was one of the relatively few people who knew he was also the Blackstaff—the White Council's officially nonexistent hit man, authorized to ignore the Laws of Magic when he deemed it necessary. The old man had fought pretty much everything that put up a fight at one point or another, and he didn't make a habit of complimenting anyone's skills.

"I can't go with you," I said.

"Aye," he said with a firm nod. "You do whatever you have to do, boy. Whatever you have to do to keep your little girl safe. You hear?"

"Yeah," I said. "Thank you, sir."

"Godspeed, son," Ebenezar said. Then he cut the connection.

I released my focus slowly until I was once more in my body in the back of the limo.

"Who was it?" Molly asked. The others let her take the lead. She must have explained the whole speaking-stone concept to them. Which made me look less crazy, but I felt twitchy about her handing out information like that to the entire car. It wasn't a big deadly secret or anything, but it was the principle of the thing that—

I rubbed at my face with one hand. Ye gods. I was becoming my mentors. Next I'd be grumbling about those darned kids and their loud music.

"Uh, the Council," I said. "Big shock, they aren't helping."

Murphy looked like she might be asleep, but she snorted. "So we're on our own."

"Yeah."

"Good. It's more familiar."

Lea let out a peal of merry laughter.

Murphy opened an eye and gave Lea a decidedly frosty look. "What?"

"You think that this is like what you have done before," my godmother said. "So precious."

Murphy stared at her for a moment and then looked at me. "Harry?"

I leaned my head back against the window, so that the hood fell over my eyes. Murphy was way too good at picking up on it when I lied. "I don't know," I said. "I guess we'll see."

It took Glenmael less than twenty minutes to get to Aurora. We got out at a park there, a pretty little community place. It was empty this time of night, and all the lights were out.

"Pitcher's mound, folks," I said, piling out and taking the lead.

I was walking with long, long strides, staying ahead of everyone. Murphy caught up to me, moving at a slow jog.

"Harry," she said, her voice low. "Your godmother?"

"Yeah?"

"Can we trust her?"

I scowled. She wouldn't be able to see the expression, with the hood and all. "Do you trust me?"

"Why do you think I'm asking you?"

I thought about it for a moment and then slowed down, so that everyone else was nearer. That included my godmother.

"Okay, folks. Let's clear the air about the scary Sidhe lady. She's under orders to go with me and to help. She will. She's got a vested interest in making sure I come out of this all right, and if she doesn't do it, she's in trouble with the queen. As long as you all are helpful to her mission, getting me in and out in one piece, she'll support you. The second she thinks you're a liability or counter-productive to her mission, she's going to let bad things happen to you. Maybe even do them herself." I looked at Lea. "Is that about right?"

"That is precisely right," she said, smiling.

Susan arched an eyebrow and looked from me to my godmother. "You have no shame about it at all, do you?"

"Shame, child, is for those who fail to live up to the ideal of what they believe they should be." She waved her hand. "It was shame that drove me to my queen, to beseech her aid." Her long, delicate fingers idly moved to the streaks of white in her otherwise flawless red tresses. "But she showed me the way back to myself, through exquisite pain, and now I am here to watch over my dear godson—and the rest of you, as long as it is quite convenient."

"Spooky death Sidhe lady," Molly said. "Now upgraded to spooky, *crazy* death Sidhe lady."

The Leanansidhe bared her canine teeth in a foxlike smile. "Bless you, child. You have such potential. We should talk when this is over."

I glowered openly at Lea, who looked unrepentant. "Okay, folks. The plan is going to be for me to stand where the fire is hottest. And if one of you gets cut off or goes down, I'm going to go back for you." I kept glaring at my godmother. "Everyone who goes in with me is coming out again, dead or alive. I'm bringing you all home."

Lea paused for a few steps and arched an eyebrow at me. Then she narrowed her eyes.

"If they can all carry themselves out," I said, "I believe that would be more 'quite convenient' than if they couldn't. Wouldn't it, Godmother?"

She rolled her eyes and said, "Impossible child." But there was a hint of a smile on her mouth. She bowed her head to me slightly, like a fencer acknowledging a touch, and I returned it.

Then I figured I'd best not threaten her ego any more than I had to. "Be careful when you speak to her," I told the others. "Don't make her any offers. Don't accept any, not even in passing, not even things that seem harmless or that could only be construed through context. Words are binding around the Sidhe, and she is one of the most dangerous creatures in all of Faerie." I bowed my head to her. "Fortunately for us. Before the night's over, we'll all be glad she's with us."

"Oh," the Leanansidhe purred, all but literally preening. "A trifle obvious, but . . . how the child has grown."

"Da," said Sanya cheerfully. "I am glad that she is here. For the first time, I got to ride in a limousine. Already it is a good night. And if spooky crazy death Sidhe lady can help serve a good cause, then we who bear the Swords"—he paused for a smiling second—"all three of them"—he paused for another second, still smiling—"will welcome her aid."

"Such charm, O Knight of the Sword," Lea replied, smiling even more endearingly than Sanya. "We are all being so pleasant tonight. Please be assured that should one of the Swords be dropped or somehow misemployed, I will do everything in my power to recover it."

"Sanya," I said. "Please shut up now."

He let out a booming laugh, settled the strap of the

shotgun a little more firmly over his shoulder, and said nothing more.

I checked my mother's memories and nodded as I reached the pitcher's mound. "Okay, folks. First leg here. Should be a simple walk down a trail next to a river. Don't get freaked when you notice the water is flowing uphill." I stared at the air over the pitcher's mound and began to draw in my will.

"Right," I said, mostly to myself. "Annnnnd here we go. *Aparturum.*"

Chapter

Forty-one

The first leg of the trip was simple, a walk down a forest trail next to a backward-flowing river until we reached a menhir—that's a large, upright standing stone, to those of you without a pressing need to find out what a menhir is. I found where a pentangle had been inscribed on the stone, a five-pointed star within a circle, like the one around my neck. It had been done with a small chisel of some kind, and was a little lopsided. My mother had put it there to mark which side of the stone to open the Way on.

I ran my fingers over it for a moment. As much as my necklace or the gem that now adorned it, it was tangible proof of her presence. She had been real, even if I had no personal memories of her, and that innocuous little marking was further proof.

"My mother made this mark," I said quietly.

I didn't look back at Thomas, but I could all but feel the sudden intensity of his interest.

He had a few more memories than I did, but not many. And it was possible that he had me outclassed in the parental-figure issues department, too.

I opened another Way, and we came through into a dry gulch with a stone wall, next to a deep channel in the stone that might once have held a river—now it was full of sand. It was dark and chilly, and the sky was full of stars.

"Okay," I said. "Now we walk."

I summoned a light and took the lead. Martin scanned the skies above us. "Uh. The constellations . . . Where are we?"

I clambered up a stiff little slope that was all hard stone and loose sand, and looked out over a vast expanse of silver-white beneath the moon. Great shapes loomed up from the sand, their sides almost serrated in the clear moonlight, lines and right angles that clashed sharply with the ocean of sand and flatland around them.

"Giza," I said. "You can't see the Sphinx from this side, but I never claimed to be a tour guide. Come on."

It was a stiff two or three miles from the hidden gully to the pyramids, and sand all the way. I took the lead, moving in a shambling, loose-kneed jog. There wasn't any worry about heat—dawn was under way, and in an hour the place would be like one giant cookie pan in an oven, but we'd be gone by then. My mother's amulet led me directly to the base of the smallest and most crumbly pyramid, and I had to climb up three levels to reach the next Waypoint. I stopped to caution the party that we were about to move into someplace hot, and to shield their eyes. Then I opened the Way and we continued through.

We emerged onto a plain beside enormous pyramids— but instead of being made of stone, these were all formed of crystal, smooth and perfect. A sun that was impossibly huge hung in the sky directly overhead, and the light was painfully bright, rebounding up from the crystal plain to be focused through the pyramids and refracted over and over and over again.

"Stay out of those sunbeams," I said, waving in the direction of several beams of light so brilliant that they made the Death Star lasers look like they needed to hit the gym. "They're hot enough to melt metal."

I led the group forward, around the base of one pyramid, into a slim corridor of . . . Well, it wasn't shade, but there wasn't quite so much light there, until we reached the next Waypoint—where a chunk the size of a large man's fist was missing from one of the perfectly smooth edges of the pyramid. Then I turned ninety degrees to the right and started walking.

I counted five hundred paces. I felt the light—not heat, just the sheer, overwhelming amount of light— beginning to tan my skin.

Then we came to an aberration—a single lump of rock upon the crystalline plain. There were broad, ugly facial features on the rock, primitive and simple.

"Here," I said, and my voice echoed weirdly, though there was seemingly nothing from which it *could* echo.

I opened another Way, and we stepped from the plain of light and into chilly mist and thin mountain air. A cold wind pushed at us. We stood in an ancient stone courtyard of some kind. Walls stood around us, broken in many places, and there was no roof overhead.

Murphy stared up at the sky, where stars were very faintly visible through the mist, and shook her head. "Where now?"

"Machu Picchu," I said. "Anyone bring water?"

"I did," Murphy said, at the same time as Martin, Sanya, Molly, and Thomas.

"Well," Thomas said, while I felt stupid, "I'm not sharing."

Sanya snorted and tossed me his canteen. I sneered at Thomas and drank, then tossed it back. Martin passed

Susan his canteen, then took it back when she was finished. I started trudging. It isn't far from one side of Machu Picchu to the other, but the walk is all uphill, and that means a hell of a lot more in the Andes than it does in Chicago.

"All right," I said, stopping beside a large mound built of many rising tiers that, if you squinted up your eyes enough, looked a lot like a ziggurat-style pyramid. Or maybe an absurdly large and complicated wedding cake. "When I open the next Way, we'll be underwater. We have to swim ten feet, in the dark. Then I open the next Way and we're in Mexico." I was doubly cursing the time we'd lost in the Erlking's realm. "Did anyone bring any climbing rope?"

Sanya, Murphy, Martin— Look, you get the picture. There were a lot of people standing around who were more prepared than me. They didn't have super-duper faerie godmother presents, but they had brains, and it was a sobering reminder to me of which was more important.

We got finished running a line from the front of the group to the back (except for my godmother, who sniffed disdainfully at the notion of being tied to a bunch of mortals), and I took several deep breaths and opened the next Way.

Mom's notes on this Waypoint hadn't mentioned that the water was *cold*. And I don't mean cold like your roommate used most of the hot water. I mean cold like I suddenly had to wonder if I was going to trip over a seal or a penguin or a narwhal or something.

The cold hit me like a sledgehammer, and it was suddenly all I could do just to keep from shrieking in surprise and discomfort—and, some part of my brain marveled, I was the freaking *Winter Knight*.

Though my limbs screamed their desire to contract

around my chest and my heart, I fought them and made them paddle. One stroke. Two. Three. Four. Fi— Ow. My nose hit a shelf of rock. I found my will and exhaled, speaking the word *Aparturum* through a cloud of blobby bubbles that rolled up over my cheeks and eyelashes. I tore open the next Way a little desperately—and water rushed out through it as if thrilled to escape.

I crashed into the Yucatán jungle on a tide of ecto-plasmic slime, and the line we'd strung dragged everyone else through in a rush. Poor Sanya, the last in line, was pulled from his feet, hauled hard through the icy water as if he'd been flushed down a Jotun's toilet, and then crashed down amidst the slimed forest. Peru to Mexico in three and a half seconds.

I fumbled back to the Way to close it and stopped the tide of ectoplasm from coming through, but not before the vegetation for ten feet in every direction had been smashed flat by the flood of slime, and every jungle crea-ture for fifty or sixty yards started raising holy hell on the what-the-fuck-was-that party line. Murphy had her gun out, and Molly had a wand in each hand, gripped with white knuckles.

Martin let out a sudden, coughing bellow that sounded like it must have torn something in his chest—and it was *loud*, too. And the jungle around us abruptly went silent.

I blinked and looked at Martin. So did everyone else.

"Jaguar," he said in a calm, quiet voice. "They're ex-tinct here, but the animals don't know that."

"Oooh," said my godmother, a touch of a child's glee in her voice. "I like that."

It took us a minute to get everyone sorted out. Mouse looked like a scrawny shadow of himself with his fur all plastered down. He was sneezing uncontrollably, having apparently gotten a bunch of water up his nose during the swim. Ectoplasm splattered out with every sneeze. Thomas was in similar straits, having been hauled through much as Sanya was, but he managed to look a great deal more annoyed than Mouse.

I turned to Lea. "Godmother. I hope you have some way to get us to the temple a little more swiftly."

"Absolutely," Lea purred, calm and regal despite the fact that her hair and her slime-soaked silken dress were now plastered to her body. "And I've always wanted to do it, too." She let out a mocking laugh and waved her hand, and my belly cramped up as if every stomach bug I'd ever had met up in a bar and decided to come get me all at once.

It. Hurt.

I knew I'd fallen, and was vaguely aware that I was lying on my side on the ground. I was there for, I don't know, maybe a minute or so before the pain began to fade. I gasped several times, shook my head, and then slowly pushed myself up onto all fours. Then I fixed the Leanansidhe with a glare and said, "What the hell do you think you're doing?"

Or *tried* to say that. What came out was something more like, "Grrrrrrbrrrr awwf arrrr grrrrr."

My faerie godmother looked at me and began laughing. Genuine, delighted belly laughter. She clapped her hands and bounced up and down, spinning in a circle, and laughed even more.

I realized then what had happened.

She had turned us—all of us, except for Mouse—into great, gaunt, long-legged hounds.

"Wonderful!" Lea said, pirouetting upon one toe, laughing. "Come, children!" And she leapt off into the jungle, nimble and swift as a doe.

A bunch of us dogs stood around for a moment, just sort of staring at one another.

And Mouse said, in what sounded to me like perfectly understandable English, "That *bitch*."

We all stared at him.

Mouse huffed out a breath, shook his beslimed coat, and said, "Follow me." Then he took off after the Leanansidhe, and, driven by reflex-level instinct, the rest of us raced to catch up.

I'd been shapeshifted one other time—by the dark magic of a cursed belt, and one that I suspected had been deliberately designed to provide an addictive high with its use. It had taken me a long time to shake off the memory of that experience, the absolute clarity of my senses, the feeling of ready power in my whole body, of absolute certainty in every movement.

Now I had it back—and this time, without the reality-blurring euphoria. I was intensely aware of the scents around me, of a hundred thousand new smells that begged to be explored, of the rush of sheer physical pleasure in racing across the ground after a friend. I could hear the breath and the bodies of the others around me, running through the night, bounding over stones and fallen trees, slashing through bits of brush and heavy ground cover.

We could hear small prey animals scattering before us and to either side, and I knew, not just suspected but *knew*, that I was faster, by far, than any of the merely mortal animals, even the young buck deer who went soaring away from us, leaping a good twenty feet over a waterway. I felt an overwhelming urge to turn in pursuit—but the lead runner in the pack was already on another trail, and I wasn't sure I *could* have turned aside if I had tried to do so.

And the best part? We probably made less noise, as a whole, than any one of us would have made moving in a clumsy mortal body.

We didn't cover five miles in half the time, an hour instead of two.

It took us—maybe, at the most—ten minutes.

When we stopped, we could all hear the drums. Steady, throbbing drums, keeping a quick, monotonous, trance-inducing beat. The sky to the northwest was bright with the light of reflected fires, and the air seethed with the scents of humans and not-quite humans and creatures that made me growl and want to bite something. Occasionally, a vampire's cry would run its shrill claws down my spine.

Lea stood upon a fallen log ahead of us, staring ahead. Mouse walked up to her.

"Gggrrrr rawf arrrgggrrrrarrrr," I said.

Mouse gave me an impatient glance, and somehow—I don't know if it was something in his body language or what—I became aware that he was telling me to sit down and shut up or he'd come over and make me.

I sat down. Something in me really didn't like that idea, but when I looked around, I saw that everyone else had done it too, and that made me feel better.

Mouse said, again in what sounded like perfectly clear English, "Funny. Now restore them."

Lea turned to look at the big dog and said, "Do you dare to give me commands, hound?"

"Not your hound," Mouse said. I didn't know how he was doing it. His mouth wasn't moving or anything. "Restore them before I rip your ass off. Literally rip it off."

The Leanansidhe tilted her head back and let out a

low laugh. "You are far from your sources of power here, my dear demon."

"I live with a wizard. I cheat." He took a step toward her and his lips peeled up from his fangs in unmistakable hostility. "You want to restore them? Or do I kill you and get them back that way?"

Lea narrowed her eyes. Then she said, "You're bluffing."

One of the big dog's huge, clawed paws dug at the ground, as if bracing him for a leap, and his growl seemed to . . . I looked down and checked. It didn't *seem* to shake the ground. The ground was *actually shaking* for several feet in every direction of the dog. Motes of blue light began to fall from his jaws, thickly enough that it looked quite a bit like he was foaming at the mouth. "Try me."

The Leanansidhe shook her head slowly. Then she said, "How did Dresden ever win you?"

"He didn't," Mouse said. "I won him."

Lea arched an eyebrow as if baffled. Then she shrugged and said, "We have a quest to complete. This bickering does not profit us." She turned to us, passed a hand through the air in our general direction, and murmured, "Anytime you want it back, dears, just ask. You'd all make gorgeous hounds."

Again, agony overwhelmed me, though I felt too weak to scream about it. It took a subjective eternity to pass, but when it did I was myself again, lying on my side, sweating and panting heavily.

Mouse came over and nuzzled my face, his tail wagging happily. He walked around me, sniffing, and began to nudge me to rise. I got up slowly, and actually braced my hand on his broad, shaggy back at one point. I felt an acute need to be gripping a good solid wizard's staff again, just to hold me up. I don't think I'd ever appreciated how much of a psychological advantage (i.e., security blanket) it was, either. But I wouldn't have one until I'd taken a month or so to make one: Mine had been in the *Blue Beetle*, and died with it, too.

I was on my feet before anyone else. I eyed the dog and said, "You can talk. How come I never hear you talk?"

"Because you don't know how to listen," my godmother said simply.

Mouse wagged his tail and leaned against me happily, looking up at me.

I rested my hand on his head for a moment and rubbed his ears.

Screw it.

The important things don't need to be said.

Everyone was getting back up again. The canteens made a round, and I let everyone recover for five minutes or so. There was no point in charging ahead before people could get their breath back and hold a weapon in a steady hand.

I did say something quietly to Susan, though. She nodded, frowned, and vanished.

She was back a few minutes later, and reported what she'd found into my ear.

"All right, people," I said then, still quietly. "Gather in."

I swept a section of the jungle floor clean and drew with my fingertip in the dirt. Martin lit the crude illustration with a red flashlight, one that wouldn't ruin our night vision and had less chance of being glimpsed by a nearby foe.

"There are guards stationed all over the big pyramid.

The girl is probably there, in the temple on top. That's where I'm going. Me, Susan, and Lea are going to move up through the gallery, here, and head for the temple."

"I'm with Susan," Martin said. "I go where she does."

This wasn't the time or place to argue. "Me, Susan, Lea, and Martin will go in that way. I want all eyes facing north when we head for the pyramid. So I want the rest of you to circle that way and come in from that direction. Right here, there's a cattle truck where they're storing their human sacrifices. Get close and spring them. Raise whatever hell you can, and run fast. Head west. You'll hit a road. Follow it to a town. Get into the church there. Got it?"

There was a round of nods and unhappy expressions.

"With any luck, that will draw off enough of them to let us pull a smash and grab on the temple.

"Also," I said, very seriously, "what happens in the Yucatán stays in the Yucatán. There will be no jokes about sniffing butts or chasing tails or anything like that. Ever. Agreed?"

More sober nods, this time with a few smiles.

"Okay, folks," I said. "Just so you know, friends— I'm in your debt, and it's one I'll never be able to repay. Thank you."

"Gush later," Murphy said, her tone wry. "Rescue now."

"Spoken like a true lady," I said, and put my hand out. Everyone piled hands. Mouse had to wedge in close to put his paw on the pile. All of us, every single one of us, except maybe my godmother, were visibly, obviously terrified, a circle of shivers and short, fast breaths.

"Good hunting, people," I said quietly. "Go."

Everyone had just gotten to their feet when the brush

rattled, and a half-naked man came sprinting almost directly into us, his expression desperate, his eyes wide with mindless terror. He smashed into Thomas, rebounded off him, and crashed to the ground.

Before anyone could react, there was a muted rustle, and a Red Court vampire in its black-skinned monstrous form came bounding out of the forest five yards away and, upon seeing us, went rigid with startled shock. An instant later, it tried to reverse its course, its claws gouging at the forest floor.

I've heard it said that no plan survives first contact with the enemy.

It's true.

The vampire let out an earsplitting screech, and all hell broke loose.

Chapter

Forty-two

A lot of things happened very quickly.

Mouse rushed forward and caught the vampire by one calf just before it could vanish into the thick brush. He set his legs as the vampire struggled wildly, trying to scream again.

Martin brought his pistol up in a one-handed grip, six inches of sound suppressor attached to its muzzle. Without hesitating for an instant, Martin took a step to one side for a clear shot and fired on the move. The gun made a sound no louder than a man clearing his throat, and blood spattered from the vampire's neck. Though it kept struggling, its screams suddenly ended, and it bounded and writhed wildly to maneuver Mouse between itself and Martin.

That stopped abruptly when Thomas's falcata took the vampire's head from its shoulders.

The half-naked man looked at us, and babbled something in Spanish. Susan answered him with a curt gesture and a harsh tone, and then the man blurted something, nodding emphatically, then turned to keep running into the darkness.

"Quiet," I breathed, and everyone dropped silent while I stood quite still, Listening for all I was worth.

I have a knack, a skill that some people seem to be able to learn. I'm not sure if it's something biological or magical, but it allows me to hear things I wouldn't otherwise pick up, and I figured it was a good time for it.

For a long breath, there was nothing but the continued rumble of the drums.

Then a horn, something that sounded a bit like a conch, began to blow.

A chorus of vampire screams arose and it didn't take any supergood hearing to know that they were headed our way.

"There. You see?" Sanya said, his tone gently reproving. "Frontal assault."

"Oh, Jesus," Murphy said, her tone more disgusted than afraid.

"He's right," I said, my voice hard. "Our only chance is to hit them hard." We had only a moment, and my mind raced, trying to come up with a plan that resulted in something other than us drowning in a flood of vampires.

"Harry," Susan said, "how are we going to do this?"

"I need Lea," I said, trying to keep my voice calm and steady. "I need Molly."

Molly made a squeaking noise.

I turned to Susan and said, "We do it in two waves."

We moved directly toward the enemy, entering the ancient gallery full of columns, and the vampires came boiling out of the shadows to meet us. I don't know how many of them there were. More than a hundred, less than a million. I stepped out in front of everyone and said, "Attack!"

Sanya's battle roar was loudest. He leapt forward,

drawing *Esperacchius*, and blazing light shone forth from the blade.

Murphy ran forward upon his right, letting out a scream of her own and holding the shining length of *Fidelacchius* in her hands. An aura of soft blue light had surrounded her. On Sanya's left, Susan ran, *Amoracchius* held aloft and wreathed in white fire, and her scream was something primal and terrible. Thomas flanked Murphy. Martin ran next to Susan, and both of them charged forward with blade and pistol in hand.

I saw the front ranks of vampires hesitate as they saw the pure, terrible light of the three Swords coming toward them, but it wasn't enough to stop the momentum of that horde. It swallowed all five valiant figures in a tidal wave of dark, flabby bodies, claws, fangs, and lashing tongues.

Suckers.

I still stood forward of everyone else, and the meeting of the two ranks of combatants brought the horde to a halt. A brief halt, true, something that lasted no more than a handful of seconds—but it was time enough for me to reach down to touch the slow, terrible power of the ley line flowing beneath my feet.

The temple atop the pyramid in the ruins was the center of the confluence, but ley lines, each one a vast, roaring current of magical energy, radiated out in all directions—and the one beneath us was an enormous current of raw earth magic. Earth magic wasn't my forte, and I knew only a couple of applications well enough to use them in a fight.

But one of them was a doozy.

I reached out and touched the power of that ley line, desperately wishing I had my staff with me to assist with the effort. I could sense the earth magic in my mind, feel it flowing by with a power that vibrated up through the soles of the big, stompy, armor-plated boots my godmother had put on me. I took a deep breath, and then thrust my thoughts down into that power.

I was immediately overwhelmed with a rush of images and alien sensations, contacting a power so intense and coherent that it nearly had its own awareness. In a single moment, I saw the ponderous dance of continents clashing against one another to form mountains, felt the slow sleepiness of the earth, its dreaming shivers felt as disasters by the ephemeral things that lived upon its skin. I saw wealth and riches beyond petty mortal imagination, gold and silver flowing hot in rivers, precious gems by the millions being born and formed.

I fought to contain the images, to control them and channel them, focusing all of those sensations into a well I could see only in my imagination, a point deep below the gallery of crumbling old stone that rested next to the pitifully temporary mortal structure on the surface.

Once I had the raw magic I needed, I was able to pull my mind clear of the ley line, and I was suddenly holding a whirlwind of molten stone in my head, seething against the containment of my will until it felt like my skull would burst outward from the pressure, and realized as I did that the use to which I was putting this pure, raw energy was almost childish in its simplicity. I was a frail wisp of mortality beside that energy, which could, quite literally, have moved mountains, leveled cities, shifted the course of rivers, and stirred oceans in their beds.

I set that well of energy to spinning, and directed its power as it spiraled up, a tornado of magic that reached out to embrace simple gravity. With the enormous energy of the ley line, I focused the pull of the earth for miles around into a circle a couple of hundred yards across and spoke a single word as I unleashed the torrent of energy, bound only, firmly if imperfectly, by my will. The spell, start to finish, had taken me a good sixty seconds to put together, and tapping into the ley line had been the last part of the process—far too long and far too destructive to use in any of the faster and more furious fights that I'd found myself in over the years.

Perfect for tonight.

For a quarter of a second, gravity vanished from Chichén Itzá, and the land for miles all around it, jerking everything that wasn't fastened down, myself included, several inches into the air. For that time, all of that force was focused and concentrated into a circle perhaps two hundred yards across that embraced the entire gallery and every vampire inside it. There, the enormous power of that much focused gravity, nearly three hundred times normal, slammed everyone and everything straight down, as if crushed by a single, gigantic, invisible anvil.

The stone columns handled it better than I thought they would. Maybe half of them suddenly cracked, shattered, and fell into rubble, but the rest bore up under the strain as they had for centuries.

The assault force of the Red Court wasn't nearly so resilient.

I could hear the bones breaking from where I stood, each snapping with hideously sharp pops and cracks. Down crashed the wave of vampires in a mass of shattered bones. Many of them were crushed beneath the falling stones of the weaker columns—each flabby black body smashed beneath a weight of scores of tons of stone, even if hit by only one piece from a single block.

The energy involved had been enormous, and as I was bounced up about a foot into the air, I was hit with the wave of exhaustion that came along with it. It wasn't as bad as it might have been. Technically, I was only channeling and rearranging forces that were already in existence and motion, not creating them from my will, or I could never have managed to affect an area so big, and to do it so violently. But believe you me, it was still hard.

I was thrown several inches up along with everything and everyone else that wasn't secured. I landed with only one foot beneath me, so I dropped to one knee, catching myself on my hands. Panting, I looked up to see the results of the spell.

A couple of acres of flat, dead, and a few horribly wounded and dying vampires lay strewn about like so many crushed ants, and standing over them, each in a combat pose, as if ready to keep on swinging, were the friends I had sent running ahead, entirely unaffected.

"Good," I said, panting. "That's enough, kid."

I heard Molly, several feet behind me, let out a sigh of relief herself, and the lights and shining auras vanished from the three figures wielding a Sword.

"Well-done, little one," the Leanansidhe said, and as she spoke the five figures themselves vanished. "A most credible illusion. It is always the little touches of truth that make for the most potent deceptions."

"Well, you know," Molly said, sounding a little flustered. "I just watched my dad a few times."

Mouse stayed close at my side. His head was turned to the right, focused upon the trees and the darkness that way. A growl I felt more than heard came from deep in his chest.

Susan stepped up to my side and looked at the crushed vampires with undisguised satisfaction, but frowned. *"Esclavos de sangre,"* she said.

"Yes," said Martin from somewhere behind me.

"What?" I asked.

"Blood slaves," Susan said to me. "Vampires who have gone entirely feral. They can't create a flesh mask. They're almost animals. Scum."

"Cannon fodder," I said, forcing my lungs to start taking slower, deeper breaths. "A crowd of scum at a top-end Red Court function."

"Yes."

It wasn't hard to figure out why they'd been there. Mouse's interest in whatever it was he sensed in the trees was deepening. "The Red Court was expecting company."

"Yes," Susan said, her voice tight.

Well. Nothing's ever simple, is it?

That changed everything. A surprise raid upon an unsuspecting, unprepared target was one thing. Trying to simply kick in the teeth of a fully armed and ready Red Court obviously expecting someone with my firepower was something else entirely. Namely, sheer stupidity.

So.

I had to change the game and change it fast.

A gong began to clash slowly, a monstrous thing, the metallic roar of its voice something low and harsh that reminded me inexplicably of the roar Martin had produced earlier. The tension got thicker, and except for the sounds of the drum and the gong, there were no other noises, not of the creatures of the jungle or any other kind.

The quiet was far more terrifying than the noise had been.

"They're out there," I said quietly. "They're moving right now."

"Yes," said Lea, who had suddenly appeared at my left side, opposite Mouse. Her voice was very calm, and her feline eyes roamed the night, bright and interested.

"That mob of trash was merely a distraction. Our own tactic used against us." Her eyes narrowed. "They are employing veils to hide themselves—and they are quite skilled."

"Molly," I said.

"On it, boss," she replied.

"Our distraction was an illusion. It didn't cost us any lives," Murphy pointed out.

"Neither did theirs, from their perspective, Sergeant," Martin said. "Creatures who cannot control themselves are of no use to the Red King, after all. Their deaths simply reduced the number of useless, parasitic mouths he had to feed. He may think of humans as a commodity, but he'd rather not throw that wealth away."

"Harry?" Murphy asked. "Can you do that anvil thing again?"

"Hell. I'm sorta surprised I got away with it the first time. Never done anything with that much voltage." I closed my eyes for a second and began to reach down for the ley line again—and my brain contorted. Thoughts turned into a harsh explosion of images and memories that left long lacerations on the inside of my skull, and even after I had moved my mind away from those images, it took several seconds before I could open my eyes again. "No," I croaked. "No, that isn't an option. Even if they gave me enough time to pull it off."

"Then what are we going to do?" Thomas asked. He held a large pistol in his left hand, his falcata in his right, and stood at my back, facing the darkness behind us. "Stand here until they swarm us?"

"We're going to show them how much it will cost to take us down," I said. "How's it coming, padawan?"

Molly let out a slow, thoughtful breath. Then she

lifted one pale hand, rotated an extended finger in a circle around us, and murmured, *"Hireki."*

I felt the subtle surge of her will wash out and drew in my own as it did. The word my apprentice whispered seemed to flow out from her in an enormous circle, leaving visible signs of its passing. It fluttered leaves and blades of grass, stirred small stones—and, as it continued, it washed over several shapes out in the night that rippled and became solid black outlines, where before there was only indistinct darkness and shadow.

"Not all *that* skilled," Molly said, panting, satisfaction in her voice.

"Fuego!" I snarled, and threw a small comet of fire from my right hand. It sailed forth with a howling whistle of superheated air and smashed into the nearest of the shadowed forms, less than a dozen yards away. Fire leapt up, and a vampire screamed in rage and pain and began retreating through the trees.

"Infriga!" I barked, and made a ripping gesture with my left hand. I tore the fire from the stricken vampire—and then some. I sent the resulting fireball skipping over to the next form—and left the first target as a block of ice where the damp jungle air had emptied its water over the vampire's body and locked it into place, rigid and very slightly luminous with the residue of the cold energy I felt in me, the gift of Queen Mab. Which was just as well—there were a dozen closing attackers in my immediate field of vision alone, which meant another fifty or sixty of them if they were circling in from all around us, plus the ones I *couldn't* see, who may have employed more mundane techniques of stealth to avoid the eye.

I wanted them to see what I could do.

The second vampire fell as easily as the first, as did

the third, and only then did I say quietly, "One bullet apiece, Martin."

Martin's silenced pistol coughed three times, and the slightly glowing forms of the ice-enclosed vampires shattered into several dozen pieces each, falling to the ground where the luminous energy of Winter began to bleed slowly away, along with the ice-riddled flesh.

They got the point. The vampires stopped advancing. The jungle became still.

"Fire and ice," murmured the Leanansidhe. "Excellent, my godson. Anyone can play with an element. Few can manipulate opposites with such ease."

"Sort of the idea," I said. "Back me up."

"Of course," Lea said.

I stepped forward and slightly apart from the others and lifted my hands. "Arianna!" I shouted, and my voice boomed as though I'd been holding a microphone and using speakers the size of refrigerators. It was something of a surprise, and I looked over my shoulder to see my godmother smiling calmly.

"Arianna!" I called again. "You were too great a coward to accept my challenge when I gave it to you in Edinburgh! Now I am here, in the heart of the power of the Red King! Do you still fear to face me, coward?"

"What?" Thomas muttered under his breath.

"This is not an assault," Sanya added, disapproval in his voice.

I ignored them. I was the one with the big voice. "You see what I have done to your rabble!" I called. "How many more must die before you come out from behind them, Duchess? I am come to kill you and claim my child! Stand forth, or I swear to you, upon the power in my body and mind, that I will lay waste to your strong place. Before I die, I will make you pay the price for every drop of blood—and when I die, my death curse will scatter the power of this place to the winds!

"Arianna!" I bellowed, and I could not stop the hatred from making my voice sharply edged with scorn and spite. "How many loyal servants of the Red King must die tonight? How many Lords of Outer Night will taste mortality before the sun rises? You have only begun to know the power I bring with me this night. For though I die, I swear to you this: *I will not fall alone.*"

I indulged in a little bit of melodrama at that point: I brought forth soulfire—enough to sheath my body in silver light—as my oath rolled out over the land, through the ruins, and bounced from tree to tree. It cast a harsh light that the nearest surviving vampires cringed away from.

For a long moment, there was no sound.

Then the drums and the occasional clash of the gong stopped.

A conch shell horn, the sound unmistakable, blew three high, sweet notes.

The effect was immediate. The vampires surrounding us all retreated until they were out of sight. Then a drumbeat began again, this time from a single drummer.

"What's happening?" Thomas asked.

"The Red King's agents spent the past couple of days trying to kill me or make sure I showed up here only as a vampire," I said quietly. "I'm pretty sure it's because the king didn't want the duchess pulling off her bloodline curse against me. Which means that there's a power play going on inside the Red Court."

"Your explanation isn't one," Thomas replied.

"Now that I *am* here," I said, "I'm betting that the Red King is going to be willing to attempt other means of undercutting the duchess."

"You don't even know he's here."

"Of course he is," I said. "There's a sizable force here, as large as any we've ever seen take the field during the war."

"What if it isn't his army? What if he's not here to run it?" Thomas asked.

"History suggests that kings who don't exercise direct control over their armies don't tend to remain kings for very long. Which must be, ultimately, what this is all about—diminishing Arianna's power."

"And talking to you does that how?"

"The Code Duello," I said. "The Red Court signed the Accords. For what Arianna has done, I have the right to challenge her. If I kill her, I get rid of the Red King's problem for him."

"Suppose he isn't interested in chatting?" Thomas said. "Suppose they're pulling back because he just convinced someone to drop a cruise missile on top of us?"

"Then we'll get blown up," I said. "Which is better than we'd get if we had to tangle with them here and now, I expect."

"Okay," Thomas said. "Just so we have that clear."

"Pansy," Murphy sneered.

Thomas leered at her. "You make my stamen tingle when you talk like that, Sergeant."

"Quiet," Sanya murmured. "Something is coming."

A soft lamp carried by a slender figure in a white garment came toward us down the long row of columns.

It proved to be a woman dressed in an outfit almost exactly like Susan's. She was tall, young, and lovely, with the dark red-brown skin of the native Maya, with their long features and dark eyes. Three others accompanied her—men, and obviously warriors all, wearing the skins of jaguars over their shoulders and otherwise clad only in loincloths and heavy tattoos. Two of them carried swords made of wood and sharpened chips of obsidian. The other carried a drum that rolled off a steady beat.

. I thought there was something familiar about the features of the three men, but then I realized that they weren't personally familiar to me. It was the subtle tension of their bodies, the hints of power that hung about them like a very faint perfume.

They reminded me quite strongly of Susan and Martin. Half vampires. Presumably just as dangerous as Susan and Martin, if not more so.

The jaguar warriors all came to a halt about twenty feet away, but the drum kept rolling and the girl kept walking, one step for each beat. When she reached me, she unfastened her feathered cloak and let it fall to the ground. Then, with the twist of a piece of leather at each shoulder, the shift slid down her body into a puddle of soft white around her feet. She was naked beneath, except for a band of leather around her hips, from which hung an obsidian-bladed knife. She knelt down in a slow, graceful motion, a portrait in supplication, then took up the knife and offered its handle to me.

"I am Priestess Alamaya, servant of the Great Lord Kukulcan," she murmured, her voice honeyed, her expression serene. "He bids you and your retainers be welcome to this, his country seat, Wizard Dresden, and offers you the blood of my life as proof of his welcome and his compliance with the Accords." She lowered her eyes and turned her head to the right to bare her throat, the carotid artery, while still holding forth the blade. "Do with me as you will. I am a gift to you from the Great Lord."

"Oh, how thoughtful," the Leanansidhe murmured.

"You hardly ever meet anyone that polite, these days. May I?"

"No," I said, and tried to keep the edge of irritation out of my voice. I took the knife from the girl's hands and slid it into my sash, and let it rest next to the cloth sack I had made from a knotted inside-out Rolling Stones T-shirt. The shirt had been in my gym bag of contraband ever since it had been a gym bag of clean clothes for when I went to the gym. I had pressed the shirt (*bah-dump-bump, ching*) into service when I realized the one other thing I couldn't do without during this confrontation. It was tied to my grey cloth sash.

Then I took the young woman's arm and lifted her to her feet, sensing no particular aura of power around her. She was mortal, evidently a servant of the vampires.

She drew in a short breath as she felt my hand circle her wrist and rose swiftly, so that I didn't have to expend any effort lifting her. "Should you wish to defile me in that way, lord, it is also well within your rights as guest." Her dark eyes were very direct, very willing. "My body is yours, as is my blood."

"More than a century," Murphy muttered, "and we've gone from 'like a fish needs a bicycle' to this."

I cleared my throat and gave Murphy a look. Then I turned to the girl and said, "I have no doubt about your lord's integrity, Priestess Alamaya. Please convey us to his seat, that I may speak with him."

At my words, the girl fell to her knees again and brushed her long, dark hair across my feet. "I thank you for my life, wizard, that I may continue to serve my lord," she said. Then she rose again and made an imperious gesture to one of the jaguar warriors. The man immediately recovered her clothing and assisted her in dressing again. The feather cloak slid over her shoulders once more, and though I knew the thing had to be heavy, she bore it without strain. "This way, lord, if you please."

"Love this job," Sanya murmured. "Just *love* it."

"I need to challenge more people to duels," Thomas said in agreement.

"Men are pigs," Murphy said.

"Amen," said Molly.

Lea gave me a prim look and said, "I've not sacrificed a holy virgin in ages."

"Completely unprofessional," muttered Martin.

"Ixnay," I said quietly, laying a hand on Mouse's shoulders. "All of you. Follow me. And don't look edible."

And, following the priestess with her lamp, we entered the city of Chichén Itzá.

Chapter

Forty-three

Chichén Itzá smelled like blood.

You never mistake blood for anything else, not even if you've never smelled it before. We've all tasted it—if nowhere else, when we lose our baby teeth. We all know the taste, and as a corollary, we all know the smell.

The main pyramid is known as El Castillo by most of the folk who go there today—literally, "the castle." As we walked up out of the gallery of pillars, it loomed above us, an enormous mound of cut stone, every bit as large and imposing as the European fortifications for which it was named. It was a ziggurat-style pyramid, made all of square blocks. Levels piled one on top of another as it rose up to the temple at its summit—and every level of the pyramid was lined with a different form of guard.

At the base of the pyramid, and therefore most numerous, were the jaguar warriors we had already seen. They were all men, all appealing, all layered with the lean, swift muscle of a panther. They all wore jaguar skins. Many of them bore traditional weapons. Many more wore swords, some of them of modern make, the best of which were superior in every physical sense to the weapons manufactured in the past. Most of them also carried a Kalashnikov—again, the most modern versions of the weapons, made of steel and polymer, the finest of which were also readily superior to the weapons of earlier manufacture.

The next level up were all women, garbed in ritual clothing as Alamaya had been, but covered in tattoos, much as the jaguar warriors were. They, too, had that same subtle edge to them that suggested greater-than-mortal capability.

Hell's bells. If the numbers were the same on every side of the pyramid, and I had no reason to believe that they were not, then I was looking at nearly a thousand of the jaguar warriors and priestesses. I am a dangerous man—but no one man is *that* dangerous. I was abruptly glad that we hadn't tried a rope-a-dope or a forward charge. We'd have been swamped by sheer numbers, almost regardless of the plan.

Numbers matter.

That fact sucks, but that makes it no less true. No matter how just your cause, if you're outnumbered two to one by a comparable force, you're gonna have to be real creative to pull out a victory. Ask the Germans who fought on either front of World War II. German tankers would often complain that they would take out ten Allied tanks for every tank they lost—but the Allies always seemed to have tank number eleven ready to go.

I was looking at an impossible numerical disadvantage, and I did not at all like the way it felt to realize that truth.

And I was only on the second tier of the pyramid.

Vampires occupied the next several levels. None of them were in their monstrous form, but they didn't have to be. They weren't going all out on their disguises, and the all-black coloration of their eyes proclaimed their inhumanity with eloquence. Among the vampires, gender seemed to have no particular recognition. Two more levels were filled with fully vampire jaguar warriors, male and female alike, and the next two with vampire priests and priestesses. Above them came what I presumed to be the Red Court's version of the nobility—individual vampires, male and female, who clearly stood with their own retinues. They tended to wear more and more gold and have fewer and fewer tattoos the higher up the pyramid they went.

Just before the top level were thirteen lone figures, and from what I could see they were taller than most mortals, seven feet or more in height. Each was dressed in a different form of traditional garb, and each had his own signature mask. My Mayan mythology was a bit rusty, but White Council intelligence reports said that the Lords of Outer Dark had posed as gods to the ancient Mayans, each with his own separate identity. What they didn't say was that either they had been a great deal more than that, or that collecting worshipers had *made* them more than merely ancient vampires.

I saw them and my knees shook. I couldn't stop it.

And a light shone in the temple at the top of the pyramid.

The smell of blood came from the temple.

It wasn't hard to puzzle out. It ran down the steps that led up the pyramid, a trickling stream of red that had washed down the temple steps and onto the earth beyond—which was torn up as if someone had cruised through the bloodied earth with a rototiller and torn it to shreds. The blood slaves, I was willing to bet. My imagination provided me with a picture of that insane mob tearing at the earth, swallowing bloody gobbets of it, fighting with one another over the freshest mud— until yours truly showed up and kicked off the party.

I looked left and right as we walked across the open courtyard. The cattle car Susan had told us about was still guarded, by a contingent of men in matching khakis and tactical vests—a private security company of some kind. Mercenaries. There were a load of security bozos around, several hundred at least, stationed here and there in soldierly blocks of fifty men.

Without pausing, Alamaya trod across the courtyard and began up the steps, moving with deliberate, reverent strides. I followed her, and everyone else present came with me. I got hostile stares all the way up, from both sides. I ignored them, as if they weren't worth my notice. Alamaya's calves were a lot more interesting anyway.

We reached the level below the temple and Alamaya turned to me. "My lord will speak to only one, Wizard Dresden. Please ask your retainers to wait here."

Here. Right next to the Lords of Outer Night, the expired godlings.

If I made a mistake, and if this went bad, it was going to go really bad, really fast. The people who had been willing to risk everything to help me would be the first to suffer because of it. For a moment, I thought about cutting a deal. Send them away. Let me face the Red Court alone. I had enough lives on my conscience already.

But then I heard a soft, soft sound from the level above: a child weeping.

Maggie.

It was far too sad and innocent a sound to be the death knell for my friends—but that might have been exactly what it was.

"Stay here," I said quietly. "I don't think this is going to turn into a John Woo film for a couple of minutes, at least. Murph, take the lead until I get back. Sanya, back her."

She arched an eyebrow at me, but nodded. Sanya shifted his position by a couple of feet, to stand slightly behind her and at her right hand.

I moved slowly up the last few steps to the temple.

It was a simple, elegant thing: an almost cubic building atop the pyramid, with a single opening the size of a fairly standard doorway on each side. Alamaya went in first, her eyes downcast. The moment she was in the door, she took a step to one side and knelt, her eyes on the ground, as if she were worthy to move no farther forward.

I took a slow breath and stepped past her, to face the king of the Red Court.

He was kinda little.

He stood with his back to me, his hands raised over his head, murmuring in what I presumed to be ancient Mayan or something. He was five-two, five-three, well muscled, but certainly nothing like imposing. He was dressed in a kind of skirt-kilt thing, naked from the waist up and the kneecap down. His hair was black and long, hanging to the top of his shoulder blades. He gripped a bloodied knife in his hand, and lowered it slowly, delicately.

It was only then that I noticed the woman on the altar, bound hand and foot, her eyes wide and hopeless, fixed on that black knife as if she could not look away.

My hands clenched into fists. I wasn't here to fight, I reminded myself. I wasn't here to fight.

But I wasn't here to stand around and let something like this happen, either. And I've never had a clear head when it comes to protecting women. Murphy says it makes me a Neanderthal.

She may be right, but I didn't seize a bone and jump the guy. I just cleared my throat really, really obnoxiously, and said, "Hey."

The knife paused.

Then the Red King lowered it and turned to face me. And I was forcibly reminded that nuclear warheads come in relatively small packages. He made absolutely no threatening gesture. He didn't even glare.

He didn't need to.

The pressure of his eyes was like nothing I had ever felt before—empty darkness that struck at me like a physical blow, that made me feel as if I had to physically lean away from him to keep from being drawn forward into that vacuum and lost to the void. I was suddenly reminded that I was alone, that I had none of my tools, that I was involved in matters way over my head, and that my outfit looked ridiculous.

And all of it was simply his physical presence. It was far too huge for the little body it came in, too large to be contained by the stone of this temple, a kind of psychic body heat that loomed so large that only a fool would not be instantly aware of how generally insignificant he was in the greater scheme of the universe. I felt my resolve being eroded, even as I stood there, and I clenched my jaw and looked away.

The Red King chuckled. He said something. Alamaya answered him, then rose and came to kneel down at his feet, facing me.

The slave on the altar remained in place, crying quietly.

I could hear another, smaller voice coming from behind the altar. Holy crap. I couldn't have cut this one much closer. I focused on my daughter's voice for a moment, small and sweet—and suddenly I didn't feel nearly so small. I just felt angry.

The Red King spoke.

Alamaya listened and then said, "You do not speak

the true tongue of the ages, wizard, so my lord will use this slave to ensure that understanding exists between us."

"Radical," I said. "Wicked cool."

Alamaya eyed me for a moment. Then she said something to the Red King, apparently conveying the fact that I had obnoxiously used phrasing that was difficult to translate.

He narrowed his eyes.

I mimicked his expression. I didn't know if he got it, but he sure didn't like it.

He said something in a short, curt tone.

"My lord demands to know why you are here," the priestess said.

"Tell him he fucking well knows why I'm here," I said.

She stared at me in shock. She stammered several times as she translated for me. I don't know if ancient Mayan has a word for *bleep* or if she used it.

The Red King listened, his expression slipping from displeasure into careful neutrality. He stared at me for several moments before he spoke again.

"'I was given a gift by she you know as Duchess Arianna,'" the girl translated. "'Are you saying that the gift was wrongfully obtained?'"

"Yes," I said, not looking away from him. "And you know it." I shook my head. "I'm sick of dancing. Tell him that I'll kill Arianna for him, take my daughter with me, and leave in peace. Tell him if he does that, it stops being personal. Otherwise, I'm prepared to fight."

The girl translated, her face once more fearful. When she finished, the Red King burst out laughing. He leaned back against the altar, his mouth wide in a grin, his black eyes utterly unsettling. He spoke a few terse sentences.

"My lord says that he will throw one of your limbs from each door if you lift your hand against him."

I snorted. "Yes. But I won't even try to kill him." I leaned forward, speaking to the Red King, not the girl, and showing him my teeth. "I'll try to cripple him. Wound him. Weaken him. Ask him if he thinks the death curse of a wizard of the White Council can deal him a wound. Ask him how well he trusts the people on the nearest couple of levels of the pyramid. Ask him if he thinks that they'll visit and send gifts when they realize he's been hurt."

Alamaya spoke in a fearful whisper, earning a sharp word of reproof and a command from the Red King. I guessed at the subject matter: "I don't want to tell you this, my lord." "Stupid slave, translate the way I damned well told you to do or I'll break my foot off in your ass."

Okay. Maybe not that last part.

Alamaya got on with her unpleasant job, and the words pushed the Red King into a rage. He gritted his teeth, and . . . things *moved* beneath his skin, shifting and rolling where nothing should have existed that could shift and roll.

I stared at him with one eyebrow lifted and that same wolf smile on my face, waiting for his reaction. He hadn't been talked to like this in a long time, if ever. He might not have much of a coping mechanism for dealing with it. If he didn't, I was going to die really horribly.

He did. He mastered himself, but I thought it was close—and it cost the woman on the altar her life.

He spun and slammed the obsidian knife into her right eye with such force that the blade broke off. She arched her body up as much as her restraints allowed and let out a short, choked scream of agony, throwing her head left and right—and then she sort of slowly relaxed into death. One leg kept twitching and moving.

The Red King ran two fingertips through the blood that was seeping from her eye socket. He slipped the fingers into his mouth and shuddered. Then he turned to face me, completely composed again.

I'd seen behavior like that before. It was the mark of an addict scoring a fix and full of contentment that he had a body full of booze or drugs or whatever, and therefore the illusion that he could handle emotional issues more capably.

That . . . explained a lot about how the Red Court had behaved during the war. Hell's bells, their king was a junkie. No wonder they had performed so inconsistently—brilliant and aggressive one moment, capable of making insane and idiotic mistakes the next. It also explained why there was strife within the Court. If the mark of power was control of one's blood thirst, indulging it only when and where one chose, and not with every random impulse, then anyone who knew about the Red King's condition would *know* that he was weak, inconsistent, and irrational.

Hell's bells. This guy wasn't just a monster. He was also paranoid. He had to be, because he *knew* that his bloodlust would be seen as a sign that he should be overthrown. If it had been happening for very long, it would have driven him insane. Even for one of the Red Court, I mean.

And that must be what had happened. Arianna had somehow tumbled to the Red King's weakness, and was building a power base aimed at deposing him. She'd been building her own power, personal, political, and social, inasmuch as the vampires had a psychotic, blood-spattered, ax-murdering version of a society. Dealing appropriately with one's enemies was critical to maintaining standing in any society—and for the Red Court, the only two enemies were those who had been dealt with appropriately and those who were still alive. She literally had no choice but to take me down if she was to succeed. And a Pearl Harbor for the White Council wouldn't hurt her any either, if she pulled it off.

Oh, I *had* to make sure this little lunatic stayed king. As long as he was, the Council would never face a competent, united Red Court.

The Red King spoke a moment later, and wiped off his fingers in Alamaya's hair as he did.

"My lord accepts your petition to challenge the duchess. This slave will be sent to fetch her while you wait."

"Not so fast," I said, as Alamaya began to rise. "Tell him I want to see the girl."

She froze between us, wide-eyed.

The king moved a hand in a permissive gesture. She spoke quietly to him.

His lip twitched up away from his teeth a couple of times. But he gave me a curt nod and gestured at the altar. Then he stepped to one side and watched me.

I kept track of him out of the corner of my eye as I approached the altar.

Maggie, wearing little metal restraints that had, ugh, been made to fit children, huddled on the far side of the altar. Blood had spilled out from the altar, and she had retreated from it until she was pressed against the wall, trying to keep her little shoes and dress, both filthy already, out of the blood. Her hair was a tangled mess. Her dark eyes were wide and bloodshot. She was shivering. It wasn't terribly cold out tonight—but it was cold enough to torment a child dressed in only a little cotton dress.

I wanted to go to her. Take those restraints off. Wrap her up in my ridiculous cloak and get her some food and some hot chocolate and a bath and a comb and a brush and a teddy bear and a bed and . . .

She saw me and flinched away with a whimper.

Oh, God.

I *ached*, seeing her there, frightened and miserable and alone. I know how to handle pain when I'm the one feeling it. But the hurt that went through me upon seeing my child, my blood, suffering there in front of my eyes—it went to a whole new level, and I had no idea how to deal with it.

But I thought it would probably start with tearing some more vampires to bloody shreds.

I took that pain and fed it to the storm inside me, the one that had been raging for endless hours and that flared up white-hot again. I waited until my rage had been stoked hot enough to dry the tears in my eyes. Then I turned to the Red King and nodded.

"Deal," I said. "Go get the duchess. I'll take out the garbage for you."

Chapter
Forty-four

Alamaya departed the temple in silence. Within a minute she was back. She bowed to the Red King—a full, kneeling bow, at that—and said something quietly.

The Red King narrowed his eyes. He murmured something to the girl and walked out. Conch horns blew and the drums began again as he appeared to those outside.

Alamaya had to raise her voice slightly to be heard. "My lord wishes you to know that this place is watched and warded. Should you attempt to leave with the child, you will be destroyed, and she with you."

"Understood," I said calmly.

Alamaya gave me a more conventional bow and hurried out after the Red King.

When she was gone, I took two steps over to the altar and the dead woman upon it. Then I said, "All right. Tell me what I'm looking at."

From the improvised Rolling Stones T-shirt bag tied to my sash, Bob the Skull said, in his most caustic voice, "A giant pair of cartoon lips."

I muttered a curse and fumbled with the shirt until one of the skull's glowing orange eye sockets was visible.

"A big goofy magic nerd!" Bob said.

I growled at him and aimed his eye at the altar.

"Oh," Bob said. "Oh, my."

"What is it?" I asked.

"The ritual curse they're setting up," Bob said. "It's a *big* one."

"How does it work? In ten seconds or less."

"Ten sec— Argh," Bob said. "Okay. Picture a crossbow. All the human sacrifices are the effort you need to pull back the string and store the energy. This crossbow has its string all the way back, and it's ready to fire. It just needs a bolt."

"What do you mean, a bolt?"

"Like the little girl hiding back behind it," Bob said. "Her blood will carry the stored energy out into the world, and conduct that energy to the target. In this case, her blood relatives."

I frowned for a second. Then I asked, "Does it have to be Maggie, specifically?"

"Nah. One bolt is pretty much like another. Long as you use a compatible knife to spill the blood, it should work."

I nodded. "So . . . what if we used a different bolt?"

"The same thing would happen," Bob said. "The only difference would be who is on the receiving end."

"It's a loaded gun," I said quietly. I frowned. "Then why'd they leave me alone with it?"

"Who you gonna kill to set it off?" Bob asked. "Your little girl? Yourself? Come on, boss."

"Can we disarm it then? Scramble it?"

"Sure. It'd blow this temple halfway to orbit, but you could do that."

I ground my teeth. "If it goes off the way they mean it to, will it kill Thomas?"

"The girl's human," Bob said. "So only the human

bits. His body, his mind. I suppose if he got lucky, he might wind up a vegetable in which his Hunger demon was trapped, but it won't spread any farther into the White Court than that."

"Dammit," I said. I started to say more, but caught motion out of the corner of my eye. I stuffed Bob all the way back into the sack, admonishing him to shut up, and turned to find Alamaya entering the temple with a dozen of the full-vampire jaguar warriors at her back.

"If you would follow me, lord wizard," the girl said, "I will conduct you to she who has wronged you. My lord wishes you to know that he gives his word that your daughter will be spared from any harm until the duel is concluded."

"Thank you," I said. I turned to look at my little girl one more time. She huddled against the wall, her eyes open but not fixed on anything, as if she were trying to watch everything around her at once.

I moved over to the child, and she flinched again. I knelt down in front of her. I didn't try to touch her. I didn't think I would be able to keep cool if I saw her recoil from my hand.

"Maggie," I said quietly.

Her eyes flashed up to me, surprise evident there.

"I'm going to take you away from the mean people," I said, keeping my voice as soft and gentle as I knew how. I didn't know if she even understood English. "Okay? I'm taking you out of here."

Her lip trembled. She looked away from me again.

Then I stood up and followed the priestess of the junkie god to face my enemy.

Outside, things had changed. The Red Court had filed down from the pyramid and were on the move, walking in calm, ordered procession to another portion of the ruins. My companions waited at the bottom of the stairs.

"Right," I said, once I reached them. "Duel time."

Sanya shook his head. "Mark my words. This will not be settled in a dueling circle. Things like this always go to hell."

"The Accords are serious," I said. "He'll play it straight. If I win, I get the girl and we're gone."

Martin shook his head.

"What?" I asked him.

"I know them," he said levelly. "None of us are leaving this place alive."

His words had an instant effect on everyone. They hit Molly the hardest. She was already pale. I saw her swallow nervously.

"Maybe you know the monsters, Martin," Murphy said quietly. "But I know the guy who stops them. And if they don't return the girl, we'll make them regret it." She nodded at me and said, "Let's go. We can watch Dresden kill the bitch."

I found myself smiling. Murphy was good people.

Once the last of the half-mortal jaguar warriors had departed, we fell into step behind them, and followed them toward what looked like another temple, on the north end of the ruins.

As we went beneath the temple doorway, though, we found ourselves passing through it into the open space beyond—a swath of green grass at least a hundred and fifty yards long and seventy or eighty yards wide. Stone walls about thirty feet high lined the long sides of the rectangle, while the far end boasted a temple like the one we'd just entered.

"It's a stadium," I murmured, looking around the place.

"Ugh," Molly said. "There are some pretty horrific stories about the Mayans' spectator sports, boss."

"Indeed." Lea sighed happily. "They knew well how to motivate their athletes."

Alamaya turned to me and said, "Lord, your retainers may wait here. Please come with me."

"Keep your eyes open, folks," I said. Then I nodded to Alamaya and followed her onto the field. Even as I started out, a woman began walking toward me from the opposite end. As she approached, I saw that Arianna had the same facial features, more or less, but she had traded in her pale skin for red-brown, her icy eyes for vampire black, and she'd dropped six inches from her height. She wore a simple buckskin shift and more gold jewelry than a Mr. T look-alike convention. Her nose was a little sharper, a little longer, but as we stopped and faced each other from about ten feet away, I could see the hate boiling behind her eyes. I had no doubt that this was the duchess.

I smiled at her and said, "I gotcha now."

"Yes," Arianna replied. Her eyes flicked up and around us in a quick circle, taking in the thousands of members of the Red Court and their retainers. "I may faint with the terror."

"Why?" I demanded of her. "Why bring the child into this? Why not just come straight to me?"

"Does it matter at this point?"

I shrugged. "Not really. I'm curious."

She stared at me for a moment and then she smiled. "You don't know."

I eyed her warily. "Don't know what?"

"Dear boy," she said. "This was never about *you*."

I scowled. "I don't understand."

"Obviously," Arianna said, and gave me a stunning smile. "Die confused."

A conch horn moaned and Alamaya turned to bow toward the temple I'd just come through. I could see the Red King seated upon a throne made of dark, richly polished wood, decorated with golden filigree and designs.

Alamaya rose and turned to us. "Lord and lady, these are the limits within which you must do battle. First . . ."

I scowled. "Hey. This is an Accords matter. We abide by the Code Duello."

The Red King spoke, and though he was more than two hundred feet away, I heard him clearly. Alamaya listened and bowed. "My lord replies that this is a holy time and holy ground to our people, and has been from time immemorial. If you do not wish to respect the traditions of our people, he invites you to return tomorrow night. Unfortunately, he can make no promises about the fate of his newest chattel should you choose to do so."

I eyed the Red King. Then I snorted. "Fine," I said.

Alamaya nodded and continued. "First," she said. "As you are both wielders of Power, you will duel with Power and Power alone. Physical contact of any kind is forbidden."

Arianna's eyes narrowed.

Mine did, too. I knew that the Red Court had dabblers in magic—hell, the first Red Court vampire I'd ever met had been a full-blown sorceress by the time she'd been elevated to the Red Court's nobility. Judging by Arianna's jewelry, her proper place had been on the eleventh tier of the pyramid—the one directly below the Lords of Outer Night themselves. It stood to reason that even a dabbler could have accrued way too much experience and skill over the course of millennia.

"Second," the mortal priestess said, "your persons and whatsoever power you use must be contained within the walls of this court. Should either of you violate that proscription, you will be slain out of hand by the wills of my lord and the Lords of Outer Night."

"I have this problem with buildings," I said. "Maybe you noticed the columns back the other way . . . ?"

Alamaya gave me a blank look.

I sighed. Nobody appreciates levity when they're in the middle of their traditional mumbo jumbo, I guess. "Nothing. Never mind."

"Third," Alamaya said. "The duel will begin at the next sounding of the conch. It will end only when one of you is no more. Do you understand the rules as I have given them to you?"

"Yep," I said.

"Yes," said Arianna.

"Have you anything else to say?"

"Always," I said. "But it can wait."

Arianna smiled slightly at me. "Give my father my thanks, and tell him that I will join him in the temple momentarily."

Alamaya bowed to us both. Then she retreated from the field and back over to her boss.

The night grew silent. Down in the stadium, there wasn't even the sound of wind. The silence gnawed at me, though Arianna looked relaxed.

"So," I said, "your dad is the Red King."

"Indeed. He created me, as he created all of the Thirteen and the better part of our nobility."

"One big, bloodsucking Brady Bunch, huh? But I'll bet he missed all the PTA meetings."

The duchess studied me and shook her head. "I shall never understand why someone hasn't killed you before now."

"Wasn't for lack of trying," I said. "Hey, why do you suppose he set up the rules the way he did? If we'd gone by the Code Duello, there's a chance it could have been limited to a physical confrontation. Really seems to be taking away most of your advantages, doesn't he?"

She smiled. "A jaded person might consider it a sign of his weakness."

"Nice spin on that one. Purely out of curiosity, though: Once you kill me, what comes next?"

She lifted her shoulders in a shrug. "I continue to serve the Red Court to the best of my ability."

I showed her my teeth. "Meaning you're going to knock Big Red out of that chair, right?"

"That is more ambitious than reasonable," she said. "One of the Thirteen, I should think, will ascend to become Kukulcan."

"Creating an opening in the Lords of Outer Night," I said, getting it. "Murdering your father to get a promotion. You're all class."

"Cattle couldn't possibly understand."

"Couldn't understand that Daddy's losing it?" I asked. "That he's reverting into one of your blood slaves?"

Her mouth twitched, as if she were restraining it from twisting into a snarl. "It happens, betimes, to the aged," Arianna said. "I love and revere my father. But his time is done."

"Unless you lose," I said.

"I find that unlikely." She looked me up and down. "What a . . . novel outfit."

"I wore it especially for you," I said, and fluttered my eyelashes at her.

She didn't look amused. "Most of what I do is business. Impersonal. But I'm going to enjoy this."

I dropped the wiseacre attitude. The growing force

of my anger burned it away. "Taking my kid isn't impersonal," I said. "It's a Kevorkianesque cry for help."

"Such moral outrage. Yet you are as guilty as I. Did you not slay Paolo's child, Bianca?"

"Bianca was trying to kill me at the time," I said. "Maggie is an innocent. She couldn't possibly hurt you."

"Then you should have considered that before you insulted me by murdering my grandchild," she hissed, her voice suddenly tight and cold. "I am patient, wizard. More patient than you could imagine. And I have looked forward to this day, when the consequences of your arrogance shall fall upon both you and all who love you."

The threat lit a fire in my brain, and I thought the anger was going to tear its way free of my chest and go after her without me.

"Bitch," I spat, "come get some."

The horn blew.

Chapter

Forty-five

Both of us had been gathering up our wills during the snark-off, and the first instant of the duel nearly killed us both.

I called forth force and fire, both laced with the soul-fire that would help reinforce its reality, making the attack more difficult to negate or withstand. It took the shape of a sphere of blue-white fire the size of an inflatable exercise ball.

Meanwhile, Arianna fluttered her hands in an odd, twisting gesture and a geyser of water erupted from the soil with bone-crushing force.

The two attacks met halfway between us, with results neither of us could prevent. Fire and water turned to scalding-hot steam in a detonation that instantly washed back over us both. My shield bracelet was ready to go, and a situation something like this one that had rendered my left hand into a horror prop had inspired me to be sure I could protect myself from this kind of heat in the future.

I leapt back and landed in a crouch, raising the shield into a complete dome around me as the cloud of steam swept down, its heat boiling the grass as it came. It stayed there for several seconds before beginning to disperse, and when it finally did, I couldn't see Arianna anywhere on the field.

I kept the all-around shield in place for a moment, and rapidly focused upon a point a little bit above and midway between my eyebrows. I called up my Sight and swept my gaze around the stadium, to see Arianna, forty yards away and running to put herself in position to shoot me in the back. A layer of greasy black magic seemed to infest the air around her—the veil that my physical eyes hadn't been able to see. To my Sight, she was a Red Court vampire in its true form, only even more flabby and greasy than the normal vamp, a creature ancient in power and darkness.

I tried not to see anything else, but there was only so much I could do. I could see the deaths that had been heaped upon this field over centuries, lingering in a layer of translucent bones that covered the ground to a depth of three or four feet. In the edges of my vision, I could see the grotesqueries that were the true appearance of the Red Court, every one of them a unique and hideous monster, according to his particular madness. I didn't dare look directly up at the spectators, and especially not those gathered on the second floor of the little temple at the end of the stadium. I didn't want to look at the Red King and his Lords unveiled.

I kept my gaze moving, as if I hadn't spotted Arianna on the prowl, and kept turning in a circle, timing when my back was going to be exposed to her before I dropped the shield and rose, panting, as if I couldn't have held it any longer than that. I kept on turning, and an instant before she would have released her spell, I whirled on her, pointed a finger, and snarled, *"Forzare!"*

Raw will lashed out and exploded against her chest just before the flickers of electricity she'd gathered could congeal into a real stroke of lightning. It threw her twenty feet back and slammed her against the ancient rock wall along the side of the ball court.

Before she could fall, I looked up at the top of the wall, seized a section of large stones in fingers of unseen will, and raked them out of their resting places, so that they plunged thirty feet down toward Arianna.

She was superhumanly quick, of course. Anyone mortal would have been crushed. She got away with only a glancing blow from one of the smaller stones and darted to the side, rolling a sphere of lurid red light into a ball between her hands as she went.

I didn't want to be on the receiving end of that, whatever it was. So I kept raking at the wall, over and over again, bringing down dozens of the stones and forcing her to keep moving, while I ran parallel to her and kept our spacing static.

We were both slinging magic on the run, but she had more one-on-one experience than me. Like a veteran gunslinger in the Old West, she took her time lining up her shot while I flailed away at her with rushed actions that had little chance to succeed. All told, I must have dropped several dozen tons of rock down onto her as we ran, inflicting nothing worse than a few abrasions and heavy bruises.

She threw lightning at me once.

The world flashed red-white and something hard hit me in the back. My legs went wobbly and I sat there for a subjective hour, stunned, and realized that whatever she had packed her lightning bolt with, it had been sufficient to throw me twice as far as my heavy punch had thrown her. I'd bounced off the opposite wall. I looked down at myself, expecting to see a huge hole with burned edges—and instead found a black smudge on my overdone breastplate, and a couple of flaws in the gold filigree where the metal had partially melted.

I was alive.

My head came back together in a sudden rush, and I knew what was coming. I flung up my shield, shaping it not into a portion of a sphere, as I usually did, but into a lengthy triangle in the shape of a pup tent. I crouched beneath it and no sooner had I done so than stones from the wall above me, torn free by Arianna's will, began to slam into the shield. I crouched there, rapidly being buried in grey stone, and tried desperately to get my impact-dizzied brain to think of a plan.

The best I came up with under the circumstances was this: What would Yoda do?

There was a tiny moment between one rock falling and the next and I dropped the shield. As the next rock began to fall, I stretched out my hand and my will, catching it before gravity could give it much velocity. Again I screamed, "*Forzare!*" and with an enormous effort of will I altered the course of the stone's fall, flinging it as hard as I could at Arianna, abetted by gravity and the remnants of her own magic.

She saw it coming, but not until it was too late. She lifted her hands, her fingers making warding gestures as she brought her own defensive magic to bear. The stone smashed through it in a flash of reddish light, and then struck her in the hip, spinning her about wildly and sending her to the ground.

"Harry Dresden, human catapult!" I screamed drunkenly.

Arianna was back on her feet again in an instant: Her shield had bled enough of the energy from the stone to prevent it from smashing into her with lethal force, but it had bought me enough time to get out of the pile of rocks around me and away from the stadium wall. I smashed at her with more fire, and she parried each shaft deftly, congealing water out of the air into wobbling spheres that intercepted the bolts of flame and exploded into concealing steam. By the fifth or sixth bolt, I couldn't see her with my physical eyes, but I did see energies in motion behind the steam as she pulled another dark sheath of veiling energy around her, and I saw her take off into an animal-swift sprint, again circling me to attack me from behind.

No. She couldn't be trying the same thing twice.

Duels between wizards are about more than swatting each other with various forms of energy, just as boxing is about more than throwing hard punches. There is an art to it, a science to it, in which one attempts to predict the other's attack and counter it effectively. You have to imagine a counter to what the opponent might do, and have it ready to fly at an instant's notice. Similarly, you have to imagine your way around the strength of his defenses. A duel of magic is determined almost purely by the imaginations and raw power of those involved.

Arianna had obviously prepared against my favorite weapon—fire—which was only intelligent. But she had tried this backstabbing ploy on me once before, and nearly got burned doing it. A wizard of any experience would tell you that she would never have tried that one again, for fear that the enemy would exploit it even further.

Arianna was an experienced killer, but she hadn't done a lot of dueling with nothing to rely on except her magic. She'd always had the cushion of her extraordinary strength and speed to fall back upon. Hell, it would have been the smart way to kill me—come straight in, shedding attacks and maybe taking some hits to get close enough to end it decisively.

Except here, she couldn't. And she wasn't adjusting well to the handicap. Flexibility of thought is almost never a strength of the truly ancient monsters of the world.

Instead of obliging her by standing in place, as I had last time she'd tried to give me the runaround, I darted forward, into the edges of the concealing steam. I got burned, and accepted it as the price of doing business. I clenched my teeth, focusing past my pain, and tracked Arianna's energy with my Sight, waiting for my shot and hoping that she didn't have the Sight as well.

Apparently she didn't, or wasn't bothering to use it, relying upon her superior senses instead. She got into position and seemed to realize that I'd gone into the steam. She began to advance cautiously, gathering more lightning to her cupped hands. I saw the instant in which she began to spot my outline, the way she drew a breath to speak the word to unleash the lightning upon me.

"*Infriga,*" I hissed, and threw both hands forward. "*Infriga forzare!*"

And the entire cloud bank of steam in the air around me congealed into needle-pointed spears of ice that flew at her as if fired from a gun.

They struck her just as she unleashed her lightning bolt, which shattered one of the spears and tore a two-foot furrow in the dirt some twenty feet to my side.

Arianna stood still for a moment, her black eyes wide with disbelief, staring down at the spears and shards of ice that had slammed deep into her flesh. She looked up at me for a second and opened her mouth.

A blob of black blood burst out and spilled down over her chin. Then she shuddered and fell, simply limp, to the ground.

From the far end of the ball court, I heard my godmother throw back her head and let out an eerie howl of excitement and triumph, bubbling with laughter and scorn.

I watched Arianna twisting upon the spears of ice. She'd been pierced in dozens of places. The worst hit came from an icicle as thick as my forearm, which had impaled her through the belly and come out the back, bursting the blood reservoir of the creature beneath Arianna's flesh mask. The pure, crystalline-clear ice showed a glimpse of her insides, as if seen through a prism.

She gasped a word I didn't recognize, again and again. I didn't know what language it was, but I knew what it meant: *No, no, no, no.*

I stood over her for a moment. She struggled to bring some other form of magic to bear against me, but the cruel torment of those frozen spears was a pain she had never experienced and did not know how to fight. I stared down at the creature that had taken my daughter and felt . . .

I felt only a cold, calm satisfaction, whirling like a blizzard of snow and sleet in the storm of my wrath.

She stared up at me with uncomprehending eyes, black blood staining her mouth. "Cattle. You are c-cattle."

"Moo," I said. And I lifted my right hand.

Her eyes widened further. She gasped a word I didn't know.

From the corner of my eye, I saw the Red King rise from his distant throne.

I poured all that was left of my fury into my hand and snarled, "No one touches my little girl."

The explosion of force and fire tore a crater in the ground seven feet across and half as deep.

Arianna's broken, headless corpse lay sprawled within it.

Silence fell over the ruined city.

I turned toward the Red King and started walking that way. I stopped on what would have been the ten-yard line in a football stadium and faced him. "Now give me my daughter," I said.

He stared at me, bleak and remote as a far mountain. And then he smiled and said, in perfect English, "I think not."

I clenched my teeth. "We had a deal."

He looked at me with uncaring eyes and said, "I never spoke a word to you. A god does not converse or bargain with cattle. He uses and dispenses with them as he sees fit. You have served your purpose, and I have no further use for you—or the mewling child."

I snarled. "You promised that she would not be harmed."

"Until after the duel," he said, and sycophantic chuckles ran through the vampires all around me. "It is after the duel." He turned his head to one side and said to one of the jaguar warrior vampires in his retinue, "Go. Kill the child."

I almost got the Red King while his head was turned, but some instinct seemed to warn him at the last instant, and he ducked. The bolt of flame I'd hurled at him blew the jaguar warrior vamp's jaw off of his head and set him on fire. He fell back, stumbling and screaming, his monstrous form tearing free of his mask of flesh.

The Red King whirled toward me in a fury, and those black eyes pressed down upon me with all the crushing weight of the ages. I was driven to my knees by a blanket of pure will—and not just will, but horrible pain, pain that originated not in my body but in the nerves themselves—pain I was helpless to resist.

I heard someone shout, "Harry!" and saw the masked

figures upon the temple with the Red King step forward. A gun went off, and then someone screamed. I heard a bellow, and looked up to see my friends and my godmother facing the masked Lords of Outer Night. Sanya was on his feet but motionless, grimly clutching *Esperacchius* in both hands. Murphy was on one knee and had dropped her P-90. One hand was moving slowly, determinedly toward the sword on her back. Martin was on the ground.

I couldn't see any of the others. I couldn't turn my head far enough. But nobody was up to fighting. None of us could move beneath the horrible pressure of will of the Red King and the Lords of Outer Night.

"Insolent beast," snarled the Red King. "Die in agony." He seized another guard by his jaguar skin and jerked him close, as if the brawny vampire had been a child. "Need I repeat myself?" he seethed, and shoved his bloodstained ritual knife into the warrior's hands. *"Place that child upon the altar and kill her."*

Chapter

Forty-six

Guys like the Red King just don't know when to shut up.

I fought to raise my hand, and it was more effort than anything I'd done that night. My hand shook and shook harder, but finally moved six inches, to touch the surface of the skull in the cloth bag on my hips.

Bob! I screamed, purely in my head, as I would have using Ebenezar's sending stone.

Hell's bells, he replied. *You don't have to scream. I'm right here.*

I need a shield. Something to ward off his will. I figure this is a spiritual attack. A spirit should be able to counter it.

Oh, sure. But no can do from in here, boss, Bob said.

You have my permission to leave the skull for this purpose! I thought desperately.

The skull's eye sockets flared with orange-red light, and then a cloud of glowing energy flooded out of the eyes and rose, gathering above my head and casting warm light down around me.

Seconds later, I heard Bob thinking, *Take this, shorty!*

And suddenly the Red King's will was not enough to keep me down. The pain receded, smothered and numbed by an exhilarating icy chill that left my nerves tingling with energy. I clenched my teeth, freed from the burden of pain, and thrust my own will against his. I was a child arm wrestling a weight lifter—but his last remark gave me some extra measure of strength, and suddenly I drove myself to my feet.

The Red King turned to face me fully again, and extended both hands toward me, his face twisting with rage and contempt. The horrible pressure began to swell and redouble. I heard his voice quite clearly when he said, "Bow. Down. Mortal."

I took one dragging step toward my friends. Then another. And another. And another, moving forward with increasing steadiness. Then I snarled through clenched teeth and said, "Bite. Me. Asshole."

And I put my hand on Murphy's left shoulder.

She'd already moved her hand halfway to the sword. As I touched her, touched our auras together, spreading my own defenses over hers, and felt the direct and violent strength of her own will to defy the immortal power brought against us, her hand flashed up to the hilt of *Fidelacchius* and drew the katana from its plain scabbard.

White light like nothing that ancient stadium had ever seen erupted from the sword's blade, a bright agony that reminded me intensely of the crystalline plain. Howls of pain rose from around us, but were drowned by Murphy's sudden, silvery cry, her voice swelling throughout the stadium and ringing off the vaults of the sky:

"False gods!" she cried, her blue eyes blazing as she stared at the Red King and the Lords of Outer Night. "Pretenders! Usurpers of truth! Destroyers of faith, of families, of lives, of children! For your crimes against the Mayans, against the peoples of the world, now will you answer! Your time has come! Face judgment Almighty!"

I think I was the only one close enough to see the shock in her eyes, and I realized that it wasn't Murphy speaking the words—but someone else speaking them through her.

Then she swept her sword in an arc, slashing the very air in front of us in a single, whistling stroke.

And the will of the Red King vanished. Gone.

The Red King let out a scream and clutched at his eyes. He screamed something, pointing in Murphy's direction, and in the same instant the rest of my friends gasped and rocked in place, suddenly free.

Every golden mask turned toward my friend.

Bob! I cried. *Go with her! Keep her free!*

Wahoo! the skull said, and gold-orange light fell from my head toward Murphy and gathered about her blond hair, even as the joined wills of the Lords of Outer Night fell upon her, so thick and heavy that I was knocked away from her as if by a physical force. The very air around her warped with its intensity.

White light from the sword flowed down and over her, and her garments literally transformed, as if that light had flowed into them, become a part of them, turning night to day, black to white. She staggered to one knee and looked up, her jaw set in stubborn determination, her teeth bared, her blue eyes, through the distortion, blazing like fire in defiance of thirteen dark gods—and with one of the most powerful spirits I'd ever met gathered around her head in a glowing golden halo.

Murphy came to her feet with a shout and a smooth stroke of the sword. The Lords of Outer Night all reacted, jerking back as if they'd been struck a blow in the face. Several golden masks were ripped from their faces, as if the blow had physically touched them—and the molten presence of their joined wills was suddenly gone.

With a scream, the jaguar warriors, half-breed and vampire alike, surged toward Murphy.

She ducked the swing of a modern katana, shattered a traditional obsidian sword with a contemptuous sweep of *Fidelacchius*, and struck down the warrior wielding it with a precise horizontal cut.

But she was outnumbered. Not by dozens or scores, but by the hundreds, and the jaguar warriors immediately fanned out to come at her from several directions. They knew how to work together.

But then, so did Sanya and I.

Sanya came forward with *Esperacchius*, and as it joined the fray, it too kindled into blazing white light that seemed to lick out at the vampires, forcing them to duck, to slap at white sparks that danced in their eyes. His booted foot caught one jaguar warrior in the small of the back, and the raw power of the kick snapped the warrior's head back with force enough to break his neck.

I followed Sanya in, unleashing a burst of freezing wind that took two warriors from their feet when they tried to flank Murphy from the other side.

She and Sanya went back-to-back, cutting down jaguar warriors with methodical efficiency for several seconds, as more and more of the enemy swarmed toward them. I kept slapping them away—not able to do any real harm, but preventing them from focusing overwhelming numbers on Murph and Sanya—but I could feel the fatigue setting in now. I couldn't keep this up forever.

There were quick footsteps beside me, and then Molly pressed her back to mine. "You take that side!" she said. "I'll take this one!"

DJ Molly C lifted both of her wands and turned the battle chaos to eleven.

Color and light and screaming sound erupted from

those two little wands. Bands of light and darkness flowed around and over the oncoming jaguar warriors, fluttering images of bright sunshine intertwining with other images of yawning pits suddenly gaping before the feet of the attackers. Bursts of sound, shrieks and clashes and booms, and high-pitched noises like feedback on steroids sent the hyperkeen senses of full vampires into overload, literally forcing them back onto the weapons of those coming behind them.

Vampires staggered through the handiwork of the One-woman Rave, not stopped but slowed and stunned by the incredible field of sound and light.

"I love a good party," Thomas shouted merrily, and he began to dance along the edges of Molly's dance floor, his falcata whipping into the limbs and necks of the jaguar warriors as they wobbled forward, struck down before they could recover. I didn't think anyone could have moved fast enough to catch them, but my brother evidently didn't agree. He struck down the foe as they came for us, and he threw in a few dance moves along the way. The part he borrowed from break dancing, where a wave traveled up one arm and down the other, was particularly effective, aesthetically, when it was bracketed by his falcata beheading one vamp and his automatic blowing apart the skull of another.

The pressure of numbers increased, and Thomas started moving more swiftly, more desperately—until Mouse leapt in to help plug the leak in the dam of confusion that held the full power of the Red Court at bay.

I had my own side of the store to mind. Again I reached into the well of cold, ready power, and with a word blanketed the field before me in smooth, slick ice. Howling wind rose to greet any foe who stepped out onto the ice, forcing them to work around to the killing machine that was Sanya and Murphy, or else circle around to attempt an approach through Molly's murderous light and sound show.

Someone touched my arm and I nearly roasted him without looking.

Martin flinched, as though he'd had a dodge ready to go if I had something for him. "Dresden!" he called. "Look!"

I looked. Up on the little temple at the end of the ball court, the Lords of Outer Night and the Red King were standing in a circle, and they were all gathering magical power—probably from one of the bloody ley lines, to boot. Whatever they were going to do, I had a bad feeling that I was reaching the very end of my bag of tricks.

I heard booted feet and saw the mortal security guards lining up along the sides of the stadium, rifles at the ready. When they were in position they would open fire, and the simple fact was that if they piled enough rounds into us, we would go down.

Who was I kidding?

I couldn't keep the field of ice and wind together for very long. And I knew Molly couldn't maintain her Rave at that intensity for long, either. Dozens of jaguar warriors had fallen, but that meant little. Their numbers had not been diminished by any significant measure.

We could fight as hard as we wanted—but despite everything, in the end it was going to be futile. We were never getting out of that stadium.

But we had to try.

"Lea!" I screamed.

"Yes, child?" she asked, her tone pleasant and conversational. I could still hear her perfectly clearly. Neat trick.

"The king and his jokers are about to hit us with something big."

"Oh, my, yes," the Leanansidhe said, looking sky-ward dreamily.

"So *do something*!" I howled at her.

"I already am," she assured me.

She removed a small emerald from a pocket of her gown and flung it skyward. It sparkled and flashed, and flew up out of the light of torches and swords, and vanished into the night. A few seconds later, it exploded in a cloud of merry green sparks.

"There. That place will do," she said, clapping her hands and bouncing up and down on her toes. "Now we shall see a *real* dance."

Green lightning split the sky, erupting with such a burst of thunder that the ground shook. Instead of fading, though, the thunder grew louder as more and more strokes of lightning flared out from the area of sky where Lea's gem had exploded into light.

Then a sheet of a dozen separate green bolts of lightning fell all at the same time onto the ground of the ball court twenty yards away, blowing smoking craters in the ground.

It took my dazzled eyes a few seconds to recover from that, and when they did, my heart almost stopped.

Standing on the ball court were twelve figures.

Twelve people in shapeless grey robes. Grey cloaks. Grey hoods.

And every single one of them held a wizard's staff in one hand.

The Grey Council.

The Grey Council!

The nearest figure was considerably shorter than me and stout, but he stood with his feet planted as if he intended to move the world. He lifted his staff, smote it on the ground, then boomed, "Remember Archangel!"

JIM BUTCHER

He spoke a single, resonating word as he thrust the tip of the implement at the Red King and the Lords of Outer Night.

The second floor of the stadium-temple where they stood . . . simply exploded. A force hit the ancient structure like an enormous bulldozer blade rushing forward at Mach 2. It smashed into the temple. Stone screamed. The Red King, the Lords of Outer Night, and several thousand tons of the temple's structure went flying back through the air with enough violent energy to send a shock wave rebounding from the point of impact.

The massive display of force brought a second of stunned silence to the field—and I was just as slack-jawed as anyone.

Then I threw back my head and let out a primal scream of triumph and glee. The Grey Council had come.

We were not alone.

The echo of my scream seemed to be a signal, sending the rest of us back to fighting for our lives. I blew a few more vampires away from my friends, and then sensed a rush of supernatural energy coming at me. I turned and caught a tide of ruinous Red power upon my shield, and hurled a blast of flame back at a Red Court noble in massive amounts of jewelry. Others in their ranks began to open up on the newly arrived Grey Council, who responded in kind, and the air was filled with a savage crisscross of exchanged energies.

The stocky figure in grey stumped up to me and said casually, "How you doing, Hoss?"

I felt my face stretch into a fierce grin, but I answered him just as casually. "Sort of wish I'd brought a staff with me. Other than that . . . can't complain."

From within his hood, Ebenezar grunted. "Nice outfit."

"Thanks," I said. "I liked your ride. Good mileage?"

"As long as there's some carpet to scuff your feet on," he said, and tossed me his staff. "Here."

I felt the energies moving through the implement at once. It was a better-made staff than mine, but Ebenezar had been the one to teach me how they were made, and both staves I had used over the years had been carved from branches of the lightning-struck oak in the front yard of his little farm in the Ozarks. I could make use of this staff almost as well as if it were my own.

"What about you?" I asked him. "Don't you want it?"

He batted a precisely aimed thrown ax from the air with a flick of his hand and a word of power, and drawled, "I got another one."

Ebenezar McCoy extended his left hand and spoke another word, and darkness swirled from the shadows and condensed into a staff of dark, twisted wood, unmarked by any kind of carving whatsoever.

The Blackstaff.

"Fuego!" shouted someone on the walls—and for a second I was hit with a little sting of insult. Someone was shouting *"fuego"* and it wasn't me.

While I was feeling irrational pique, guns started barking, and they aimed at me first. Bullets rang sharply as they hit my armor, rebounding from it and barely leaving a mark. It was like getting hit with small hailstones: uncomfortable but not really dangerous—unless one of them managed a head shot.

Ebenezar turned toward the walls from which the soldiers were firing. Hits thumped into his robes, but seemed to do little but stir the fabric and then fall at his feet. The old man said, mostly to himself, "You took the wrong contract, boys."

Then he swept the Blackstaff from left to right, murmured a word, and ripped the life from a hundred men.

They just . . . died.

There was absolutely nothing to mark their deaths. No sign of pain. No struggle. No convulsion of muscles. No reaction at all. One moment they were firing wildly down at us—and the next, they simply—

Dropped.

Dead.

The old man turned to the other wall, and I saw two or three of the brighter soldiers throw their guns down and run. I don't know if they made it, but the old man swept the Blackstaff through the air again, and the gunmen on that side of the field dropped dead where they stood.

My godmother watched it happen, and bounced and clapped her hands some more, as delighted as a child at the circus.

I stared for a second, shocked. Ebenezar had just shattered the First Law of Magic: Thou shalt not kill. He had used magic to directly end the life of another human being—nearly two *hundred* times. I mean, yes, I had known what his office allowed him to do. . . . But there was a big difference between appreciating a fact and seeing that terrible truth in motion.

The Blackstaff itself pulsed and shimmered with shadowy power, and I got the sudden sense that the thing was *alive*, that it *knew* its purpose and wanted nothing more than to be used, as often and as spectacularly as possible.

I also saw veins of venomous black begin to ooze their way over the old man's hand, reaching up slowly, spreading to his wrist. He grimaced and held his left forearm with his right hand for a moment, then looked over his shoulder and said, "All right!"

The farthest grey figure, tall and lean, lifted his staff. I saw light gleam off of metal at one end of the staff, and then green lightning enfolded the length of wood as he thrust the metal end into the ground. He took the staff back—but the twisting length of green lightning stayed. He drove the staff down again about six feet away, and again lightning sheathed it. Then he removed the staff, reversed his grip on it, and with a sweep of his arm drew another shaft of lightning between the two upright columns of electricity, bridging the gap.

He was opening a Way.

There was a flash of light, and the space between the bolts of lightning warped and went dark—then exploded with black figures bearing swords. For the first moment, I thought that they were wearing odd costumes, or maybe weird armor. Their faces were shaped something like a crow's, complete with a long yellow beak. They were wearing clothes that seemed to be made from feathers—and then I got it.

They actually were beak-faced creatures, covered in soft black feathers and carrying swords, each and every one of them a Japanese-style katana. They poured out of the gate by the score, by the *hundreds*, and began to bound forward with unnaturally long leaps that seemed only technically different from flying. They looked deadly and beautiful, all grace, speed, and perfection of motion. The wild light of the One-woman Rave glittered off of their blades and glassy black eyes.

"The kenku owed me a favor," Ebenezar drawled. "Seemed like a good time to call it in."

With sharp whistles and wails of fury, the strange creatures bounded up out of the ball court and began to engage the Red Court in numbers.

It was too much to take in. Sorcery flew beside bullets on a scale larger than anything I'd ever seen. Stone weapons clashed against steel. Blood flew: the black of the vampires, the blue of the kenku, and, mostly, flashes of scarlet mortal blood. There was too much terror and incongruous beauty in it, and I think my head reacted by tuning out everything that wasn't threatening my life, or was more than a few yards away.

"Maggie," I said. I grabbed the old man's shoulder. "I've got to get to her."

He grimaced and nodded his head. "Where?"

"The big temple," I said, pointing at the pyramid. "And about four hundred meters north of the temple, there's a trailer cattle car," I said. "It was guarded the last time I looked. There are human prisoners still in it."

Ebenezar grunted and nodded. "Get the girl. We'll take care of the Red Court and their Night Lords." The old man spat on the ground, his eyes alight with excitement. "We'll see how the slimy bastards like eating what they've been dishing out."

I gripped his hand, hard, then put my other one on the old man's shoulder and said, "Thank you."

His eyes welled up for an instant, but he only snorted and squeezed back. "Get your girl, Hoss."

The old man winked at me. I blinked a few times myself and then turned away.

Time was running out—for Maggie, and for me.

Chapter

Forty-seven

"**G**odmother!" I shouted, turning toward the pyramid.

Lea appeared at my side, her hands now filled with emerald and amethyst light—her own deadly sorcery. "Shall we pursue the quest now?"

"Yeah. Stay close. We'll round up the team and move."

Molly was nearest. I went to my apprentice and shouted in her ear, "Come on! Let the birdmen take it from here! We've got to move."

Molly gave me a vague nod, and finally lowered the little wands as the kenku's charge drove into the Red Court and took the pressure from our flanks. The tips of her wands, both of them made of ivory, were cracked and chipped. Her arms hung limply and swung at her sides, and she looked even paler now than she had going in. She turned to me, gave me a quivering smile, and then suddenly sank to the ground, her eyes rolling back in her head.

I stared at her in shock for a second, and then I was on my knees next to her, my amulet glowing as I used its light to check her for injuries. In the chaos, I hadn't seen that one of her legs, at midthigh, was a mass of blood.

One of the wild shots from the security goons had hit her beneath the armored vest. She was bleeding out. She was dying.

Thomas crashed to the ground next to me. He ripped off his belt and whipped it around her leg as a tourniquet. "I've got this!" he said, looking up at me, his expression remote, calm. "Go, go!"

I stared at him for a second, uncertain. Molly was my apprentice, my responsibility.

He regarded me and his calm mask cracked for a second, showing me his tension, the fear he was holding in check at the scale of the conflict around us. "Harry," he said. "I'll guard her with my life. I swear it."

I nodded, and then clenched a fist, looking around. That much spilled blood would start drawing vampires to the wounded girl like bees to flowers. Thomas couldn't care for her *and* fight. "Mouse," I called, "stay with them!"

The dog rushed over to Molly and literally stood over her head, his eyes and ears everywhere, a guardian determined not to fail.

Then I ran to Murphy and Sanya, who both bore small cuts and abrasions, and who looked like they were about to charge into the nearest portion of the fray. Martin tagged along with me, apparently calm, and by all appearances unaware that he was in the middle of a battle. Say what I would about Martin, his blandness, his boring demeanor, and his noncombative body language were very real armor in this situation. He simply didn't look like an important or threatening target, and he was untouched.

I looked around them and picked up a sword that had been dropped by one of the warriors they had killed, a simple Chinese straight sword known as a jian. It was light, razor-sharp on both edges, and suited me just fine.

"We're going to the pyramid," I called to Murphy and Sanya. A group of thirty or forty kenku went over us, witch shadows against the rising moon, and entered the fray against the jaguar warriors who still stood between us and an exit from the ball court. "There!" I said. "Go, go, go!"

I suited action to my words and plunged toward the opening Ebenezar's allies were cutting for us. There was a surge of magic and a flash of motion ahead of us, as another vampire noble tossed another flare of power at me. I caught a small stroke of lightning on my mentor's staff—it was shorter, thicker, and heavier than mine—conducting the attack down my arm, across my shoulder, and out the tip of my newly acquired sword. The lightning bolt chewed a hole in the belly of the Red Court noble. He staggered as I closed on him. I spun the staff to the horizontal, and checked him in the nose as I went by, dropping him to the ground.

We went past the remains of the temple and out into the open space between the buildings. It was chaos out there. Jaguar warriors and priest types were everywhere, and most of them were armed. Mortal security folks were forming into teams and racing toward the ball court to reinforce the Red Court. I realized that at some point Murphy, her clothing shining with white light, her halo a blaze of molten gold, had begun racing along on my right side, with Sanya on my left. The brilliant light of the two Swords was a terror to the vampires and half-breeds alike, and they recoiled from that aura of power and fear—but that wasn't the same thing as retreating. They simply fell back, while other creatures closed a large circle about us, drawing it slowly tighter as we moved toward the pyramid.

"We aren't going to make it," Murphy said. "They're getting ready to rush us from all sides."

"Always they are doing that," Sanya said, panting, his cheerful voice going slightly annoyed. "Never is it anything new."

They were right. I could sense the change in motion of the villains around us, how they were retreating more slowly before us, pressing in more closely behind us.

I felt my eyes drawn up to the pyramid ahead—and there, standing on the fifth level of the pyramid, looking down, was a figure in a golden mask. Evidently, one of the Lords of Outer Night had been knocked all the way over to the pyramid by Ebenezar's entrance. And I could feel his will at work in the foes around us—not used to overcome an enemy with immobility now, but to infuse his troops with confidence and aggression.

"That guy," I said, nodding at him. "Gold mask. We take him down and we're through."

Murphy scanned the pyramid until she spotted him. Then her eyes tracked down to the base of the stairs and she nodded shortly. "Right," she said.

And she raised *Fidelacchius*, let out a scream that had startled a great many large men working out at her dojo, and plunged into the warriors of the Red Court like a swimmer breasting a wave.

Sanya blinked.

Holy crap, I hadn't meant she should do *that*.

"Tiny," Sanya said, letting out a belly laugh as he began to move. "But *fierce*!"

"You're all insane!" I screamed, and plunged forward with them, while Martin backpedaled and tried to keep up with us while simultaneously warding off the vampires closing in from behind.

Murphy did what no mortal should have been able to do—she cut a path through a mob of warrior vampires. She went through them as if they'd been no more than a cloud of smoke. *Fidelacchius* blazed, and no weapon raised against the Sword of Faith, neither modern steel nor living relic, could withstand its edge.

Murphy hardly seemed to actually attack anyone. She simply moved forward, and when attacks came at her, bad things happened to whoever had attempted to strike her. Sword thrusts were slid gently aside while she continued onward, her own blade seeming to naturally, independently pass through an S-shaped slash upon the opponent's body on the way through, wreaking terrible damage with delicate speed. Warriors who flung themselves upon her found their hands grabbing nothing, their bodies being sent tumbling through the air—and that horrible Sword of light left wounds in each and every opponent, their edges black and sizzling.

They'd come at her in twos, and once, three of the jaguar warriors managed to coordinate an attack. It didn't do them any good. Murphy had been handling opponents who were bigger and stronger and faster than her, in situations of real danger, since she was a rookie cop. The vampires and half-breeds, swift and strong as they were, seemed no more able to beat her down than had all of those thugs and criminals. Stronger though her enemies were, the blazing light of the Sword seemed to slow them, to undermine their strength—not much, but enough to make the difference. Murphy dodged and feinted and tossed warriors into one another, using their own strength against them. The three-on-one she faced almost seemed unfair. One of the jaguar warriors, armed with an enormous club, wound up smashing his two compatriots, courtesy of the intern Knight, only to find his club sliced into three pieces that wound up on the ground next to his own severed leg.

Karrin Murphy led the charge, and Sanya and I tried to keep up. She went through that sea of foes like a little speedboat, her enemies spun and tossed and turned and disoriented in her wake. Sanya and I hacked our way through stunned foes, pushing and chopping with unsophisticated brutality—and that big Russian lunatic just kept laughing the whole time.

We hit the stairs, and resistance thinned sharply. Murphy surged ahead, and the Lord of Outer Night raised a bejeweled hand against her, his sheer will causing the air to ripple and thicken. Sanya and I hit it like a brick wall and staggered to a halt, but it seemed to slide off of Murphy, as had every other attack to come at her, her halo burning still brighter. Panicked, the enemy raised a hand and sent three shafts of sorcerous power howling at her, one right after another. Murphy's feet, sure and swift on the stairs, carried her into a version of a boxer's bobbing dance, and each shaft went blazing uselessly past her.

Sanya yelped and dropped, dodging the bolt that nearly clobbered him. I blocked one on my shield and took the other in the shin. My godmother's armor protected my flesh, but I hit the stone stairs of the pyramid pretty hard.

I jerked my eyes up in time to see Murphy rush the Lord of Outer Night and speed straight past him, her sword sweeping up in a single, upward, vertical slash.

The gold mask fell from the vampire's head—along with the front half of its skull. Silver fire burned at the revealed, twisted, lumpy lobes of the vampire's brain, and as its blood flowed out and touched that fire, it went up in a sudden pyre of silver-white flame. The Lord of Outer Night somehow managed to scream as fire consumed it, and flung more bursts of magic blindly and in all directions for several more seconds, until it finally fell into blackened ash and ugly smears on the stone.

Only *then* did the barrier of its will vanish, and Sanya, Martin, and I hustled up the stairs toward the temple.

Still, the enemy pursued us—there were so damned *many* of them—and as I gained more height I was able to look back and see that the Red Court had begun to contain the kenku incursion. The battle was still furiously under way within the ball court, and though the feathered warriors were the match of any two or three vampires or half-breeds, the enemy had numbers to spare. I could only be grateful that so many of their spell-slingers were duking it out with the Grey Council instead of getting in our way.

"Dammit," I said, looking up the steps toward the temple at their summit. Shadows moved inside. "Dammit!" I looked around me wildly and suddenly felt a hand grasp mine, where I clutched my staff.

Murphy shook my hand until I looked at her. "Sanya and I will stay here," she said, panting. "We'll hold them until you get Maggie."

I looked down the slope of the pyramid. Hundreds of the Red Court were coming up, and they were tearing free of their flesh masks now, revealing the monsters beneath. Hold them? It would be suicide. The Swords gave their wielders immense power against things out of nightmares, but it didn't make them superhuman. Murphy and Sanya had both been fighting for twenty minutes—and there *is* no aerobic exercise that compares with the physical demands of combat. Both of them were breathing hard, growing tired.

Suicide.

But I needed to get up there.

"Dresden," Martin called. *"Come on!"*

I hadn't even realized he was shaking me, trying to get me up the stairs.

I guess I was getting pretty tired, too.

I narrowed my focus to Martin, to the stairs up, and tried to ignore the burning in my arms, my legs, my chest. I drew in a sharp breath, and it was like inhaling sudden cool, clean wind. I thought I heard someone whispering to me, something in a tongue I didn't understand—but I knew my queen's voice. I became aware that a cloud of white mist and vapor was gathering around me as I continued, a little faster, the humid air of the Yucatán boiling around the frost that had formed on my armor.

Then the cold washed away the hot fatigue, and I felt the ice flowing into me, implacable, merciless, relentless. My legs began to churn like the pistons of an engine. Suddenly one step per stride simply wasn't enough, and I started flying up them two at a time, rapidly leaving Martin behind.

I reached the top and a half-breed jaguar warrior flung himself toward me. I snarled, batted his sword aside with mine, and lashed out with one foot, landing a stomping kick in the center of his chest.

His sternum cracked audibly, and he flew backward as if rammed by a truck. He hit the stone wall behind him hard enough to shake dust from the roof overhead, and crumpled like a broken toy. Which was exactly the kind of power the Winter Knight was *supposed* to have, and as I watched the poor idiot drop, I felt nothing but satisfaction.

The square temple had four doorways, one on each side, and in the one to my immediate right a vampire torn free of its flesh mask appeared, a jaguar skin still draped over its shoulders. It clutched an obsidian knife in its hand—the Red King's dagger. It was the vamp he'd dispatched to kill Maggie.

"Fog of war, huh?" I asked him, and felt myself smiling. "Buddy, did you ever walk through the wrong door at the wrong time."

Its eyes flicked to the floor to my left for an instant, and I looked, too. Maggie crouched there, directly between the altar and the door on my left, chained and shivering, huddling low to the ground as if hoping to be overlooked.

"Go on," I said, looking back at the vampire. I bounced the sword in my hand lightly. White mist poured off the blade. So did a few snowflakes. "Go for it, tough guy. Take one step toward that girl and see what happens."

The door opposite me suddenly darkened.

The Red King and no fewer than four of his Lords stood there, gold masks shining, throwing back weird reflections from the dazzling array of flickering lights and fires in the darkness outside.

His face twisted with rage, and his will and the wills of the Lords behind him fell upon me like blows from individual sledgehammers. I staggered, planted my mentor's staff firmly on the stone floor, and barely kept myself from being driven to the ground.

"Now," the Red King said, his voice strangled with fury. "Put that little bitch on the altar."

One of the Lords stepped forward and bent down to seize the child by her hair. Maggie screamed.

"No!" I shouted.

The Red King went to the altar and kicked the corpse of the dead woman from it. "Mortal," he spat. "Still so certain that his will matters. But you are nothing. A wisp. A shadow. Here and then gone. Forgotten. It is fated. It is the way of the universe." He jerked the ritual knife from the hands of the warrior and glared at me, his true nature writhing and twisting beneath his skin. The Lord dragged the shackled, screaming child to the altar, and the Red King's black eyes gleamed.

"This is your only role, mortal," he said, "your only grace, the only thing you are truly meant to do." He stared at Maggie and bared his teeth, all long fangs, slaver running out of his mouth and down over his chin. *"Die."*

Chapter

Forty-eight

The Red King raised the knife over my daughter, and she let out a quavering little scream, a helpless, hopeless wail of terror and despair—and as hard as I fought with the new strength given me by Queen Mab, with the protection granted by my godmother's armor, I could not do a damned thing about it.

I didn't have to.

White light erupted over the altar from no visible source, and the Red King let out a scream. The shackles of his will vanished, even as his right hand, the one holding the stone knife, leapt off of his arm and went spinning through the air. It fell to the stone floor, still clutched hard around the leather-wrapped hilt of the knife, and the obsidian blade shattered like a dropped dish.

I let out a shout as I felt the Red King's will slip off of me. The others still held me in place, but I suddenly knew that I could move, knew that I could fight. As the Red King reeled back screaming, I lifted a hand, snarled, *"Fuego!"* and sent a wash of fire to my right, engulfing the jaguar warrior who still stood a couple of feet inside the doorway. He tried to flee, and only wound up screaming and falling down the deadly steep steps of the

pyramid while the soulfire lacing my spell found his flesh
and set it aflame.

I whirled back to the Lords facing me from the far
side of the altar. I couldn't have risked throwing destructive energy at them with my daughter lying on the altar
between us, and I'd had no choice but to take out the
immediate threat of the warrior so that I could focus on
the Lords and the Red King—otherwise it would have
been relatively simple for him to come over and cut my
throat while I was engaged by the vampire elite.

But two could play at that game—and my physical
backup was a hell of a lot better than theirs.

I drew on my own will and lifted my borrowed staff—
and as I did four more beings in golden masks entered
the temple.

Where did all these yo-yos *come* from?

"Hold the wizard!" snarled the Red King, and the
pressure of hostile minds upon me abruptly doubled. My
left arm shook and the staff I held in it slowly sank down.
My right arm just ran out of gas, as if the muscles in it
had become totally exhausted, and the tip of the sword
clinked as it hit the stone floor.

The Red King rose, and stared for a moment at the
altar and at the column of shimmering light over it. As he
did, his freaking hand began to writhe like a spider—and
a second later, it flipped itself over and began to crawl
back over toward him. The king just stood there, staring
at the light. I tried to fight my way out of the mass of dark
will directed against me. The light could only be Susan,
veiled behind the Leanansidhe's handiwork and wielding
Amoracchius. I mean, how many invisible sources of holy
light interested in protecting my daughter could there be
running around Chichén Itzá? She hadn't attacked yet,
instead standing over Maggie—I wanted to scream at her

to take him, that it was her only chance. If she didn't, the Red King and his Lords could take her out almost as swiftly and easily as I had the jaguar warrior.

But he didn't—and in a flash of insight, I understood why he didn't.

He didn't know what the light *was*.

He knew only that it had hurt him when he had tried to murder the child. From his perspective, it could have been almost anything—an archangel standing guard, or a spirit of light as terrible as the Ick had been foul. I thought back to the voice coming from Murphy's mouth, pronouncing judgment upon the Red Court, and suddenly understood what was making the Red King hesitate, what he was really thinking: that the entity over the altar might be something he did not think actually existed—like maybe the *real* Kukulcan.

And he was afraid.

Susan *couldn't* do anything. If she acted, if she revealed what she was, the enemy's uncertainty would vanish and the conflict would immediately ensue again. Outnumbered so heavily, she wouldn't have a chance.

But she knew what she had, in uncertainty and fear, and she neither moved nor made a sound. It was a weapon as potent as the wills of the demigods themselves—it had, after all, paralyzed the Red King. But it was a fragile weapon, a sword made of glass, and I felt my eyes drawn to the broken pieces of obsidian on the floor.

I couldn't move—and time was not our ally. With every moment that passed, the more numerous enemy would become more organized, recover more from the shock of the sudden invasion of a small army smack in the middle of their holiday celebration. I needed an opportunity, a moment, if I was going to get Maggie out of this mess. And I needed it soon.

I strained against the wills of the Lords of Outer Night, unable to move—and keeping their attention locked upon me. One by one, my gaze traveled over each of the golden masks. I focused on the last one for a time, then began again with the first, tried to test each individual will, to find out which would be the weakest point of attack when my moment came.

Just then, Martin ghosted into the temple through the fourth door, making absolutely no sound, and it looked to me like the moment was freaking nigh. All of the Lords present were focused on me. The Red King stood intently distracted by Susan's light show, while his severed hand crawled its way up his leg and hopped over to his wounded arm, where rubbery tendrils of black ooze immediately extruded from whole and wounded flesh alike, and began intertwining.

Martin had walked into what had to be a Fellowship operative's wet dream: the Red King's naked back, and no one to stop him from going medieval on the leader of the vile edifice of power and terror that was the Red Court.

He took the machete from its sheath without a whisper of steel on nylon and drew back, readying himself to strike. There was an intensity of focus in his face that I had never seen before.

He closed the last two steps in a superquick blur, went into a spin, and I was getting ready to cheer—

—when his foot swept up to streak savagely through the air beneath the glowing white light.

I heard Susan let out a cry as she fell, startled by the blow. Martin, moving with his eyes closed, got close to her, his arms lashing out, and caught something between them. He ripped hard with his left arm, twisting the machete up with the right as he did—and suddenly Susan was fully visible, bowed into a painful arch by Martin's grip on her. The feather cloak had fallen from her, and the blade of Martin's machete rested against her throat.

I screamed in rage. It came out as a sort of vocalized seethe.

The Red King took a swift step back as Martin attacked, his eyes intent. Then, when Susan appeared, his head tilted as he worked through what he was seeing.

"Please excuse me, my lord," Martin murmured, giving a slight bow of his head to the Red King. "Drop it," he said in a flat voice to Susan. He twisted his body more, bending her painfully, and pressing the machete's edge against her throat even harder, until Susan's fingers opened and *Amoracchius* fell to the floor, its light slowly dying.

"A trick," said the Red King. Anger began to pour off of him. "A charlatan's trick." His eyes moved from Susan up to Martin. "And you have revealed yourself."

"I beg your forgiveness, my lord," Martin said. "It seemed the proper time. On my initiative, strike teams began removing Fellowship personnel and safe houses two hours ago. By this time tomorrow, there won't be an operative left alive south of the United States. And our financial division will have taken or destroyed well over ninety percent of their accounts."

"You son of a bitch," Susan said, her voice overflowing with pain. "You fucking traitor."

Martin's expression flickered at her words. But his eyes never left the Red King. "I give you the Fellowship of St. Giles, my lord," he said. "And I beg you to grant me my reward."

"Reward," Susan said, loading more contempt and hate into the word than should have been possible. "What could they possibly give you, Martin, to make it worth what you've done?"

The Red King stared at Susan and said, "Explain it to her."

"You misunderstand," Martin said calmly. "I have not betrayed the Fellowship, Susan. This was the plan from the moment I joined it. Think. You've known me for less than a decade and you've seen how near some of our scrapes have been. Did you truly believe I had survived a hundred and fifty years of battle against the Red Court, outlived every other operative ever to serve the Fellowship on my own merits?" He shook his head. "No. Escapes were provided. As were targets. It took me fifty years and I had to personally kill two of my fellows and friends working much as I was to win the trust of the Fellowship. Once they admitted me to the inner circle, their time had come. Trust is a poison, Susan. It took another century to ferret out their secrets, but it is finally done. And our people will finish removing the Fellowship, in every meaningful sense, by tomorrow. It is over."

Susan's eyes flickered over to me, and Maggie continued to weep quietly, huddling in on herself. Susan's face was twisted with pain. There were furious tears in her eyes as she looked at me.

And I couldn't even speak to her.

"And what do you get?" Susan asked her, voice shaking.

"Ascension," said the Red King. "I have no interest in admitting bloodthirsty lunatics to the nobility of my Court. Martin has proven himself—his dedication, his self-control, and, most important, his competence, over the course of decades. He was a priest for fifty years before he was even permitted to attempt this service."

"Honestly, Susan," Martin said, "I told you many times that you can never let emotion interfere with your duties. If you had listened to me, I'm certain you would have caught on. I would have been forced to kill you, as I have several others who were too wise for their own good, but you would have known."

Susan closed her eyes. She was shaking. "Of course. You could make contact as often as you wished. Every time I visited Maggie."

"Correct," he said quietly. He turned back to the Red King. "My lord, I beg your forgiveness. I sought only to give you that which you wished, and the timing made it necessary for me to act, or see the opportunity pass us by."

"Under the circumstances, I think I will not object, priest," the Red King said. "If the strike teams are as successful as you predict, you will have your reward and my gratitude."

Martin bowed his head to the Red King, and then looked up at me. He studied my face for a moment before he said, "The wizard has Alamaya's dagger in his sash, my lord, should you wish to complete the ritual."

The Red King took a deep breath and then blew it out, his expression becoming almost benevolent. "Martin, Martin, the voice of practicality. We've been lost without you."

"My lord is too kind," Martin said. "Please accept my condolences on the loss of Arianna, my lord. She was a remarkable woman."

"Remarkably ambitious," the Red King said. "Determined to cling to the past, rather than exploring new opportunities. She and her entire coterie, determined to undermine me. Had she destroyed this animal and then made good upon her promise to break the back of the accursed White Council, she would have been a real threat to my power. I take no pleasure in thinking on it, but her death was meant to be."

"As you say, my lord," Martin said.

The Red King approached me, smiling, and reached for the dagger in my sash.

Susan bared her teeth, still straining, but Martin was more than her equal, it seemed.

There was nothing I could do. The deck had been stacked so hard against me that even with Martin on our side, things had looked grim. His treachery had come at the ideal moment, damn him. Damn them all. There was nothing I could . . .

Long ago, when I was little more than a child, my first lover and I had devised a spell to let us speak silently to each other in class. It was magic much like the speaking stone Ebenezar had crafted, but simpler, with a much shorter range. I had never used to it communicate with anyone but Elaine, but Susan had been intimate with me—and I thought that at that moment, the only thought on our minds was Maggie.

It might be enough to establish the link, even if it was only one-way.

I grasped for the minor magic, fighting to pull it together through the dragging chains of the wills of the Lords of Outer Night, and cast my thought at Susan as clearly as I could. *He doesn't know all of it*, I sent to her desperately. *He doesn't know about the enchantment protecting your skin. He only knows about the cloak because he saw you use it when we got here.*

Susan's eyes widened briefly. She'd heard me.

The altar, I thought. *The ritual meant to kill us can be turned back upon them. If one of them dies on that knife, the curse will go after their bloodline, not ours.*

Her eyes widened more. I saw her thinking furiously.

"Martin," she asked quietly. "Why did Arianna target my daughter?"

Martin looked down at Susan, at Maggie, and then away. "Because the child's father is the son of Margaret LeFay, the daughter of the man who killed her husband. By killing her, this way she would avenge herself upon all of you."

If I hadn't already been more or less motionless, I would have frozen in place.

Margaret LeFay. Daughter of the man who had killed Arianna's husband (and vampire child), Paolo Ortega.

Duke Ortega. Who had been destroyed by the Blackstaff.

Ebenezar McCoy.

One of the most dangerous wizards in the world. A man of such personal and political power that she would never have been able to take him down directly. So she had set out to strike at him through his bloodline. From him to my mother. From her to me. From me to Maggie. Kill the child and kill us all.

That was what Arianna had meant when she said it wasn't about me.

It was about my grandfather.

Suddenly it made sense that the old man had put his life on the line by declaring himself my mentor when the Council would have killed me for slaying Justin Du-Morne. Suddenly it made sense why he had been so patient with me, so considerate, so kind. It hadn't just been an act of random kindness.

And suddenly it made sense why he would barely ever speak of his apprentice, Margaret LeFay—a name she'd earned for herself, when her birth certificate must have read Margaret McCoy. Hell, for that matter, he probably never told the Council that Margaret was his daughter. I sure as hell had no intentions of letting them know about Maggie, if I got her out of this mess.

My mother had eventually been killed by enemies she had made—and Ebenezar, her father, the most dangerous man on the White Council, had not been there to save her. The circumstances wouldn't matter. No matter what he'd accomplished, I knew the old man would never forgive himself for not saving his daughter's life, any more than I would if I failed Maggie. It was why he had made a statement, a demonstration of what would happen to those who came at me with a personal vengeance—he was trying, preemptively, to save his grandson.

And it explained why he had changed the Grey Council's focus and led them here. He had to try to save me—and to save my little girl.

And, some cynical portion of me added, himself. Though I wasn't even sure that would be a conscious thought on his part, underneath the mountain of issues he had accrued.

No wonder Arianna had been so hot and bothered to use the bloodline curse, starting with Maggie. She'd avenge herself upon me, who hadn't had the good grace to die in a duel, and upon Ebenezar, who had simply killed Ortega as you would a dangerous animal, a workaday murder performed with expedience and an extremely high profile. Arianna must have lost a lot of face in the wake of that—and my ongoing exploits against the Reds and their allies would only have made her more determined to show me my place. With a single curse, she'd kill one of the Senior Council and the Blackstaff all at once. My death would be something to crow about, too—since, as Arianna herself had noted, no one had pulled it off yet—and I felt I could confidently lay claim to the title of Most Infamous Warden on the Council, after Donald Morgan's death.

For Arianna, what a coup. And after that, presumably . . . a coup.

Of course, if the Red King was holding the knife, he got the best of all worlds. Dead enemies, more prestige, and a more secure throne. No-brainer.

He took the knife from my belt, smiling, and turned toward the altar—and my daughter.

Dear God, I thought. *Think, Dresden. Think!*

One day I hope God will forgive me for giving birth to the idea that came next.

Because I never will.

I knew how angry she was. I knew how afraid she was. Her child was about to die only inches beyond her reach, and what I did to her was as good as murder.

I focused my thoughts and sent them to Susan. *Susan! Think! Who knew who the baby's father was? Who could have told them?*

Her lips peeled away from her teeth.

His knife can't hurt you, I thought, though I knew damned well that no faerie magic could blithely ignore the touch of steel.

"Martin," Susan said, her voice low and very quiet, "did you tell them about Maggie?"

He closed his eyes, but his voice was steady. "Yes."

Susan Rodriguez lost her mind.

One instant she was a prisoner, and the next she had twisted like an eel, too swiftly to be easily seen. Martin's machete opened up a long cut on her throat, but she paid as little attention to it as a thorn scratch gained while hiking.

Martin raised a hand to block the strike he thought was coming—and it was useless, because Susan didn't go after him swinging.

Instead, her eyes full of darkness and rage, her mouth

opened in a scream that showed her extended fangs, she went for his throat.

Martin's eyes were on mine for a fraction of a second. No more. But I felt the soulgaze begin. I saw his agony, the pain of the mortal life he had lost. I saw his years of service, his genuine devotion, like a marble statue of the Red King kept polished and lovingly tended. And I saw his soul change. I saw that image of worship grow tarnished as he spent year after year among those who struggled against the Red King and his empire of terror and misery. And I saw that when he had come into the temple, he knew full well that he wasn't going to survive. And that he was content with it.

There was nothing I could do in time to prevent what was coming next, and I wasn't sure I wanted to. Martin said that it had taken him years and years to run a con on the Fellowship of St. Giles. But it had taken him most of two centuries to run the long con on the Red King. As a former priest, Martin must have known of the bloodline curse, and its potential for destruction. He must have known that the threat to Maggie and the realization of his betrayal would be certain to drive Susan out of control.

He'd told me already, practically the moment he had come to Chicago, that he would do anything if it meant damaging the Red Court. He would have shot me in the back. He would have betrayed Maggie's existence, practically handing her to the murderous bastards. He would betray the Fellowship to its enemies.

He would destroy Susan.

And he would die, himself.

Everything he had done, I realized, he had done for one reason: to be sure that I was standing here when it happened. To give me a chance to change everything.

Susan rode him to the stone floor, berserk with terror and rage, and tore out his throat, ripping mouthful after mouthful of flesh from his neck with supernatural speed.

Martin died.

Susan began to turn.

And that was my moment.

I flung myself against the wills of the Lords of Outer Night with everything in my body, my heart, my mind. I hurled my fear and my loneliness, my love and my respect, my rage and my pain. I made of my thoughts a hammer, infused with the fires of creation and tempered in the icy power of the darkest guardian the earth had ever known. I raised my arms with a scream of defiance, bringing as much of the armor as I could between my head and theirs, and wished for a fleeting second that I had just worn the stupid hat.

And I threw it all at the second Lord from the left— the one whose will seemed the least concrete. He staggered and made a sound that I'd once heard from a boxer who'd taken an uppercut to the nuts.

With that, the last Lord of Outer Night to enter the temple—the one wearing the mask I had seen once before, when Murphy had sliced it from its owner's head— raised her hands and sent ribbons of green and amethyst power scything through her apparent compatriots.

The blast killed two of them outright, with spectacular violence, tearing their bodies to god-awful shreds and spattering the inside of the temple with black blood. All of the remaining Lords staggered, screaming in surprise and pain, their true forms beginning to claw their way free of the flesh that contained them.

My godmother, too, discarded her disguise, flinging the gold mask at the nearest Lord as she allowed the illusion that concealed her true form to fade away, taking

with it the clothes and trappings that had let her insinu-
ate herself among the enemy. Her eyes were bright, her
cheeks flushed. Bloodlust and an eager, nearly sexual desire to destroy radiated from her like heat from a fire.
She howled her glee and began hurling streaks and bolts
and webworks of energy at the stunned Lords of Outer
Night, spinning power from her flickering fingertips even
as they brought the force of their wills and their own
sorcery to bear upon her.

Not one of the Lords of Outer Night remembered to
keep me down.

I was suddenly free.

I hurled myself at the Red King's back with a scream,
and saw him spin to face me, knife in hand. His dark
eyes suddenly widened, and the awful power of his will
descended upon me like a dozen leaded blankets.

I staggered, but I did not stop. I was hysterical. I
was not well. I was invincible. My armor and my grandfather's staff and the sight of my frightened child and
the cold power flowing through my limbs allowed me to
push forward one step, and another, and another, until I
stood nearly toe-to-toe with him.

The Red King's restored right hand snapped forward
to bury the obsidian knife in my throat.

My left hand dropped the staff and intercepted his
wrist. I stopped the knife an inch from my throat, and his
eyes widened as he felt my strength.

His left hand shot out to clench my throat with
crushing power.

I formed the thumb and forefinger of my right hand
into a C-shape, ice crackling as it spread over them, rigid
and crystal clear.

I plunged them into both of his black, black eyes.

And then I sent my will coursing down my arm, along with all the soulfire I could find as I screamed, *"Fuego!"*

Fire seared and split and cooked and steamed, and the king of the Red Court, the most ancient vampire of their kind, the father and creator of their race, screamed in anguish. The sound was so loud that it blew out my left eardrum, a novel new agony for my collection.

And when the Red King screamed, every single member of his Court screamed with him.

This close to him I could almost feel it, feel the power of his will calling them, drawing vampires to him with a summoning beyond self-interest, beyond reason. But even if I hadn't been there touching him, the sudden storm of cries from outside would have told me the same story.

The vampires were coming toward us in a swarm, a storm, and nothing on earth would stop them from going to their king's aid. His grip on my throat faltered, and he staggered back and away from me. My fingers came free of his head, and I grabbed his knife hand at the wrist with both hands. Then, screaming in rage, coating his arm with frost, I snapped his forearm in half—and caught the dagger before it could fall to the floor.

Freed, the Red King staggered away, and even blinded and in sanity-destroying pain, he was dangerous. His will, unleashed at random, blew holes in the stone walls. Sorcery lashed out, the scarlet lightning that seemed to be a motif around here raking over one of his own Lords and cutting the struggling vampire in half.

The eldest vampire of the Red Court screamed in his agony as a tide of his creatures came to obliterate us.

And the youngest vampire of the Red Court knelt on the ground over Martin, staring at her hands.

I watched for a second as the skin around her fingers seemed to burst at the tips. Then I saw her fingers begin to lengthen, nails growing into claws, muscle tissue tearing free of skin with audible, obvious torment. Susan stared at them with her all-black eyes, shaking her head, her face a mask of blood. She was moaning, shuddering.

"Susan," I said, kneeling down in front of her. The howl of sorcerous energies filled the temple with a symphony of destruction. I took her face in my hands.

She looked up at me, terrified and tortured, despair written over her face.

"They're coming," she rasped. "I can feel them. Inside. Outside. They're coming. Oh, God."

"Susan!" I shouted. "Remember Maggie!"

Her eyes seemed to focus on me.

"They wanted Maggie because she was the youngest," I said, my voice cold. "Because her death would have taken us all with her."

She contorted around her stomach, which was twisting and flexing and swelling obscenely, but she kept her eyes on my face.

"Now you're the youngest," I hissed at her, my voice fierce. "The youngest vampire in the entire and *literally* damned Court. You can kill them *all*."

She shuddered and moaned, and I saw the conflicting desires at war within her. But her eyes turned to Maggie and she clenched her jaw. "I . . . I don't think I can do it. I can't feel my hands."

"Harry!" screamed Murphy desperately, from somewhere nearby. "They're coming!"

Lightning split the air outside with thunder that would register on the Richter scale.

There was a sudden, random lull in the cacophony of sorcerous war, no more than a couple of seconds long.

Susan looked back at me, her eyes streaming her last tears. "Harry, help me," she whispered. "Save her. Please."

Everything in me screamed no. That this was not fair. That I should not have to do this. That no one should *ever* have to do this.

But . . . I had no choice.

I found myself picking Susan up with one hand. The little girl was curled into a ball with her eyes closed, and there was no time. I pushed her from the altar as gently as I could and let her fall to the floor, where she might be a little safer from the wild energies surging through the temple.

I put Susan on the altar and said, "She'll be safe. I promise."

She nodded at me, her body jerking and twisting in convulsions, forcing moans of pain from her lips. She looked terrified, but she nodded.

I put my left hand over her eyes.

I pressed my mouth to hers, swiftly, gently, tasting the blood, and her tears, and mine.

I saw her lips form the word, "Maggie . . ."

And I . . .

I used the knife.

I saved a child.

I won a war.

God forgive me.

Chapter
Forty-nine

Everything changed the night the Red Court died. It made the history books.

First, for the unexplained destruction of several structures in Chichén Itzá. A thousand years of jungle hadn't managed to bring the place down, but half an hour of slugfest between practitioners who know what they're doing can leave city blocks in ruins. It was later attributed to an extremely powerful localized earthquake. No one could explain all the corpses—some of them with dental work featuring techniques last used a hundred years before, some whose hearts had been violently torn from their chests, and whose bodies had been affected by some kind of mutation that had rendered their bones almost unrecognizable as human. Fewer than 5 percent of them were ever identified—and those were all people who had abruptly gone missing in the past ten or fifteen years. No explanation was ever offered for such a confluence of missing persons, though theories abounded, none of them true.

I could have screamed the truth from the mountaintops and blended right in with all the rest of the nuts. Everyone knows that vampires aren't real.

Second, it made the books because of all the sudden disappearances or apparent outright murders of important officials, businessmen, and financiers in cities and governments throughout Latin America. The drug cartels took the rap for that one, even in the nations where they weren't really strong enough to pull such tactics off. Martial law got declared virtually everywhere south of Texas, and a dozen revolutions in eight or ten different countries all kicked off, seemingly on the same night.

I've heard that nature abhors a vacuum—though if that's true, then I can't figure why about ninety-nine zillion percent of creation *is* vacuum. But I do know that governments hate 'em, and always rush to fill them up. So do criminals. Which probably tells you more about human beings than it does about nature. Most of the nations in South America proper kept their balance. Central America turned into a war zone, with various interests fighting to claim the territory the vampires had left behind them.

Finally, it made the books in the supernatural community as the night of bad dreams. Before the next sunset, the Paranet was buzzing with activity, with men and women scattered over half the world communicating about the vivid and troubling dreams they'd had. Pregnant women and mothers who had recently delivered had been hardest hit. Several had to be hospitalized and sedated. But everyone with a smidge of talent who was sleeping at the time was troubled by dreams. The general theme was always the same: dead children. The world in flames. Terror and death spreading across the globe in an unstoppable wave, destroying anything resembling order or civilization.

I don't remember what happened when the ritual

went off. There's a blank spot in my head about two minutes wide. I had no desire whatsoever to find out what was there.

The next thing I remember is standing outside the temple with Maggie in my arms, wrapped up in the heavy feather cloak her mother had left behind. She was still shivering and crying quietly, but only in sheer reaction and weariness now, rather than terror. The shackles lay broken on the ground behind me. I don't remember how I got them off her without hurting her. She leaned against me, using a fold of the cloak as a pillow, and I sat down on the top step, holding her, to see what I had paid for.

The Red Court was dead. Gone. Every one of them. Most of the remains were little more than black sludge. That, I thought, marked the dead vampires. The half-breeds, though, only lost the vampire parts of their nature. The curse had cured them.

Of course, it was the vampire inside them that had kept them young and beautiful.

I saw hundreds of people on the ground aging a year for every one of my breaths. I watched them wither away to nothing, for the most part. It seemed that half-breeds came in a couple of flavors—those who had managed to discipline their thirst for blood, and thus carried on for centuries, and those who had not been half-vampires for very long. Very few of the latter had ranked in the Red King's Court. It turned out that most of the young half vampires had been working for the Fellowship, and many had already been killed by the Reds—but I heard later that more than two hundred others had been freed from their curse.

But for me, it wouldn't matter how many I'd freed in

that instant of choice. No matter how high the number, it would need to be plus one to be square in my book.

Inevitably, the Red Court had contained a few newbies, and after the ritual went off, they were merely human again. They, and the other humans too dim to run any sooner, didn't last long once the Grey Council broke open the cattle car and freed the prisoners. The terror the Reds had inflicted on their victims became rage, and the deaths the Reds and their retainers suffered as a result weren't pretty ones. I saw a matronly woman who was all alone beat Alamaya to death with a rock.

I didn't get involved. I'd had enough for one day.

I sat and I rocked my daughter until she fell asleep against me. My godmother came to sit beside me, her gown singed and spattered with blood, a contented smile upon her face. People talked to me. I ignored them. They didn't push. I think Lea was warning them off.

Ebenezar, still bearing the Blackstaff in his left hand, came to me sometime later. He looked at the Leanansidhe and said, "Family business. Please excuse us."

She smirked at him and inclined her head. Then she stood up and drifted away.

Ebenezar sat down next to me on the eastern steps of the temple of Kukulcan and stared out at the jungle around us, beneath us. "Dawn's about here," he said.

I looked. He was right.

"Locals stay hidden in their houses until sunrise around here. Red Court would meet here sometimes. Induct new nobility and so on. Survival trait."

"Yeah," I said. It was like that a lot, especially in nations that didn't have a ton of international respect. Something weird happens in Mexico; twenty million people can say that they saw it and no one cares.

"Sun comes up, they'll be out. They'll call authorities. People will ask questions."

I listened to his statements and didn't disagree with any of them. After a moment, I realized that they were connected to a line of thought, and I said, "It's time to go."

"Aye, soon," Ebenezar said.

"You never told me, sir," I said.

He was quiet for a long moment. Then he said, "I've done things in my life, Hoss. Bad things. I've made enemies. I didn't want you to have them, too." He sighed. "At least . . . not until you were ready." He looked around at the remains of the Red Court. "Reckon you more or less are."

I thought about that while the sky grew lighter. Then I said, "How did Arianna know?"

Ebenezar shook his head. "A dinner. Maggie—my Maggie—asked me to a dinner. She'd just taken up with that Raith bastard. Arianna was there. Maggie didn't warn me. They had some scheme they wanted my support on. The vampires thought I was just Maggie's mentor, then." He sighed. "I wanted nothing to do with it. Said she shouldn't want it, either. And we fought."

I grunted. "Fought like family."

"Yes," he said. "Raith missed it. He's never had any family that was sane. Arianna saw it. Filed it away for future reference."

"Is everything in the open now?" I asked.

"Everything's never in the open, son," he responded. "There're things we keep hidden from one another. Things we hide from ourselves. Things that are kept hidden from us. And things no one knows. You always learn the damnedest things at the worst possible times. Or that's been my experience."

I nodded.

"Sergeant Murphy told me what happened."

I felt my neck tense. "She saw it?"

He nodded. "Reckon so. Hell of a hard thing to do."

"It wasn't hard," I said quietly. "Just cold."

"Oh, Hoss," he said. There was more compassion in the words than you'd think would fit there.

Figures in grey gathered at the bottom of the stairs. Ebenezar eyed them with a scowl. "Time for me to go, looks like."

I nudged my brain and looked down at them. "You brought them here. For me."

"Not so much," he said. He nodded at the sleeping child. "For her."

"What about the White Council?"

"They'll get things sorted out soon," he said. "Amazing how things fell apart just long enough for them to sit them out."

"With Cristos running it."

"Aye."

"He's Black Council," I said.

"Or maybe stupid," Ebenezar countered.

I thought about it. "Not sure which is scarier."

Ebenezar blinked at me, then snorted. "Stupid, Hoss. Every time. Only so many blackhearted villains in the world, and they only get uppity on occasion. Stupid's everywhere, every day."

"How'd Lea arrange a signal with you?" I asked.

"That," Ebenezar said sourly. "On that score, Hoss, I think our elders ran their own game on us."

"Elders?"

He nodded down the stairs, where the tall figure with the metal-headed staff had begun creating another doorway out of green lightning. Once it was formed, the space beneath the arch shimmered, and all the hooded figures at the bottom of the stairs looked up at us.

I frowned and looked closer. Then I realized that the metal head of the staff was a blade, and that the tall man was holding a spear. Within the hood, I saw a black eye patch, a grizzled beard, and a brief, grim smile. He raised the spear to me in a motion that reminded me, somehow, of a fencer's salute. Then he turned and vanished into the gate. One by one, the other figures in grey began to follow him.

"Vadderung," I said.

Ebenezar grunted. "That's his name this time. He doesn't throw in often. When he does, he goes to the wall. And in my experience, it means things are about to get bad." He pursed his lips. "He doesn't give recognition like that lightly, Hoss."

"I talked to him a couple of days ago," I said. "He told me about the curse. Put the gun in my hand for me and showed me where to point it."

Ebenezar nodded. "He taught Merlin, you know. The original Merlin."

"How'd Merlin make out?" I asked.

"No one's sure," Ebenezar said. "But from his journals . . . he wasn't the kind to go in his sleep."

I snorted.

The old man stood and used his right hand to pull his hood up over his face. He paused and then looked at me. "I won't lecture you about Mab, boy. I've made bargains myself, sometimes." He twitched his left hand, which was still lined with black veins, though not as much as it had been hours before. "We do what we think we must, to protect who we can."

"Yeah," I said.

"She might lean on you pretty hard. Try to put you

into a box you don't want to be in. But don't let her. She can't take away your will. Even if she can make it seem that way." He sighed again, but there was bedrock in his voice. "That's the one thing all these dark beings and powers can't do. Take away your ability to choose. They can kill you. They can make you do things—but they can't make you *choose* to do 'em. They almost always try to lie to you about that. Don't fall for it."

"I won't," I said. I looked up at him and said, "Thank you, Grandfather."

He wrinkled up his nose. "Ouch. That doesn't fit."

"Grampa," I said. "Gramps."

He put his hand against his chest.

I smiled a little. "Sir."

He nodded at the child. "What will you do with her?"

"What I see fit," I said, but gently. "Maybe it's better if you don't know."

Both pain and faintly amused resignation showed in his face. "Maybe it is. See you soon, Hoss."

He got halfway down the stairs before I said, "Sir? Do you want your staff?"

He nodded at me. "You keep it, until I can get you a new blank."

I nodded back at him. Then I said, "I don't know what to say."

His eyes wrinkled up even more heavily at the corners. "Hell, Hoss. Then don't say anything." He turned and called over his shoulder, "You get in less trouble that way!"

My grandfather kept going down the stairs, walking with quick, sure strides. He vanished through the doorway of lightning.

I heard steps behind me, and turned to find Murphy standing in the entrance of the temple. *Fidelacchius* rode over one shoulder, and her P-90 hung from its strap on the other. She looked tired. Her hair was all coming out of its ponytail, strands hanging here and there. She studied my face, smiled slightly, and came down to where I sat.

"Hey," she said, her voice hushed. "You back?"

"I guess I am."

"Sanya was worried," she said, with a little roll of her eyes.

"Oh," I said. "Well. Tell him not to worry. I'm still here."

She nodded and stepped closer. "So this is her?"

I nodded, and looked down at the sleeping little girl. Her cheeks were pink. I couldn't talk.

"She's beautiful," Murphy said. "Like her mother."

I nodded and rolled one tired and complaining shoulder. "She is."

"Do you want someone else to take her for a minute?"

My arms tightened on the child, and I felt myself turn a little away from her.

"Okay," Murphy said gently, raising her hands. "Okay."

I swallowed and realized that I was parched. Starving. And, more than anything, I was weary. Desperately, desolately tired. And the prospect of sleep was terrifying. I turned to look at Murphy and saw the pain on her face as she watched me. "Karrin," I said, "I'm tired."

I looked down at the child, a sleepy, warm little presence who had simply accepted what meager shelter and comfort I had been able to offer. And I thought my heart would break. Break more. Because I knew that I couldn't be what she needed. That I could never give her what she had to have to stand a chance of growing up strong and sane and happy.

Because I had made a deal. If I hadn't done it, she'd be dead—but because I had, I couldn't be what she deserved to have.

Never looking away from the little girl's face, I whispered, "Will you do me a favor?"

"Yes," Karrin said. Such a simple word, to have so much reassuring mass.

My throat tightened and my vision blurred. It took me two tries to speak. "Please take her to Father Forthill, when we get b-back," I said. "T-tell him that she needs to disappear. The safest place he has. That I . . ." My voice failed. I took deep breaths and said, "And I don't need to know where. T-tell him that for me."

I turned to Murphy and said, "Please?"

She looked at me as if her heart were breaking. But she had a soul of steel, of strength, and her eyes were steady and direct. "Yes."

I bit my lip.

And, very carefully, I passed my little girl over into her arms. Murphy took her, and didn't comment about the weight. But then, she wouldn't.

"God," I said, not two full seconds later. "Molly. Where is she?"

Murphy looked up at me as she settled down to hold the child. The girl murmured a sleepy complaint, and Murphy rocked her gently to soothe her back to sleep. "Wow. You were really out of it. You didn't see the helicopter?"

I raked through my memories of the night. "Um. No."

"After . . ." She glanced at me and then away. "After," she said more firmly, "Thomas found a landline and made a call. And a navy helicopter landed right out there on the lawn less than an hour later. Lifted him, Molly, and Mouse right out."

"Mouse?"

Murphy snorted gently. "No one was willing to tell him he couldn't go with Molly."

"He takes his work seriously," I said.

"Apparently."

"Do we know anything?" I asked.

"Not yet," Murphy said. "Sanya's manning the phone in the visitors' center. We gave Thomas the number before he left."

"Be honest, Sergeant Murphy," the Leanansidhe said quietly as she glided back over to me. "You gave the dog the number."

Murphy eyed her, then looked at me and said defensively, "Thomas seemed to have enough on his mind already."

I frowned.

"Not like that," Murphy said sternly. "Ugh. I wouldn't have let him go with her if he'd seemed . . . all weird."

"Yeah," I said. "Yeah. Mouse wouldn't have, either, would he."

"He was in no danger of losing control," my godmother said calmly. "I would never let such a promising prospect be *accidentally* devoured."

Sanya appeared, jogging around the lower end of the pyramid from its far side. *Esperacchius* hung at his side— and *Amoracchius*, still in its sheath on Susan's white leather belt, hung from his shoulder.

I stared at the belt for a moment.

It hurt.

Sanya came chugging up the stairs, moving lightly for a big guy with so much muscle. He gave my godmother a pleasant smile, one hand checking to be sure that *Amoracchius* was still on his shoulder.

"Next time," Lea murmured.

"I think not," Sanya said, beaming. He turned to me. "Thomas called. He seemed surprised it was me. Molly is on navy cruiser on maneuvers in Gulf of Mexico. She will be fine."

I whistled. "How did . . . ?" I narrowed my eyes.

"Lara?" Murphy asked quietly.

"Got to be," I answered.

"Lara has enough clout to get a navy chopper sent into another country's airspace for an extraction?" Murphy kept on rocking Maggie as she spoke, seemingly unaware that she was still doing it. "That's . . . scary."

"Yeah," I said. "Maybe she sang 'Happy Birthday, Mister President.'"

"Not to be rude," Sanya said, "but I saw some people come up road in car and drive away very fast. Now would be a good time to . . ." He glanced over his shoulder and frowned. "Who left that lightning door there?"

"I arranged that," Lea said lightly. "It will take you directly back to Chicago."

"How'd you manage that?" I asked.

The Leanansidhe smoothed her gown, a hungry little smile on her lips, and folded her hands primly in her lap. "I . . . negotiated with its creator. Aggressively."

I made a choking sound.

"After all, your quest must be completed, my child," my godmother said. "Maggie must be made safe. And while I found the swim bracing, I thought it might not be safe for her. I'm given to understand that the little ones are quite fragile."

"Okay," I said. "I . . ." I looked back up at the temple. "I can't just leave her there."

"Will you take her back to Chicago, child?" my godmother asked. "Allow your police to ask many questions? Perhaps slip her into your own grave at Graceland Boneyard, and cover her with dirt?"

"I can't just leave her," I said.

The Leanansidhe looked at me and shook her head. Her expression was . . . less predatory than it could have been, even if it wasn't precisely gentle. "Go. I will see to the child's mother." She lifted her hand to forestall my skeptical reply. "With all the honor and respect you would wish to bestow yourself, my godson. And I will take you to visit when you desire. You have my word."

A direct promise from one of the Sidhe is a rare thing. A kindness is even rarer.

But maybe I shouldn't have been surprised: Even in Winter, the cold isn't always bitter, and not every day is cruel.

Sanya, Murphy, and I went down the stairs and through the lightning gate. Murphy politely refused Sanya's offer to carry Maggie for her. He didn't know how to work her the right way to get her to accept help.

I offered to carry her gear.

She surrendered the Sword and her guns willingly enough, and I lagged a few steps behind them while I settled the straps and weaponry about myself. I hung the P-90, the only object Murph was carrying with enough open space in it to hide an itinerant spirit, so that it bumped against the skull still in the improvised bag on my belt and murmured, very quietly, "Out of the gun."

"About time," Bob whispered back. "Sunrise is almost here. You trying to get me cooked?" Orange light flowed wearily out of the apertures of the P-90 and back into the safety of the skull. The lights in the eye sockets flickered dimly, and the spirit's slurred voice whispered,

"Don' gimme any work for a week. At least." Then they flickered out.

I made sure the T-shirt was still tied firmly, and that the gun wasn't going to scratch the skull. Then I caught up to the others, and was the first one through the gateway.

It was like walking through a light curtain into another room. A step, a single stride, took me from Chichén Itzá to Chicago. Specifically, we emerged into Father Forthill's storage room–slash–refugee closet, and the lightning gate closed behind us with a snap of static discharge.

"Direct flight," said Sanya with both surprise and approval, looking around. "Nice."

Murphy nodded. "No stops? No weird places? How does that work?"

I had no idea. So I just smiled, shrugged, and said, "Magic."

"Good enough," Murphy said with a sigh, and immediately settled Maggie down onto one of the cots. The child started to cry again, but Murphy shushed her and tucked her beneath the blankets and slipped a pillow beneath her head, and the little girl was out in seconds.

I watched Maggie without getting involved.

Her mother's blood was on my hands. Literally.

Sanya stepped up next to me and put his hand on my shoulder. He nodded toward the hallway and said, "We should talk."

"Go ahead," Murphy said. "I'll stay with her."

I nodded my thanks to her, and went out into the hallway with Sanya.

Wordlessly, he offered me *Amoracchius*. I stared at the Sword for a moment.

"I'm not so sure I should have that," I said.

"If you were," he said, "I wouldn't want you to have it. Uriel placed it in your care. If he wanted it moved, he should say so."

After a moment, I took the sword and hung its belt over the same shoulder as *Fidelacchius*. The Swords felt very heavy.

Sanya nodded. "Before he left, Thomas said to give you this. That you would know what it was." He passed me a key.

I recognized it from the stamp on the head reading, *WB*. It stood for the name of the *Water Beetle*, Thomas's beat-up old commercial fishing boat. It had a bathroom, a shower, a little kitchen, some bunks. And I had a couple of changes of clothing there, from overnight trips to one of the islands in Lake Michigan.

My brother was offering me a place to stay.

I had to blink my eyes several times as I took the key. "Thank you," I said to Sanya.

He studied my face for a second, thoughtfully. Then he said, "You're leaving now, aren't you?"

I looked back toward Forthill's quiet little haven. "Yeah."

He nodded. "When will Mab come for you?"

"I don't know," I said quietly. "Soon, I guess."

"I will talk to Michael for you," he said. "Tell him about his daughter."

"I appreciate it," I said. "Just so you know . . . Murphy knows my wishes regarding Maggie. She'll speak for me."

"*Da*," he said. Then he reached into his pocket and produced a metal flask. He sipped from it, and offered it to me. "Here."

"Vodka?"

"Of course."

"On an empty stomach," I said, but took the flask, tilted it to him in a little salute, and downed a big swallow. It burned going in, but not necessarily in a bad way.

"I am glad that we fought together," he said, as I passed the flask back. "I will do everything in my power to help make your daughter safe until you can return."

I lifted my eyebrows. "Returning . . . isn't really in the cards, man."

"I do not play cards," he said. "I play chess. And in my opinion, this is not your endgame. Not yet."

"Being the Winter Knight isn't the kind of job you walk out of."

"Neither is being Knight of the Sword," he said. "But Michael is with his family now."

"Michael's boss was a hell of a lot nicer than mine."

Sanya let out a rolling laugh, and took another sip from the flask before slipping it back into his coat. "What will be, will be." He offered me his hand. "Good luck."

I shook it. "And you."

"Come," the Russian said. "I will call you a cab."

I went down to the *Water Beetle*. I took off the armor. I hid the swords in the concealed compartments Thomas had built into the boat for just such an occasion, along with Bob's skull. And I took a long, long shower. The water heater on the tub wasn't much, but I was used to not having hot water. Being the Winter Knight didn't help when it came to the cold water, which seemed a complete rip-off to me—in other words, typical. I scrubbed and scrubbed at myself, especially my hands. I couldn't decide if Susan's blood was coming off my skin or just sinking in.

I moved mechanically after that, with the routine of a longtime bachelor. There was chicken soup and chili in the kitchen—sorry, galley. I heated them both up and ate them. I had a choice between white wine, orange juice, or warm Coke to go with them. The orange juice was about to go bad, so it won the decision. Hot soups and cold juice got along better than I thought they would, and I lay down on a bunk. I thought I would sleep.

I couldn't.

I lay there feeling the gentle motion of the great lake rocking the boat. Water made soft slaps and gurgles against the hull. Sunlight warmed the cabin. I was clean and dressed in an old pair of sweats and lying in a bed that was surprisingly comfortable—but I couldn't sleep.

The old clock on the wall—sorry, bulkhead—ticked with a steady, soothing rhythm.

But I couldn't sleep.

Chicken soup and chili. That was one hell of a last meal.

Maybe I should have had the cab stop at Burger King.

As noon closed in, I sat up and stared at my god-mother's armor, which had stopped bullets and lightning bolts and maybe worse. I'd found several marks on the back and sides, but no corresponding memories match-ing them to any of the attacks I knew about. Evidently, it had handled a number of hits I hadn't noticed, and I knew that without the ridiculously ornate stuff I'd be dead.

The little ticking clock chimed twelve times at noon, and on the twelfth chime the armor changed. It . . . just melted back into my leather duster. The one Susan had given me before a battle a long, long time ago.

I picked up the coat. There were gaping wounds in it. Slashes. Patches burned away. Clearly visible bullet holes. There was more hole than there was coat, really, and even the surviving leather was cracked, dried, stiff, and flaking. It began to fall apart while I stood there examining it.

I guess nobody tried making a pie out of Cinderella's pumpkin once it got through being a carriage. Though in some versions of the story, I guess it had been an onion. Maybe you could have made soup.

I dropped the coat into the lake and watched it sink. I washed my face in the bathroom and squinted at the little mirror. My mother's amulet and gem gleamed against my bare chest.

Three days ago, my life had been business as usual. Now that little bit of silver and stone was just about the only thing I had left. Not my office. Not my house. Not my car. Not my dog—or my cat. God, where had Mister gone after the fire? Not my integrity. Not my freedom. Not my friends—not after Mab finished with me.

What was left?

A little bit of silver and a tiny rock.

And Maggie.

I sat down and waited to see what happened.

Footsteps came down the dock and then onto the boat. A moment later, Murphy knocked on the door, and then let herself into the cabin.

She looked like she'd come straight here from the church, since she was still in her whitened battle wear, and from her expression she hadn't slept. She exhaled slowly and nodded. "I thought so."

"Murph," I said, "maybe you shouldn't be here."

"I had to see you," she said. "You . . . you just left."

"Wanted to say good-bye?" I asked.

"Don't be stupid," she said. "I don't *want* to say it." She swallowed. "Harry . . . it's just that . . . I was worried about you. I've never seen you like this."

"I've never murdered my child's mother before," I said tonelessly. "That's bound to take a little adjustment."

She shivered and looked away. "I just . . . just came to make sure that you aren't doing this to punish yourself. That you aren't going to . . . do anything dramatic."

"Sure," I said. "Nothing dramatic. That's me."

"Dammit, Dresden."

I spread my hands. "What do you want from me, Murphy? There's nothing left."

She came and sat down next to me, her eyes on my face, on my chest and shoulders, taking in all the scars. "I know how you feel," she said. "After Maggie was settled, I called in to the office. There's . . . been another investigation launched. That putz Rudolph." She swallowed, and I could practically smell the pain on her. "The game's rigged. Stallings thinks he can get me early retirement. Half pension."

"Jesus, Murphy," I said, quietly.

"I'm a cop, Harry," she whispered. "But after this . . ." She spread her hands, to show me that nothing was in them.

"I'm sorry," I said. "I got you into this."

"The fuck. You. Did." She turned angry blue eyes to me. "Don't try that bullshit with me. I knew what I was doing. I took the risks. I paid for it. And I'll keep doing it for as long as I damned well please. Don't try to take that from me."

I looked away from her and felt a little bit ashamed. She was probably right. She could have backed off from me a long time ago. She'd chosen to be my friend, even though she'd known the danger. It didn't exactly make me feel any better about myself, but it made me respect her a little more.

Is it wrong of me to admire a woman who can take a

hit? Take it with as much fortitude as anyone alive, and stand up again with the fire still in her eyes?

If it is, I guess I can blame it on a screwed-up childhood.

"Do you want the Sword?" I asked.

She let out a quiet groan. "You sound like Sanya. That was the first thing he said." She twisted her face into a stern mask wearing a big grin and mimicked his accent. " 'This is excellent! I have been doing too much of the work!' "

I almost laughed. "Well. I must say. It looks good on you."

"Felt good," she said. "Except for that pronouncement-of-doom thing. It was like someone else was using me as a sock puppet." She shivered. "Ugh."

"Yeah, archangels can be annoying." I nodded toward the hidden compartment. "There's a space behind that panel. You ever want the Sword, check there."

"I'm not rushing into anything. I've had rebound boyfriends. Not interested in a rebound career."

I grunted. "So. What are you going to do?"

She shrugged. "I don't know. I don't want to think about it. I don't want to make any more decisions. So . . . I think I'm going to go get really drunk. And then have mindless sex with the first reasonably healthy male who walks by. Then have a really awkward hangover. And after that, we'll see."

"Sounds like a good plan," I said. And my mouth kept going without checking in with the rest of me. Again. "Do you want some company?"

There was a sharp, heavy silence. Murphy actually stopped breathing. My heart rate sped up a little.

I wanted to curse my mouth for being stupid, but . . .

Why the hell *not*?

Bad timing is for people who have *time*.

"I . . ." She swallowed, and I could see her forcing herself to speak casually. "I suppose you exercise. It would make things simpler."

"Simple," I said. "That's me."

Her hand went to her hair and she forced it back down. "I want to . . ." She took a breath. "I'll pick you up in an hour?"

"Sure," I said.

She stood up, her cheeks pink. Hell's bells, it was an adorable look on her. "An hour, then," she said.

Before she could leave, I caught her hand. Her hands were small and strong and just a little rough. She had bandages over a couple of burst blisters the sword had worn on her during half an hour or so of hard work. I bent over it and kissed the back of her fingers, one for each. I let her go reluctantly and said, my stomach muscles twitching with butterflies, "An hour."

She left and I saw her walking very quickly toward her car. Her ragged ponytail bobbed left and right with her steps.

The only thing certain in life is change. Most of my changes, lately, hadn't been good ones.

Maybe this one wouldn't be good either . . . but it didn't have that feel to it.

I took forty minutes shaving and putting on my nicest clothes, which amounted to jeans and a T-shirt and my old fleece-lined denim jacket. I didn't have any cologne, so the deodorant and soap would have to do. I didn't allow myself to think about what was going on. In a dream, if you ever start realizing it's a dream, poof, it's gone.

And I didn't want that to happen.

After that, I spent a few minutes just . . . breathing.

Listening to the water around me. The ticking of the clock. The peaceful silence. Drinking in the comforting sense of solitude all around me.

Then I said out loud, "Screw this Zen crap. Maybe she'll be early." And I got up to leave.

I came out of the cabin and into the early-afternoon sun, quivering with pleasant tension and tired and haunted—and hopeful. I shielded my eyes against the sun and studied the city's skyline.

My foot slipped a little, and I nearly lost my balance, just as something smacked into the wall of the cabin behind me, a sharp popping sound, like a rock thrown against a wooden fence. I turned, and it felt slow for some reason. I looked at the *Water Beetle*'s cabin wall, bulkhead, whatever, behind me and thought, *Who splattered red paint on my boat?*

And then my left leg started to fold all by itself.

I looked down at a hole in my shirt, just to the left of my sternum.

I thought, *Why did I pick the shirt with a bullet hole in it?*

Then I fell off the back of the boat, and into the icy water of Lake Michigan.

It hurt, but only for a second. After that, my whole body felt deliciously warm, monstrously tired, and the sleep that had evaded me seemed, finally, to be within reach.

It got dark

It got quiet.

And I realized that I was all by myself.

"Die alone," whispered a bitter, hateful old man's voice.

"Hush, now," whispered a woman's voice. It sounded familiar.

I never moved, but I saw a light ahead of me. With the light, I saw that I was moving down a tunnel, directly toward it. Or maybe it was moving toward me. The light looked like something warm and wonderful and I began to move toward it.

Right up until I heard a sound.

Typical, I thought. *Even when you're dead, it doesn't get any easier.*

The light rushed closer, and I distinctly heard the horn and the engine of an oncoming train.

Author's Note

When I was seven years old, I got a bad case of strep throat and was out of school for a whole week. During that time, my sisters bought me my first fantasy and sci-fi novels: the boxed set of *Lord of the Rings* and the boxed set of Han Solo adventure novels by Brian Daley. I devoured them all during that week.

From that point on, I was pretty much doomed to join SF&F fandom. From there, it was only one more step to decide I wanted to be a writer of my favorite fiction material, and here we are.

I blame my sisters.

My first love as a fan is swords-and-horses fantasy. After Tolkien I went after C. S. Lewis. After Lewis, It was Lloyd Alexander. After them came Fritz Leiber, Roger Zelazny, Robert Howard, John Norman, Poul Anderson, David Eddings, Weis and Hickman, Terry Brooks, Elizabeth Moon, Glen Cook, and before I knew it I was a dual citizen of the United States and Lankhmar, Narnia, Gor, Cimmeria, Krynn, Amber—you get the picture.

When I set out to become a writer, I spent years writing swords-and-horses fantasy novels—and seemed to have little innate talent for it. But I worked at my writing, branching out into other areas as experiments, including SF, mystery, and contemporary fantasy. That's how the Dresden Files initially came about—as a happy accident while trying to accomplish something else. Sort of like penicillin.

But I never forgot my first love, and to my immense delight and excitement, one day I got a call from my agent and found out that I was going to get to share my newest swords-and-horses fantasy novel with other fans.

The Codex Alera is a fantasy series set within the savage world of Carna, where spirits of the elements, known as furies, lurk in every facet of life, and where many intelligent races vie for security and survival. The realm of Alera is the monolithic civilization of humanity, and its unique ability to harness and command the furies is all that enables its survival in the face of the enormous, sometimes hostile elemental powers of Carna, and against savage creatures who would lay Alera to waste and ruin.

Yet even a realm as powerful as Alera is not immune to destruction from within, and the death of the heir apparent to the crown has triggered a frenzy of ambitious political maneuvering and infighting amongst the High Lords, those who wield the most powerful furies known to man. Plots are afoot, traitors and spies abound, and a civil war seems inevitable—all while the enemies of the realm watch, ready to strike at the first sign of weakness.

Tavi is a young man living on the frontier of Aleran civilization—because let's face it, swords-and-horses fantasies start there. Born a freak, unable to utilize any powers of furycrafting whatsoever, Tavi has grown up relying upon his own wits, speed, and courage to survive. When an ambitious plot to discredit the Crown lays Tavi's home, the Calderon Valley, naked and defenseless before a horde of the barbarian Marat, the boy and his family find themselves directly in harm's way.

There are no titanic High Lords to protect them, no Legions, no Knights with their mighty furies to take the field. Tavi and the free frontiersmen of the Calderon Valley must find some way to uncover the plot and to defend their homes against the merciless horde of the Marat and their beasts.

It is a desperate hour, when the fate of all Alera hangs in the balance, when a handful of ordinary steadholders must find the courage and strength to defy an overwhelming foe, and when the courage and intelligence of one young man will save the realm—or destroy it.

Thank you, readers and fellow fans, for all of your support and kindness. I hope that you enjoy reading the books of the Codex Alera as much as I enjoyed creating them for you.

—Jim

Furies of Calderon, Academ's Fury, Cursor's Fury, Captain's Fury, Princeps' Fury, and *First Lord's Fury* are available from Ace Books.

WANT TO KNOW WHAT HAPPENS
AFTER THE END OF *CHANGES*?

READ

SIDE JOBS
Stories from the Dresden Files

Here, together for the first time, are the shorter works
of Jim Butcher—a compendium of cases that Harry
and his cadre of allies managed to close in record
time. The tales range from the deadly serious to the
absurdly hilarious.

Also included is "Aftermath," a new, never-before-
published story that takes place hours after the
cliff-hanger ending of *Changes*.

**Available wherever books are sold or at
penguin.com**

R0066

ROC

JIM BUTCHER
The Dresden Files

The #1 *New York Times* bestselling series

"Think *Buffy the Vampire Slayer* starring Philip Marlowe." —*Entertainment Weekly*

STORM FRONT
volume two

HARRY DRESDEN RETURNS!
by Jim Butcher, Mark Powers & Ardian Syaf
Monthly from Dynamite Entertainment!

WWW.DYNAMITEENTERTAINMENT.COM